# Illegal Dreams

To M.J.
Happy reading
J. Mwangi

Joel Mwangi

Published by Dreamsooth Publishers

Paperback ISBN-13: 978-1-7398420-0-0
eBook ISBN-13: 978-1-7398420-1-7

Printed in the United Kingdom



Cover design and layout by www.spiffingcovers.com

*Dream, dream, for this is also sooth.*

William Butler Yeats 1865–1939

To Ruth my love, wife and friend.
To our cheeky children Turi, Imara and
Shiro who make us smile lots

To all those who relentlessly pursue their dreams,
hold onto your dreams for this is also sooth

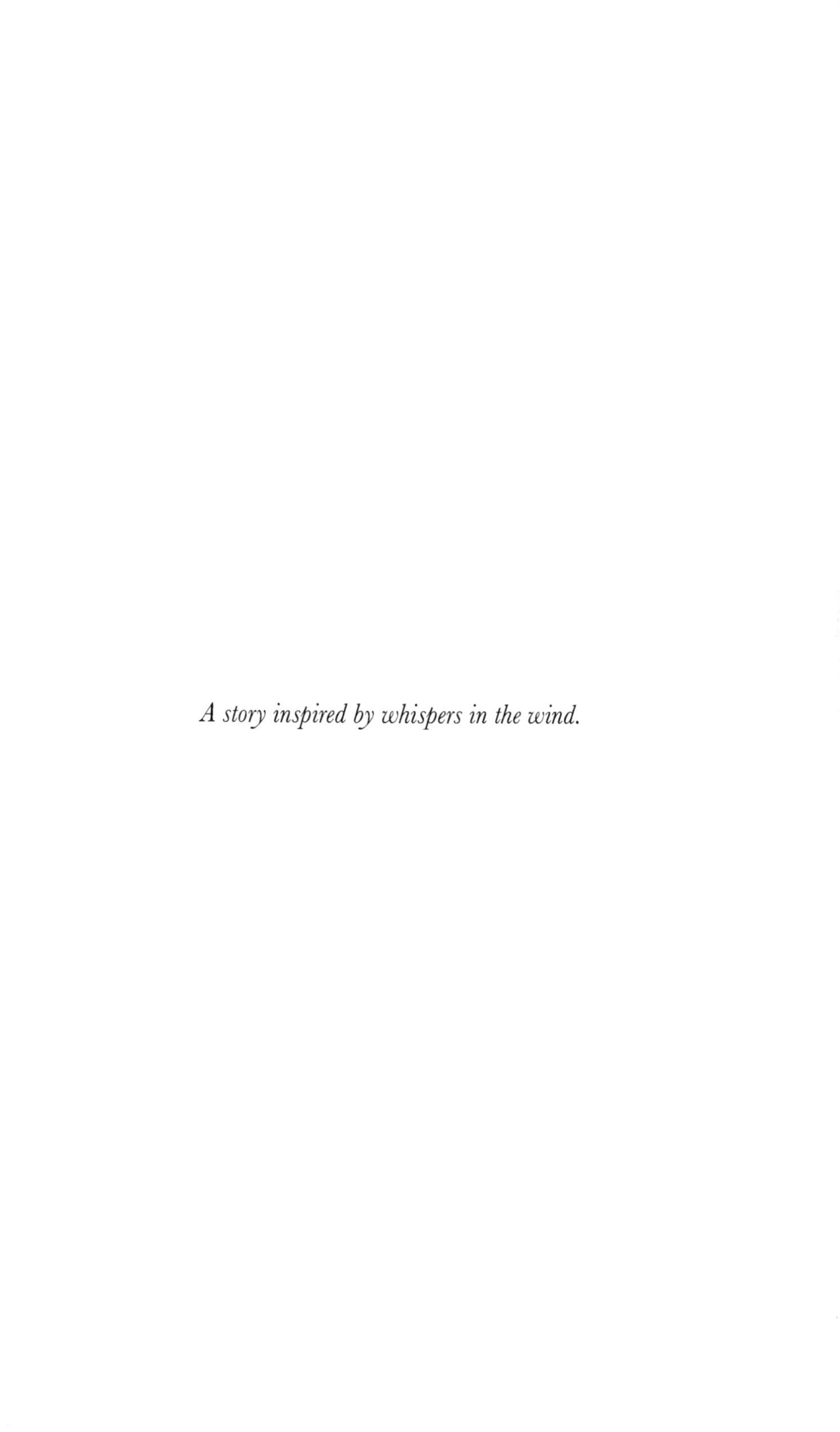

*A story inspired by whispers in the wind.*

# 1

The rubber wasted on the tarmac with a loud screech that tore into the falling darkness. Fuso negotiated the Roysambu roundabout like a crazy boy racer high on something illegal. Taking the first exit, he turned left off Nairobi-Thika highway towards Kahawa West. At the first bus stop he struggled to slow the seething Subaru meandering through the chaotic commuter minibuses popularly known as *matatu*. Passengers shoving to get into them scampered for safety as the surging car swayed precariously towards them. That gave Fuso a clear break. He floored the gas pedal, sending the rumbling car hurtling down towards Mirema Drive. A traffic jam had formed there but he wasn't stopping for anybody. He pulled out dangerously, overtaking five cars in a row. Fuso could see there was a vehicle coming from the opposite direction, a matatu, and considering what indisciplined matatus subjected other motorists to daily, he figured there was lots of room off the road which the other driver could make use of. The car charged like a cross rhino on a collision course with the oncoming matatu. Realising Fuso's car wasn't stopping, the matatu driver scampered onto the kerb and the pavement to give him room to pass.

"Stupid!" the matatu driver shouted, sticking his head out of his window and wagging his middle finger at Fuso.

"Thank you!" Fuso shouted back mischievously and zoomed off, drunk with adrenaline. Lulu, his girlfriend, was her usual self beside him. She was always calm. There was this side of her that fascinated Fuso. Speed thrilled her, gave her a high. He worried about the day she would learn to drive. She also believed nothing could go wrong when he was in control. That was a good thing, for the 'love thing' and his ego, but dangerous and, at the back of his mind, it read 'stupid' in bold capitals. The matatu driver he just encountered had the right of way after all... but hey, look who's said it! The only rule matatu drivers know about road use, from their own book, is; if there is any space, grab it, run over pedestrians, push other cars off the road, move against traffic, but take the space no matter what.

Fuso was in a mad rush to get to his sister Kendi's place, where his parents and a few assorted relatives waited for a small send off gathering. It was now 7.30 pm and Fuso had a flight to catch at 10 pm. This was his day and he hadn't even taken a bath, a fact that he was well reminded of by his T-shirt sticking on his sweaty back. There was also the matter of the twenty-odd miles drive to the airport and he was supposed to check in at least an hour before his flight, thanks to the turbaned and bearded one in some cave wherever, and his deranged disciples.

The car, an old but still proud Subaru WRX, was taking the abuse relatively well. The dilapidated road, full of potholes, was ordinarily a tedious, slow, winding journey through what remained of the tarmac. The shock was minimised by the fact that the speed didn't allow the car to get into the mini craters; it simply flew over them. Just before he got to Kamiti Prison he turned right towards Kahawa West. There was a couple, Bob and Dene Njagi, who he was to pick up at Fanaka Complex, a seven-floor residential flat. He had sold them his car and they were to keep it after dropping him off at the airport. Even from a distance he could tell there was a power outage, a common occurrence in this part of the world. It was unusually dark, a dangerous thing in this crime-ridden estate. Trust things to go wrong when you can hardly afford it. His frustration was growing as he watched the precious minutes tick away, waiting for the couple to grope their way down the flat's winding stairs.

When he got to his sister Kendi's house, he quickly dropped Lulu off and asked her to get rid of some of the clothes and books that were making his luggage too heavy. Fuso didn't want the hassle of having to repack at the airport to reduce excess weight or pay extra for it under the accusing eye of a check-in attendant. Hurriedly he left for the Kenol fuel station where he was to meet his high school buddy, Moya, who had come to help him ferry his well-wishers to the airport. On his way to Kahawa West he had called Moya and told him he was on his way but when he got there Fuso couldn't find him. Apparently, Moya thought Fuso would be late – like always – so he drove around the estate just to cheer himself and Jean his girlfriend up. Both Moya and Jean hadn't been to Kahawa West before and they took the advantage to have a tour around at the expense of Fuso's precious time. The minutes drifted on and now Moya was lost. He couldn't find his way back to Kenol and being the man he is, and against his girlfriend's advice, he didn't ask for directions. That cost Fuso some twenty minutes to his chagrin. Fuso would have liked to strangle him when he finally showed up without remorse but that could have taken more of his fast-dwindling time.

"Hi, dude," Moya saluted when he finally spotted Fuso. "Been on a neighbourhood tour, took a little more time than I anticipated." He waved his long arms and shrugged with his broad rugby player shoulders.

"Hi, Jean," Fuso said to Moya's girlfriend, ignoring Moya. She was small and barely reached Moya's chest. Fuso felt sorry for her because Moya had a habit of tucking her head in his armpit whenever he held her.

"C'mon guys, let's go, we're running late."

"Won't say sorry if that's what you expect," said Moya, full of mischief.

"Suit yourself," Fuso said.

"He always does things the last minute," Moya said to his Jean. "Would sit till he watched the cast at the end of a film before running out of a burning house. I bet he hasn't even taken a bath."

"Oh, shut up, Moya!"

"See, true or false?"

Moya knew Fuso very well and how he always used to race the last day to finish his assignments. Fuso wasn't in a mood to discuss his little flaws; he just revved up his car and asked Moya to follow.

In his sister's house, Fuso found his mum, Rachel, his dad, Karani, and an assortment of relations, some who he didn't have the foggiest idea how they were related to him. They were all anxiously waiting for him. His dad was in an elegant suit he had convinced Fuso he needed through sophisticated persuasions. Fuso's aunt Neta was there with a nephew she supported through school. Probably she had brought him to learn from Fuso and see what goodies education could swing his way. Well, Fuso was a model to be emulated, a hero. He could see the young boy envied him and he thought he saw a look of resolve on the boy's face that he had better watch it. He wasn't going to remain the only hero for long. Also present was his brother-in-law Martin, his little baby nephew Kiki and several in-laws from his sister Kendi's side. Martin and Kendi were at their wits end worrying about the logistics of putting up so many people for the night. Where they would sleep was still a mystery, and only one of the least worrying of problems. Already the toilet was in a mess. A village relative had swung the flash handle with too much force – the only way he was used to, swinging hoes when tilling land – and broke it. The excitement of doing a number two without a dash to the bush or the dreadful pit latrine was such a convenience to behold. Now that the chain was broken, one had to use a bucket to flush the mess down after use but, being used to drop-and-go pit latrines, few did so. Kendi had to promise the house help extra pay when she threatened to quit immediately. The poor girl had the unenviable role of carrying bucketfuls of water to flush down the disgusting aftermath of the frequent visits to the loo.

Fuso was a celebrity. Everybody had something to tell him but he wasn't listening. There was no time. He rushed to the bathroom and asked Lulu to iron the clothes he was to wear for the trip. He had to be smart for his first major air travel, you see. His mum threw Lulu a curious look and his dad grinned… *Aha, so my son is normal after all!* They hadn't met Lulu nor heard about her and Fuso knew in his absence they wondered aloud what the matter with him was, socially. It must have been confusing for them because in his high school days they were always worried about his escapades with girls, but now that he had a good job and was all mature and stable, he never introduced any girls home.

All freshened up and ready, he called Lulu to an inner room and kissed her, probably the last in a long time. He was not sure he would be able to do that at the airport with his parents and kinsmen watching, it just isn't the done thing in Africa. When he emerged, he introduced Moya and Jean and also introduced everybody to them. Finally he introduced Lulu as his 'official' girlfriend.

"And finally, here's Lulu," he said, "my friend, my good friend, my girlfriend!" There was dead silence, and then everybody laughed.

"So Lulu, where're you from?" his dad said. Fuso answered the question for her, sensing she needed time to recover her breath. She was so nervous now that all eyes were on her. Trust Fuso's dad. Immediately, he shifted his attention to her, chatting like he had known her for ages. His mum wore an uncertain face, stealing suspicious glances at Lulu but Fuso thought he also read some emotion there, female bonding, probably sympathy with the poor girl. Mum was going to miss her baby boy so much and she understood it must have felt painful to his girlfriend as well.

Karani, Fuso's dad, was in his late fifties. He stood at five feet eight, slim and wore a look of wisdom and dignity. Karani never liked using one word where two would do. His garb skills went into overdrive, especially in farewells. He loved people, loved socialising; a very unusually emotional African man. If he were a millionaire, his life would have been one long party and travel. He hated to see people leave and if you visited him you were better off if you indicated your intention to leave half an hour before you hoped to depart. There was no way you would leave sooner. It was 8.30 when Karani took over after the introductions. Fuso hoped he understood when he explained he didn't have much time left so could he, Karani, be as brief as he could.

Karani started with his gratitude that his son's long-time dream was now being fulfilled, moved on to moralistic examples of others who went abroad and never returned to good old Mother

Africa or, worse, fell to vice; drugs and stuff. He talked about the wisdom of trusting in God for guidance all the time and in all places and more so in a foreign land where it was reputed godliness is scarce. Fuso fidgeted so much, wondering how to cut him short. Everyone except Karani kept sneaking glances at the wall clock but he didn't pick the cue. Finally he suggested two people should pray, one from among the up-country relations and the other from Nairobi. *Double prayers!*

The prayers were said, a lengthy one by the up-country lot as usual and a shorter one by Fuso's sister Kendi, who understood there was little time left. To their horror, Karani never believed any prayers well said if they weren't concluded with the Lord's Prayer and the Grace Prayer. The Amen after the grace was, however, said too soon. Someone was in a desperate attempt to stifle a fart with a cough, failing miserably. It not only rumbled in the abrupt silence but also the attempt to hide it with a cough was topped with a loud belch.

There was lots of food to eat that night, at Fuso's cost of course, and many didn't waste such an opportunity. Food in the village wasn't always cooked with flavour in consideration, to find enough food was sometimes hard enough. In the ensuing discomfort and embarrassment, people hurriedly got into the two available cars and a van. The van wasn't big enough to take everybody, earning Fuso a few enemies instantly. His up-country people considered such moments as important as a once-in-a-lifetime occasion. Of course, anybody could get on a bus and visit the airport any day, but seeing a relative off at the airport meant so much to them that if one was left out it was a marker of who ranked low in the clan. They had to scramble for the few spaces. With no apologies, Fuso had no time to sort out who to take and who to leave and even if he had, he wasn't going to be drawn into it. It was such a delicate family diplomacy issue.

The drive to the airport was, in a word, suicidal. Within minutes, Fuso's car was approaching the first roadblock at the heavily guarded Jomo Kenyatta Airport. If disrupting and inconveniencing everybody's lives was Osama's goal, then he had succeeded big time.

"Is this your car?" the policeman asked, leaning on the window, inspecting inside the car and taking time to study every face, perhaps expecting one tattooed with 'terrorist' on the forehead.

"That's right."

"Open the boot, please."

Fuso pulled the boot lever below the driver's seat and instinctively glanced at the time on the dashboard. It was 9.27 pm; he was late for check-in by more than twenty minutes. He wanted to scream and tell the cop that he was no terrorist.

"Please step out," he said.

*Oh, whatever for!* "Why, is anything wrong?"

"Not yet, just open the boot for me please."

The policeman was trying to be polite as he read Fuso's frustration. Fuso was trying to be calm. The cop wanted Fuso to lift the boot himself perhaps fearing he had a bomb in there that would go off when the lid lifted. If so, Fuso thought, then the cop was an idiot because he was right next to him and if there was an explosion it couldn't possibly miss him. The policeman quickly rummaged through the boot and told Fuso it was okay to shut it. He didn't even ask Fuso to open his luggage. Some inspection all right!

"What was all that for?" Fuso mumbled in exasperation.

"Sorry?" Luckily the cop didn't get that one.

"I said have a good evening officer."

"Nice trip sir."

*Sir, what sir?* Fuso hissed.

When Fuso got to the departures lounge he ran to the British Airways reception with Lulu in tow. At the entrance to the main Departures foyer, he found a small queue of latecomers like him and a massive security officer who was pushing away those who were seeing off their loved ones. He treated everybody like a potential terrorist or an accomplice. Certainly he was over enthusiastic about his boss's directive for extra alertness, these were troubled times of sick fanatics. Only passengers were allowed into the main foyer, a cruel move, especially to his Lulu who was in tears but there was nothing Fuso could do with a giant bully security officer between them.

After his bags were inspected he moved to the next desk where he found a middle-aged man who wore a face of calm defeat, resigned to the fate of sitting behind a desk for the rest of his life. He wanted to know where Fuso was going.

"To the UK for studies."

"Do you have a letter of admission to support that?"

Fuso produced his Bournemouth University admission and acceptance letter. The man fiddled with his passport, keenly inspecting it and occasionally throwing a glance at Fuso's face as if he wasn't sure of the semblance between the picture in the passport and the face before him. Finally he handed the documents back to him, satisfied.

"So you're a teacher?"

"Was, I quit a year ago."

"What are you now?"

"Work for NEMA, the environment agency."

"Oh, and if I'm not mistaken it's a government agency, right?"

"Right," Fuso mumbled.

"So you're a civil servant. Any letter from the ministry allowing you to travel?"

"None," Fuso sighed, alarmed at this line of questioning.

"You look honest. I like that. You better not say what you've just said at the third immigration counter or they won't let you leave. See this guy here?" Fuso looked at a distraught fellow next to the desk. "He too is a civil servant. They're demanding a letter from the ministry authorising his travel." Fuso sympathised with him. He imagined being stopped by overzealous immigration wardens from taking a journey that was a life's dream because you work for a government that ordinarily treats civil servants like a disease and then complains about brain drain. Instinctively, he looked outside where he could see his anxious loved ones watching just in case they might be taking him back home with them. When he was allowed to proceed, they raised the thumbs-up sign to him. He responded with a discreet nod, *so far so good.*

After the first desk, he moved on to the British Airways counter where he was welcomed by a gorgeous African beauty. She gave him a departure card to fill and chatted with him happily. He liked her. She helped him lighten up. The thought that someone could stop his trip when he had come this far had unsettled him quite a bit.

"Did you pack your luggage or did someone do it for you?" she asked, sweetly.

*Oh c'mon, my beautiful girlfriend of course, who else, and neatly so.* "Packed it myself."

"Has anyone else handled your luggage?"

*Oh yeah, all my kinsmen. How else could they share in the glamour of their hero?* "Oh, no-no, not at all."

At the adjacent desk, he could see Paul Tergat, the accomplished athlete with quite a few marathon world records in his name. He was putting his luggage on the scale and filling the departure form as well. If he was relaxed, Fuso would have run to him and asked for an autograph. You don't bump into a world record holding athlete every other day, but this wasn't an ordinary day. Well, he hoped he would be able to see him on the plane or in the waiting lounge upstairs. At least he was travelling on the same flight, probably even sitting next to him and that wasn't bad at all, although he didn't expect a man of that status to travel economy. In the meantime, he had his own hurdles to jump, so to say.

At the third counter, an immigration control point, he found the almighty immigration nightmare-makers. There were three of them, all in their fifties or sixties and wearing stern professional faces. Fuso gave one of them his passport and put on a brave face. The other two studied every inch of him. Somehow he felt very confident, even though the other two stared blankly at him. This was his life's dream and nobody was *gonna* take it away.

"I see you're a teacher," one of them stated.

"Was," Fuso said, as boldly as he could muster.

"When did you stop?"

"Last year."

"What do you do now?"

"Promoting cleaner environment," Fuso was trying to be vague. He was certain it would take ages before they figured a connection between civil service and environment.

"What's the purpose of your travel?"

"Further studies."

"Enjoy your flight," the one who held his passport said and stamped it.

"Next," he called. *Phew!*

Thoroughly relieved, he wished that he could go out and quickly hug everyone goodbye. Instead, Fuso headed straight for the departure lounge, which was probably a good thing because soon his mobile was ringing continuously.

After the phone rang persistently, he fished it out of his trouser pocket expecting another kind word from another distant relative, but instead it was Nimo, one of his many girl buddies. He picked the call expecting a word of goodbye and a reprimand because he only told her he was leaving the previous night.

"Hi Nimo."

"You're a bad boy. I'll smack you when you get out here."

"Out where, what have I done now?"

"I'm out here, outside main Departures, when done with check-in, get out here *haraka."*

"Nimo, I won't be coming out."

"What do you mean, you won't be coming out? I'm outside and you just can't leave without… a hug, a kiss, you… we haven't… you have to say a proper goodbye to me."

"Nimo, I'm already in the boarding lounge. It's too late. You didn't tell me you were coming to see me off." There was a long silence on the other side but he could hear she was sobbing. *Crying?* Was she crying because he didn't say a proper goodbye? Were they really that close?

"Nimo, please… I'm sorry… I…"

"It's all right. I'll miss you. I love you." There, she blurted it out.

"I love you so much." That blew him over. Someone told him once, a long time ago, that there was nothing like being 'just friends' between compatible men and women. At least one of them will always have a niggling wish the friendship graduated to something deeper. Now he saw the wisdom especially when the said 'just friends' were young compatible singles. Fuso thanked the circumstances because he didn't know how he could have handled the situation with both Nimo and Lulu present. He sighed and concentrated on answering last quick calls from well-wishers, envious of his prospective life of glamour.

Soon it was time to board the plane. He was doing well for a first timer so far, thanks to movies, safe for showing the boarding staff his passport instead of the boarding ticket, a small mix-up really. He trooped on like a veteran through the air bridge to the door of the huge BA Boeing 747. To welcome the passengers on board was a beautiful, smartly dressed steward and a captain who stunk of charisma. He cut a fatherly image, made Fuso feel safe. The only hitch was when he took the wrong seat and a tough-looking middle-aged lady, firmly but respectfully pointed it out to him that he had taken the wrong seat, her seat. He apologised profusely, hurriedly taking his hand luggage with him to the right seat.

There was movement all over the cabin. Passengers were trying to find their seats and putting their hand luggage in the compartments above. It now seemed silly the pains he had gone to, buying new clothes befitting the class of 'highflyers'. All around were clothes in different stages of wear and a few in stages of tear. A teenage Asian guy was in shorts that were once jeans, now cut and the edges purposely frayed out around the thighs. Fuso could tell his turbaned much older companion, perhaps the father, disapproved but had heard something about letting the young be and hoped the boy would grow past his teenage years fast before he tried ugly tattoos and piercings whether conventional or in dodgy places. Fuso could also tell the shorts the teenager wore had had little association with water in recent days and the fade did little to hide it. A middle-aged white woman had a T-shirt that attracted attention with its rampant holes that revealed too much for decency. It also had an inviting message around the bust that read: I have F, C and K all I need is U. A young black guy's attempt to emulate those rappers you see on music channels had tragically backfired. If you heard a knock at your door and when you answered were met at the door by his face in his dark sunglasses and an ugly bandana to go with it you would have a heart attack. He looked horrendous. Did he really need the sunglasses in the cabin?

Fuso was still trying to convince himself that this was real, that his dream was becoming true, when the captain's voice came through the speakers.

"This is your captain, Carlton Edwards. Welcome aboard British Airways, flight 64. We're going to spray the plane for bugs and flies. Please bear with us, it's not harmful and has no smell."

The captain then made a few more announcements about safety and the expected weather on the flight path. He also humorously said something about smoking.

"Please note that this BA flight has a strict no-smoking policy. I'm allowed to report offenders to my grandmother, a formidable anti-smoking activist you don't want to mess with." That elicited laughter across the cabin.

After a little while the huge plane taxied to the runway. It was time for the skies. It surged forward with a little jerk and picked speed. Fuso was relishing every second of the moment. He had been on a small plane before, a Cessna something or other, but this was different. The plane lazily lifted off, not as fast as he expected but he wasn't afraid, not when his life was beginning. He had a long life ahead of him, where his dreams lay waiting for him to realise them, where they had been waiting to soothe him.

# 2

The glowing lights in Nairobi city below were beautiful. Fuso stared in delight, trying to make out the familiar places; a futile indulgence for it all looked like a simmer of dancing glow. It was to be a long time before he set foot on his home city again and a nostalgic cloud hovered above him but he quickly suppressed it. He had dreams to chase, soothing dreams that had kept his ambitions alive. Achieving them was going to take a while. He wasn't going to get homesick within minutes of his departure.

Not too long after take-off the safety belts signs went off. It was time for dinner. Fuso was hit by a bout of craving for some wine to go with his meal but he strongly repelled it. An evil destroyer of principles kept whispering in his ears that it was okay, that no one was looking, that in any case 'everybody' was doing it. The voice in his head also said that when he arrived abroad, apparently wine was offered at every meal. The other voice however, the voice of reason, reminded him of his Christian convictions, his version disapproved of taking any alcohol. Besides he reckoned he needed to be sober for the final hurdle at the entry point.

One of his friends overseas had sent him a text message saying that it was important he had proof of financial capability to support himself through his university course. He didn't have one. Mistakenly he had sent the bank statement of his 'sponsor' with his visa application and they don't give back application documents except the passport. He was now beginning to get worried but he wasn't going to do much of that on an empty stomach. It had been a very busy day with hardly a moment to even take a bite. In any case, the young, pretty and elegant cabin crew were smiling appetite into him. But some of the cabin crew were not so young and Fuso wondered what they were still doing in a job like that, trying so hard to conceal stretch marks on their faces with layers of make-up. He was to understand later about labour rights and stuff… *but pleeease…* an illegal thought came to his mind, *sssh… isn't it understood the world over that some roles are better handled by younger blood?* Anyone who doubted that should ask his deceased grandpa, may his very brave soul be well rested; he married a new wife every new decade! Oh, and there were still a dozen or so children dotted around the neighbourhood and nearby villages – surprisingly all rascals, hotheads, crazies or all of these – who resembled him too much to be coincidental.

The assorted dishes that were set before him were a real mystery. Fuso didn't know what to start or end with. He could tell there was some form of rice, some flesh of an animal or other, leaves that might as well have been plucked from a murky pond. Constantly he sneaked glances across the middle aisle and followed how a smartly dressed gentleman went about this fork and knife business. For a time, he was doing fine, concentrating more on how to hold the fork and knife than on the taste of the food. Well, when he finally picked the taste he immediately decided to starve than die of food poisoning. *What's that stuff they've just served me?* he thought. Fuso's good old judgement whispered to him that he was the safer drinking coffee only. He gestured at a middle-aged, beautiful Asian or Latino hostess, who was still serving the middle aisle, that he wanted coffee.

"Coffee inn't?" she said, and looked at him quizzically.

"*Innay what?*"

"Coffee… did you say or tea?" she asked slowly after seeing the confusion in his face. She flashed her mystically beautiful eyes with unusually long natural eyelashes and waited for a response.

"Oh, coffee." *Innayte, what on earth…* and then it clicked in his mind this *innit* business; his brain had taken a while to process that.

When coffee came she might as well have given him a concoction of antiseptic, aspirin and bleach. It tasted horrible.

*Why are they so keen to poison me?* he kept asking in his mind. To save his life, and his taste buds, he settled for apple juice. At least that tasted close to human food.

The soft hum of the engines wafted lazily like smoke that on inhalation sent people to sleep, eagerly assisted by full stomachs. It was as if someone had rung a bedtime bell. Almost everyone in the cabin fell asleep after the meal. Never underestimate the power of food. Well, a few passengers like Fuso who didn't tuck in much, and a lady in the seat in front of him who cleared everything and was still asking for a bite of this and a sip of that, were still awake. Fuso had lots of things to worry about… but there was still time. Meanwhile he explored the channels on the in-flight entertainment system until he landed on some slow lulling music. He needed his nerves calm for later.

Waking up with a start, Fuso took a brief moment to recall where he was. He must have drifted to dreamland. Almost everybody was asleep in the semi-lit cabin. A few guys still had their reading lights on, shuffling through papers that only they knew what they were about. A sense of panic began to germinate in him. A quick check of his watch said it was 2 am. Whatever time zone it was, it didn't matter. All that mattered was that he was getting closer to the point of entry into the land of his dreams. He had to be prepared for it. Fuso had heard that folks like him were treated with suspicion, guilty till proven innocent; he had to be ready, to prove his innocence.

Thinking of proving his genuineness, his mind drifted to the issue of the bank statement. He cursed himself for lacking foresight. He should have made copies. When he went back to his distant auntie who had given him the statement, the alleged sponsor, she didn't seem comfortable with getting him another one. Fuso didn't blame her. A bank statement isn't something you go dishing out every time someone requests it.

"I did what I could, son," she had said to him. "Now you've got a visa, you're an educated person. You should know how to go about accomplishing your goals. In any case, you speak their language, tantalise them with it." Tantalise all right!

"I'll try *shangazi*, I will try. Thanks a lot for your help. I'll always remember."

"Don't mention it, son."

The issue of his being educated, as she said, caused him embarrassing self-reflection. Here was an old lady, older than his mum by far and, more astounding, illiterate. She had to be taught for years just to sign her name. The multinational bank was bored with her signing with a thumbprint but wanted her money. Single-handedly, she had built a small scrap metal business into a multi-million outfit and had huge investments in real estate. Even in Queen's pounds her wealth would run into a few million, quite impressive. She was now challenging Fuso that he was supposed to be doing better, yet there he was leaving his good job for greener pursuits overseas. She never left Kenya even once… but then she hadn't seen many movies either.

Fuso had to think of a way to prove his financial capability to see him through university but he didn't have a clue how. Saying a prayer sounded brilliant. It is amazing how trouble arouses the spiritual in lots of people. He promised God lots of things like keeping the way of righteousness if God saw him through this and invoked the name of Christ, reminding Him that he owned everything including Great Britain and that he was just an ambitious child who wanted to visit another part of what Jesus owned… they were buddies you know… a friend in deed is a friend in need and that sort of thing.

Reaching overhead, Fuso pulled down his small bag where he had stashed the Bournemouth University brochures. Familiarity of facts was an asset here. He studiously went through them like an exam leak until he was satisfied nobody would catch him off guard with anything about Bournemouth. He knew everything from its history to the geo-coordinates and how much the coach would charge him from King's Cross Station, or from wherever, to Bournemouth. However, Bournemouth would have to wait forever.

At dawn he could tell they were already in European airspace. There were millions of sparkling lights below unlike the massive expanse of darkness that covers Africa. *Oh, Africa!* Soon the pilot announced that they were flying over Paris. Fuso was excited and peered through the window to see if he could make out the Eiffel Tower. *Paris too had better wait for me.* He made a mental note that he had to visit Paris before his tour of 'operation brighter day' in Europe was over.

If you are to get into trouble, Fuso thought, then it better be on a full stomach. This is what his wisdom suggested when breakfast was served. He felt revulsion when he remembered the previous meal but this time he took what seemed familiar and remembered to take tea instead of coffee although they gave him only a drop of cream and a few particles of sugar. Fuso instantly missed Kenya where tea is brewed and served differently: lots of it with lots of milk, lots of sugar and lots of warmth. Tea drinking in Kenya was almost like a ritual.

Not long after breakfast, the captain announced that the plane was going to land at Heathrow Airport in twenty minutes and repeated the security highlights about remaining seated till the plane came to a complete halt and not using mobile phones till complete stop. Fuso threw a tired look down as the huge jumbo descended for the approach to landing. *Okay, this is it,* he said to himself, and felt a surge of adrenaline rush through his body. Finally, the inevitable was about to happen. The next half hour was to either fulfil or shatter his life's dream.

When the gigantic bird came to a complete halt, Fuso retrieved his hand luggage from the locker above his head and arranged his documents in a way that would enable him to readily produce them on demand. The million interviews he had gone through in search of jobs had conditioned him. He also took a *Highlife* magazine and a gift pack the airline gave to all its world traveller passengers, not knowing he would have an unpleasant encounter with the pack later. The gift pack had a toothbrush, paste and a pair of socks. Maybe they figured folks needed to freshen up after such a long haul, especially those who still had connecting flights. The pack was like a souvenir to him; ever give thanks for small mercies, Mama taught him early in life. He wasn't sure if he was to take the magazine though but he figured he had paid the moon for the flight and a magazine couldn't dent the mega profits of the mighty BA.

Out of the plane, Fuso joined the tired travellers into the air bridge that led to corridors and halls and more corridors. He simply followed the directions, marvelling at the sophistication of a big modern airport. It almost sounded laughable that Nairobi's Jomo Kenyatta Airport was called 'international'. *All of it was only the size of one of Heathrow's terminals!* Fuso trooped on like a pro, barely concealing his fascination with the small technological conveniences like the escalator-like 'thingy' that you just stood on and it moved you down the corridor like a treadmill. Yeah, he had seen escalators, but this wasn't one. It was flat on a flat corridor, so what did they call it?

Deep within him he was sure he would get through immigration but was resigned to whatever happened. Anything that was to go wrong would go wrong. However, somehow he felt he would get through. He was still whispering prayers when he found himself face to face with the immigration officials at the arrivals reception desk – the people who were going to determine his future. The foyer was deceptively welcoming for this is where many a life was shattered. Fuso distracted himself from panicking by wondering what so many old folks – mostly Asian and black people – were doing there just to organise the queues and dish out arrival forms, which anyone could pick from the wall rack anyway; weren't they too old to be out at night in the cold? But sssh… that's an illegal thought! He had filled his arrival card on the plane so straightaway he joined the queue. There was a lady who looked motherly and humble and a hulk of a guy who seemed in a hurry to finish his shift and go home. It was 5.15 in the morning local time and the human body will always rebel against crazy night shifts no matter how routine they become. Back to basics, night is night – people sleep and rest; day is day – folks rise and work. But then the world's economy would slump, or wouldn't it? Two other officials were a bit too far away for him to read their temperament. He prayed and hoped he would land at the lady's desk. That reassuring look was just what he needed.

Like it is wont to happen, an Asian-looking girl ahead of him might have been thinking the same thing. Instead of going to the hulk's desk she dropped her bag either intentionally or not and in that split second the lady's desk became vacant. She purposefully marched there with Fuso's burning eyes watching her mess his life. An impatient guy behind him tapped his shoulder, pointing at the hulk's desk. *This was it!* He walked there with assumed confidence, though his heart beat a hundred times a minute, sending floods of blood to his head making him feel woozy. He silently started saying his prayers.

"Is this your first time to the UK?"

"Yes sir."

"Which flight were you on?"

"Nairobi–London."

"You're a student, right?"

"That's right."

"Will you be taking residence at the college?"

"Yes sir." He hadn't looked up so far. That wasn't bad because Fuso was mumbling the name 'Jesus' over and over again. Now he looked up. *Bad.*

"Has the college asked you to bring a chest X-ray scan?"

"No."

"Then you need to take one. You go down the hall, right through the blue door to the reception inside. You'll be directed where to take the X-ray." He stamped Fuso's passport and gave it back to him. Its fruit, his people and the good book said, judges a tree. At that moment that was the best guy in the whole wide world. Fuso could have given him whatever he owned if he asked.

"Oh, and please let us know your exact address when you settle at the college because what we have there is the office address, we'd want the residential address as well."

"I'll do that. Thank you." If he was keen he could have noted the emotion Fuso attached to the last statement. Fuso had met an angel.

When he passed the seemingly kind lady's desk she was still

haggling rudely with the Asian girl over her documents. The girl was now in tears and was being told to step aside to allow other passengers get attended. Her papers had been handed to other officials in a glass office behind the desk who were now busy studying them suspiciously. Fuso thanked Jesus and proceeded to the blue door for his X-ray. An elderly nurse took him to a booth and told him to remove his shirt, closely studying every inch of his upper body. It felt awkward. She was like his grandma checking if he had had a bath in the last week, but what was he to do? She took his X-ray and told him to wait at her desk. She returned moments later to tell him that he was all clear, fine. That too gave him some relief. What was it about, TB scan? No health hitches were going to deter him from his dream. She gave him a report card and told him to post it back to her when he got to know his exact address. A fine lady, kind and welcoming she was. It may sound silly but months later it filled Fuso with much guilt that he never sent the card back to her.

Close to heaven is what Fuso felt when he got behind the immigration officials on his way to pick his luggage. It had happened! Oh boy it was happening! He wanted to scream, crow, sing and do a shimmy. Quickly he went through the complicated maze of stairs and escalators to the luggage collection foyer below. He found an Asian-looking guy, a security officer or something that directed him where to pick his luggage. When he found it, the handle was broken but he didn't care a hoot about it. He could have given BA the box with its contents if they wanted it safe for his photos, which he greatly valued, as for his papers they were in his handbag. On a lighter thought he figured if he was a local, with the compensation culture raging, perhaps he would sue for damages and a host of lifelong psychological trauma asking for compensation that could see him retire comfortably. He wondered why universities didn't include modules on successful compensation claims in their business courses, or did they? Sssssh, but those are illegal thoughts…

Out in the arrivals foyer he joined the hundreds of other travellers scurrying in all directions. There was controlled chaos of exaggerated hugs, of reunited loved ones, the odd lost and anxious lonely soul, creepy unlicensed cab operators discreetly wooing passengers, and a cacophony of announcements that few listened to. Fuso strolled to a forex bureau and changed a fiver into coins so that he could make a call.

"Hello, I'm here," he happily said to his cousin Makena when she picked the phone. He could tell she was still in bed.

"Oh, hi boy, you're early. Your pilot should be done in for speeding. I wasn't going to be out of bed for another hour. Don't worry though, just get some place to sit and wait for me, won't be long."

Fuso could wait for as long as anyone cared. He was in Queen's GB, the heart of the great empire that once marched on his very village like colossus, treading on the poor locals; killing, imprisoning, detaining, torturing and all. The primitive natives had to be civilised, pulled out of the dark ages. It was a divine mission, bestowed by the Almighty and if the natives didn't cooperate, a little pushing was in order. Well, they had to respect their saviours, you see, hats off when the *Johnnies* drove past and that sort of thing. If they didn't, the young well-trained Queen's soldiers would help them remove the dirty hats. See, their guns were oh so accurate… but accidents happen. Once in a while the hat came off laced with the murk of spilt mixture of brains and blood… but those were accidents… and the native was to blame for not removing the hat… why were some natives so disrespectful? Such were the illegal thoughts that passed in Fuso's mind now that he had come for some retribution. Luckily there were no mind readers around.

He joined two teenagers who were on the same flight as him. Fuso could tell they were Kenyans just by looking at their faces. There's something about identifying your own that is ingrained in humans. You just recognise them but can't pin down what it is that is distinctive about them. You just know.

"Hi, my name's Fuso, Kenyan," he said.

"Ann, Kenyan too," the girl said, unsure what Fuso was up to.

"Mutuku, can tell from *ma* name. Kenyan as well," went the

dandy youth, with a supposedly trendy levelling of shoulders.

"Well, what brings you to the UK?"

"Study, A levels," said Ann, a little settled now.

"Me," went dandy boy, "books man, and *chums* if I get them. Must make enough dough to buy a convertible *Beema*." Fuso resisted rolling his eyes. He couldn't argue with another person's priorities and aspirations.

They were soon chatting like they had known each other for ages. It is funny how folks who never communicated beyond a hasty bored wave or nod back on their turf find they have enough to make a conversation when they meet in strange places. Ann was from the wealthy Kenyan families who drove monster 4x4s, that rivalled military tanks in size, might and fuel addiction but here she was happy that she had someone who could at least understand her *Engsheng*. That was a supposedly superior form of *Sheng*, the slang language of the young concocted of English, Swahili and an assortment of Kenya's numerous local languages. Ann was also relieved to have someone on whom she could spill some of her now recovering attack of nerves. A kinsman had been so worried that their sweet princess wouldn't get a proper Kenyan meal in such a long time she had packed for her half a freezer of ready foodstuff. Ann had been so anxious throughout the flight, worried sick that she would be asked to open her luggage by immigration officials and the first stuff to roll off would have been several dozen ready sausages and chapatis. As it turned out, none of that happened and though she scorned at the irony of a few days' food supply to wean her into European food, she was glad she had a bite of something that could answer to the name food. She had, like Fuso, found the in-flight meal too much for her stomach.

Ann was the first one to be picked. A huge fellow adorning a diamond ear stud came stomping into the lounge to where they sat. She saw him just before he reached them and jumped hugging him and hung on him like a teddy bear. It was an emotional experience complete with tears, more from the guy than from Ann. It was strange what the West could do to a full-blooded circumcised African warrior. The emotions spent and tears wiped, Ann introduced them to her big brother who studied at some university or other. He had been in the UK for a long time having studied his A levels in Britain. These were the cream of the elitist Kenyans who owned holiday homes abroad. It was not surprising to find such a student lived in a five-bedroom apartment in an upmarket London suburb and drove a convertible Porsche. The biggest challenge they had in life was not what they could afford but on making the 'difficult' choice of what is it that they wanted in life. Fuso squirmed, peering past the gloom stretched before his eyes into the smog that was his future. *I have a dream Europe, I have a dream… that one day I won't strain groping in the dark for a way out of the tunnel… that my children will look at tomorrow with a reassured hope and not with anxiety and fear… and here I am, paying the price for it… for that dream. Will you help me fulfil it?* He was almost going philosophical there, Martin Luther's messages replayed in his mind.

Fuso was the next one to be picked. Mutuku's brother was coming from Gloucestershire and that was going to take a while. Fuso's cousin arrived after almost an hour. She had lost some time after going to Terminal 3 only to realise he was in Terminal 4. Relief welled in him when he saw her. Fatigue was catching up with him and the teenager's *Sheng* was straining his ears. Fuso's *Sheng* being rusty, he had to form the words slowly in his brain before processing the meaning. That wasn't something the mind fancied after a nine-hour flight. Fuso bade the lad goodbye and left him Makena's number, which he requested, promising he would call. It was obvious the poor guy was afraid he might not get many other Kenyans to socialise with and wanted contacts of the one available… a bird at hand…

Drunk with anticipation, Fuso followed his cousin Makena out through the automatic doors, to the pick-up area outside. The world outside was dazzling in the clearing morning. The cars were so clean and posh and the coaches looked magnificent. Cabs were lined up so orderly on the clean roads devoid of any dust and rubbish. As a matter of fact, that was something that was to confound him a lot. Dust and rubbish was rampant in Nairobi.

The hot sun and poorly maintained roads and pavements ensured that your eyes were thoroughly tortured by dust, a signature of wild Africa?

"Help me put this one in the boot, *meit*," the cabbie said to him politely, in a hurry to put Fuso's luggage in and get them going. It was this box-type black cab, no doubt a more recent model of the ones found in Kenya. This one was immaculately clean and groaned less noisily. Smoothly the cab eased out of the airport and headed west after the roundabout towards Staines. The cars once again fascinated him. Admittedly he had a serious love for cars. A nice clean car raised his adrenaline to highs and when cars did a real stunt Fuso got drunk. In his dreams, his ultimate machine was the Range Rover, the class car a Mercedes, add taste to class and you have a Porsche, if young and still love a life you've earned, step forward Golf GTI and the old love… respected, to keep in rickety mobility and stuttering heart… VW Beetle. Fuso's dream was to own these four and he always fantasised of remaking a Beetle; give it a sunroof, metallic grey or blue coat, alloy spoke rims, a digital music system… that sort of thing. Pretty cars left him speechless. He was now in a good country, he could tell, and his interest was going to be indulged to the full.

In less than twenty minutes they were on Staines Road approaching Ashford hospital and turned left on Desford Way where his cousin Makena and Wambúi, Makena's roommate since high school, lived in a one-bedroom flat. It was a short drive from the airport indeed. It took Fuso a minute to take in the surroundings. The serenity of the place made him notice just how quiet everything was around. As if from a reverie he noticed for the first time that he hadn't heard anyone honk. Fuso shook his head when he thought about the maddening blare of so many decibels of car horns in downtown Nairobi. He could still hear them in his head and he could still hear the drug-crazed *matatu* touts shouting for passengers.

His cousin lived in a small cosy first-floor single-bedroom flat but he had the facts and knew that he was going to be accommodated somehow. When you come from a place where at some point in your life you had to share the little there was with many siblings and relatives you get used to these things. Better, actually, if you didn't ask many questions and waited for things to take their course. At times things worked, mostly so, but once in a while they didn't and small squabbles and fights followed. Nothing lasted long though, for that was the situational peculiarity of the African communal lifestyle. Jet-lagged and consoled that finally he was on a highway to where his dreams lay, he mumbled catching-up stories with his cousin till he dropped into a deep sleep on the couch.

He must have left some sentence about his ambitions half finished because his first dream was about his cousin visiting him in his villa on some island and him filling her in on how his beautiful wife and two kids – a boy and a girl who were now playing besides his Range Rover – were doing. The second dream – actually a mental replay – was about how it all started that he was now in the land of the great and the royals. Of a people who affected his history so much, of a dream that was coming to be… a life of fantasy actualised and it played in his mind, how it all started.

# 3

Fuso was named Irúngú Karani at birth. When Mathendi, one of his wealthy uncles, bought a ten-wheeler Mitsubishi Fuso truck little Irúngú, then four, went mad. He was a hopeless petrol head and his love for cars started early. So hopelessly he was in love with the huge machine, so drunk with its power; the virile hum of its new engine, its musky diesel smell and the baritone of its engine's brake-assist pressure system he ate, talked, played... and lived the truck. Arguably he was the most knowledgeable four-year-old about Fuso trucks. To ease the youngster's obsession with the truck and get him out of his lorry, Mabeca bought him Fuso branded T-shirts, caps and toy trucks. His little mates started calling him Fuso, mainly because that's all they heard from him, then the name stuck with everybody. After a big fight, even his dad conceded to calling him Fuso despite his discomfort with the connection to its origin. He had an icy relationship with his wealthier brother but it was not jealousy. 'Wrong chemistry' he called it.

Fuso's best friend in the initial years of schooling was a likeable fellow called Bryan. He was a son of a wealthy and respected farm manager on a white man's coffee estate far from home at Kíganjo in Kíambu. Only such folks could afford fancy names like Bryan, wherever they got them from. A generous kid like Bryan was always ready to share goodies he brought from home and it was from him that Fuso first saw a sausage – a real one that is. The ones he had eaten before were just chunks of half-cooked intestines, ends tied with banana-stalk fibre, stuffed with anything from raw blood to indefinable pieces of meat you couldn't dare eat if you saw it raw. It was a miracle that folks didn't die from eating these sausages going by the fancy name *mútura*, but fancy name or not, though people didn't die from eating them, if they caught you on a wrong footing, they had a way of irritating the bowels. What followed was serious 'driving', a local euphemism for diarrhoea.

Besides the sharing of delicacies, Bryan also brought back coloured magazines after school holidays, which he always spent in the farms at Kíganjo playing with the white kids of the farm directors. The pictures in the magazines were magical, almost heavenly, portraying exotic Western places and countries with foreign names like Canada and Australia. There were pictures of horses, of smoothly mowed lawns, of expansive fields with friendly welcoming well-tended grass and well-trimmed hedges.

The kids at his school spent hours dreaming about exotic places as portrayed in the magazines. They imagined and fantasised how it would be like if they ever found themselves in places like that. As his best friend, Bryan lent Fuso some of the magazines knowing, of course, he never intended to return them. Fuso still had one in his possession all these years that he might return someday. Fuso's fantasies were transferred home where he compared the dirt floor of his house with the beautiful, tiled floors he saw in the pictures, all sorts of tiles and other floors adorned with beautiful carpets. He revelled at the thought of how it felt like to live in a house where he could walk barefoot and still jump into bed without his mama screaming that he had to wash his feet... being a rural village boy that was utopia.

His love with the West had just begun, especially the pictures with serene sceneries of wheat fields and horses and low, wooden or stone fences. They made him ache with longing. The country boy in him became salient. He even imagined himself up on the gentle hills watching the lazy slope, whistling to the sheep, cows and horses. A desire burned in him to travel, to visit places, to go round the world and experience this magic. Suddenly, his village looked ugly. The trees were wild and the fences were overgrown to grotesque shapes. Their silhouettes in the moonlight filled the kids with terror at night when that unwelcome call of nature echoed and they had to walk the few odd agonising yards to the 'long drop' pit latrine outside. The fireside tales that mostly featured child-eating ogres didn't help either. Many were the times the 'relief act' was done halfway through the path to the latrine, opting to face Mama's wrath rather than the ogres lurking in the bushes. The terror was so real in their young minds, almost tangible.

Few people trimmed their fences like his paternal grandpa Njúgúna did. He had learnt this from the *mzungu* he worked for, an Englishman who not only taught him a few positive things like neatness, cleanliness and all, but he also taught Grandpa the negative, a little of English mostly dwelling on the four-letter words. Enough words though – the mentionable ones that is, which Grandpa used with abandon when his short temper got the better of him – had more than four letters like 'bloody' and 'swine'.

Sadly, for understandable reasons, Bryan was transferred to a modern independent farm school where his white friends studied and went to live with his dad. Gíthima Primary School, which was two miles away from Fuso's home, was no place for the pampered, soft-skinned lot like Bryan. The school was built on a hill, the highest peak in the village, hopefully to give the impression of a citadel of enlightenment. It was the biggest in the location, handling upwards of fifteen-hundred pupils and with such a population, coupled by a raw neighbourhood, villains and rascals abounded. Discipline therefore had to be strict. Reporting time was seven in the morning, yet Fuso was never punished for lateness unlike his wealthier friend who always arrived late but then, like his mother, the teachers were lenient with him. It helped if your dad was the village who's who. Fuso was also never dragged to school by an irate mum like some boys who found playing *mbiira* and riding *tiri* more fun than making audience to cane-wielding teachers determined to whip ignorance out of them. Truancy was rampant. Fascinated by cars and the skills matatu touts had swinging and hanging like chimps on moving matatu's doors, enough of the boys' ambition was to become matatu touts. That didn't require much education except perhaps having strong biceps to swing off van doors and basic arithmetic to give the correct change to the passengers.

Some teachers contributed too by behaving like jail wardens looking after dangerous perverts. The boys nicknamed them accordingly. Mr Kamanú was called *Cuma* – iron, for his iron-fisted punishments. Mr Kíirú was called *Mara ma thumuni* for his love of fifty-cent-worth of roasted goat and beef intestines. He had a weakness for the odd offals that he ever munched to fill his sagging belly. Mr Micah was called *Ngui* for dog. He was appropriately nicknamed because when angry he portrayed psychopathic traces akin to a rabid dog and attacked the pupils like a maniac; he used to scream, mouth frothing, kick and call kids dogs too. He injured many but those were the days when people didn't know their rights. One of his favourite punishments was to cane the pupils as they squatted, arms at the calves under the inside of the knee, hands on the ears. If you took your hands off the ears, the count was lost and he caned you all over again.

Fuso had this experience once after skiving Micah's art and craft lesson. The pupils were meant to bring a completed art project but Fuso had none. Weighing the consequences of not having an art project or skiving, he gambled with the possibility that perhaps Micah's rabid instincts also made him forgetful. And if asked about skiving he would say he had a headache or something like that, he would deal with it when it got to that.

And getting to that it did. Fuso and three other boys in a similar dilemma hid in the bushes on the lower side of the school overlooking Waigwe's farm. True to the rumour that Micah could sniff skivers and truant pupils from miles away, he appeared from nowhere and stood at the entrance to the hideout. What followed was not unlike rats trying to escape from a hole a cat had positioned itself at the mouth of. The wallop was swift and brutal. Afterwards the four boys were rounded up in the staffroom for the 'official' punishment, despite the fact that they were already in a bad way from the hideout encounter. Only Fuso's good reputation and pleas from other teachers made mad Micah reduce the punishment to only ten lashes. He caned the boys swearing at them and calling them dogs for breaking wind – they couldn't help it in that lip-frog posture he had ordered them to take and from the searing pain. Micah was so incensed his mouth frothed like an exhausted bulldog.

As it is said, 'every dog has its day'. Micah's day came after the boys he was used to terrorising had had enough. He had gone on one of his torturous sprees whipping and whacking anyone who as much as crossed his path. Micah was on duty that week and his duty weeks were known for strict discipline. Pupils behaved their best. None wanted to nurse an injury by falling prey to his rabid instincts. It had rained so much the Sunday preceding Mr Micah's duty week. It always happened that when it rained came mud-sliding, a 'sport' every boy relished but which was banned at school. The boys simply made a stretch of the muddy ground very slippery with water from the puddles then competed who would slide the longest and fastest barefooted without losing balance. The boys couldn't wait for Monday, Micah or no Micah. This was, however, a no-no when Micah was on duty. He was so cross he rounded the participants, nearly half the boys in the school, and with the help of other like-minded spoilsport teachers, persecutors of mud-sliding faithful, caned the boys so much they couldn't sit on their bums afterwards.

Fuso didn't subscribe to the 'sport'. There was no way he could be involved in such a major violation of school rules. Apart from his encounter with Micah for skiving off an art and craft lesson, the only other offence he ever committed was to take a pocket mirror to school. This was considered contraband, supposedly its sole motive being to peep up girls' skirts. The mirror had accidentally dropped to the floor but the scandalised girls in his class were having none of it. In a rare unity of mission, the girls led by Wangeci, the most militant of the lot, trooped to the staffroom to report the abomination to the class teacher. Much as the teacher wanted to hear Fuso's side of the story, aware of Fuso's reputation to be a good boy, this had become such a hot political issue and the girls had to be appeased. See, unlike the boys, the girls were considered innocent until proven otherwise. It was their word against his from the start. The punishment was immediate and thorough, fifteen lashes in all to pacify the fifteen girls. Fuso never took another mirror to school and neither was he found on the wrong side of school rules again.

To the other boys his obedience meant he was either chicken-hearted – a sissy – or he was a traitor. They therefore didn't make him privy to the plot they had to 'do in the dog'. At 4 pm after classes that day in late March, Fuso saw a big group of the super rascals, the mud-sliding martyrs, congregate at the extreme end of the field that they called 'coast' and he instinctively knew there would be trouble. He kept a distance when they lowered their voices and herded themselves closer, their eyes expressing their displeasure at his presence. It was clear he was unwelcome.

"The dog has messed too much with us," said Gatiba. He was small statured but tough as nails. Being the mud-sliding priest, he was surrounded by his agitated adherents.

"Yieeh," they mumbled in agreement.

"Sliding is here to stay. It's our right, our fun, right?"

"Right!" the boys shouted, nodding their little heads in agreement, and some still scratching their burning buttocks.

"The teachers either slide or we slide and coz they won't then they let us be." He was now getting philosophical. A few boys clapped to his wisdom.

"The school isn't theirs, neither are the grounds, yieeh?"

"Yieeh!"

"The water isn't theirs as well, God rained it," he barked, his fist clenched, his activism becoming passionate. He got more nods for that. "A dog is just that; a dog. Let's kill the mongrel."

"Yieeh," they agreed, their little faces stern with resolve.

"You are either with us or forever on your own. Those in for this, let's go. Get enough stones, let them rain, let the dog take them all in his porridge-filled skull. I have the cable." Gatiba spoke with zest and led the boys down through Mwíhaki's forest, down to Gathima-iní by Henderson's well (Hendersoni is what the local tongue could manage), crossed River Karura and went up the hill towards Kahethu. They trooped on in single file, purposefully, not unlike a military drill. Any military commander would have been impressed. Fuso had to rush home immediately lest he be associated in any way with the looming catastrophe.

True to his instincts, news trickled in the following day. Mr Micah was reported to have had a terrible motorbike accident the previous day at Kahethu when riding home and had broken both his legs. The first people to arrive at the accident scene said they found lots of stones and a cable partly entangled in the bike's spokes. The cable had been tied to a tree and run across the road to the other side. It was evident it had been used to trip poor Micah to his near fatal crash. The culprits were not immediately known and Fuso couldn't tell what he knew for fear of reprisals. Those rascals could do anything. It added weight to his already overburdened conscience. Gatiba had a way of scaring everyone into secrecy about his many freaky exploits.

To divert attention from an imminent probe about the accident by the suspicious teachers, Gatiba the chief mischief-maker came up with another of his impish firsts. Mr Mbúgua was caning everyone who had not done homework. When it came to his turn, Gatiba retrieved the crushed yolk of a raw egg he had in a bottle and quickly put its contents in his mouth. By the third lash he threw himself to the floor groaning and foaming and spat out the yolk. The class screamed in horror. The rest of the school came running and joined in the hysterical wailing for the dying boy. Most of the pupils ran home in panic, triggering village frenzy in the neighbourhood. Gatiba was rushed to Kigumo Dispensary by the terrified headteacher, Mr Njakú, in his car with the villagers baying for a bloody vengeance. In his entire teaching career, no child had died under his care. At the dispensary, when the freaked-out headteacher rushed to get the medics, Gatiba slipped out of the battered Ford Cortina whose doors didn't lock properly anymore, but was Mr Njakú's pride and joy, and sneaked out of the hospital. He disappeared to the embarrassment of the panic-stricken headteacher.

"Believe me, I had a patient," Njakú said, scratching his shiny, bald head, "a pupil in my school."

"Well, can't see anyone," said one of the lady nurses to the other, balancing a stretcher in her hands. "Looks like you need admission yourself, erm, Mr Headmaster?" The nurses laughed, beckoning him to the stretcher, and left him outside thoroughly mortified.

What followed the next day was massacre if the mud-sliding caning was persecution. Almost all the boys, including Fuso, were rounded up into the expansive workshop which doubled as the school hall surrounded by all the teachers baying for vengeance. It was the only venue big enough to round up all the boys. Mr Njakú was not relenting. He led the onslaught, thirsty for blood, until his chagrined ego was adequately appeased.

Many boys, Gatiba among them, dropped out of school after this incident, their dream career as touts starting earlier than they expected. This became the end of Gatiba's short but adventurous school life full of mischief and extremities. One of his favourite exploits was giving the teachers' water the *'Roiko flavour treatment'* as he called it. The 'treatment' had nothing to do with *Roiko,* a brand of curry, but had to do with open flies and lacing the teachers' water with pee. Woe unto the boy sent by the teachers to draw the water for them from Henderson's well. Such a boy was caught between his conscience and the murderous brute. Most chose to deal with their conscience. They figured it would hurt less.

It could have hurt less if Fuso too never went back to Gíthima School. His bum hurt so bad he wondered aloud how he was going to sit on those hard wooden desks the following day. His mum and dad pretended not to hear him and a clever attempt at feigning sickness only drew a warning glare from Dad. His protestations of innocence did not alter Dad's attitude. What the boys had done was horrendous. They could have killed someone. If all the boys were punished it set a good example for the others that fooling around had limits. *Which others, the girls?* However, those were the days when the teacher's decision was law and although the villagers were horrified by the incident when Gatiba was allegedly injured, they now knew the truth and fully supported a crackdown. What they wanted were good results and disciplined children. Njakú delivered, supported by his discipline crew like Micah, Kiirú and

Cuma, so the parents had confidence in him. There was therefore no way Fuso was going to win sympathy from his dad.

Come early morning, Fuso slowly walked to school, careful that the crispy khaki uniform he wore did not hurt his sore buttocks. He was angry that he had been punished for something he had not done and for a moment he wished he had joined Gatiba's army on its mission-kill-the-dog. Most boys did not turn up that day but trickled in later in the week. Many did not return at all, starting their dim lives of touting early, but others, like Bryan, had a brighter side to this injustice. His mum wept when he limped home. She couldn't believe anyone could do that to her baby. Unlike the rest, Bryan was taken to hospital that night for a check-up and perhaps a treatment with steaming lavender to soothe his bottom. He spent the following day in bed recuperating over fried eggs, sausages, assorted exotic fruits and stuff like that while frantic arrangements were made to transfer him to a private school in Thika. His parents were determined that those savage barbarians disguised as 'enlighteners' were not to touch their baby again.

Much as Fuso and Bryan were inseparable buddies, they lost touch and the few times they met afterwards they couldn't connect. Fuso didn't blame him. Bryan had become 'cultured', so refined, complete with fluency in both English and Swahili, whereas Fuso was still the raw village boy, devoid of any sophistication. With his stuttering, halting English, Fuso was fascinated reading the foreign magazines Bryan had lent him over and over again and committed every picture to memory. He went through them with microscopic attention, enjoying finding that speck of detail he had missed previously. The kids in the magazines became his friends and he gave them names like Joan and Jack; the dogs he called Timmy. The dog's name must have come from one of the 'Famous Five' story series he had stumbled on sometime. With Bryan away to explain to him about what his white friends said about their countries, he lost a little of the motivation he had to disappear to faraway lands but he still harboured the desire and the resolve that someday he would travel the world.

# 4

Fuso's dream to travel out of Africa was revived when he joined Mang'u High School and took aviation as one of his options. The class had started as a club, a mark of the school's privileged position and sophistication but later aviation was offered as a taught and examinable optional subject, if only at a relatively basic level. Fuso took to it like an obsession; gluttonously taking in anything he could lay his hands on about the subject. He had fallen in love with aircrafts. The weekend American movies shown in the boarding school reinforced the dream. He belonged there with the movie characters. He wanted to be them, wanted to be where they were, wanted to fly out of the constrictor that was the Kenyan life. Soon he acquired a fake American twang and nicknamed himself 'Homeboy'.

In his second year, an American chain-smoking Peace Corp volunteer called Ms Dobson came to teach aviation in Fuso's school. She was tall and slender and carried an air of quiet authority. When she looked at you it always felt like she knew all about you. Her off-the-topic comments about American life captivated him. He had to do something to get there. After acquiring addresses from the *Flight* magazine, he applied for a place to train as a pilot in a Californian flying school. When the response came in the affirmative Fuso wanted to die with excitement. He sneaked out of school on a weekend and went home to break the good news to Dad.

"Dad, I've been offered a place to train as a pilot in America," he cautiously said, when the opportunity arose. He had been vague about why he had come home so early in the term, lying about forgotten items, although he could tell his dad wasn't convinced.

"Complete with a scholarship?" he asked, without enthusiasm.

"No... just offered a place."

"How much does it cost?"

"Erm, guess about $20,000 or something... why about the money?" Somehow he expected Dad, a train locomotive fitter, to easily sort out that small money issue. He was still a bit inclined to that stage in life that views dads as supermen.

"Guess? Anyhow, got ideas how you'll meet the cost?"

"Dad?" he was now confused, he could see where this was leading to.

"How old are you son?"

"Fifteen, almost."

"And only in form two of your secondary studies in case you forgot."

"Dad... I..."

"Can you shake your head a little, you know, check whether all nuts are intact."

"I thought you'd be happy for me..."

"I am very much, a very imaginative son. Now here's your bus fare." He put a hundred-shilling note on the table. "Take whatever it is you said you forgot here, better if it's being in touch with reality, then go back to school and put a little of your creative mind to your studies, real studies that is."

With that, Fuso's dad boarded a bus and left for Nairobi where he worked in the week. He only came home on weekends. Reluctantly, Fuso left for school after a talk with Mum, who tried hard to show him how irrational his idea was but in kinder words. Trust good old mums, they are not afraid to take time to search for the right words if it made one feel better.

When he got back to school, he grudgingly took a little of Dad's advice and concentrated on his O level studies. Fuso still watched the movies and dreamed on, holding the belief that he would get there someday.

By the time he joined Kenyatta University for a bachelor's degree in Education, he had sobered enough and had started to understand the way of life, not always giving people the beat they would like to dance to. However, this didn't mean that he gave up on his dream, only that he dwelled on it less than 24 hours a day. Fuso knew he was going to push it till he could push no more then, maybe he would accept his fate, but the question was how much push was hard enough. He had heard that visa applications for postgraduate studies were easily approved. That sounded like his best bet but only time could tell.

After graduating, Fuso was posted to Boro Secondary School at the foothills of the Aberdare Range. Boro is a beautiful place, green all year round and mostly carpet covered by restful tea bushes. The greyish mountain in the background on clear mornings gave a breathtaking view of natural harmony. The cascading valleys, covered by hanging pockets of fog and mist, were therapeutic. They evoked something close to a spiritual experience. The only problem with Boro was its remote location. There was no electricity and the place rained most of the year making the dry weather roads impassable. The school was not performing at all and he felt wasted. Much as he put efforts drumming the Queen's English to the disinterested youths it all went down the drain. Mostly the school held the first position in the district league tables: if you read the list the wrong way up and the kids found it so funny, they laughed and joked about it, to Fuso's annoyance.

In his 'I can make a difference' fresh-from-uni enthusiasm, he wanted so much to make an impact that was frustratingly not forthcoming. Nothing, therefore, filled him with ire like the students laughing at their own failure rather than be sad. Being a day school, most of the students were from the neighbourhood, graduates of the primary school just across the fence. Those who joined the secondary school were those that didn't pass well enough to secure places in the bigger district, provincial or national schools and the few unfortunate ones who did but couldn't afford to join the better schools.

Fuso's fake twang was then as misplaced as he was himself, a self-professed city guy. Since he joined secondary school, he passionately disassociated himself with anything village, always running to put up with his brothers and sisters in Nairobi on holidays. Those are some of the privileges of being a lastborn. At least in most cases you have someone to tolerate you. The sojourns were not in vain. He acquired urbanite mannerisms complete with a self-induced stutter in his first language, Kikuyu. He also had a good command of the urbanites' *Sheng,* and a reasonably all right accent in English and a fake twang that the kids envied. It was at times frustrating to realise the students who seemed so keen in class were actually listening to *how* he was talking and not *what* he was teaching after a whole eighty-minute double lesson.

The evenings were worse at Boro. There was nothing much to do with himself. He tried jogging around the village and working out in the big school play field but gave up after the bewildered villagers started whispering that all was not right in his head. Grown-up men were meant to engage in more important adult matters of life than running around like children. In such places your affairs become everyone's business and teachers, especially, were always under the microscope. It didn't help much that most of them were young unmarried males in a mixed school and the gossip was about which teacher was dating which student. Somehow, his name wasn't dragged into the scandals but once in a while there were rumours of some girl he was apparently planning to date sometime on an educational tour. Some of his colleagues were not so lucky though and got a real smear, but Fuso also doubted they were totally innocent; some of the teachers were over familiar with the girls, but he could not prove anything.

At night, the teaching staff met in one place and watched tiny black and white TVs, which was all the batteries could manage, and many were the times the battery fainted mid-news or in the middle of a major international league match that they had waited for all week. Fuso therefore couldn't wait for the weekend. He looked forward to escaping to Nairobi where he could watch a colour TV. He wanted out of that Boro hell, fast.

His restlessness drove him to apply for a transfer. This was to turn out a nightmare when finally he was moved to a worse place – Gíthúya. Boro was remote, inaccessible at times, but green and beautiful and later, perhaps too late, he realised the folks were not that bad. Gíthúya was remote, dry and ugly. The Maragúa River valley nearby was all rocky, full of thorn bushes, sisal and aloe vera. The neighbouring community was hostile, callous and still practised dodgy cultural rites. Dropout rates were high, drugs were rife in the neighbourhood and even the students rampantly smoked cannabis.

All the teachers who didn't come from the neighbourhood lived at Maragúa, seven kilometres away where there was electricity and a tarmac road. There was no way of staying at Gíthúya. Crime was the norm and being a salaried teacher was being a ready target. The thugs believed they could always find cash on you. Never mind if it was a few hundred Kenyan shillings. At least it guaranteed them another few days' supply of *chang'aa*, an illicit drink; a concoction of God-knows-what that evidently a car engine could run on. It left their lips red, burning their pigment off after prolonged use. What it did on the inside was anybody's guess.

Going to Gíthúya was a harrowing experience. Getting transport was like a chance game, only about ten times in a three-month term. One therefore needed a good set of appendages for the long walk. When it rained, then the teachers wallowed in misery. Maragúa being a few ridges away, one had to wade through the muddy valleys down below. There was one steep climb up Gathúngúri Hill that was a test of the spirit. Slipping and landing on the mud were not unusual if you didn't grip the fence properly. Then you were left to figure out how to make yourself presentable to the curious students. Every time Fuso got to the hill's apex, whether it had rained or not, he stood and watched the valley below where he had come from and felt like crying. This wasn't him. He had to be in a bad dream. Most of his friends, who had little or no city affiliation, had been posted to posh schools in towns with the best of facilities. He, the allegedly cultured one, had been thrown into mediocrity. He had never imagined himself in this kind of a situation. It was a bad dream, a sick joke. He had to get out but Kenya isn't where you resign from a permanent job at a whim. There are not enough of them to go round.

Watching the lady teachers worrying how they would teach in their mud-stained clothes after a nasty fall filled him with pity. At least the male teachers easily wiped the mud off their jeans with a wet cloth but the ladies didn't wear jeans. Somewhere in the code of practice jeans were frowned at, and absolutely never where female teachers were concerned, but this was like a war situation that required unorthodox measures. Nobody really cared about men wearing jeans so long as you were decent. The women teachers however weren't so lucky. It scared the peace out of Fuso that he was going to remain in this misery. He feared he might resign himself to fate and do nothing about it like most teachers, who did nothing but whine for years on end about their predicament.

Some of the teachers were visionless, just wiling away time waiting for their pay at the end of the month. Many of them were content just to crawl through life. This was what life had handed them, so be it! There were millions who were doing worse and being a secondary school teacher you were in a privileged position in the society. Many of them were so unhappy with their job and every day was an endurance journey, but there was no motivation to change their circumstances or at least try and like the job a little. Fuso didn't like it himself and that's why he wanted out so bad.

Many of his teacher friends looked at him with sceptical amusement, letting him know that they started like him; restless and wanting out, but now they knew there was no way out. He was better off contented, they advised. Fuso therefore told them he would leave them someday soon and stopped sharing with them his dreams of travelling out of the country. It was of no use because they considered this as hallucinations of a frustrated frayed mind. They reasoned that he joined his current school as a teacher last and might as well be the last to leave, especially being an English teacher, a specialism that was in demand so schools did all they could to hold on them.

The big break came when he was invited for an interview after applying to a newspaper ad for an environmental representative job at the National Environment Management Agency, a semi-autonomous state-owned environment agency. The qualifications needed for the position were environmental studies or teaching degrees. Apparently the teachers were preferred because they were effective at reaching out to communities. Fuso saw a window of opportunity and dived for it. The fact that he would have to go through extensive training as he had little environment management skills didn't deter him.

When he entered the interview room he nearly fainted when in the panel he saw Professor Gladys Opok, a renowned author of many books on environmental issues, and a former assistant government minister. She was a member of the agency's board of directors. Surprisingly the interview went well and he could sense they were pleased with him. Finally they asked him whether he had anything to say.

"When do I start?" he asked boldly, eager to know his fate. That elicited bemused smiles from the panel. They could read his anxiety.

"Patience is a virtue, young man," responded the bald but heavily bearded Mr Tirop, the managing director.

Fuso thanked them and slithered out, carefully closing the door behind him lest he offended the panel. He had a thing with doors: always seemed to apply too much force than necessary ending with an unwelcome slam. His dad always joked that he didn't open them but rather walked right through them. Fuso also had issues when holding things – at times they just fell off and broke, the reason why he preferred using china and glasses at the table where he could quickly put them back down, and he never held newborn babies. Not that he ever dropped any baby but he never wanted to find out. As for glasses and stuff, that's a different matter. He still owed Mum several treasured unique sets she had been given as presents on her wedding in 1966. Fuso didn't consider himself clumsy though; heavy-handed was a more acceptable description.

When the interview results were out, Fuso got the job. To say he was in nirvana, would be the understatement of the century. No more wading through mud, no more drumming rules of syntax into marijuana-dazed teenagers and no more fourteen-kilometre daily trek. He was going back to civilisation, where he belonged.

Initially Fuso was assigned to the senior regional representatives and moved to various provinces in the country for his orientation. He enjoyed the travel so much, he didn't know Kenya was so beautiful. The drives too were good fun, his love for cars run deep. They were paying him to do what he loved. Finally through with orientation, he was assigned his own region, which covered most of the Central Province, a vast region indeed. This is a beautiful place with both Mt Kenya and the Aberdare Range visible from all sides. His work was to visit schools, factories, businesses and all sorts of institutions, promoting better waste management, water use, recycling, soil conservation and stuff like that. Fuso was also to organise any promotional events he deemed appropriate to pass the 'cleaner environment' message across. This was fun. Mostly the representatives were left on their own to do the job to their discretion. He loved it so much, cruising all over in a good, agency-maintained car and visiting the schools. The teachers envied him – especially when they learnt that he used to teach. Many wanted to know how he had escaped the drudgery of the classroom and the lady teachers literally scrambled for his business cards.

With the change of government in late 2002, there began a shake-up of government institutions. After a couple of months, the agency CEO, a political appointee of the reigning government, was forced to retire and in came another political appointee of the new government. That's the African way for you and evidently also in many other parts of the world – out goes the wolf, in comes another in sheepskin. For some reason, the new chief executive immediately started blaming the regional representatives for the failures of the agency, even though soon the agency was swarming with his kinsmen as messengers and drivers that weren't needed. Just how many office messengers does a two-hundred staff establishment need? He suggested many changes including that the regional representatives move permanently to their respective regions to cut costs and be closer to their locations all year round. Whatever the rationale he employed, Fuso wasn't going back to the countryside now that he had settled in Nairobi where he always sneaked back on weekends. He had run away from that life and he wasn't going back to it. Besides, that meant the per diem allowance was no more. The representatives always saved so much on their daily allowances making for themselves a tidy pile on the side at the end of the month.

The CEO seemed so hell-bent on implementing these changes that Fuso revived his old dreams to go and see the world out there. He immediately applied for a place at Bournemouth University to do a master's degree. How he was going to finance his studies was an enigma he hoped to sort out someday along the way but apply he did, and was accepted.

The next thing was to apply for a visa at the UK High Commission in Nairobi. Those who know about it would tell that this is like a 'baptism by fire' experience. If you got the visa, that was a miracle and you were considered favoured by the gods. In fact, you were so valued, so popular that you could find love instantly from people who barely gave you a glance previously. More than half the young people in the country wanted out. They felt trapped in mediocrity, suppressed by ancient geezers who held on to everything and always sung of the youth being tomorrow's leaders. Nothing was as frustrating to the job-seeking graduates as watching a seventy-year-old cabinet minister, also made chairman of some corporation, a director of a government organisation and a member of some commission or other, drawing pay and allowances from each of these positions. Besides, the African youth of the day was confused about identity having been socialised by the media to think like the West and see themselves as missing out if they didn't conform to the world culture; read West. They dressed West, attempted with varying degrees of success to talk and behave West. The movies and TV were full of the West, Africa having little in production of its movies and shows. With meagre budget to work on, the filmmakers in Africa could only do so much.

Most of these young people therefore identified themselves with the West and knew almost everything about America and Europe and much of other developed places. Sadly they didn't want to know much about their own country. Those who were born and brought up in Nairobi and other major towns considered those from the countryside as second-class, uncultured, *washamba*. Anything that happened outside their comfortable towns might as well have happened in some remote hamlet in the Arctic. It was as if they were on loan to Kenya waiting to go back home to the West.

Fuso wanted out too, but his motivation was not to become a rap star or some Hollywood celebrity or something… that was what many fantasised about. His motivation ran deeper than this. It started with the early childhood magazines Bryan gave him. There had to be another way to live than in the drudgery of Africa. Fuso wanted to broaden his mind, see the world and get to know what it was that the West had that made them achievers. Probably he was to return to make things work. Africa had too many tragic stories. A total let-down by its leaders – gluttonous bloodsuckers who weren't ashamed to raid the nation's treasury and keep the money in their private Swiss accounts. If their people starved they would go and beg for aid from friendly developed countries, use some and stash the rest in their other accounts in the Cayman Islands. Of course, their lenders and 'donors' knew all about it but so long as their interests in these African states were secure the dictators could annihilate everyone for all they cared.

Fuso's first love was America. He loved their dream of freedom, of personal growth, of democracy, loved their might. They were the heroes in all their movies but he was convinced they deserved it. They were so brave and all they wanted was to save the world from forces that threatened the dream of democracy and freedom. Someone had to do it and to him they were the fair cop. He loved the way they went out of their way to save one of their own in their movies and loved their outgoing and loud lifestyle. There were many in Kenya, wonderful people, especially the missionaries.

One, Mr Dean was the main pastor in Fuso's church. If there was ever a vote for the best human beings he had ever met, Dean could appear in the top three. He was selfless, dedicated to God's service and loved people regardless. He was kind, and had an ear for everyone, a true follower of Christ who wasn't afraid to take the back seat at times and wasn't afraid of being corrected either. It was understandable then why Fuso shed a tear when the enemies of freedom bombed the American embassy in Nairobi in 1998, killing many, most of them his fellow Kenyans.

In 2002, Fuso had applied for a visa to the US. He had joined a group of traders who were going for an exhibition cum conference exploiting the American AGOA act – the African Growth and Opportunity Act, which was signed into law on May 18, 2000, as Title 1 of The Trade and Development Act of 2000. The Act offered tangible incentives for African countries to continue their efforts to open their economies and build free markets. Fuso had to pay the NGO director, a distant relative, an aunt or something, to include his name in the group's list. Of course, he had to tell a few lies, including that he was a trainer for fabric designs, if he was to use his passport that stated that his profession was a teacher. He was also advised to state that he was married since single guys were frowned at on the assumption that they travelled for the sole purpose of marrying Americans to acquire citizenship.

Come the interview day, his brother drove him to the US embassy off Mombasa Road very early in the morning. The embassy had leased a huge, greyish architectural masterpiece after the bombing of their old embassy building in the city centre by those who shed innocent blood in the name of God. Fuso was surprised to find a snaking queue of about two-hundred people and more were still coming. After going through a thorough search at the gate and leaving behind watches and mobile phones, the people were let into a huge outdoor foyer. One by one the interviewees were called to the glass-partitioned desks, where dreams were ruthlessly shattered. Many left in tears, others had to be dragged out by security guards, screaming and kicking after heated arguments with the interviewers – you can't always slay dreams quietly. Some interviewers barely glanced at their papers and rudely pushed them back to them. Reason: 'You don't look like you'll ever come back.' Now pray, what do people who don't look like they will return home look like?

Fuso twisted the ring on his finger this way and that way in anxiety, feeling odd about the unfamiliar metal. His application said he was married so he had to have some symbol. This was turning out a comedy of sorts. He quietly observed the Americans' sense of humour. All males below the age of forty-one had to fill a form stating whether they had ever received any military training or firearms training anywhere and whether they were terrorists or were planning to carry out any terrorist activities. Fuso imagined they expected terrorists to be honest about it and write something like, 'Yeah, me bad news, gonna blow up planes and towers, I'm also good in hijackings and usually practise cricket with grenades and mines. I'm also not afraid to die if I can shed the blood of Americans and Zionists.' Fuso also found the age marker unrealistic. Did they imagine terrorists retired after they turned forty-one?

There was, particularly, one slim, terse lady interviewer who appeared to be in charge of the others. Fuso didn't see her give anybody a visa and was afraid to land at her desk. She didn't look like she had smiled in a long time and if she had she must have forgotten how. To his relief he was called to a desk next to hers. The proximity wasn't comforting. Fuso didn't want her overhearing what he had to say. His interviewer was a motherly, expectant lady. She asked him questions in a kind tone and even smiled at him. After the questions, she disappeared with his papers for a long time. This was a harrowing wait. His fate was being put on hold together with his dream, his whole life. He quietly prayed, vehemently thanking God that the positive was happening. All the people who had been denied visas were dismissed immediately so the delay meant he was lucky.

When she finally appeared, she was still smiling.

"Mr Keirein-ai, we have a slight problem. We've been unable to verify some of your documents. My advice is you contact your exhibition organisers to send you verifiable documents, all right?"

"Will I have to reapply for another interview?"

"Sadly, yes."

"But that might take more than a week and the trade fair starts next week."

"I wish there's anything I can do about it," she said sweetly. "Try anyway, good'ay Keirein-ai." He knew he was being dismissed. He gathered his numerous papers and clumsily stuck them into his laptop bag and left in a daze.

Fuso was still smiling with disbelief when he got out of the building to the warmth of mid-morning Nairobi sunshine that would be on another day welcoming. There, his dream that had seemed so near had gone bust. He had lost a lot of money too, paying for the documents that stated he was a member of the NGO. Later he was also to learn that some Ksh 35,000 he had given to his aunt, supposedly to book for the exhibition booth he was to display his stuff in, was actually to be paid to the exhibition organisers on registration in Washington DC. His aunt had already left for the US. She held a ten-year multiple-entry American visa. The whole lot of the NGO's exhibitors, both genuine and not so genuine, had been conned out of hundreds of thousands of Kenyan shillings. It hurt so bad that he had been conned by his own relative, a respectable much older relative, he trusted very much. The betrayal hurt badly and for once in his life he felt a very strong urge to hate someone.

As for his hero Americans, he didn't know what to make of them now. He had seen them treat some applicants with contempt, throwing their papers back at them like they had anthrax. Almost everyone was treated like a terrorist or an illegal immigrant. True, many like him had forged papers and honestly wanted to overstay and make enough dollars to brighten their doomed lives when they returned – if they returned. It didn't make him feel better considering that pretty much every American can get a visa to Kenya without any hassle. That was so unfair. Africa is generally unwelcome in other places but everybody thinks Africa should be grateful for the privilege of the rest of the world wanting to visit her. Well, he guessed the West had to put restrictions if they were to curb the influx of illegals. The world was so ridiculously unbalanced with some countries so rich while others so poor it was only natural for the poor ones to want to escape to the rich ones. Nobody should open their doors to all undesirables but at least all people should be treated with respect.

Fuso had paid Ksh 5,400 for the US visa application. That, multiplied with the three-hundred plus applicants he saw that day, was a lot of money in any language and multiplying that by five days a week it was a rip off. This was a goldmine for the embassy; something to do with, 'those who have little even the little they have will be taken away from them', or 'if you wanted to visit me so bad and more so uninvited then I might as well charge you for being a nuisance'.

Oh America, how could he let her know how much he loved her? How could he now justify the defence he put up for her in discussions that put America on the receiving end? How could he make her know how much he preached the strength and advantages of her foreign policies? How could she ever know how much he longed to land on her bosom closer to her heart and there redefine himself preaching and practising her dream, the American Dream. How could she ever know that he was distressed when her embassy in Kenya was bombed, that he, a full-blooded African male, circumcised and all, shed a tear when he saw the New York's WTC twin towers come down in smoke, dust and debris?

# 5

The betrayal by the Americans was total and hurt so deep like a teenager's first heartbreak. He didn't know what to make of the whole thing so he moved on. The next best option was the UK. Fuso had been taught their history, knew a lot about Churchill and the whole lineage of kings and queens, knew their manners and etiquette. He spoke the Queen's language, with an accent of course. Kenya shared many things with Britain having been a British colony and in his preparatory school years sung songs like 'London is burning' or something like that. In fact, Queen Elizabeth II technically became a queen in Kenya when her father died while she was on a holiday, at the Treetops Hotel in Nyeri to be exact. That was in the heart of Kikuyuland, Fuso's turf. *Good old Queen's land, here I come*, he thought.

After the American heartbreak eased off many months later, Fuso arrived at the British High Commission at Upper Hill, Nairobi at 5 am, the wiser to beat the queue. He had heard about the excruciating experiences people went through in an attempt to get visas, that ticket to paradise. It was said that some camped there for as long as a week or more, mostly missing an interview at a whisker when the commission closed to applicants at 11 am. Surprisingly, when he arrived he only found just a few cars parked outside the premises with a few souls inside waiting for opening time. This was a relief to him. He knew there was always a difference between reality and gossip or so he thought. Contented, he reclined the car seat and listened to his favourite Darlene Zschech music, waiting for the embassy to open.

At 6 am he figured he better take his position if he wanted to be among the first to go in. He joined a group of women that came from the Kenyatta Hospital direction headed for the High Commission. Out of nowhere, a GSU paramilitary police officer appeared.

"Hey and where do you think you're going?"

"To the embassy, why?"

"Why?" he sneered. "Don't try to be smart with me."

"Smart? I came for an interview at the embassy and that's where I'm going. Am I too early?"

"What time did you come here?"

"5 am."

"And you drove here." It was an accusing statement. He said it as if it was a sin Fuso was supposed to be ashamed of. "Can you go up there," he indicated a place a hundred yards away, "and see what I mean?"

Reluctantly, Fuso walked the few yards to where he was supposed to find a revelation. What he saw he wasn't prepared for. Half of Kenya was there. Folks of all walks of life; the old, the young, different shades and hues all clad in heavy wear to ward off the cold. Some creative ones had lit a bonfire a distance from the queue to warm themselves but some couldn't risk being so far from the queue in case they lost their place.

Everyday people took numbers. Fifty lucky ones got to be invited for the interview but only about twenty or thirty actually managed to be interviewed. The remainder were the first to get a chance the following day, that is, if they stuck the queue all night. It was therefore necessary to have good relatives and friends as your back-up to take turns at guarding your position, often overnight, so that you arrived for the interview fresh. The industrious cops were also seriously interested in the affairs of the queue. If you had several thousand shillings to shake their hands with then you could save yourself the hassles and simply get to the front of the queue. Some unemployed Kenyans became creative as well. They queued for you at a fee. That actually worked perfectly since they had entered some kind of a deal with the cops to fix them first positions in the queue and then of course split the money. If the cops sensed one of these men won't make it, they disrupted and broke up the queue pushing people away on grounds of security, then allowed them back ensuring their men got a lead position. It was very frustrating for the applicants after a night of vigil to see well-groomed people come fresh in the morning to take up their secured positions from these enterprising queue brokers.

To Fuso's dismay he was put at position 186 on the informal list that was being handled by self-appointed organisers. When he asked how long he would take to get to be interviewed he was told that with some luck that was to take about four days.

"And that is if you're present every night," said the guy with the informal list.

"And if I'm not?"

"Well, pay these brokers but as for me I can't pay anybody. I need every coin," he said, moving up the queue checking who might have jumped in.

"How long have you been here, mate?"

"Three days, today I'm number fifty-seven. With some luck I'll get an interview tomorrow."

Looking at the desperation of the prospective travellers, Fuso pitied them. This was July, the season many sought visas for studies in the UK with most courses starting in September. Many were genuine and many others not. Travelling as a student was the easiest way to get that coveted document to where their dreams waited. Many people did not even have the money for the plane ticket and resorted to asking family and friends to raise the amount to send them to glory land. The embassy was serious about proof of financial capability to pay for the course, accommodation and all. This wasn't a deterrent to prospective dream-chasers. It was easy because most people borrowed bank statements from willing rich relatives and friends. Some forged statements while others bought them from rich people who weren't afraid to let you know what they had in the bank. They charged you for the risk anyway. Others bought them from unscrupulous bankers who made copies from their rich customers, complete with a letter of commitment. All the commission did was contact the bank to ask if there was such an account then they phoned the said 'sponsor' whose number was provided in the letter of commitment. The number provided of the alleged sponsor was actually the number of the crooked banker, who then confirmed sponsorship. How you survived when you landed in your country of destination was your problem. Most people had relatives and friends abroad who hosted them for some time before they found their way round the system and work.

This was more than Fuso could handle. There was no way he was going to spend a night in the cold just to get a visa. *You got to bend but never crawl... have a little pride* a voice whispered in his mind. His sense of morality did not allow him to bribe anyone to fix him at the lead of the queue and he found it so unfair to all those poor freezing souls. He got into his car and drove off to think of the best alternative strategy.

Later in the day, a few minutes before 11 am, Fuso returned to the High Commission. There was still a good number of the day's lucky fifty in the queue, now resigned to frustration with only a few minutes before interviews closed. He parked the car a distance away from the embassy and the paranoid paramilitary security officers. Osama was affecting the world big time. Security was running erratic all over the world but the guys in Nairobi were overenthusiastic. Every approaching motorist was treated like a suicide bomber. In their glaring stare, Fuso put the relevant documents in an envelope and then into the drop box. This method was unpopular with most applicants who had so much to hide and couldn't trust their papers to speak for them. They preferred one-on-one interviews so that they could dodge that tricky question that might expose them.

He didn't care about the outcome, whatever it was. He had a good job he enjoyed doing. So what if he didn't get a visa? A dream would be broken but he wasn't going to die from it. In any case there was no way he was going to spend a night freezing to secure an interview. His pride didn't allow him and his spirit and body were unwilling.

For the next month and a half he waited anxiously for his fate. It was like waiting for a suspended response to a proposal made to the girl of your fantasies, the love of your life, and didn't know if it would be an exhilarating 'yes' or a heart breaking 'no'.

When finally the response came it was from Securicor Courier Service. They said they had a parcel for him from the British High Commission. He immediately knew his fate with destiny was sealed. The wait was not in vain. His dream was coming to be.

After he went for the parcel from the courier's Embakasi depot he felt a strong emotion, his hands were shaking as he cautiously opened the dirty brown envelope. This was happening to him finally. He was going to fly, to chase his biggest dream. The childhood pictures of beautifully mowed fields and horses and nicely trimmed hedges came rushing through his mind. He was finally allowed to travel to the land of the great. It was like an abandoned child finally accepted by a repentant mother. He sent a text message to his cousin Makena: 'Tell the Queen, Fuso is on his way.'

# 6

Fuso was initially very self-conscious when out of the house. He felt strange surrounded by so much *whiteness.* It didn't matter that southwest London is multicultural. He felt as if everyone could tell he was a fresh foreigner. In his paranoia he thought he read their unwelcoming stares biting into his face. Then the real shocker was the language. He, the English teacher complete with a bachelor's degree and a literary graduate, couldn't understand most of what they said. Was this London or what? The language barrier so frustrated him that he almost took offence when he spoke and people looked at him in puzzlement and said, 'Sorry, what was that?' He felt like screaming: *I speak English damn you!*

Curiosity burned in him. He was rearing to go out and see Great Britain. Trouble was, London is a busy and expensive city. Few people could afford missing out on a day's pay to indulge the wishes of the new fellow on the block. Fuso had to wait for the weekend. The alternative was to take directions and visit places blindly and at random. This sounded like an exciting idea.

Makena took him to Hounslow Bus Station, the nearest major bus station, and explained to him all the buses that began and ended their routes there. The idea was that Fuso take one to its final destination, visit the high street there and the surroundings, and then return on the same bus.

Hounslow therefore became his point of reference whenever he got confused about directions. Admittedly he felt lost and dazed. It was like a floating-in-space sensation that left him in a state of vertigo. He couldn't quite locate the directions on his mental compass. What felt like east one day felt like south the next day.

Fuso's first solo visit was to Slough. He took a red London bus route 81 at Hounslow and headed west although it felt east then. The bus was neat and spacious with emergency doors left clear for easy exit and a section for the disabled complete with an exit ramp for the wheelchair. In his imagination he contemplated the shock his mum would register on her face if he told her the buses 'bend their knee' like a camel for easy access for the old and the buggies. This was different from the congested Nairobi buses. Nairobi bus operators would shed tears, imagining what a waste it was to leave useless spaces all over. Some of the new London buses were built so safety-conscious they couldn't move if the doors were open. Londoners would have instant heart attacks if they saw how folks in Nairobi jumped into and out of moving buses.

When he arrived at Slough Bus Station, Fuso crossed to the other side via the subway under the main road, past the Thames Valley campus to the high street. He visited the Queensmere mall, mesmerised by the sparkling elegance of the shops inside. Never mind that he wasn't buying anything. Window-shopping was in itself a fulfilling experience. The fact that he was in the great UK mixing with all those sophisticated people in the midst of the sophistication of the twenty-first century in a developed country was an accomplishment in itself.

Next Fuso visited Ealing Broadway, then Kingston upon Thames, where he lost himself in the magnificence of the Bentall Centre. After that he went to Staines High Street and Uxbridge where he marvelled at the sparkle of the Pavilions mall. Next Fuso went to Hayes and the Charter Place in South Harrow and many other places in between, blowing much of the money he brought from Kenya on meals at KFCs and McDonald's and on fancy clothes at the GAPs and the Debenhams in these high streets, with the belief that many more pounds will soon start rolling his way. This was the great Queen's GB with the strongest currency in the world! Surely there must be enough for everyone.

Fuso was becoming a veteran; hardly had he asked much for help on directions. One common feature of all these places was the perfect signposting, making it easier to find your way around.

He felt sorry for Kenya where signs often disappeared to fix a leaking roof on a shack or to be sold for a few shillings as scrap metal.

It was in these initial exploratory travels that Fuso encountered the British children on the buses. He was horrified by the behaviour of some. Often he encountered a rowdy rude lot whose most common vocabulary seemed to start with the letter 'F'. This was most unfortunate as he was later to learn that the British are a swearing society. Their ordinary speech featured an unhealthy amount of the 'F' word or similarly spiced ones.

He couldn't understand the complacency of the adults in these buses who squirmed and did nothing. In fact, most of these adults seemed terrified of the children and didn't want to sit anywhere near them. A child could occupy two seats with feet up on the third seat and nobody dared tell them anything. Fuso imagined if it was in Nairobi the brats would receive a proper smacking. He came to understand later that it was something to do with the law that you even had to be careful when talking to your children lest you raised your voice and it was taken as 'verbal abuse'.

Whereas Fuso didn't advocate battering and abusing kids he was sure a few years back, the world over, kids were a little more respectful of authority because parents were stern. The numerous smacks he himself received were well deserved and perfectly instilled appropriate behaviour. Fuso couldn't believe that the kids here, in his view, almost ruled. They screamed in buses, insulted passengers, and did gymnastics on the bus and painted rude graffiti all over. They even opened emergency doors when the buses were still in motion if they fancied doing so, just for laughs.

On a sad note, he remembered something he had seen in the papers about a young twelve-year-old boy who was killed when teenage yobs pushed and shoved and messed around sounding the horn and then grabbed the steering wheel from a double-decker driver. The driver lost control trying to push the teenagers off the wheel and ploughed the packed bus into a tree. The little lad was crushed to death by a branch. After his death, the family lobbied for all school buses to be fitted with seatbelts.

Belts are good but could achieve nothing without a change of attitude in children who grow up without taking responsibility for anything at all. Probably this death could have been prevented. It was so needless. This was a whole generation of kids who if not properly guided were going to become dangerous zombie adults with no morals or regard for anything else but the self and mischief. Mischief is all right, it is what gives youngsters a laugh but it should go only so far and when one carries it on to adulthood then that needs a psychiatric definition. Children need guidance and there is no guidance without discipline. If only adults reflected on their own youth, they would see how wrong they were on so many issues yet now they wanted to give their children extreme *laissez faire*. When they grow up they will hate their parents for it rather than thank them. They will say they were never taught that the world was realistic and harsh and had little regard for the fact that when little you were given fancy tags at home like 'darling', 'angel' or 'princess'. It was very interesting to see young criminals just past their eighteenth birthday horrified that they were facing the wrath of the law and possible incarceration. They were so accustomed to getting away with anything then *Booom!* They land in trouble at eighteen and nobody thinks they are cute anymore.

Fuso had started toying with thoughts of going back to teaching but he was not sure anymore. Much as teaching was a respectable profession, he was now terrified of managing such kids. No wonder fewer people were keen on the profession nowadays. Parents pushed their responsibility on teachers while all along waiting for an opportunity to pounce on them if they as much as told off their little angels. He wondered what to make of a parent who takes a teacher to court because her son got injured on a field trip when the son disobediently sneaked away from the rest of the group and went where he had been forbidden?

All in all, Fuso liked the fact that children here were assertive and bold enough to express their opinion about things that affected them. He wished he were allowed to tell his dad what he thought of him when he used to give him measly pocket money to last him a whole term. On deeper reflection, Fuso thought that maybe he was beginning to grow old, slipping into that stage in life where only things of yesteryear seem better. Who was he to judge children from a culture he was yet to fully comprehend? Were there no rascals back where he came from? Weren't a few of his friends reformed imps who used to join juvenile gangs to raid beehives and farms at night in the neighbouring villages for honey and sugarcane? Britain was still among the leading nations of the world and probably he needed to understand her culture before he took a higher moral standing. In any case, youths in Africa may not use an f-laced expletive to their teacher but they too were trouble in their own way. This was becoming a global phenomenon or maybe age was clouding his judgement.

Come the weekend, Wambúi, his cousin's mate, bought him a ticket to go on the tube. Makena could not join them because she had to go to work. Together Fuso and Wambúi travelled to central London where he was dying to set foot. Getting off at Green Park on a cloudy but bright September day, they first went to Buckingham Palace and Westminster, some of the initial favourite spots for most newcomers and tourists. Fuso wanted to see the Houses of Parliament and the Palace that were symbols of the empire that had rendered many countries colonies. Most people from these former colonies wanted to see where most of the decisions that shaped the destiny of their nations, and therefore their lives, came from.

The massive collection of concrete at Buckingham Palace was imposing. Its greyish hue hid the excellence of its architectural superiority. This was also common in Central London with lots of huge old greyish buildings so intimidating and sturdy. Some were quite ugly too compared to buildings in other major world cities but that applied only before you went inside. The interiors were a touch of comfort and design, warm and delicately decorated. What amazed Fuso was that these buildings were built hundreds of years ago but were still sophisticated and strong. He admittedly felt despair for Africa; so many years later and people were still putting up grass-thatched, mud-walled huts. Many African brothers would argue that only a few isolated people were still making grass-thatched huts anymore but it was incredible that anyone was still making them in this century. 'It's poverty,' someone may want to argue. Poverty there may be, but there are enough rocks in Africa. If someone collected several everyday one would have a good load for a few walls in a short time.

They visited Westminster Abbey, the Houses of Parliament, the Aquarium, the Saatchi Gallery and the London Eye. They joined crowds of excited tourists playing at the fountains in Trafalgar Square and took enough photos, a record of his journey into the heart of the 'promised land'. They toured the beautiful Hyde Park and went to Kensington and Olympia. By the time they got back to Piccadilly Circus he was freezing and tired. He wanted to go home. A mild sunshine was doing a poor job of warming anything. This was a good lesson for him that not all that lights up in Britain is warm. One had to mistrust the British weather. The weather could turn to sudden gloom and rainfall or to freezing temperatures with your deceiving sunshine still shining.

They went down to the Piccadilly underground through the maze of escalators to the westbound Piccadilly Line platform and waited for the train to Heathrow. The underground itself was a complicated engineering masterpiece. The fact that there were three escalators to reach this platform was amazing and the fact that this was made many decades ago astounding. Fuso's wonder was whether Africa will ever get this far before Christ returned.

By the second week, the honeymoon was over. Fuso had started getting restless spending the day in the house surfing the internet. He needed work to keep him busy. In his environmental management job in Kenya he was his own manager. He determined when to wake up, where to go and what to do. It is amazing that people with a drive work best when they are left to do their thing without unnecessary interference. Fuso worked so hard, pushed himself so hard, he had no time for lunch. He set impossible targets for himself. It was fun doing this and he was sure if anyone tried to lord over him he couldn't have achieved much. Now here he was, jobless, and spending days lazing in the house. He had registered with several employment agencies both for industrial and teaching jobs but little was forthcoming. The teacher agencies particularly had a problem with the fact that Fuso hadn't been teaching in the past one year, had no British experience and needed his results to be verified by UK Naric – the National Recognition Information Centre. This is the designated United Kingdom national agency for the recognition and comparison of international qualifications and skills. The experience bit was the 'chicken and egg' question. Which comes first; the chicken or the egg, the job or the experience?

While he registered in these agencies he was also chasing some UK documents that his system-wise advisers thought necessary. Most important was a National Insurance number but that had to wait until he joined college – if ever he did. The NI people might get snoopy and smoke someone out and before you knew it see yourself on a plane back to Africa. If deported this way, in disgrace, you would go on record as the fellow who went to the land of opportunity and came back empty-handed – read dishonour. One returned only if they had saved some money to start a better life than when they left or if they got an education that guaranteed a better job. Africa is full of unemployment. Jobs are not easy to find.

The other important document was a utility bill or a voter's registration. Fuso had no bill under his name. They were all in Makena and Wambúi's names and that wasn't going to change soon enough. An alternative was to register as a student in a bogus college that didn't require a lot of deposit money. With this and a letter of a job offer he could apply for a NI number and start working without fear. Many of these bogus colleges, he was told, operated a cartel with the illegals. They knew the students were never going to attend any studies but who cared if they paid so much for a few enrolment forms and a student ID? Fuso did not want to go down this route. He dropped the idea; besides a few of his advisers had worked for several months with a temporary NI number. If the taxman sent letters asking for details, one simply ignored them until you joined college. The taxman was not going to come chasing after you for earning a few hundred pounds a month without NI, there were bigger problems chasing after multi-million-pound tax dodgers.

If it was a consolation, the papers were talking about the lack of a link between the various government institutions. For example, if immigration liaised with the taxman it was then so easy to catch the illegal workers. This disharmony was music to the illegal workers fraternity. There was also another problem. What about those whose employers knew they were illegal but didn't care? Some paid their employees in cash or by cheque, happy themselves that they paid them less than the minimum wage or just happy to evade the complication of paperwork, submitting tax returns and stuff? In fact, there were many employers who were glad for the availability of much-needed hands that were not shy to wade in muck for the valuable pound, hands that Britain seemed short of.

It helped if you had a British driving licence, either a full one or provisional. The British are very proud of their institutions and documents as Fuso found out with the teacher agencies. Many that had frowned at his unattractive Kenyan degree certificate beamed at the sight of the UK Naric statement of comparability when he got it. This confidence in their stuff worked both for and against them. The driving licence was a weak point. All that was required to get a provisional DL was to send an application to DVLA Swansea with your passport and some twenty-nine pounds. Within a week you had a provisional DL, a document that was easily accepted in many places including opening a bank account. Fuso had heard of people who got fake passports, took provisional DLs and then opened accounts supported by utility bills. After using the account for some time, the generous UK banks would persuade them to take a loan. This is a method the bank uses with abandon to get you hooked and slowly earn huge profits off you. Not always, though, for some illegals then take the maximum loan they can get and take the next plane home. With the obscene profits the banks make and don't hesitate to brag about it, few people felt sorry for them.

A GP's (General Practitioner) registration was essential although it didn't do much in the way of helpful papers. Some employment agencies asked for the GP just in case something like an accident happened at work, or so he thought. Fuso went to Stanwell Road Surgery, the nearest to his home and close to Ashford High Street. An elderly lady at the reception called Gladys didn't know what to do with him. His visa said he was a student so why wasn't he registered with the university's health centre? That was tricky to answer. How could he tell her that he hadn't joined university yet? After some enquiries from a colleague who was in an adjacent room, Gladys was told so long as he lived locally then it was okay since he wasn't taking residence at the university. One of the other ladies at the surgery wasn't very pleased though. Fuso overheard her tell Gladys, "Might not even be staying in the UK for long. They come from all over the world, no medical insurance, nothing. They want it free, strain the NHS and we pay for it."

"This one's a student, might be here a while."

"You never know. Anyhow, can't do policing at the same time, can we?"

"No, can't turn him away either." Fuso pretended he didn't understand a word of what they said and nodded to Gladys' wisdom. She booked a general check-up appointment for him immediately.

Without having a bank account of his own when he started working, Fuso had to make do for some time with one of his cousin's accounts. He opened an account much later with Barclays after some struggle. His advisers had said that Slough's Barclays branch was worth trying because there were many immigrants in the neighbourhood. So, said his advisers, the branch was not fussy about foreigners. When he arrived at Slough, however, the situation was different. A blue-eyed young Asian lady who looked at him with suspicion said he had to have an account with another bank in the UK. Armed with his Kenyan Barclays account details and cards, he tried to explain to her that he had banked with Barclays for many years but she was adamant. She said that Fuso had to have lived in the country for at least six months to open an account with Barclays. He had been in the country for only three months. 'Pop', up went his dream in smoke.

Fuso felt sick. This girl was standing between him and his dream. He wanted to hate her but she was so gorgeous with those blue eyes that he thought was odd for an Asian person but he couldn't bring himself to it. Letting pass a cloud of a racist thought he walked out in a daze. He had hoped to get an account and a good credit limit to enable him to join Kingston University which had offered him a place for a master's degree in Environmental and Earth Resources Management Studies starting in February, the coming year. That way he was going to kill several birds with a single stone. For one, he was going to legalise his immigration status and then he was also going to get a proper NI, and dream of returning home with an education. The appeal of living in Britain had started to wear thin. Fuso just felt he didn't belong.

The following day he went to the Ashford branch. To his horror he found himself face to face with another Asian lady. This one was different though. After Fuso showed her his passport and she realised that he was a teacher by profession, Fuso saw respect reflect in her face. She asked him for a driving licence and a utility bill but she accepted his payslip that was from an agency she knew, a few blocks away down the Ashford High Street. She was also very impressed with his Kenyan Barclays visa credit card. Fuso could tell she didn't think they had those in Africa. All along she chatted about Kenya and talked of wanting to take a holiday there to 'connect with my roots', she said. Her grandparents had emigrated from there. She encouraged him not to worry about working in warehouses because soon he would get a teaching job. Fuso liked her very much. She was so kind and he felt ashamed that he had made a generalised racist mental remark the previous day at Slough. By the time he left the bank he was whistling *There is a miracle when you believe,* a chequebook already in his pocket.

# 7

His first job was mail sorting in an out-of-way warehouse in Colnbrook. Fortunately the agency that got Fuso the job offered transport. Quiet and afraid, the four of them picked for the day were driven to work in an elegant Mitsubishi Challenger. There was a Liberian guy called Martin and two other Asian guys – Sanjeev and Indevir. The young Asian lady, Parminder, from Firsts Recruitment Agency in Hayes, drove them there and treated them to choice Punjabi lyrics on the way which sounded strange to Fuso's ears. Fuso was beginning to like her a little, if only for her looks. She was absolutely beautiful.

In an earlier encounter when he went to register with the agency he had wanted to hate her when she made him sit a juvenile test about the spelling of places like Ireland and do kindergarten addition sums. Armed with a photo, a passport and a temporary NI that everybody kept singing about, he had dragged himself through the agency doors to register after visiting many others in other high streets. That's when he encountered Parminder for the first time. His advisers had warned him to use a temporary NI until he legalised his status as a student, if he joined uni at all. Studentship now seemed unlikely. Fuso was beginning to get worried when he realised the authorities had a system of identifying illegal workers, a tag he didn't want to label himself with. What he was to do as yet he didn't know but he was determined to get himself into college one way or other.

Twice he had had to take a detour at Hounslow High Street when he saw cops stopping black people and asking for papers. Fuso had a legal visa, yes, but he hadn't joined any college. It could have turned tricky if he was questioned about that. It felt horrible having had to avoid cops. He had always been a law-abiding individual, always wanting to do the right thing and, in a few instances, helping police do their work. Now he was almost an illegal, running afraid that he would bump into some cop who didn't like him or, worse, hear a knock on the door and when he opened it get whisked away and deported immediately. It wasn't a very pleasant feeling, jumping out of her skin at every knock on the door.

Much as he protested to Parminder about the cheap patronising test and firmly let her know that he had a bachelor's degree from Kenya, she was bluntly adamant that he must do it and Fuso thought he saw her sneer at his CV. *Oh God, what was happening to me?* he thought. How could he make these people understand that he was an environmental representative in charge of a whole province almost the size of England? Nobody really cared that he had a degree from wherever. He was a foreigner who neither had a proper NI nor a proper accent.

When Parminder dropped them at the Colnbrook warehouse she told them, dismissively, that the Iver train station was three-hundred yards away and if they found their way there in the evening they could find their way home. Well, that was an afterwork worry, first things first. Timidly they approached the mammoth metallic warehouse written 'Logistic Solutions…' something or other. After introducing themselves they were assigned positions, sorting out heaps of mail, mostly magazines, advertisement brochures and organisations' mail that were posted out on mass scales, call them bulk junk. Most of the people working there were Asians and you might as well have been in Bombay. Fuso didn't like the fact that they seemed not to care that there were people who didn't understand their language. They chatted on excitedly, shutting everybody out. In the course of his warehouse employment Fuso was to realise that this was duplicated in many other places.

The job was easy but monotonous and boring. The break took so long to come and the lunch break even longer. For lunch, Fuso went to a nearby canteen where he ate a four-pound pizza and a cold drink. It escaped his understanding the reluctance of his employment agency friends to take a meal that cost so little. He still had a little of his savings from Kenya and the concept of the strength of the pound hadn't properly registered in his mind. Besides, he wasn't paying any bills yet, save for his weekly bus pass and his mobile top-up. There was no way Fuso was going to watch a man starve at work when he had money in his pocket. Feeling generous, he bought Martin the Liberian guy some lunch. Martin profusely thanked Fuso, saying 'that's what *brodas* are for'.

Nothing lasts forever and soon the end of day was nigh. That Iver train station that Parminder talked about didn't look so near. A possibility of getting a lift to a bus stop was much welcome. Unfortunately, nobody seemed amicable enough to be approached. When the place closed at 5 pm almost everybody scurried out. Indevir headed for the car park, apparently having been offered a lift by one of the Asian permanent employees, a lady who had been fussing all over him all day. No amount of Indevir pleading for his agency colleagues to be dropped at a bus stop softened her heart. She made it clear to him that he was the only one welcome in her Rover 75. Indevir looked their way and shrugged his shoulders. They understood.

All day Fuso had watched the lady curiously. He thought Indevir wasn't prepared for what was likely to follow. The lady had literally forced him to work at her workstation. Later on, Fuso saw her whispering things to the visibly irritated Indevir. At lunchtime she put some money in his pocket but Indevir with due respect handed it back to her. She had taken his mobile phone at some point and scrolled through his phonebook and text messages to the dismay and annoyance of the young man. He didn't know how to react to a fussy forty-something-year-old in a new work place and the woman seemed like she had a say in the business too. Whatever happened to Inder, as they called him, will remain a mystery because he never came back. Fuso thought he began to understand when the following day the same lady picked on another young Pakistani guy from Lahore who had replaced Indevir, engaged him in endless chatter, fussing all over him with no respect for his personal space and with unnecessary touching and drooling stares, and eventually gave him a lift home in the evening.

Fuso ended up getting a seat in a Volkswagen camper van owned by one of the employees. It soon turned out that each of them was supposed to cough up one pound fifty to be dropped at Heston from where they could pick a bus. Luckily, he had the money and could pick up his bearings from Heston quite well. This was a capitalist economy. There was always a bill to pay wherever you turned.

The following day came with new challenges. The van owner was working overtime so Fuso and his lot had to look for other means. Down to Iver they walked and waited for a train. Their guide was a tall, elderly, South African woman who advised them to get a permit ticket from the automatic machine for as little as 10p. If the inspectors asked they produce a ticket on the train they were to show the permit and say they would pay with a card at the exit station. When they arrived in Southall they disembarked from the train and walked right out. Once outside Fuso asked her where they were supposed to pay and she had a knowing smirk on her face.

"What payment?"

"For the train," Fuso said in his naivety.

"You're out of the station. Get a bus and go home."

There, he had just had a lesson on evading paying for the train. He felt terrible that he was sinking into crime. If he was as clean as he imagined, he reasoned, he should have gone back in and paid but he hadn't and now he was headed home all guilty and everything. Some people had been in Britain for a long time and knew the system inside out. They knew how to dodge paying if they could get away with it. Besides this was a rich country that could do with a few less train tickets on its balance sheet. Many felt Britain owed them something, having plundered their countries during the colonial days. Others just felt they didn't belong, that they were unwelcome. Why be loyal to a society that considered you as scum and never wanted to give you good jobs with decent pay or reward you reasonably in a way you could afford to pay all the taxes, pay for train tickets and still leave you with a little to spend. The medal went to Nikolai, a smooth operator bloke from Kosovo, a friend of one of Fuso's neighbours at Ashford. Nikolai used a single train ticket for a whole year. Whatever he had done with it to pass through the barriers was a secret he didn't want to divulge. Some crooks are very sharp upstairs.

A week into his work at Logistic Solutions they said they didn't require agency staff anymore, so Fuso had to look for another job. After much searching, he got one at Colnbrook bypass, in the Lakeside Trading Estate, past Waterside. It was another warehouse job in a company called Jive. The first time Fuso went there he took a number 81 bus to Slough and got off at the Colnbrook Garage. To his distress he realised it was a long way to the Lakeside on foot. He had to take a bus and go back to Bath Road and then take a taxi at the Sheraton Hotel. Someone had told him that no buses went through the bypass and if there were then it didn't stop at Lakeside. Still fresh in London, he was charged ten pounds by the cabbie for the short distance to the Lakeside. Nobody had told him that he should ensure the cab meter was running when he got in.

It was a twenty-minute walk from waterside to Jive on a lonely and deserted road. The bypass over the M25 motorway usually had no souls on foot and Fuso was almost always alone treading the odd industrial neighbourhood. This should tell how enthusiastic he was doing the distance in the temperamental British weather.

Jive was contracted by British Airways to manage orders for lots of the consumer stuff the airline required for passengers. His job was to do cutlery and passenger toiletry kits. It was another easy but monotonous and boring job.

In his first day at Jive, Fuso was almost turned back because he didn't have safety boots. After numerous accidents that led to unimaginable obscene compensation claims, the company had become paranoid about safety. Fuso was told he had to wear them if he wanted to continue working there. He also had to wear a luminous high visibility jacket 'to see others and be seen'. In the warehouse there were designated walkways that one had to adhere to. Well, they had a point – with all those trolleys and forklifts racing about madly to beat targets, accidents could happen.

The manager of the returns section was a bulky Scot called McManus, an ex-navy guy who knew little about management. He was always munching something or other. Fuso imagined his stomach was like a busy lab run by a psychotic professor who was constantly mixing, always struggling to sort and digest all the stuff he put in there. He found it disgusting for a man to keep eating all day and feared for MacManus' health. If he ever stopped working or stopped being active he was simply going to blow up into a mess of fat and flesh.

His way of motivating staff was calling them to silly meetings and going: "I have targets to meet, I have the big shots on my arse, they kick mine I kick yours. Anyone who's not performing is just as well misplaced and should go home. If you feel you don't like it here, just tell me and I'll show you the door out if your daft head can't remember. If you're staying you have to hit your targets. Else I'll kick your arse out that gate." That was the soldier in him all right. Give orders and expect unquestioned adherence. This was no military though. People grumbled so much; some just left every time he ranted his commands. What was the use of threatening temporary employees who would soon leave anyway? Human beings hate to be lorded over. Any wise manager knows threats lead nowhere and the surest way to get better output was to win your employees over.

The team leader was a tall, slim, red-haired Russian woman called Alexia whose turquoise eyes shone like laser beams off her chisel-featured face. She had the coldest look Fuso ever saw. She didn't push staff but just her green-eyed look drilled a chill into anyone. In the department there were two pensioners, Dave and Evans, doing cutlery. Both talked of having had very good jobs all their lives but they had to work to clear their mortgage. Fuso couldn't quite understand why someone who had a senior job before retirement could be doing menial warehouse jobs as a pensioner. Surprisingly, Evans had been a senior marketing officer for BA with postings all around the world. He also always talked of lots of exotic places he had been on holidays all over the world. This line of thought was strange to Fuso. Why would one take so many expensive holidays abroad when one still had lots of balance on their mortgage? Dave wasn't any better. His wife had left him a few years back. Why couples would stick together for over forty years and then divorce at sixty or seventy was beyond his comprehension. Dave was frustrated and still had a few thousands to clear on his mortgage. Fuso thought people like Dave and Evans needed someone to teach them a thing or two about saving when still young.

Next were teenagers Sheila – tall, bulk torso, non-existent bottom and Sharon – skinny, bad teeth and bad hygiene, who spent the whole day playing and laughing. Sheila talked non-stop and most of it nonsense, antagonising everybody. She had no respect for anyone or anything including herself and neither did she have any values nor morals, a perfect composition of stupidity. She could say anything despite Dave and Evans' presence. Well, Dave didn't quite mind. He usually joined the teenagers in swearing matches. How a sixty-year-old could sit with teenagers and 'eff' about was intriguing to Fuso's African upbringing. The girls were soon sacked to everybody's relief.

There was also Derek and Mary who lived in a world of their own. They were strange friends with a bond beyond this world. Surprisingly, apparently it wasn't a romantic relationship. You can always tell when people are romantically involved, the eyes always a sell-out. These weren't but there was no separating them. They didn't bother anyone and preferred to be left alone to do their work and do silly play. This involved darts – not real darts but a biro pen fitted with paper fins and wings and shot at a target on a carton box but Alexia didn't mind their play as they made as much cutlery as everybody else. If either Derek or Mary was absent the other endured the day quietly feeling like a slug on salty sands.

There were many people from all over the world but mostly from Asia and India who seemed hell-bent on cutting everybody else out of their discussions. Fuso had a good relationship with most of them, especially Rezaul, a nice fellow who he shared with many of his fears and dreams. A young lady called Ramah didn't think much of him though and either out of loathing, poor hearing or language barrier she never responded to his greetings for the first few weeks until he stopped trying. Later on she surprised Fuso when she actually started greeting him. Perhaps she realised he was going to be there for a long time and she could do herself much good if she made some effort to tolerate him. Kumar was the warehouse's man without specific portfolio. He swept, was sent around for whatever was needed and did numerous errands. He was a nice guy and liked greeting Fuso with '*jambo*', which was as far as his Swahili went. One day he went to Fuso's workstation to take the output figures for the day's cutlery sets on behalf of Alexia who was busy in the office.

"How many did you make?"

"Three hundred ninety," Fuso answered. He moved on to Singh, Fuso's cutlery workmate who spoke very little English. Now Fuso understood why Firsts Recruitment made him sit that silly test.

"You?" Kumar asked Singh.

"Four hundred twenty."

"He works very hard. Always makes more than me," said Fuso complimenting Singh. It was true that he always made more than everybody else. Not that there was any competition but that was just the way it was. He was good at making cutlery sets.

"Yeah," added Kumar. "You lazy or vhat? You must vork as hard as my Indian friend here. Ask him to teach you how, lazy lazy lazy, just like your people."

Fuso felt like he was about to 'go into labour'. That is how his good friend Kamau would put it. Kamau had a funny way of comparing any unpleasant feeling with labour pains as if he was a mother. Fuso wanted to pass out immediately. An imbecile who only knew how to run errands and push trolleys was telling him that he and 'his people' were lazy. Kumar's education, and that of the rest doing manual work, was minimal and there he was, the educated one being advised to learn from a guy who could hardly write his name.

Fuso felt hot tears well up behind his eyes and the frustrations he had accumulated in the last few weeks threatened to burst out. He had been reduced to doing menial jobs that required little brain in an out-of-way warehouse, where he had to walk twenty minutes in the winter weather. And there surrounded by idiots with little schooling, telling him how superior they were. Once again, he wanted to hate somebody.

He thought about Kenya and about his lost privileged status. Thought about the fabulous agency car, a 4x4 Mitsubishi Pajero, he used to drive and his own lovely Subaru WRX that he sold to finance his travel. He thought about the foreigners in Kenya – Asians, British, Americans and how much they enjoyed peace there – thought about how they thrived in business because nobody bothered them. Now here was a little moron drumming his superiority into him. In an unguarded moment, Fuso was attacked by a bout of racist feelings.

Fuso didn't even wait for Rezaul before starting his frustrating walk to Waterside to pick the H30 bus. Kumar must have realised Fuso was offended just before he walked out the door and tried to explain that he just wanted to draw him into a discussion because he had been quiet all day. Fuso ignored him and walked on, hurting so bad he felt like he was carrying weight in his chest. He now hated them, hated Jive, hated Britain and hated his life. He loathed his relatives and dubious friends in Africa who constantly sent him text messages asking for money. They believed he swam in riches and put unrealistic expectations on him adding to his sorrows. He was angry with himself for having been lured by his king-sized ego and ambitious dreams to seek fortunes abroad. It was hard not to think about his former job, smart suits and relaxed itinerary, his car, his girlfriend and all his buddies. Memories of his Sunday outings with his mates came flooding in his tortured mind, the places they visited, the pizzas they demolished. If returning home was as simple as boarding a plane like one would a bus, he would have headed to Heathrow Airport and boarded a plane still in his ugly safety boots.

Fuso had heard stories that some immigrants thought the British were lazy; that they thought they themselves were so hardworking. He had also heard rubbish gossip that some of the immigrant communities virtually controlled almost all corner shops because apparently the British were too lazy to sit through the boredom of shopkeeping, but he had dismissed it as gossip. Now he was beginning to think that there were actually people with that sort of attitude.

This was frightening to Fuso. He couldn't believe this was he getting racist. All his life he hadn't cared much about races. He wasn't sure he was going to remain that way much longer. Hoping he was going to get over this small incident as soon as possible he trudged on, his soul seriously wounded.

The walk to Waterside that day was most laborious. He was sick with frustration and fear. In his mind played a documentary that he had watched on BBC a few days earlier about racism in the Manchester Police Department. Fuso had watched it in horror as the undercover journalist exposed his experiences through training as a cop. Fuso, together with Makena and Wambúi, watched with trepidation at the revelation of what some police officers really felt about black people. It was most appalling to say the least. Dreadful thoughts of cops lurking at the corner waiting to pounce on someone just because they were black filled their minds.

He remembered talks that were going on in the Conservative Party with the party's shadow home secretary recommending that the government should detain asylum seekers on offshore islands like Lundy, off north Devon, Drake's island in Plymouth and the Scilly Isles while their claims were processed. With fear, Fuso remembered the Conservatives' anger that the Labour Party was too lax with immigrants and that Britain was becoming some dumping ground for all sorts of undesirables. They suggested that the immigrants should get an electronic tag that identified where they were at all times. This was enough to make Fuso dislike the Conservative Party and he wished that they would never win. Down with Conservatives, victory to Labour, war or no war. It was with glee when he read in a newspaper that someone had said that the Conservative Party leader's name sounded like a disease. Fuso couldn't agree more.

Why were folks fussing so much about the war, their newfound love for Iraqis? No, they just wanted to exercise their 'freedom of expression' and all the more exciting when the object of the said rights was the PM, accusing him of 'lying'. A walk in history reveals an acute shortage of leaderships that didn't have to tell a lie in its reign. Political leadership is often about being economical with truth, the more convincingly the better.

It was understandable if they were accusing the prime minister of lacking convincing lying skills. Saddam was not exactly a saint and it was an open secret that the world knew the war wasn't about WMDs, it was the oil, oil and power, stupid. A mad man interfering with such vast oil resources and causing such an impact on world stock markets was too much of a risk. Also a lot of British businesses benefit much from the relationship with their partners across the pond. You don't let a friend tough it out in a fight when you can lend a hand. Fuso's view was that Britain's support for the war was therefore strategic. The British people surely knew that but they didn't have to mouth it all over. Ask any son of a wealthy dodgy businessman and he would tell you he was glad there was food on the table. He may have suspicions about where the money came from but never let his mind dwell on it and would die before he discussed its source with outsiders. The British need the oil. Could you imagine what would happen if there were a shortage of oil? That would start a civil war. What, with their attachment to their cars that would be easy and the prime minister was the wiser to provide the oil, even if he had to lose credibility for it.

Fuso found an uneasy relief in the Liberal Democrats who he ordinarily couldn't stand. They had dismissed the Conservatives as trying to appeal to the most base of populist prejudices. At least someone had the voice of reason.

As he waited in the lonely Waterside bus stop, memories of that particular police constable portrayed in the BBC documentary with a white Ku Klux Klan hood over his head came back and filled him with anxiety. What if a like-minded supremacist found him at the lonely bus stop? There were bushes all around and the only building, a British Airways office complex, was four-hundred yards away. The way the PC demonstrated on TV what he would like to do to an 'effing Paki bastard' made Fuso shudder. Where did that leave him, them, the black people? He recalled Matthew a bulky white guy, a temp who quit from Jive and who used to offer him lifts home. He always wanted to draw him into racist discussions. Constantly he complained that all that the 'effing Paki' thought of was money, money and more money. In guarded confusion he refused to be drawn in. Where did he stand in all this? What did Matthew and his friends say about black people when he wasn't there?

What was it in humans that drove them to hate, drove them to xenophobic instincts? What was it that made people think they were better humans than others? What are the criteria of judging a superior human than the other? These thoughts tortured him as Fuso trod one heavy step after another. On one side were the likes of Kumar, feeling all superior, yet the likes of the police constable on the TV programme considered them as scum. They may want to shout 'discrimination' but in other situations they themselves discriminated. Fuso felt that the racists were just losers, driven by a sense of insecurity, crude shabby witches on broomsticks. And thinking of witches, Fuso amused himself with the question why witches were depicted riding broomsticks and never upgraded to riding vacuum cleaners.

In his anger, frustration and straying imagination he wished he could get a forum to ask Britain why she was becoming xenophobic. For hundreds of years Britain ruled over vast parts of the world. They plundered and killed and lorded over. Definitely the current generation couldn't understand what formed the basis of their comfortable lives, and their strong economy. Some of the wealth came from all over the world; from America to Asia and Africa. How could he, Fuso, tell the current generation that the British government murdered his forefathers because they dared fight for their rights? The Mau Mau movement was termed terrorists by the British. To the British these freedom fighters were barbarians who refused the divine mission to bring 'light' to their lives. What were the people to do when the British had stolen virtually every arable land in the country for their settlers and had banned the Africans from growing cash crops? How would the British people react if he told them that to date Kenya couldn't actively use the waters of Lake Victoria, one of the biggest lakes in the world, because colonial Britain signed an unfair treaty, the Nile treaty, in 1929 and later renegotiated it in 1956 giving total control of the Nile waters to Egypt and Sudan.

In the agreement, the riparian countries couldn't initiate projects that would affect the volume of Nile waters without the permission of Egypt. Apparently the British and the Egyptians were doing exciting profitable things up the Nile in Egypt like irrigating the Sahara Desert and building the mammoth Aswan High Dam. Never mind that most of the water catchments and tributaries that feed the Lake Victoria basin are from all the countries neighbouring the lake, but nobody gave regard to them. How could he explain to today's British people that to date the Delamere family still held land the size of an entire district, land that they simply took from its native owners?

The first of the Delamere family to settle in Kenya was the legendary Hugh Cholmondeley, the Third Baron Delamere, otherwise known as Lord Delamere. Born in 1870, the Third Baron Lord Delamere originally visited Kenya in 1895 on a hunting expedition and fell in love with the country. He went on to become leader of elected British settlers in the Legislative Council between 1910 and 1930. The Third Baron Delamere was, in the 1920s, instrumental in encouraging other Britons to settle in Kenya. This eventually led to the country's colonisation. How could Fuso explain to the British people that Europeans still dominated the upper market estates like Karen where many locals can only dream of owning property? How could he let them know that the Mt Kenya foothills and the Nanyuki plains, one of the most beautiful places in the world, are almost a reserve for Europeans and especially the British who own thousands of acres of farms and ranches?

They are free here to roam the plains in showy 4x4s fitted with lots of exciting fancy off-road accessories. They actually lived better lives than most of their countrymen back home, safe for a few lacking infrastructures like tarmac roads. They were revellers on a one-long-summer ball and the locals just watch indifferently, not bothering them in the least. Nanyuki town, situated at the foothills of Mt Kenya, and the nearby towns were hunting grounds for the amorous British soldiers – popularly known locally as *Johnnies* – who have a training base nearby at Archer's Post. They drink and brawl and indulge and debauch and rape. The soldiers did things that, if it happened in Europe, would put them in jail for life. Young girls, some underage, lured by prospects of riches from the moneyed soldiers – the Kenyan shilling is about 120 to the pound on average – ran off to Nanyuki. The evidence is unmistakable. Some of the poor girls returned home with trophies – light-complexioned, mixed-race babies. Only recently did non-governmental organisations and child protection agencies start blowing the whistle.

Well, this was a strange world indeed. Yesterday's terrorists were today's heroes. Yesterday's pariah Gaddafi was today's symbol of reformed troublemaker with an official welcome in Brussels and official visits in dusty tents by European leaders. The way of life was about power and control. Probably the Third World mourned so much because it had been on the receiving end for so long but you only need to think *What if the tables were turned?* Looking at it that way, one would make sense of the source of rising xenophobic attitudes. Human beings are territorial. Everybody seeks self-preservation, to hold on to their own and maybe that was what the racist cops featured in the TV programme were trying to do, but their tact was in short supply. If the British were to return to Africa and elsewhere in the numbers and manner they did in the colonial days, they'd be torn to pieces. This perspective made Fuso start to understand. The British people had reason to feel uncomfortable with the encroachment of their society by strange aliens.

When he reported to work the following day, Fuso's nerves had relaxed a bit. He was determined to put the previous day's incident behind him. Keen to forget it, he met up with Rezaul, a truly nice guy who he found easy to share his dreams and fears with. This was their daily routine. They used to meet at Hatton Cross tube station from where they picked the free H30 bus to Waterside. Their misery normally began not at Hatton Cross but at Waterside. The waterlogged grounds, and hence its name, were freezing and deserted and now the mornings were usually dark in the approaching winter. Walking to the Lakeside industrial estate from Waterside required nerves or desperation, whichever was the stronger. They had to walk to the bypass over the M25 motorway. This called for a brave soul, for on the flyover bridge blew the strongest of winds that threatened to blow them onto the motorway below. The drama got more interesting when it was raining and one had those one-pound umbrellas. Loathing cheap things, the wind twisted the umbrellas into a useless mess of wires and rags. They had to give up carrying them unless they were prepared to spend several pounds each week on umbrellas.

If Kumar was an idiot, Rezaul was a genius. A remarkable young fellow who had his life all mapped out, if only currently experiencing a rough stretch. Having qualifications in ACCAs he had experience in accounting, but the very nature of his origin put some sand on his cog. His strong accent was so bad not many employers were eager to offer him an accounting job. He was from Pakistan but had lived in the UK for seven years. One of his big dreams was to start a business of his own, probably a mobile phone shop where no McManus would shout about kicking his arse. After saving enough money he hoped to start a new life in Canada where his brother lived. At times he expressed distaste for relatives who had promised to host him when he arrived from Pakistan but who went on to charge him rent and bills immediately before he even got a job. Some twist of luck saved him from having to sleep rough on a bench in a park somewhere when he got contacts for a distant aunt who took him in. He still lived in her house, and wisely and happily volunteered to pay all bills. Those were some of the many woes of immigrants all over, being kicked out in the cold in a strange land.

Good friendships must be tried and theirs wasn't different. The cause: one Anna Sawyers. She was a beautiful, mature, sensible student doing her undergraduate in education at Leicester University. Christmas was approaching so she needed to make some extra cash during the short Christmas break. Apparently she couldn't stand the silly chatter of Sheila and Sharon, Dave and Evans were too old, Derek and Mary closed themselves in their world and Kumar's lot shut her out with their Punjabi. Rezaul and Fuso welcomed her to their table and made her feel comfortable. There are few thoroughly good people in the world. Anna was one of them. She had the best of attitudes, loving people for who they are. A clean heart topped her personality so deliciously one just had to fall in love with her inner beauty. When people describe someone as having inner beauty one tends to imagine they must be unattractive physically – wrong. Anna was a stunning beauty adorned with those delicate full curves. The African in Fuso was atoned. Where he came from they never liked their women too big, but neither did they like them so skinny, bones and all.

Come evening, Anna offered to give Rezaul and Fuso a lift to Ashford where she lived and saved them the agony of the torturous walk. This was too good for the two guys. She was so trusting she had no problems giving a lift to two young, coloured, male foreigners she just met. Others may argue it wasn't wise but that was Anna. She chose to see people positively until they proved otherwise. When she dropped them at Ashford Hospital, Rezaul was breathless. He wasn't sure which part of the Quran talked of only marrying a fellow Muslim.

As fate would have it, Rezaul had an interview appointment the following day, a Tuesday. Fuso had Anna all to himself. He spent the day with her working and during breaks they talked about the teaching career. At least they had a shared interest and that helped with enough material to keep the conversation going. Well, once in a while the talk detoured to social life. Fuso was very interested to hear her views about matters of the heart. Not that he was having ideas, besides he missed his girlfriend in Kenya like crazy. But, any man would admit when confronted by certain situations one just flips and teeters before sense takes charge. It's the charm instincts where blokes explored possibilities even if they didn't want to go all the way. Ask any man why he gets jealous when he sees a girl he dumped in the arms of another man.

In the evening, Anna dropped Fuso home and promised to pick him up Thursday. Again, as fate would have it she had a doctor's appointment the following day, Wednesday. She therefore gave him her number so that he could call her and confirm whether she was to come to work on Thursday because she feared the doctor might recommend a visit to a consultant on Thursday. That Wednesday, Fuso met Rezaul at Hatton Cross and went to work as usual. He was eager to know how it went with Anna and if Fuso managed to secure her telephone number but Fuso wasn't forthcoming. Rezaul was curious to know if she would pick Fuso up on Thursday morning but Fuso said she wouldn't. He wasn't sure whether she would be happy if he gave out her number to Rezaul and with picking both of them every day. It seemed courteous to ask her first, do the gentlemanly thing.

She picked him up Thursday all right. When Fuso asked her about picking both him and Rezaul she had no problem. By the time they arrived at Jive, Rezaul was nowhere to be seen and hadn't appeared at the clock-in time. He was to arrive an hour later, panting and frozen. Throughout the day he was in a foul mood and didn't want to talk to Fuso. He sensed he had gotten a lift from Anna – something he must have arranged either on Tuesday or on the phone. At lunch break, Fuso called him aside and inquired what the problem was.

"What's up with you today mate?" Fuso asked cautiously.

"I don't want to talk to you."

"Why, mate? We're friends."

"So I thought."

"What have I done now?"

"You had her number." It was a statement.

"Yes... I mean..."

"You knew she was to pick you today."

"It's not like that, Rezaul. I wanted to ask her about both of us first. We're still much of strangers and you can't extend favours just like that."

"So now I'm the unwelcome one? How come she gave the both of us a lift on Monday without having to request and did not ask us to pay?"

"C'mon Rezaul, be reasonable."

"I'm reasonable. Forget about all that, Fuso. What I'm mad about is you lying to me about her number and about picking you up today."

"First I wanted to ask her if it was all right, you know, lifts every day."

"You should have explained that when I asked yesterday instead of lying. I could've understood if you fancy her. I would have had no objection, but this… I feel like you treated me… like a small boy."

"Oh Rezaul, you can't say that. I'm so sorry." Fuso felt guilty, felt stupid. It was incredible that within four days Anna had caused friction between them and not for any fault of hers. In fact, she wasn't aware of any friction. He wondered whether the problem was in the 'lie' or some rising rivalry. All the same, it felt bad for him too. Rezaul had been his friend for some time. They had endured the walk from Waterside many times in horrible weather. Rezaul had a way with people, managing to get both of them lifts from colleagues once in a while to a place where they could pick a bus. If he could reverse the time he would stick by him, Anna or no Anna. There was never going to be anything with Anna and though he thought Rezaul was overreacting he felt like Peter when he disowned Jesus at his arrest. Fuso had betrayed a friend because of a girl he knew little about. Well, not quite betrayed because he didn't see it that way but the fact that she had come between him and a good friendship unsettled him. That evening they drove home in silence, with Rezaul letting him 'have her all' and Fuso feeling horrible and tense about the whole thing. They sat back and listened to sweet Anna trying to cheer them up; if only she knew why her passengers were so quiet that day.

The problem resolved itself on Friday when Anna quit the job. She said it was too monotonous and that it didn't engage her mind at all, 'like you were stupid'. If only Anna knew, that was Rezaul and Fuso's exact view of their work but they didn't have much choice. They couldn't afford a week without pay to go look for better work elsewhere. The break could dent their income so badly it could cause all sorts of bill trauma.

In her absence it was Waterside and the bypass all over again. The tension lifted and the two blokes were buddies again, though they both missed her very much. Often they talked about her and always fantasised about holding her in the moonlight.

# 8

There was a house on Nestles Avenue, Hayes, with a massive carved wooden fist sticking out in the middle of its lawn. It housed nine black immigrants owing to some complicated arrangement. Next door to this house lived a sweet little white girl with sparkling blue-grey eyes and curly blonde hair. She knew one of the occupants, Grace, a friend of her mum. Grace used to drop by once in a while to play with the little angel. When the child was old enough to venture out on her own, she loved to sit on the doorstep and, wearing an angelic smile on her round little face, wave at whoever passed by. She knew Grace was their immediate neighbour but she had never been there. In her young mind a house contained a mummy, a daddy and a baby. She therefore called all the ladies who lived next door 'Auntie Grace' and all the guys 'Uncle B' but many times confusion was written all over her face when a different 'Grace' appeared. Finally she resigned herself to the belief of a Grace and an Uncle B who took many forms. She played with all of them but they were all one until two of them appeared at the same time and then her blue-grey eyes would flutter in amazement; *strange creatures, these black neighbours.*

The house with the imposing wooden carving in its lawn was a three-bedroomed house that was home to nine people on a house-share arrangement. London is a very expensive city. You didn't come all the way from Africa to work to enrich the already wealthy British landlords. The cheaper you lived the more you saved to return home in glory, both real and imagined. Grace and Ben were in a relationship and shared a bedroom. Shiko – short for Wanjikú – and Múgo were married and took the second bedroom. Kamau and Dan used to share the third bedroom but

Dan was kicked out when Kamau's girlfriend Jane arrived from Kenya. Njambi, who was Ben's sister, and Múmbi, who had been badly betrayed by Ben, briefly shared one of the bunk beds in the curtain-partitioned living room before Múmbi moved out to live on her own. Dan took the other bunk bed. He had to train himself to shut his uncooperative eyes when the girls dressed. Abdi, a one-day-at-a-time chap, happily slept on the couch.

It was a crowded happy home, made up of young people brought together by their desire for a better life. All being from the Kikuyu community of Central Kenya except Abdi, a Somali, they had strong traditional communal sense. In fact they referred to themselves as 'Múhíríga' – the clan. Well, they had their fights – especially in the morning, when it got tricky taking turns for the bathroom. There were unstated designated times for each to take a shower depending on job shifts but once in a while one jumped the queue. There were screams and shouts and name-calling, but nothing escalated to a fight.

These were souls who had been brought together by their dream of a better life, a desire to break free and fly. They sought to realise their potential in an obsession of sorts, legally or illegally. Most people from the developing world are driven by tales of a paradise, of a world of sheer beauty, elegance, and abundance. The prospect of a 'Garden of Eden' type of place full of ripe and succulent fruits for their picking was irresistible. Travelling abroad – or 'flying out' as Kenyans called it – was the 'in thing'. Those from the countryside who still had communal lifestyles especially idolised those who had been abroad. It wasn't surprising to find loads of hired minibuses going to the airport to see off one of their own 'making it big'. It was a mark of progress, of achievement, of greatness with expected rewards to the community when such lucky people returned. A local authority representative might be present to express the authority's solidarity in pursuit of greatness.

Many never returned of course, to the distress of the villagers, and their names were embedded in the proverbs that others may not tread their stray path. A good count of how many young people a village had sent overseas was a source of pride. It was therefore usual to hear of a fundraiser to send a youngster abroad. Many happily stretched their hands to share in a noble gesture with the expectations of rewards to the community. Such a youngster was supposed to join a college abroad and get a good education that landed him a good job. That, hopefully, in turn gave clout to the community some day. They then could talk about 'our son' with pride. Alternatively he could seek wealth in the land of opportunity and return someday to be counted among men, *real men*. That too worked the same way. Wealth gives clout even to the dull, the ugly and the boring. That explained why being deported from abroad was a horror to these disillusioned souls.

The Nestles Avenue house occupants came from a plethora of background, each with a convoluted tale that was preferably not told. Ben, an accounting graduate from University of Nairobi, first occupied the house. When he arrived in Britain he had come for an accounting seminar in Northern Ireland, or so he stated in his visa application papers. Getting an invitation was easy. He simply applied using a fictitious company complete with a website. Getting a visa wasn't hard either because his bank account, never mind if it was genuine, spoke for itself. Ben had no genuine nerve in his body. He never believed in getting anything the straight way, including buying you a meal. He had to complicate it by first asking that you split the bill but then gave back all your money as 'change' hours later.

He was a smooth operator, a master of intrigue, who understood systems better than the veterans. A smooth talker too, so perfectly adorned with the gift of the gab he could sell you a free brochure – even with the words 'not for sale' written in bold on top. If you weren't careful he could easily get you sign into some deal to sell your own blood. Call it conning but he always made you have a part in it so that in the end you blamed yourself as much as him for allowing yourself to be taken in.

Coming for a seminar, then, he only got a visitor's six-month visa. That posed a problem because he had to find some way of getting Blunkett's Home Office papers and not poor forgeries from East Europe. Soon he teamed up with Grace, an ambitious, slim, light-complexioned and beautiful nurse, who found his plans for 'making it big' very interesting. She was about five feet four, and standing next to Ben – who was a foot taller than her – gave her a sense of wanting to be dominated. That was Ben's specialism. He took the cue and overshadowed her in many aspects but still kept romance on hold. What she didn't know was that he was biding his time, slowly entangling her in his web. He wanted to use her both as a front for his shoddy business and also trick her into formalising their relationship before his visa expired because her papers were clean. She had an indefinite-leave-to-remain visa having gotten her work permit after training as a nurse in the UK. There was a huge shortage of nurses in the UK.

Ben could tell that he enthralled Grace but he had to play his cards shrewdly. He applied what he called the 'shock and awe' method – so close yet so far. It was prudent that he pretended not to be excited about the relationship. This drove Grace to the edge. She wanted him so bad but he wasn't pushing the relationship beyond friendship.

All the times he took her out he always walked her as far as her door and then politely declined to enter, content to give her a light goodnight peck. He used to say when a friendship moved to another level it was to be forever so one had to be sure it was what they wanted. A favourite of his was a quote from Achebe's *Things Fall Apart*, a Nigerian proverb: When a handshake extends beyond the elbow it becomes something else. She knew he wasn't slow, knew he had understood all the prompts she threw him yet he refused to take action. This was killing her. Did he find her so unattractive or what? That couldn't be true. He had expressed how much he appreciated her shapely curves. She had seen him lose breath at the sight of her cleavage and his eyes never left her when they were together. Why was he behaving this way then? She felt insecure and wondered if there was anything wrong with her, wondered if she smelled or if she was so devoid of charm.

"Please come in today," begged Grace one cold winter night after a happy night out. Ben shook his head.

"Oh c'mon, Ben, you can't leave me like this…" she trailed off, gesturing with her hands that she was cold.

"Are you sure it's what you want?"

"Yes Ben. I know it is what I want."

"And you won't wake up to a guilt breakfast?"

"I'm a grown woman Ben. I..." She never finished what she was about to say. He had lifted her to himself, his mouth all over hers, and carried her inside kicking the door shut with his leg, thanks to the movies.

When she moved in with him they set up a website for an organisation that was supposed to help accountants worldwide find jobs in the UK. Many people crazy about their unrealised dreams readily paid a processing fee that guaranteed a job placement at three hundred and fifty pounds if one only wanted to be in the exclusive database without guarantee of placement.

Things were going well. Ben was beginning to realise big money come his way. He had bought a Toyota Celica, two years old but as good as new. He had dreamt of owning a sports car for many years; the car occupied him so much, to the chagrin of Grace who was seeing less and less of him now. She had to pinch herself, formerly a staunch believer that men would never worry her again, how could she get jealous? They weren't even married and it was a car that was occupying him – not *some other woman*.

Ben wanted to expand his business by visiting Kenya and set up an office there to give his business some genuineness. Most of the suckers who gladly sent him the cash were Kenyans so it was only fair to give them a form of physical reference to the gate through which they dreamt of getting a better life.

'Every dog has its day,' someone said. In his quest for riches he stumbled into Obika and Oniwo, some like-minded blokes from Nigeria. When their friendship developed to buddy-buddy level they presented him with a 'small problem' one night when out for a drink in a pub.

"We need help, Ben," said Obika, who was the talkative of the two, supposedly a graduate of a Bulgarian University he talked nothing about.

"Shoot, mate, that's what friends are for." Ben was now a little tipsy, gesticulating in slow motion.

"We have a cheque we need cook but got no chef if you know what I mean." Oniwo nodded to this in agreement. He was a man of few words even when heavy with drink. Standing at seven feet and heavyset, his size intimidated any male wherever he went. He had never had to fight in a pub brawl. No one ever tried to mess with him, a formidable character whose pitch black pupils on clear white eyes on a very dark face made you feel like he saw inside you.

"I'm all ears."

"It's a forty thousand pounds delicacy, can't cook it ourselves. Our damn books are not proper."

"I understand."

"Glad you do. Don't want to draw attention to ourselves else the Dogman got our scent and shoved us back to damn Lagos." Dogman was the visually challenged home secretary who used a guide dog.

"What're brothers for?"

"Good, when do you fix it?"

"*Kesho* – that's Swahili for tomorrow."

"Good, erm, *abeg broda*. You'll be greatly rewarded."

"What's my cut?"

"What're *brodas* for? You used those words *yoself*, a third, equal for each of us."

"One missing ingredient," Ben said. "My books aren't clean either. My girl's is. She can fix this."

"Cool *broda*, no worries, in that case each gets a quarter of the cake, today you help, tomorrow I help."

Smacking his lips in excitement he took the cheque, amused that they thought he was so stupid he couldn't see through their lie. However, a fair cut from forty thousand wasn't bad at all.

The good book says bad company corrupts good morals. When he took the cheque to Grace she readily accepted 'the deal' and went to cash it through one of the accounts Ben had made her open with a strange name and passport more than a year before. *They can't tell you apart if your brother wore your clothes* Ben had convinced her. He had foresight, always saw things from a distance. For more than a year the account had seen little activity except a few small amount cheque deposits. That was about to change now with the deposit of the £40K cheque. When it matured the money was to be shared among the interested parties. However, there was another 'small problem'. The cheque belonged to Onuka who hadn't been mentioned earlier and who, it was alleged, had to see the whole loot before it was shared out.

The four of them went to South Harrow to meet Mr Onuka but unfortunately his wife, whom they found in the house, said he had left briefly and was not going to be long. Six hours later Onuka hadn't turned up. Grace was getting late for her nightshift. Being unsafe to move about with so much money they all agreed to take a thousand each and return the following day to share the money. It was therefore with profound consternation when Ben and Grace returned the following day and found an empty house. The neighbours said the occupants had moved out. When Ben inquired about Oniwo and Obika he was told reliably that they had flown out of the country the previous night.

"Bastards," was all Ben said, and knew he had been taken this time. At least he had two thousand pounds he hadn't worked for. Well, one thousand pounds belonged to Grace but it was as good as his. His adrenaline was boiling, imagining those Nigerians taking off with all that loot. Ideas clashed in his mind like snooker balls. He had to pull one big hustle himself. That cheque thing was too easy.

This was never to be. A few days later a police car appeared at Nestles Avenue. Grace was not in and those who were in said they didn't know anyone by that name. 'All blacks look the same' seemed to apply here. The cops seemed confused about the appearances of the ladies before them and insisted that each prove they were not Grace. After having a look at the few dodgy papers they had – those who had no valid visas claimed their passports were at the Home Office and interestingly the cops couldn't tell the girls apart – they said they would return but they didn't say why they were there. It was therefore critical that drastic measures were taken. The whole Múhíríga moved out.

Ben organised the Múhíríga's move to Hounslow Road in Feltham. He advised them to lie low for a while and be on the lookout. Uncomfortable with the lull, he selfishly bought a ticket to Kenya to set up the Kenyan office of his dubious recruitment company. If anything happened to the Múhíríga he was safe himself, some solidarity!

He landed in glory with some seven thousand he had managed to save, well almost, because that included Grace's thousand from the Nigerian deal. He set up an office in the new, sparkling Bazaar Plaza and launched a branch of Accounting Guru UK Ltd. The good book says there will always be poor people in the world… and so there'll always be suckers. The money kept coming. His consultations sounded so genuine, so well planned that some victims had already booked their flights. As the money came in, so did Ben blow it in lavish spending. For starters he bought a second-hand personalised sports car from a departing expatriate, a metallic grey Nissan 300ZX adorned with all sorts of flashy auxiliaries; including gleaming golden alloy spoke wheels and chest-bursting music. The rest of the dough, he dished out loads of it to relatives and friends, if only to maintain an image of 'made it big'. He had become a hit in Nairobi, doing stunts on the streets in the exceptional car. Heaps of broken hearts littered in his trail.

After four months he was running out of cash fast and needed to do something immediately. He couldn't return to the UK because he had heard the police were looking for him. The solution was to re-invent himself.

Most of the people seeking UK visas in East Africa were Kenyans, having had a little more exposure to the outside world than their neighbours, thanks to tourism. Kenya was a popular destination for safaris and holidays with its rich game reserves, unmatched beaches and weather that rarely lost its temper. Uganda, therefore, was a likely successful point to apply for a visa due to the lesser number of applicants. The days of the exodus of Ugandans of Asian origin that sought refuge in Britain after Idi Amin expelled them were long gone. Also the number of

Ugandans who sought refugee status following the successive wars and oppressive regimes that nearly destroyed a beautiful country was also reducing in the now more relatively stable country.

Ben moved to Kampala to establish links with fellow forgers. Soon he was armed with a Ugandan passport and all the papers he needed – and some that he didn't, at least not yet. They ranged from a fake church baptism card supposedly to have been issued when he was at the age of six, to a land title deed for a parcel of land in Entebbe. He applied for a student's visa to travel for a master's degree in Business Administration (MBA) at Thames Valley University and his visa application was approved immediately.

He laughed his way to Heathrow Airport, a man at peace with himself and his achievements. He was unafraid, confident nobody would know. "All blacks look the same," he muttered with amusement. It worked fine for him. If they had problems telling the black people apart, so be it. It worked fine for him. Let them figure out whether that was good or bad for them. He approached the arrivals desk, still whistling.

"Which flight were you on, sir?" the sweet brunette behind the desk asked him, studying his tall frame. The 'sir' tag suited him well. A single-breasted dark blue suit and gold-on-black Marks and Spencer tie brought out the image of a gentleman in him. *This student took life a little too seriously,* the lady thought.

"Egypt Air, Kampala–Cairo–London."

"Will be taking residence at the University?"

"Yap."

"How long is the course?"

"Slightly over a year."

"Hope you enjoy it here. My parents been to Uganda," said the lady and stamped his passport.

"Oh, that's nice. Have you been there?"

"Not yet, hope to someday."

"Hope I'll be there to show you around," he said all honey and charm. The lady smiled and motioned for the next passenger to approach.

Out of Terminal 3 arrivals lounge he whistled, a happy song

in his heart, and took a 285 bus to Hounslow Road, Feltham – the Múhíríga's new abode.

All he thought in the bus was how much the current generation laughed at the previous one for the fact that they didn't have computers and stored their data in paper files. Yet paper passports and old manual stamps were still in use in this age of digital technology. There should have been an electronic identity of sorts, say, that identified the passport holder by their fingerprints or the eyes or something like that. He had just made a mockery of the system and laughed at them in his heart, happy that such a technology was yet to be widely applied. But then there will always be a way to beat any foolproof system. Let the systems change and the authority watch all the borders for all he cared, he would cross borders and use airports anyway. He was a wanted man yet he wasn't smuggled through in some smelly truck. He got in through the airport and was welcomed back. He almost secured a date!

Grace met him at the door. She had requested a Zimbabwean colleague to cover her shift so she could welcome him when he arrived. He had told her there was no need for her to pick him up from Heathrow. He was travelling light. She was seething lava on the inside, so angry with him having heard from her friends in Kenya that he had become a Casanova. Diplomacy, however, demanded that she didn't confront him immediately after the long flight. He needed to shake off the jetlag.

"Tell me what mischief you've been up to," she said when he woke up all fresh from his rest a few hours later.

"C'mon love, what kind of question is that? You haven't even told me you missed me." He knew all was not well. Grace had missed him so much and though angry with him she was glad to see him. All the missiles she had prepared for him seemed unreasonable now. She wanted to ask him about the alleged affairs but she didn't know how to start.

"So, did you meet any girls?"

"Jealous?" he said, grinning mischievously. "Plenty… told them I was married to a goddess."

"If only I didn't know… I mean know you." He read something in her tone but let it pass.

"Of course you know me. Admit it, you seduced me."

"No! That's not true!" she screamed.

He had turned over her offensive approach. Grace was now on the defensive. She didn't know how to confront him without a fight. A part of her wanted him like crazy. She doubted if all the things she had been told were true. In any case, her friends might have been jealous of her man. Probably they wanted to break her relationship. Just then Ben took her in his arms, overwhelming her with his might. She loved the feeling of his power over her and much as she had her doubts, she let them remain just that.

They lived on, supposedly happy, Ben drawing a lot of money from Grace. His Accounting Guru UK business was doing poorly, people having long realised it was a sham. There were some victims that were on his case and wanted to roast him, wherever he was in the world. Some had parents with influence who even contacted Interpol. He had to slow it a bit but he needed money. Much as Grace pushed him to get a job, he refused and spent days on the internet trying to con someone or set up a con website. Grace was beginning to detest having to pay for his upkeep. She had to pay his bit of the house-share bill as well as finance his travel all over Britain and beyond in his pursuit of 'deals'. Slowly it began to sink in that he had put her on the wrong side of the law once. From his clandestine escapades she felt it wouldn't be long before she was on the run again. She was never caught but she hated the flighty feeling whenever she saw a cop and having to avoid eye contact with the police all together. She had had to abandon the account she had used to cash that fateful cheque and give up some five hundred pounds still in it. To make matters worse, Ben had also taken her share of the Nigerian loot. It wasn't funny anymore.

Several months later she surprised the Múhíríga when she announced she was leaving.

"Where to?" they asked in unison.

"Why?" asked Abdi, who was closer to her than anybody else.

"Change of scene," she responded enigmatically, and left them thinking it was a joke. That night she gave Ben her all, used his own 'shock and awe' strategy as he used to call his unpredictable tricks. In the morning she wasn't in a hurry to wake up and get ready for work.

"C'mon, honey, you'll be late for work," mumbled Ben, still reeling from the absolute satiation of the previous night.

"It's my day off today."

"Hadn't told me."

"Forgot."

"Great, will make you breakfast in bed, you know, like them white folks. It's supposed to be so romantic."

"Too late."

"You've not had no breakfast. It's only seven in the morning."

"I'm leaving, Ben."

"What do you mean you're leaving? Where to? Quitting job?"

"It's over, Ben, between us."

Ben looked her in the face for a clue that she was joking and found none. He had dominated her, controlled her and knew he was like a drug to her. She needed him.

"Get serious, Grace. What have I done now?" he laughed, nervously afraid that she sounded serious.

"Nothing. I just want to be free awhile. Be sure this is what I want, you know, that sort of thing."

"I don't believe you. Is it because I've been taking money from you?"

"No, Ben... please understand."

"Look, I've gotten papers, real papers, and Blunkett's stuff for that matter. My contact gave me an indefinite stay. Whoever said the West wasn't corrupt? Got them from an understanding white guy. It's a capitalist place and everybody can do with a little quid on the side. Hadn't told you, wanted it to be a surprise. Got lots of dough coming too, will let you know about it when it's all in the bank."

"Shock and awe?"

"Sort of, we could get married now if you want, start a family."

He was getting frantic. He ran to the drawer and came with his passport, hurriedly opening it to display the valid visa. She was surprised, wondered how he had pulled that one off, but it just gave her all the more reason she wanted out of his life. She didn't want to live all her life with her nerves on edge, fearing there were cops at the door every time she heard a knock.

"It's over, Ben," she stated, and pulled a stack of photographs from a drawer cabinet next to the bed, which she handed him. She sat up, leaning on the headrest and watched Ben's face change through confusion, to consternation to resigned guilt and defeat. In a daze, he put on his jogger bottoms, trainers and an old T-shirt. He walked to the door in a trance and stopped. When he turned his eyes were moist.

"Would it help if I said sorry, that I do really love you?"

"If it had happened earlier, yes."

"Please," he said faintly.

She shook her head, wanting to cry herself. She loved him, wished it didn't end this way. It was heartbreaking watching him so vulnerable, a fatally wounded lion. She pointed to photos of him and the myriad of girls he dated when he escaped to Nairobi after the Nigerian cheque, leaving her behind to face the law alone. She had asked her friends in Nairobi to send her evidence when they expressed concern about his behaviour. He avoided looking at the photos.

"You said I seduced you. I started it, I end it."

Ben slipped out for a walk in the chilly autumn morning, his mind too preoccupied with the meaning of all this to mind the cold. He needed to sort his head, convince himself he wasn't dreaming. A gust of fresh cold air felt like all he needed to calm him. Else he thought if he stayed on he would lose control and do something stupid.

When he returned, Grace had packed all her stuff into a rental van outside. She had wanted to do it in a hurry lest he returned and refused her permission to leave or possibly convince her to change her mind. She loved him and she would miss him terribly but she felt this was the right thing to do now. He didn't say anything. He didn't even try to stop her. What was the use anyway? He had lived with her and knew that she took time to make serious decisions but once they were made that was it. To Grace's surprise, he didn't put a fight when she said she was taking the sports car.

"Why would you want to do that?" he asked in resignation.

"Because you owe me lots of money."

"Suit yourself," he said, and went to the bedroom. Guilty and sick with what she had just done, she thought it was unfair to take the car. He had so much attachment to it the thought of losing it would depress him. The fact that he didn't fight for the car portrayed how much this had hit him. She left the car keys with Ben's sister Njambi to give them back to him and rushed out to the van leaving the shocked Múhíríga now living at Feltham dumbfounded by the new developments. Was this the initial crack of the clan's imminent break-up?

# 9

The Múhíríga was shaken. They all worried how Ben lived but nobody expected anything drastic from Grace. She was so focused, so in love with him in spite of his flaws. Nobody saw that one coming but then it was a case of him swallowing his own bitter pill. He had badly betrayed Múmbi, his former girlfriend who had stood by him for many years.

Ben and Múmbi's love had blossomed fully to the knowledge of their families from their teenage years. He really wanted Múmbi to join him in Britain so that they could start a family. He also figured she could help him with his immigration status. Having become a teacher after graduating from Kikuyu campus of the University of Nairobi with a Bachelor of Education degree, Ben knew with the demand for teachers in Britain she could easily get a work permit. That way, if they got married, he too would get to legalise his stay as a dependant. However, Múmbi's attempts at getting a visa were not successful until soon after Ben had given up and turned his attention to Grace. There was no way of breaking the news to Múmbi that he was now with someone else. With all his conniving skills he just couldn't find enough courage to stop her travelling to join him. In any case, he figured, she always wanted to travel abroad to try her luck. If she couldn't stand the new developments she could always move out and live on her own.

Both Ben's family and Múmbi's family saw her off at Jomo Kenyatta Airport, Nairobi, all happy that she was joining Ben to start a family. When she arrived at Heathrow Airport, Ben was there to welcome her, complete with kisses and all the lovely words. His stomach did somersaults when he saw her. She was stunning, just the way he loved her. For a moment, love tugged at his heart. He almost felt like running away with her and living elsewhere but that was going to complicate so many things at the moment.

He took her to the Múhíríga at Nestles Avenue where they all waited for the new addition, worried sick of the moment the truth would hit her. It came late at night when they had had their meals and fun and done all the talking. Grace went to bed first, saying she needed to wake up early the following day to go to work. Everybody was uncomfortable with what was to follow; all of a sudden they excused themselves scampering to the safety of their bedrooms. Dan, Abdi and Njambi, who slept in the lounge, decided to do a late night walk but her domineering brother stopped Njambi at the door.

"Where d'you think you're going so late at night?" growled Ben.

"For a walk, got safe company as you can see and I'm a big girl," she answered, aware this wasn't about her safety. She always went to work late in the night anyway.

"Leave night walks to boys, Njambi, Múmbi here needs company."

"I'm all right, let her be, she's a big girl," said Múmbi, in Njambi's defence. They had grown very close before Njambi travelled abroad. "Besides, don't you think we need some time alone?" she added and winked.

Ben ignored her and directed his attention at Njambi. "I'd like you to stay and show Múmbi where to sleep," he said, without looking at Múmbi. "She'll make sure you're comfortable, g'dnight." He said the last bit with a brief glance at Múmbi's confused look, before disappearing into his bedroom to join Grace.

She cried all night with Njambi holding her close. Njambi cried too, knowing how deeply hurt she was but there was nothing she could do about it. They both fell to sleep at dawn, exhausted from emotional trauma.

The next few weeks, everybody tried hard to act normal and did their best to avoid Múmbi's eyes. Grace defiantly went about her business; she did not want to know. This was an issue between

Ben and his ex. True, she was uncomfortable with Múmbi around and especially for the fact that Múmbi was so beautiful. However, Grace's humane side understood that you didn't kick out someone who had come thousands of miles from home before they even knew which bus to take to the local high street. She was biding her time for the opportune moment to ask her to leave.

Ben cleverly went for his intriguing trips all over Europe for several weeks, completely denying Múmbi audience. His absence helped ease tensions a little until he returned about a month and a half later to find that she had found a job as a supply teacher and moved out of the Nestles house.

He didn't know what to make of that. He wished he had been a little patient before moving in with Grace. The reason Múmbi was unable to travel was that she had been delayed by the agency she had applied for a teaching position with; they didn't want to approve her visa until she had her Kenyan police criminal disclosure certificate. Despite all her efforts, including lots of bribes, her certificate of good conduct application had been lost in the messy red tape and corruption in the police force and in their own wisdom she couldn't apply for another until they ascertained what had happened to the other one.

Ben was gutted. Did he make the biggest mistake of his life? Grace was all right but it was Múmbi he loved. They both had too much history together to simply throw away. Even a smooth wheeler-dealer conman like him had a soft side to his heart. However, history and true love aside, Grace had seen him through very bleak moments. He was a rather mixed-up man.

Being the cheeky rascal he was, when he reappeared from his continental escapades he asked Múmbi for a meeting. Múmbi, ever so graceful and controlled, gave him a lunch date.

"You look stunning," he said, when she came through to his table at the Chinese restaurant in Shepperton.

"I'm surprised you noticed," said she, sarcastically.

"I mean it," he said, regarding her lovely face and that smile that revealed a seductive gap between her front teeth. Much as the gap was an outdated marker of beauty among the Kikuyu,

Múmbi's fitted like a rare dark ruby along her perfect teeth. Ben was fidgety, filled with choking emotions. He couldn't believe what a sucker he was to let such a beauty slip out of his life.

"Why did you want to see me?" She changed the subject, uncomfortable with the way he looked at her. Wary of the hold he had on her heart, she was afraid he might win her all over again.

"Catching up, you know, I hear you're doing all right."

"I'm coping. Njambi pitied poor me and showed me around, you know, where to find teacher employment agencies. God bless her. The one who invited me here dumped me."

"I'm sorry. I had to be away on business."

"Yeah? Is that all you're sorry for?"

"I understand you're disappointed… but…"

"Disappointed, Ben? You broke my heart. What happened to all our experiences of all these years together? Why did you let me come thousands of miles just to show me what scum you think I am?"

"That's unfair, lovie, I…"

"Lovie? Thanks Ben, for letting me know who you really are before I made the biggest mistake of my life. I wish you happiness. It's because of you that I lost my faith in a God I was so committed to and probably I'm being punished for it. It was foolish but I loved you so much. I've now asked Him for forgiveness… and… as for you Ben… You're pathetic, goodbye Ben."

She walked out, trying not to cry, and left Ben imagining the many things he could do with a beauty like that and, of course, her new status as a teacher.

When she finally got home, the troubled young lady flung herself on the carpet and let go all the rot that was within her. She cried her insides out as if the pain was nauseating food she needed to vomit out for relief. Five hours later she drifted into a deathlike slumber out of exhaustion to wake up fifteen hours later, almost noon the following day.

She could only remember crying on the carpet. How she ended in bed she couldn't remember. Surprisingly, she felt refreshed and calmed. Ah, the power of tears! Now that a part of her had died she felt reincarnated. For once she didn't know what to make of God. He had been her friend all these years since she had learnt her alphabet but now he had let her down. She felt short changed. But wait a minute. Was it not her who deserted God for that despicable heartbreaker Ben? Maybe God was punishing her, wanted her to learn a lesson the hard way. And thinking of God, she thought of the step of faith she had taken in the form of a wedding gown. She had brought it all the way from Kenya for her wedding with Ben, a wedding that was never to be. Like one possessed, she dashed into her bedroom in her rented flat in Sunbury-on-Thames and opened the wardrobe. The gown hung there and imposingly so. Damn, it was beautiful, so dazzling with all those laces, beads, gems – the works. It was tantalising in her eyes but ugly too in her heart. It represented her misery, her failure, and her doomsday. It represented death and evil. Evil that was her past life's dream. She had to kill that *now!*

In a screaming rage she ran to the sideboard drawer and took out a pair of scissors. She picked up the gown and sheared it to shreds, to hell with her dreams, to hell with… faith? To hell with whatever!

# 10

Grace adjusted the load of fresh wet coffee berries on her back and trudged on. Koru coffee factory was only a few hundred yards away but seemed miles away. Well, the factory was a couple miles from her home, near Mananga Primary School, but with a heavy load of coffee on your back it was continents away. The slimy juices from the coffee berries were seeping through the sisal bag to the plastic sheet on her back that was meant to keep the wetness off her clothes. The juice from the berries then snaked down her back and dripped on her legs making sticky streaks. She hated this, hated the village life she lived and the fact that she was doing all these menial chores.

It had been six months since she sat her O level examinations at Kíría-iní Girls' Secondary School, about five miles from her home. She had been some sort of a star. An avid basketball freak, the school team never felt brave enough to play in her absence. Topping this, with her graceful sprouting beauty, the young male teachers had a fond eye for her but there was no scandal. Her innocence was written all over her, a naïve, well-behaved lassie who never hurt anyone. She was loved and pampered and given treats by all, both students and teachers. It was only natural that she was made a prefect and later elevated to school captain.

Having not performed well enough to secure a place in the public universities, she had to look for a college to train in some skill or get tertiary education. Her dad had promised to get her into some course but six months later nothing had come up. She had a younger brother, Miki, now in his second year at Wahúndúra Secondary School, a school whose records read like 'what a school shouldn't be'. She had protested to her dad fearing her brother would get into drugs but her dad was adamant.

"He can take drugs if he fancies them. We have a proverb that says: your house is built with the material you provide."

"Oh c'mon, Dad, he is only a child," Grace pleaded. She was very free with her dad, unlike other girls her age. It wasn't usual in the community.

"Child?" her dad asked, sarcastically. "Then why did he go for circumcision? He is taller than me now, he should reason like an adult. If he needs advice, he can consult Joto." Joto was a local loony who sank into madness out of drug abuse. The nickname meant 'heat' in Swahili.

"They influence each other, Dad. The students do."

"He's lucky he has someone to tell him before he joins. Please tell him not to get influenced."

"Oh shut up, the two of you! How you go on like I'm not here, I can take care of myself," Miki shouted from his room.

"See, told you he can take care of himself," said Grace's dad, in a voice that was meant to carry. Grace glared at him.

Her sister Janet studied two ridges away at Gítugí Girls' Secondary School, a good school both in behaviour and performance with a good number of the national big names in its alumni list. Being a famous district school it was more expensive than Wahúndúra or Kíría-iní. Obviously her dad, who was a junior accountant with Nairobi County Council, couldn't afford seeing all three of them through school at the same time. Grace was therefore resigned to fate, watching her formerly flawless skin begin to get spots from the strain of all the chores in the house and in the small family farm. There was little in the way of rescue that could possibly come her way any time soon.

After sorting the coffee berries and weighing them on the ancient Avery weighing machine that she doubted anyone ever calibrated, she left for home. She had milking to do, locking up the cattle and poultry and she still had supper to prepare. It was a life of drudgery for this country beauty, a life she never imagined living when she was in school. When you are young everything seems all mapped out. The possibilities are numerous and your dreams take shape instantly but only in your mind. The real world is often a shocker, so unwelcoming and callous. This was, however, too much for her. It was as if her mother had pushed all responsibilities into her hands but she wasn't loudly complaining. She couldn't believe that this was the life her poor mum had lived all these years. Much as she felt suffocated, she felt obliged to help her mum who needed a helping hand with the myriad daily chores.

That night, her dad arrived as expected. It was a Friday, the day he usually came for weekend break from Nairobi where he worked. He lived in a tiny bedsitter he rented at Kariobangi South. There was no need for a big house because his family lived in the countryside and only his wife visited overnight once in a while. When the kids visited Nairobi they had to put up with their paternal uncle who lived in a three-bedroom company house in Embakasi. After all the talk catching up on the week's village happenings her dad dropped the good news.

"So, Grace, how'd you like to do a secretarial course and computers, you know… that sort of thing?"

"Oh, that'd be fine Dad, I'd love to. You found a college for me already?" she asked, excitedly.

"That's right. Getting a place wasn't the problem, the fee was, but now it's okay."

"Which college am I to join?"

"Universal College."

"Please say I'll start immediately."

"Does that mean you're tired of staying with me?" her mum asked, in mock accusation. She was happy for her because she had noticed Grace had lost her laughter.

"Far from it, Mama, but I need to move on, you know, get some training. I'll need a job."

"Right, big girl, with my blessings."

"You join Monday so you travel Sunday with me. You'll be staying at your Uncle Múíhia's house in Embakasi. I already talked to him, he has no objections."

Grace was delighted. The drudgery was over. She had visited

her uncle's house in Embakasi Pipeline Estate. Múíhia worked for the Kenya Pipeline Corporation, a government pipeline network that supplied fuel in the country. The house was big with big spacious rooms. It had beautiful Meru oak-tiled floors that blended well with the cream white walls. The Estate itself was a unique community by itself, complete with a shopping centre that had everything from a pub to a basketball court. With her passion for basketball she was in heaven. The Estate had a concrete wall all around it, its access was through one gate with round-the-clock security officers in charge.

Her uncle was an engineer with the corporation. His family lived in Eldoret, a bustling lovely town in the Rift Valley Province. His wife, Aunt Viv, taught at Chebisaas High School just outside the town. Uncle Múíhia had worked for ten years in Eldoret himself before he was transferred to Nairobi. The family loved Eldoret and felt it was not good to disrupt the children's education. Furthermore they had a thriving beauty salon business in Eldoret town. It was therefore agreed it was better if he visited home on weekends or whenever he was free. That was easy because his job included travelling all over along the pipeline, wherever his expertise was required and the pipeline had a depot in Eldoret. Many were the times he was rushed hundreds of kilometres by helicopter to attend emergencies on the pipeline. On such calls he was often dropped home at Eldoret if the call was in the Rift Valley region to the excitement and pride of his family. He was held in high esteem in the neighbourhood. Not every Tom, Dick and whoever was dropped by a helicopter in their own backyard.

Grace thus was more or less left on her own, her uncle choosing to spend many nights in the nearest town close to where he was on duty. Such was the nomadic lifestyle of the field engineers but they didn't mind because the night jobs came with beautiful overtime allowances. Once in a while he dropped by and left her wads of money she didn't need. She was only a student and besides buying the latest trendy wear, a few books, her make-up, hairdo, lunch and bus fare she didn't need that much money. The fridge was ever stocked and Uncle Múíhia never took a meal in the house.

Most times, he came swaying with a little too much drink, smiling boyishly and trying in futility to hide that he was drunk. Such are the ways of drunks. They always think nobody can tell they've taken alcohol. With a hurried chat about whether she was all right he would then quickly excuse himself and go straight to his bedroom. The following day Grace would wake up to find more money on the coffee table in the living room. She had no way of telling him she didn't need it. Already she had several thousand that she really didn't know what to do with. She wasn't an outdoor kind of person, never went to discos or clubbing and didn't take alcohol. For a noble purpose, she used to give treats to her hard-up peers. They were always broke, having blown their money on 'hengs', slang for wild clubbing, possibly coined from 'hanging out'. She also managed to send her sister and brother pocket money. It wasn't always easy for her when she was in secondary school. There was nobody to come to her rescue when she was broke at school so she understood her siblings' plight. Not that her parents were mean; on the contrary, they went out of their way to provide for her while she could tell they were cleaned out themselves. Now that she had more money than she needed, she secretly sent her siblings pocket money and unknown to her parents, paid for all the extra-curricular events like school trips. She wanted to ease pressure on her parents.

It was lonely for a young lady living in a huge house all by herself. Most times she sat late watching TV and wondering why life was so unbalanced. Here was her uncle living in a three-bedroomed, beautiful house that he rarely used, whereas her dad lived in a single room, only slightly bigger than a closet. She was certain her father must have agonised over asking her uncle to host her. Her dad had pride, asking for favours stressed him immensely. He must have only thought about her good. Respect and pride for her father welled up within her. He had laid aside his pride to see her through her studies. Being the firstborn her dad expected her to be a role model to her siblings. She therefore promised not to let him down.

One time an American politician, Donald Rumsfeld, when

he was a defence secretary engaged journalists in gobbledegook about unknown unknowns that become known and other knowns that are unknown. That means there are things that you didn't know that you didn't know them and which you get to know… or something like that. A rainy September day became such a moment for Grace. It was past the midnight hour when she had just slipped into her nightdress, having watched a movie on video to while away the night. There was some fumbling with the outer lock, a thing that she was used to because her uncle often crept in at such odd times, wet like a sponge, both externally and with drink. Ashamed of staggering in her niece's presence he normally spent as little time with her as possible. It was therefore a bit of a surprise when on this day he seemed to linger after asking whether she was all right. She had peeped out into the hall, just to make sure it was him, so she stood at the door to her room, clad in her robe. All of a sudden he came towards her.

"We have to talk," he drawled, with drink.

"What about, anything the matter Uncle Múíhia?"

"No, not at all," he said, already at her door and indicating he wanted to get in. Grace was surprised but not shocked. This was her uncle and this was his house; he could go into any room he wanted. Besides, the man was drunk.

"What is it then?" Grace asked, and moved beside him, peering into his eyes with her wide and innocent eyes. Suddenly he grabbed her and pushed her against his body.

"You're a beautiful woman, Grace, no longer a little girl."

She gasped, surprised, and recoiled at his foul, beer-laden breath. He attempted to kiss her.

"What're you doing, Uncle? I'm your niece," she said, terrified and hurting from his vice-like grip. She tried to fight him off but he was too strong for her. A scream formed in her mouth but no sound came out. Conflicting voices gave commands in her head like an aeroplane's system gone mad. One said she should scream, the other said it would embarrass her uncle. For heaven's sake, she respected him like a father. What would people think? Would they believe that the respected, helicopter-flying engineer was a rapist?

He pushed her onto her bed, tearing her robe off in a frenzy. He was like a man possessed. The terrified girl tried to pull her legs from under him but he pinned her down with his unbearable weight. She fought him with anything she laid her hands on; jars of make-up, mirrors, books and stuff, all the time crying over and over again. "Please don't hurt me." This went on for some time until the trauma overwhelmed her and she started referring to herself in the third person. Her cry now became an echolalia of, "Please don't hurt Grace."

At this point it was as if she was lifted from her body and watched from a point high above her but still felt the pain. It hurt so badly despite her plea for him not to hurt 'Grace'. Somewhere, through the ordeal, she travelled out into a world of flowers and butterflies where there were no drunks and no evil. She was afraid to return to where her dignity was shredded.

She woke up feeling like a high-speed train had hit her. For a time, she couldn't remember where she was or why it was that she wasn't happy to wake up. Slowly, like a slow computer opening a photo, a few pixels at a time, the events of the previous night replayed in her mind to reveal the horror. She couldn't remember how long it took nor when her uncle left. Instinctively she did what she didn't want to do – survey the mess. What she saw overwhelmed her. Her bedding was stained with her blood. She wanted to die. Were some people created to suffer and others to tramp upon them? There, all her innocence was spilt in an unholy mess and left for her to clean up. What was the use preserving herself, believing in purity and waiting for that special wedding night if old drunks could take it in an instant by force? Was God that unkind? Why did he allow it?

It took her quite a few more hours in bed wishing she could fall into a deep slumber and wake up to find it was all a bad dream. Finally she got a hold of herself, hurting terribly, both physically and emotionally. She wept throughout as she cleaned up everything. She then went to the bathroom and spent hours in the tub but no amount of cleaning made her feel clean. She didn't go to college that day. Her brain was blank, refusing to absorb the magnitude of what had happened. Should she call the police? But she had destroyed evidence. Should she tell her dad? No way! He would break down permanently. Who could believe her? Uncle Múíhia was a respected figure in all circles. It was going to be his word against hers. Besides, she knew this could break her mum as well, who adored her; worse, her dad could do a terrible thing – her dad's pride was awesome and he could easily kill Uncle Múíhia for something like that. What about Aunt Viv, Múíhia's wife? She would think Grace had seduced her husband and call her a slut.

The world was divided into two races, the rich and the poor, those who had and those who didn't have. All other divisions were secondary. Those who had felt it was their right to have whatever they wanted and it was to the detriment of anyone who stood in their way, the worse if it was the poor, then their wrath was total. Whichever way she looked at it, her uncle was going to win. Afraid, she didn't feel strong enough for a scandal.

When she got to the living room there was Ksh 2,000 on the coffee table. She looked at the money with loathing. What was it for? Penance for last night's abomination? She took the money and shredded it into minute pieces and left them on the table, a statement for her uncle.

There is an African story of an evil man who used to be left behind to look after the children while the strong villagers went to work the farms. He had a problem though: he wanted to be young and strong again, unhappy with the progress of his age. After consulting a witchdoctor he was advised that if he took the heart of young lambs he would grow young again. He therefore embarked on a spree, killing the young animals and blaming it on wild animals. No amount of hunting by the community warriors managed to capture the elusive predator that was destroying the young lambs. By now he had developed a craving for this unique delicacy and in his evil he turned on the children. One by one the children disappeared. Filled with dread, the villagers consulted the same witchdoctor who answered them in a proverb: what bites you hides in your clothes. They therefore laid a trap by leaving behind some warriors to do secret surveillance on the village while the rest tilled the farms. It was hence with great shock when they found out that the old man entrusted with the care of the children while the younger and stronger villagers went to work in the farms was the culprit. All the villagers were called back and the council of elders hurriedly convened a court. The verdict was unanimous; the old man was put to the sword.

Unfortunately, unlike the cannibalistic old man, Uncle Múíhia continued his abuse with no warriors to lay an ambush on him. He only sobered when Grace got terribly ill after an abortion. She hadn't even bothered to tell him she was pregnant. What would he care? He was a cannibal, a wolf with a craving for its own cubs. She had suffered all alone and wished to fetch herself out all by herself. The problem with that kind of abuse is it becomes habitual if it isn't reported the first time and the offender feels less and less guilty. He now took her as he wished. She never fought him anymore. There were two Graces living in her. As soon as he attacked, she simply switched off and took off to a land of butterflies and flowers where no person wanted to hurt another. In any of these moments she never heard him leave. She simply wasn't there.

"Oh, Grace, why didn't you tell me?" he asked, terrified as he watched the frail caricature of Grace. He had been away for a week and she hadn't eaten for four days.

"And reverse the time, I hope?" she responded, feebly.

"Oh, God, what have I done now?" he wailed, head in hands. "Was I the father?" Being a typical bloke he asked that predictable question many cowardly men in similar situations always ask in an attempt to evade responsibility. He immediately regretted it.

"What do you think? Maybe your little seven-year-old son visited while you were away. Dogs sire dogs, right?" He let that one pass, faced with a dire question in his mind: what if she died?

In a panic, he got her a live-in nurse and contracted a doctor to check her over every so often. Her dad, his elder brother, would kill him if he found out and he wasn't sure the pipeline company would be impressed either. The company union, which also extended to the Estates' community welfare, would cause an uproar saying their children were not safe anymore.

Within two weeks she was eating normally and by the third she was almost fine. A lot of weight had dripped off her, leaving her frame frail and her countenance pale. She had missed so many lessons at the college she didn't know how she would recover. That was not necessary for soon her uncle was frantic trying to cover up his mess. He wanted to send her out of the country.

It was in the run up for multiparty politics in Kenya in the early 1990s. The dictatorship reigning at the time was getting scared with the general malaise with its rule and the public agitation for political freedom and plurality. Two charismatic multiparty activists had convened press conferences and public rallies – popularly known as kamukunji, named after Kamukunji Grounds where campaigns for Kenya's freedom from British colonial rule used to be held. The grounds therefore became a symbol of freedom, a representation of man's desire to break the chains, any chains, and especially of the oppressive kind.

'Multipartyism' and 'pluralism' were indeed strange words to the rulers who had suppressed the masses so much for so long they thought they were infallible. Now the words became common among the masses, though people had to look behind their backs because the intelligence machinery had been let loose to seek out the dissenters.

Panicking, the regime instigated ethnic clashes, especially in their power bases in the Rift Valley region where it had most support from the Kalenjin community. The rulers wanted to kick the other tribes out to destabilise them in such a way that they wouldn't vote at all and, even if they did, not in big numbers to sway the outcome. Most of the minority tribes that had settled in these trouble spots were the enterprising and farming Kikuyus. Evidently, the Kikuyus supported the opposition and that was the source of their troubles. People were massacred, houses burnt and whole communities displaced in the infamous tribal clashes with the government's blessings, a government that had the responsibility to protect its citizens and leaders who had sworn on oath as much.

The love of money has always defined the lowest to which man can sink, so the Bible says. In atrocities, other men see opportunities. In other people's pain they see their gain. It's a common vice the world over. The Holocaust records point to European banks that benefited immensely by what was robbed from the Jews. Marika was such a man who dreamt, ate and drank that extra penny. He would rather go out and beg, clean somebody's windscreen or steal than not make an extra penny each day. Not that he was poor. On the contrary, he was a constant traveller to Dubai and Europe on business that ranged from second-hand motor vehicles to horticultural export, but it wasn't unusual to see him on a street corner in muddy welly boots, vending fresh milk from his farm on the back of a battered pickup truck. With the onset of the clashes he saw a window of opportunity.

Getting a passport in Kenya in those days wasn't automatic. You had to be pushed this way and shoved that way and present affidavits and evidence of a strong reason why you needed to travel. With his links at the Department of Immigration all he required was Ksh 10,000 in cash and you would get your passport in a week. When the business became too lucrative he graduated to the next level. He wanted to start smuggling people abroad.

The world knew there was some trouble in Kenya though on a small scale. However, the evidence was all there in the news; of burnt houses and thousands of displaced people living in deplorable plastic shacks on church mission grounds. It was rumoured that the Rift Valley mafia, the ruthless power barons around the president, were even training private militia in the expansive Maasai Mara game reserve. A young British woman was murdered there and her body burnt beyond recognition in mysterious circumstances. Much as her distraught hotelier father tried to pursue justice, it came to nothing. The rumour doing the rounds was that she was a spy and had gone to the reserve not as a tourist – though she had all the paraphernalia of a tourist – but as a spy to gather intelligence on the militia. She might have been an adventurous tourist who got lost in the expansive Mara Reserve and stumbled into the camps of the ruthless militia whose masters were powerful people in the government. Some issues are let be if they stood in way of trade and money. The British government didn't want to intervene, considering their other, higher interests with the Kenyan government. All governments have a dodgy side. They have to tell lies and trade favours under the tables while shouting against each other in public. A young woman's death was unfortunate but practically there were other priorities – multi-million-pound interests.

Marika figured the unrest favoured him perfectly. The world knew about the clashes and the condemnations were trickling in. Pictures of people with arrows sticking in their bodies flashed on millions of TVs around the world. They even caught the eye of the onetime American presidential hopeful, Jesse Jackson, who visited the victims. Which government would turn away such victims? Marika organised meetings in the famous Uhuru Park for people who were interested. He figured the grounds were a safe place to discuss the illegal deals. 'Walls have ears', so some wise folk said, that's why he chose the park. It was a perfect location with so many other groups, some religious, others just family outings, nobody would be interested in what they were doing. This was just what Múíhia wanted. He had paid Marika some Ksh 10,000 to get Grace a passport. Marika had even hinted he could help her travel abroad. This was music to Múíhia's ears. He was supposed to cough up some Ksh 50,000 to 'fix' a UK visa. Money is understood in any language, including at the Queen's High Commission.

That's how Grace found herself at Uhuru Park with about a dozen young people, united in their dream of a better life. Marika, in an executive suit, was going through the training like a good professor. This was his first lot and if he pulled it off he was going to love reading his bank statements.

The instructions were simple: destroy your passport on the plane. Tear it up and throw the pieces somewhere, better if you flush them down the toilet. Eat it if you can. Get some story about death and pain and torture. Spice it up with how you watched your families wiped out. Be distraught because you don't know where your family members are. Talk as little as you can and for your own sake stick to your story. Brand the facts in your brain with whatever it is that makes your brain work when you need it to. These three words are very important: cry, cry and cry. The more genuine you look on this the better. If they needed a little help with the tears Marika had some stuff in small bottles that stung the eyes and made the tears flow, but that was an extra Ksh 500. All the ladies went for it, some guys too.

When Grace landed at Heathrow Airport she was a mess of tears and misery. No efforts to calm her by the immigration officers could comfort her, not even the ladies who were called for assistance, the men having given up. Men have never quite mastered the art of handling tears. She was put in a room with some soft drinks to give her time to get a hold of herself.

An hour later she regained some composure, though she sighed and heaved so much in distress.

"What's your name, dear?" asked a massive lady immigration officer.

"Grace," she sniffed out.

"Where're you from, Grace?"

"Kenya."

"Ah, lovely place, been there myself couple times." Grace nodded and blew her nose.

"Now, may I ask, where's your passport?"

"Don't have it."

"How's that Grace?"

"They… it… they…" she trailed off, engulfed in more tears, "burnt our house."

"Please calm down. Who burnt your house?"

"Soldiers… they killed her, they killed her… oh, my God, they killed her."

"Who was killed, Grace?"

"They killed her," she cried. "Oh, Mama," she moaned, irreconcilably distraught. In her mind she saw the other, innocent

Grace, the one who loved flowers and butterflies, the Grace who was killed late one rainy night by her own uncle. Torrents of tears flowed out unrestrained with the knowledge that she was now free. No more foul drink-laced breath and huge-bearded spout licking her lips. No more crushing weight of a 15-stone ogre over her body. No more pain down there, oh how it hurt. She cried so much now, genuinely so. Inspector MaryAnn was moved with the pain of a mother, seeing a child so traumatised she reached for her and held her close to her bosom.

"Please don't hurt me, please don't hurt her, please don't hurt Grace," she wept and recoiled in real terror. She was no longer comfortable with any physical contact.

"It's okay; it will be okay, Grace." MaryAnn reassured her and wept with her.

This was the third case she was handling this week. After the first one the immigration officers had gotten aware of the clashes in Kenya. A search for details revealed an escalating situation of ethnic cleansing. It was amazing the things that went on in the world while the developed countries whined about and considered a crisis of mammoth proportions, issues such as obesity and whether it was okay to advertise junk food on TV. Inspector MaryAnn had contacted the Home Office immediately the first one arrived. Most likely she was genuine is what she was told. They had in fact been expecting a situation like that. Apparently, the High Commission back in Nairobi had been reporting ugly skirmishes and bloodshed and of course the news said as much. MaryAnn couldn't understand. What is it about these Africans? Can't they stop fighting and concentrate on feeding their hungry?

Grace could now enter Britain but there was a lot of processing, paperwork, interviews and consultations. Somehow she was lost in the bureaucracy, being tossed from one asylum-processing centre to another. After about a year, however, a decision was made – a terrible decision. She was moved to the newly opened Campsfield Detention Centre at Kidlington, Oxford, in early December while her case was addressed. The centre was an ugly place with a twenty-foot high razor wire-topped fence. She felt like a prisoner, it wasn't much different from a prison with all those surveillance cameras trailing you. They made you feel so vulnerable. The security company officers who ran the place for private profit looked and at times acted mean. Life became so unbearable she wanted to die. She felt trapped in a cage that she thought she could never get out of. Why was she here anyway, because some low-life wanted to cover his smelly backside? True, she had always dreamt of travelling abroad from the humdrum of Kenyan problems but this wasn't any better. At least back home you always had a battery of friends to help you keep strong. Besides, most people lacked luxuries so you were never alone in poverty and life was full of laughter.

By a twist of fate, Inspector MaryAnn happened to be in a group of inspectors from immigration who were touring detention and refugee reception centres after protestations by human rights groups. She was horrified to see Grace bored and withdrawn among the hundred or so inmates.

"Hello," she said, uncertain, and went to her, to the curiosity of the other officials. "We've met, haven't we?"

"Yes, ma'am, Heathrow Airport when I arrived from…"

"Kenya," MaryAnn finished for her. "Oh, poor you, please don't tell me you've been through another ordeal?" Grace just shrugged in resignation.

"Surely one can only handle so much." She was now talking to herself – as MaryAnn the mother, not the immigration official. "I'll look into this," she whispered to her, and hurried onto the bus where the rest of the officials were waiting.

From then on her life took a turn, a positive turn. In two days MaryAnn had gotten her out on an approved refugee status and fixed her up with a council flat at Hayes in London. This was the best Christmas gift for Grace. Life couldn't have been better. In July the following year she went on to join the Florence Nightingale School of Nursing and Midwifery, a constituent of King's College London, on Waterloo Road, for her nursing degree. In three years she graduated and became a junior nurse at the busy Middlesex hospital. She felt fulfilled now, felt secure, happy with life and herself. Her dreams now were full of flowers and butterflies and spectacular dunks on basketball rings. Those other terrible experiences never happened. At least for now, nobody tried to hurt Grace.

# 11

Only one other person was ahead of him in the queue. It had been a long wait this one but it was worth it. In a few minutes he would know his fate, most likely make or break his aspirations forever. He held on to optimism because there was no other way of sustaining the confidence he needed in the next couple of minutes. This was what almost all his aspirations were based on. It had to go right.

Most of his life, since he took his initial tottering steps, Kamau developed a curiosity for what lay beyond the borders. First it was the next room, second the doorstep, then he ventured to the backyard and before long his mum had to keep a close eye on him or else she was going to hunt the whole neighbourhood looking for the adventurous tot. By the time he finished university, he knew Kenya like the back of his hand and had travelled to all the neighbouring countries on enigmatic tours that baffled most who knew him. His ultimate dream travel though was to the mighty US of A but those ones had become stingy with the precious document. *Maybe the Queen's folks wouldn't fuss about being visited*, he thought. *In any case, they never asked us when they visited us and overstayed for a whole century pretending that they did not notice us fidget wanting them to go home.*

When his name was called he got up quickly and swiftly went to the desk adjusting his tie like he used to see people do. He hated the small stranglers so much he had refused to learn how to tie one saying he will never need one. Now that he did need one his dad had to do it for him that morning, having tried to teach him how but he argued there was no need because he wanted it just for a day. Now he regretted it, wondering what he would do if it untied. The interviewer at the desk was a young white bloke, probably not much older than he was but you couldn't tell in this age of cosmetic surgeries. He had to be young, not many older people would gel-spike their hair like he had done. This raised his hopes, confident that a young man would understand another young man's desire to travel and what a tragedy it was for a young and restless person to be locked in a humdrum place like Kenya.

"Hello, Kamau." The young man behind the counter saluted, reading his name from a list as Kamau sat down.

"Hello… " *Should I call him sir, if not, what? Hell.*

"You all right, mate?" He was trying to make his interviewee relax.

"I'm fine, thank you."

"Your documents, please." Kamau opened the folder he had and handed over lots of documents from his sports certificates to his dad's old truck's logbook.

"So you want to study a masters in Business Administration in Britain?" Spiky-hair asked, shuffling through the documents without much attention to any in particular.

"That's right."

"Have you considered the cost?"

"Yes." Kamau didn't want to volunteer any information, the simpler the answer the safer. *Keep the lie simple; you won't have trouble retelling it!*

"It's more than Ksh 1,000,000," he stated with emphasis, and looked up at Kamau for effect. Kamau didn't know how to react to that. "I wonder how much it costs here in Kenya; do they offer the course anyway?"

"Yes, they do," responded Kamau. There was no point lying about such obvious things. The facts were just a call or a mouse click away. Damn the internet.

"And how much do they charge for it, Kamau?"

"About four hundred thousand."

"So in other words, Kamau, you're telling me you want to travel thousands of miles away to study a course you can take here and leave you with enough change to start a business and buy you whatever any young person like you would desire?"

"It's not exactly like you state it."

"Convince me."

"See, Dad parts with the cash only if I'm studying. He thinks it's more prestigious studying in your country. I too agree. If I take the course here he will never pay for me because he figures it's not a lot of money. I might as well sweat for it. In any case, he figures a local MBA won't land me a job with the multinationals, which favour foreign degrees. Call it a case of putting your money on the winning horse. Surprisingly, if I study abroad he pays for everything."

"That's unfair."

"Wish he could see it that way."

"Well, Kamau, why do I feel that's not the only reason you want to travel?"

"Don't know, you tell me."

"Tell me what you want to do with your MBA."

"I told you, Dad would be disappointed if I don't work with a multinational."

"Do I then conclude that you're doing this for your dad?"

"Not exactly, I want it too."

There was some silence then Spiky-hair stood and disappeared for a few minutes. When he returned he had changed but Kamau couldn't tell exactly what, he just looked different.

"Tell you what, Kamau, try to convince your old man to release that dough to you. Spend some time to convince him. If that fails, then we may consider your application."

Kamau felt nausea. He knew when something bad happened in all its constituent meanings. This was one big BAD. He sat there looking at the young man stamping his passport. Why was he doing that? If he wasn't giving him a visa why then blot his passport as well with useless stamps that read things like 'application received'. What was unstated was obvious, it translated into 'visa denied, marked for scrutiny'. He looked at the young man sitting so comfortably at his desk in an office at Upper Hill Nairobi. This was Kenya, Kamau's country. He could have wished to hold the fellow and toss him into a plane to his country. *You don't let me into yours, you don't stay in mine.* But others made those decisions, boot lickers who went all jelly in the presence of these foreigners with their bankrupting donor money. Why do they use the word 'donor' anyway? Hell they're loans that are paid at bizarrely high interest rates!

"Ever had a dream, erm, what do I call you?" said Kamau, surprised at his audacity. There was nothing more to lose.

"My name's Brown, I'm Scottish, and yes my biggest was to travel the world before I was twenty-five. The other was…"

"Never mind the others," said Kamau, feeling in charge now. It's amazing the things a man could do when nobody had a hold on him. "I thought you might understand."

"Hey, if you'd love to travel you're supposed to apply for a visitor's visa. I could give you a form if you want."

"Kind of you but never mind, the guards at the gate have copies." He collected his papers and stood up. "Pursue your other dreams as well, Brown, I'll still hold onto mine." He walked out, his head up in the air, the spirit of his great-grandfather chief Waiyaki whispering its pride in him.

In a daze he walked west down Upper Hill Road towards Haile Selassie Avenue. Somehow he managed to cross the busy road without shattering anybody's windscreen but that doesn't mean there were no near misses. When he got to the other side, he turned left towards Uhuru Park near the Railway Club and walked through the upper side of the park close to the Community area. Finding a comfortable place under a tree to shelter from the blazing Nairobi mid-morning sun, he sat down and threw the folder with his documents aside.

He must have drifted into blankness because when he got up the park had a lot of people – a sign that it was lunch hour when most people stole a moment at the park from their workplaces; some with lunch boxes, others to buy snacks from the hawkers, but many to imagine what it would be like if they could afford lunch every day. The Nairobi skyline was sprawled in its full splendour below him but to him it was just a mess of sprouting ugly grey.

Again he drifted to his happier days when he was a boy and hadn't much to worry about. If you were not bought that toy you wanted it felt bad but then you forgot all about it. It didn't sink and make you feel a failure. Now he was an adult and even your personal dreams were put under scrutiny. If you didn't achieve it you were termed a loser and that felt really bad, a feeling that lingered.

When he got up again the park was less crowded. He felt fresh and wanted to think. He had no visa and he was not going anywhere. Having graduated with his bachelor's degree in Commerce from University of Nairobi just a few months earlier, he hadn't bothered to look for a job. He wanted to travel out of the country so he immediately embarked on preparations. It was a time of trying experiences, even for simple documents like a passport with the immigration people wanting to know why you wanted to travel. Wasn't a passport a citizen's right? Then there was that stupid English proficiency test Leicester University required before offering him a place and he had to book and sit one at the British Council. *Hell, I'm Kenyan, was taught in English since my first elementary year!* Now all that was an exercise in futility.

What bothered him was how to break the bad news to everybody. He hated how his dad, Mr Hinga, a fading politician, would handle it. His dad was once a civic councillor in Lari and later became the area member of parliament. Since he was ousted after one term, he became addicted to power hunting, a power broker of sorts, happy to mingle with the powerful men. No doubt he earned a lot from it, especially in the way of ego and enemies. Kamau's mum tried to dissuade his dad from politics but he was relentless. Like most politicians he was a showman and a loudmouth, saying things he shouldn't and always in a twisted version if he could benefit from it. When he learnt Kamau was planning to travel out of the country, he commandeered the plans and even got his politician friends on it. Soon there was talk of a fundraiser. Kamau wanted to die and confronted the old geezer.

"Dad, there's something I'd like us to talk about."

"Shoot son, this must be big," he beamed, in mock expectation. He was happy today; the minister for transport had agreed to be the guest of honour at his son's fundraiser.

"What's this talk I'm hearing of a fundraiser?"

"Oh, it's for you son, you need lots of money for your studies."

"You didn't ask me if I wanted one, Dad."

"Isn't it obvious, do you have a million somewhere? If you do, please let us know."

"C'mon, Dad, I can work to support my own studies. People fly abroad, work for some time and save money for studies. If you bring people in on this, they will always lay claim on you. They'll always think you owe them."

"Now you're being illogical, son. I'm a famous person." This was said with lots of pride. "I've been a public figure and this family has always helped people since the days of your great-grandpa Waiyaki. You've no clue how much money I've pumped into other peoples' fundraisers and other events devised to con the innocent public. It's payback time."

"And I become the pawn?"

"Too many books have gone into your head, Karl Marx, Stalin or Mahatma Gandhi? Anyway, even if you want to work for your own money as you say, hoping it's that simple, you still need some money to get you started. Yes, we can afford to send you to the UK and probably a little money to get you started but the fees are too high. This family needs every coin, let the money come if you don't need it, we can use it for other needs."

"Dad, I don't even have the visa yet."

"Don't worry, you'll get it, I can talk to the minister for transport and communication."

"This is a different authority, Dad. They don't shudder because a local minister said they should give the son of, erm, a friend a visa."

"Trust me on this one, son; these people are always exchanging unofficial favours. I've seen it happen in parties and lobbies."

"What if – and I emphasise if – I don't get a visa? It will be a scandal. Please wait until I get the visa then you can have a fundraiser."

"Impossible, the minister fixed the date in his diary and it's hard to get him again if we postpone."

"Dad, I might not get a visa."

"That's not the great-grandchild of the great chief I'm hearing." That's the way Hinga always finished his discussions with his children if he didn't agree with you or he was dismissing you.

Now here Kamau was, under a tree and without a visa. This was surely going to be a scandal. People will say he never intended to travel, that the family just wanted to con people out of their hard-earned cash, probably to fund Hinga's campaign in the next elections. Kamau wondered how he was going to walk the streets again and felt sick. He knew that all family was going to suffer embarrassment – save for their dad. At least he was lucky he was a politician, a species that was yet to evolve and develop such advanced emotions as embarrassment.

A solution was to be sought, a decision made. There was no way of refunding the money. No records were kept of who gave what. Unless the money funded a public project but even then people would still read scam. He also knew his dad would never let him control the fund though it was raised in his name. That aside, he still had a dream deep within his innermost being. He had to get his passion, Brown or no Brown. What did Brown say, that he wanted to travel the world before he was twenty-five? That in Kamau's mind was every young person's dream. It was a question of if you wanted to for non-Africans and a question of if you were allowed to for poor Africans. Why were things so hard if you came from this part of the world? Maybe because of the poverty the rest of the world thinks you might be nothing more than a begging nuisance. But there were lots of people with a lot of money in this part of the world. Too bad, the rest didn't have it and if everybody was allowed to roam the world there would be an influx of immigrants seeking better lives in the West; they would cause all sorts of problems. Maybe that was true but if there were efforts to bridge the gaping gap between the rich and the poor countries that would probably solve most problems.

Kamau plotted in his mind and made a decision. He stood up,

collecting the folder, and looked undesirably at it. It felt heavier than in the morning. Taking a last glance at the skyline below, he headed for the steps down the pedestrian walk and, trying to sound like Martin Luther King Jnr, said aloud, "I have a dream. I'll hold on to my dream."

He walked down past the permanent pavilion, which hosted so many events every so often from political rallies to public holiday celebrations and religious gatherings. Past the small bridge connecting the two sections of the small lakes in the park he walked on towards Uhuru Highway. The lake was full with canoes. Kamau envied the people so happy and free that they even had time to do stupid rowing on a hot Thursday afternoon. He wondered if he was ever going to be so much at grips with his life to do stupid things like rowing on a boat with a girlfriend on a mid-week afternoon. When he got to Uhuru Highway he crossed to the other side near the Hotel Intercontinental. He couldn't fail to notice that he had just crossed Uhuru Highway that linked to Waiyaki Way to the west, a road that was named after his great-grandfather. *I'm your great-grandchild and if you were so great they named a road after you then I've your genes in me. I'll be great,* he thought.

Waiyaki wa Hinga, his great-granddad, was a Kikuyu pre-colonial chief who ruled around Dagoretti. The British came calling in his chiefdom around 1890 when he signed a treaty with Frederick Lugard of the Imperial British East Africa Company (IBEA), who later pitched their tent at Dagoretti. Stretching the welcome too far, Lugard and his men harassed the Kikuyu people demanding their food and their women. In retaliation, the Kikuyu burnt down Lugard's fortress at Dagoretti. This was sacrilege to the marauding settlers. In 1892, the colonial administration kidnapped the patriarch Hinga, forced him to dig his own grave and buried him alive along the coast of Kenya.

When he got to city hall, Kamau found a public telephone and called his dad on his mobile. He knew he must be around somewhere, brokering some political intrigue or other.

"Hi there, me boy, so when do you leave?"

"Not so fast, Dad."

"We're Waiyakis, we're not slow. So how did it go boy?"

"Well, I got it."

"That's my boy, full-blooded Waiyaki; I knew you'd get it. The minister had promised to throw in a kind word."

"Dad," Kamau almost said 'shut up'. "I wish to travel as soon as possible."

"Of course, son, I'm at Parliament Grounds, hoping to have a word with the minister for agriculture. It's about heavy stuff about pyrethrum politics, think I told you about it, didn't I son?"

"Huh? Well, maybe."

"Good, this calls for a celebration. Why don't you come down here? We could go for *nyamachoma* after I meet the minister. In any case, you're a man now. I can help you establish contacts with these big shots, you know, introduce you. There's more to it than you ever imagined." If there was anything Kamau would have hated it was to be groomed into amateur power brokering, stuck with a bunch of boring, conniving old geezers, listening to them talking big.

"Some other day, perhaps. Dad, I need to buy the ticket immediately."

"Of course, no problem. Have a friend of mine who runs a travel agency at Bruce House. I could take you there and push him to give you a good rate."

"Dad, you've just said I'm a grown man now, when will you ever let me do anything by my own?"

"Well spoken, a real Waiyaki. Still, a cheaper ticket is as good as a …"

"Daad!"

"Okay, boy, so now you want the money, fine with me. If you come here I could withdraw the money for you from a bank nearby but only the ticket money."

"I'll need a little more, you know, got things to buy like new clothes and stuff that I'll need."

"So how much are you talking about?"

"Four hundred thousand."

"Four hundred, for ticket and clothes?"

"Won't spend it all; just want to feel good that I ever held that much dough in my hands, at least this once. Isn't it meant for my schooling? Can't blow it unless I don't want to study, I'm all grown now you just said."

"Now you're playing me. Come here anyway, I'll see about that."

"No, Dad, just put it in my account," he said, and hung up.

That night there was some sort of party at their Lari home. Luckily, Hinga did not drag home a host of politicians of dubious political ambitions as he usually did. Everybody was happy for Kamau and wished him well. His dad started talking of Kamau returning someday to reclaim the Lari parliamentary seat back where it should always be – in the Waiyaki family. He also confirmed that he had deposited the money Kamau had requested in his account.

Kamau felt awful, laden with guilt that he had to lie but he reasoned that sometimes *'a man gotta do what a man gotta do'* for a 'higher purpose', even if what had to be done was full of unorthodox stench. He was an honest person and hated the lies his dad and other like-minded men told and lived but he now almost felt justified to have to lie. Maybe people will understand someday, maybe.

# 12

Two days after Kamau's dad transferred some of his study fund to his account he was in a Tawfriq bus on the Great North Road, the Kenyan chapter, towards Namanga border post. This road was an obsession in the hearts and minds of the early European pioneers who intended it to run from Cape Town to Cairo. It represented the man's insatiable love for exploration beyond the horizons, a chase after dreams. Kamau had withdrawn the money and bought himself a ticket on the bone-unfriendly trip down south before he called his girlfriend Jane and let her know that he would be away for some time but refused to say how long and where he was going.

There were many enterprising Kenyan business people who found the airfare to South Africa a bit too high. They were not the rich, high-flying business wizards. These were ordinary small-scale but hardworking business people who were not afraid to venture into the unknown to bring in that elusive profit. Surprisingly, those who started the travels down south quickly brought in lots of profitable ventures in all sorts of stuff from clothes to second-hand motor vehicles. Quite a number of them prospered too. It is amazing the troubles they went through to get to South Africa – sometimes through six other countries. There were lots of problems finding connecting transport in the next country and the journeys took more than a fortnight.

Soon, word reached Hazim the enterprising and successful lord of bus transport from Mombasa, the Kenyan coast capital. His business advisers gave him the nod to try the new lucrative route down south. After secret meetings with diplomats from different countries, money changed hands, lobbying was done and help from government leaders solicited. He was allowed by the various governments to pass through their countries all the way to South Africa. The route was established and became an instant hit. The Tawfriq Bus Company was doing very well.

In six days, Kamau was in a guesthouse in the old part of Gaborone, the capital of Botswana, a place they called Village. Kamau was feeling like he had been run over by a chain-wheeled earth digger. The trip was much cheaper than by air but he wondered whether the fatigue was worth it. It had been a test of everything from nerves to mind to spirit. The bus had left Kenya through Namanga to Tanzania and took two days to traverse the country through Arusha, Dodoma and Mbeya before crossing to Zambia. In another two days the bus laboured through Zambia via Mpulungu, Kasama and Lusaka before crossing to Botswana through Kasane, a town that is at the border among the three countries including Namibia. Another two days saw them through Maun and Mahalapye before finally arriving in Gaborone. He was one of the three people who alighted at Gaborone; the other two, Njeri and her boyfriend Mbaú, were teachers. Njeri had been offered a position by the Botswanan Ministry of Education and brought her boyfriend along, optimistic he would also get a job. Facing a serious shortage, Botswana was fishing for qualified teachers from other African countries. The rest of the passengers were business people and a few dream-chasers who were travelling to South Africa to see for themselves if it had as much gold as people claimed it had.

Gaborone, the capital of Botswana, was built from scratch to house the new government when the country got its independence from the British in 1966. The country was formerly a British protectorate called Bechuanaland, a wonderful place. Like many other African nations it boasted an impressive share of wildlife in places like the Chobe National Park, Gemsbok National Park and the Makgadikgadi saltpans that attracted loads of flamingos and wildebeests, which flocked the pan for a lick. The country is almost entirely a broad subtropical plateau adorned with some hills in the eastern part and, to the west, the awesome Okavango

River empties into the Kalahari sands creating the largest inland river delta in the world – the source of the saltpans.

When the country got its independence from Britain, it luckily stumbled on to some of the richest diamond mines in the world, placing the country at number three among the biggest producers. And while Lady Luck was still smiling, the leaders had the presence of mind to seize the moment. They didn't totally subscribe to the way of the other African leaders. Much as they minded their own stomachs, they still spared enough for the country, creating a formidable economy that ever looked extremely competitive on the exchange rates with major world currencies – at less than ten Botswana pula to the British pound that was pretty impressive. The country's population at less than two million might also have helped by putting little strain on the diamond proceeds. By most world standards, Botswana was a success story.

It was the combination of such factors that the world smiled at Botswana and extended a welcoming hand. Nobody wants losers at their doorstep and Botswana was far from losing. Botswanans were therefore not required to have a visa to travel to most of the countries in the world. As you would expect, a successful mate always attracts flocks of friends if only to share in the glory or any crumbs that might fall off the table. It was in this spirit of 'friendship' that Kamau found himself in Botswana.

He was woken by the shriek of kids playing somewhere three floors below his window. Exhausted and disorientated, he slowly tried to comprehend this place, wondering what he was doing here. The noises and sounds he heard outside were unfamiliar and very strange indeed, and then he remembered. Instinctively he reached for his watch, squinting as a bright sunbeam tore through a gap on the blind and reflected on his watch, hurting his eyes. It was half ten. He must have devoured close to sixteen hours of sleep still fully dressed, a very rare occurrence because he preferred sleeping stark naked. He used to joke that he would like to die in his sleep. He came to this world naked; he might as well depart the same way.

Dragging himself out of bed, he staggered to the window

feeling like a sausage wrapped in his grumpy creased clothes. A spectacular view of the city greeted him, daring him to join the flurry of scurrying mobs in whatever race they were in for. This way and that way dashed everyone; most of the people seemed to believe what they had to do had to be done immediately or it was going to be the end of the world. Kamau too remembered he was a man on a mission – a once in a lifetime make or break mission. He could not go wrong or he was neither going to return home nor get to his dreams.

A long hot bath had roused his lazing nerves and now he was all set for the execution of his plans. Chest bulging with perceived purposefulness, he strode down the steps to the foyer on the first floor, which functioned as both the guesthouse's reception as well as a restaurant. The seductive aroma of coffee invitingly whiffled from the kitchen area sending instant craving up his glands. He sat at a table close to the far right window, hoping an elderly waitress lady whose apron looked like it needed some attention would not serve him. Luckily for him, a young waitress who obviously took both her job and hygiene seriously dashed to take his order: a coffee pot; sausage rolls; bread and butter, and lots of jam. There had to be sweet stuff, lots of it thanks to his incredible sweet tooth. He then settled back, grabbing a copy of the *Daily Echo*, a local paper, from a neighbouring table hoping to get some insight into what sort of place this was.

Having slowly worked through his breakfast he strolled outside after leaving the key to his room at the reception. It was almost noon and the midday sun was blazing like a pyre with a blinding brightness that almost made him dizzy. However, he was a man on a mission and little inconveniences like heat were too small to bother with. He took a bus and headed to Gaborone's Main Mall between the railway station and the army garrison. This was a good starting point for his tour of the city, if only to solve his disorientated bearings. It was the heart of the city, which he thought might give him an insight into what to expect. Like any self-respecting mall in any world city it boasted housing banks, shops, business offices and other assorted facilities, including craft stands that sold you unique mementos and souvenirs. Kamau strolled down the walkway, taking his time with the knowledge that he had lots of hours to kill before he made his first serious move about 'Operation Destiny' as he chose to call it. At the eastern end of the mall was the Civic Centre that housed the public reference library but he wasn't in any reading mood except perhaps the paper and a map.

Opposite the Civic Centre was the Pula Arch, commemorating the independence of Botswana. Stopping briefly at the arch, he mused at the pride Africa portrayed in whatever symbol of independence they chose. However, technically, it was a farce because lots of whatever happened was controlled from Western capitals, yet it was better this way. Any freedom is better than nothing – at least Africans did not have to take hats off for anyone anymore, not physically anyway.

Still with time to kill, he went to a public phone and called home. Glad to catch his mum, he told her he wanted to be away for some time to sort a few issues and nobody should worry about him. He also lied that he would be back in a few days to organise his travel. Though surprised that her son could delay travelling after acquiring the coveted visa, Mum wasn't alarmed. The family had nicknamed him Msafiri because of his love for crazy adventurous travel to strange places.

After speaking to Mum he felt partly relieved of the guilt of having to do what he had done. He took a taxi to Mochudi; a town established by the Bakgatla tribe about 1871 and still having the traditional *kgloto,* the traditional meeting places with traditional houses and courtyards. Surprising even himself, he found himself in the Phuthadikoho Museum going through the collection of photographs and artefacts relating to the Bakgatla people and also the famous explorer and missionary Dr David Livingstone whose exploits had taken him into the depths of Bechuanaland. Such historical figures inspired him. Here was a man who had travelled thousands of miles from the comfort of Europe at a time when air travel was still in the minds of dreamers. Yet the missionary had penetrated his way into the heart of Africa, facing unimaginable obstacles, but he had endured and now he was a legend, a representation of endurance.

Bubbling with inspiration, he left the museum determined to penetrate Europe where he felt his dreams would acquire life. Let the obstacles come. At least he was not facing any lions or malaria-injecting mosquitoes like Livingstone did. He wasn't groping in the wilderness clearing bushes to create paths, not in the same way as Dr Livingstone. He made his way back to his Kgosi Guesthouse for a rest and freshen-up before nightfall. 'Operation Destiny' would start tonight at the Gaborone Sun Hotel and Casino on Chuma Drive.

When Kamau got to the luxurious Sun Hotel and Casino on Chuma Drive it was throbbing with fun-seeking Gaboronians and international guests, bewitched by its immaculate glitter that was much like Botswana's diamonds. The hotel offered everything from presidential suites to budget accommodation, a gathering point for professionals, business people and fun-chasing locals and tourists. He slowly traced his way to the dancing hall, carefully inching past the early dancers and strategically chose a seat near the bar. His plan was to have a vantage position from where he could survey everything before he made his move. With a glass of Martini in his hand, chilled just the way he liked it, he swung the high stool and took the hall in.

The dance floor was half full but he expected it to be packed before midnight. A few other people were seated, conversing in small groups and in couples on the seats, both at the rear and front of the hall next to the bar. The music boomed from powerful speakers that were so fantastically blended with the interior decor that they were almost impossible to spot. Lights flashed and danced and twirled in a sophisticated kaleidoscope, creating the aura of a man-made paradise. However, their beauty was no match for the tightly and mostly skimpily dressed revelling girls on the dancing floor. Kamau wished his girlfriend Jane was with him but he quickly brushed aside the thought. Sentiments were the last thing he wanted to entertain. He had a mission at hand and he had to accomplish it.

His problem now was that none of the girls seemed ideal for his mission. They all looked like professionals out for a cooling-off night out. He wasn't fooled though. The Sun Hotel wasn't the kind of place for low-class hookers to turn up with overdone make-up and in their twilight-prowling high boots. Now relaxed, thanks to the alcohol, his eyes roved analysing the girls to see which one was most approachable.

On his right there was a group of young girls, probably on the verge of seeing the end of their second decade. There was a light-skinned one in an open-necked crop top and tight jeans that did justice to her perfect curves, but she talked too much and kept the pack giggling all the time. Kamau never trusted a person of many words. There was the chocolate-skinned one, with a generously endowed bust and in an inviting miniskirt who seemed the most controlled of the lot. Kamau thought she didn't look approachable but her knowing appearance was tempting. The third was a restless flirt to the core, giggling and making gestures at every man who so much as looked her way. She was beautifully clad in short nightwear that Kamau thought was gorgeous with all those glittering speckles. She was the most approachable of the three but Kamau wondered just how long he could make her concentrate on him to explain what he wanted.

As the hours trickled and refilled glasses of Martini found their way into his hands and their contents farther down his throat, Kamau now felt slightly tipsy. He could not believe that so far all he had done was admire the dancing women, debating in his mind with several versions of himself who he should approach for Operation Destiny. He had not even danced to a single song. He glanced at his watch and realised it was 2 am. If he was to get started it had better be now.

"Going somewhere?" a girl's voice asked, just as he put his glass down and began to get off the high stool. He turned round and came face to face with a confident, pretty face on a fabulous body.

"Hello."

"Foreigner?"

Kamau smiled and sized up the girl from the face down and

then up again. She was about five and a half feet tall, had a very pretty face and a medium-sized bust and hips chiselled to perfection – the type that inspires fantasy. Her brief, open-top dress revealed a flawless ebony skin and a cleavage that could be a lusty drooler's paradise. Slowly, Kamau looked up, high up to her croissant-shaped hairstyle, then back to her face.

"What makes you think I'm a foreigner?"

"There, that confirms it!"

"What does?"

"Never mind," she said sweetly, and turned to the waiter at the bar. "A shandy and another drink for my hulk here." Kamau begun to protest about not taking drinks from strangers and especially women but she put one long, shapely, well-manicured finger across his lips to silence him.

"I'm Pumla," she said, just as Kamau was about to ask her name. He briefly considered lying about his but thought it was no use.

"Kamau," he said, extending his hand.

"See, I was right." It was a statement. "Kenyan, right?" she added, holding his hand with both hers in childlike confidence.

"Right," he said. "So what makes me so… recognisable?"

"Don't know, just can tell you aren't local."

When the drinks came, Pumla raised her glass to his for a toast. Kamau made a face, puzzled by the drama.

"To the foreigner," she said, smiling and giggling mischievously.

"To me," said Kamau, for lack of anything else to say, "and to the beautiful local," he drawled, as the glasses clinked.

"So what brings you down south?"

"Beautiful girls."

"Been lucky so far?"

"I just got lucky."

"Fat chance," she said, unconvincingly. "How long have you been in the country?"

"Several years."

"Kidding," she hissed.

"Haven't you heard a day is like a thousand years and a

thousand years like a day?"

"Yes, I've heard that from the good book and only God sees it that way. I can tell from the way you look at my cleavage that you're nothing like him."

"It's not exactly hidden."

"And neither exactly on display."

"I'm in a mood for… erm, shopping."

"Kamau!"

"What?"

"I'm offended; I didn't expect you to see me that way."

"Which way now?" Kamau asked. He was furiously looking for a detour in the line of conversation. Strange creatures these women are. He remembered the million times he had rows with Jane just because she picked a word, a phrase or a line from him and gave it the weirdest interpretation. No amount of explaining ever convinced her, and she would then rave and rant and pull moods and emotions that left him so emotionally drained he would have preferred a physical fight. He didn't relish a row right now and the danger signal was beginning to go off.

"Forget I said anything." He tried changing the subject. "So what do you do?"

"I'm a student."

Kamau wasn't convinced. Student is a good tag for twilight business. Nobody wants lots of pretty brawn with little ugly grey matter in the face anymore.

"Whereabouts and what is it that you do?"

"UB, Home-EC."

"Wow, whatever that is, sounds heavy. I guess it involves modules on looking yummy."

"University of Botswana you dummy, and yes you're nearly right about 'yumminess', I'm doing home economics." *Oh yeah? and twilighting on the side,* Kamau thought.

"Home I understand but economics of home… is it about saving on salt and gravy and stuff like that?" he attempted at a joke.

"You're a sick Northerner. Seriously though, what brings you south?"

"Thought I told you that; girls, girls and more girls."

"Those you'll get all right. With a body like that and a foreigner," she said, surveying him, "you'll only need to beckon and they'll fall all over you in heaps."

"Because I'm a foreigner?"

"Ever heard grass is always greener across the fence?" Kamau nodded. "People want to have what others don't have, what is considered exotic, what supposedly brings a tinge of strangeness to their excitement. It is an exploration into the enigma."

"Do you see me that way?" asked Kamau. She gave him a long, confident look.

"You'll find out later."

"Why not now?"

"Oh you silly boy, you're drunk now, because it'll be private. Quick, you finish your drink and Pumla will take you home."

With one gulp he downed his glass and got off the high stool. His legs were numb with too much sitting and had trouble keeping pace with Pumla. She led him with a tight grip in her small hand, cruising right through the dancers on the floor. In his drunken swagger, Kamau bumped into several dancers but he couldn't stop to apologise, Pumla couldn't let him. When they got to the exit they stopped briefly at a table to say goodbye to some friends of hers. There was a dandy Pumla called Frank who was at a table surrounded by several girls who seemed to hang on every breath he took. It was understandable. The fellow had enough diamonds on his fingers and on one ear to make each of the girls rich. Such stones as he wore were rare, even in Botswana. In any case, it's not as if the precious stones were found under every speckle of dust on any alleyway in the country. There were also some blokes at the table who only spoke when Frank felt it was all right. Kamau wondered whether he was some kind of an underworld baron, drugs and things like that. If he had been suspicious of Pumla, he was now worried. People who kept friends like these were not always the safest or healthiest to mix with.

After Kamau was introduced, the girls made mock jealous

noises and the guys winked knowingly. They got out, escorted by one of Frank's goons, a development that made Kamau all the more uncomfortable. Thankfully, the goon dashed off and called out for a taxi. He even opened and shut the doors for both of them, making Kamau wonder. It was only when they got to the hotel exit that Kamau felt in control again and he asked where they were going.

"My place, you idiot; where else? I was to show you what I think of you, remember?" she whispered in his ear.

"Do they allow girl students to take back strange foreigners to their hostels?"

"Who said anything about hostels?"

Kamau didn't want to be led down the abattoir's path. It was either his guesthouse or some other neutral place. He told the cabbie to go to Kgosi Guesthouse but Pumla was having none of it. She only relented when the cab driver stopped, agitated, after receiving a million conflicting directions from his arguing passengers. Kgosi Guesthouse it was to be but not before Pumla asked which rat would be so tasteless as to want to stay at Kgosi Guesthouse. Kamau let that one pass.

# 13

At the guesthouse there were enough patrons to keep a local amateur band and the tiny bar busy. Kamau collected his key from the reception and took to the stairs, this time Pumla on tow amid the jealous look of Kgosi's girls. Why hadn't he picked any of them? That was unfair.

Pumla was in the mood for love, despite the fact that she considered the place gutter. She hardly got into the room before she clung to him and gave him a deep long kiss. Kamau wasn't exactly excited. There was this part of him that was very moral. He had never thought it was necessary to betray his girlfriend no matter where he was or in whatever circumstances. He definitely didn't find it necessary now despite the booze. Besides, the AIDS virus ravaged Botswana. The thriving economy had taken worries from the minds of Botswanans, replacing it with an abandon to pleasure, mostly of the flesh kind. Kamau didn't want any pleasure that would result in a rotten body. He begun to regret why he had brought Pumla back to his room, cursing the drink that must have veiled his mind but it was too late now – or was it? He remembered his girlfriend back in Kenya and cringed at the very thought of her even imagining him in the situation he was in. Or, worse, he imagined her in a similar situation with some other bloke; he felt sick. Initially he kept Pumla off thoughts of love by spelling out his 'Operation Destiny' but that couldn't take much time no matter how superfluously worded a tale it was.

Finally the inevitable had to happen. When Pumla couldn't take it anymore she pulled him to bed and literally nearly ate him. She kissed him and cuddled and clung and touched places in a way only she knew how she learnt. She could teach Jane a thing or two… and now remembering Jane he had to act immediately. The situation was getting too heated for his comfort. Cleverly he extricated himself from her, excusing himself expertly. He wanted to go look for the important 'sock'. It was understandable, the world was never the same again and whoever went to war without protective armour was putting himself directly in harm's way, even horny Pumla knew that. She could only curse that such a seemingly intelligent bloke was not armed beforehand.

"Don't be long, love," she hissed with emotion.

"It's not exactly possible to shorten it."

"Don't mean *that* you ass."

"Will be back in a minute, she-ass!" He responded quickly, getting into his T-shirt which Pumla had torn off him in such a rush the stitches were now loose and the neck several sizes wider. When he got through the door, he sighed with relief. As he went down the stairs, he kept looking behind him almost expecting some life-size crawling viruses chasing after him. He now saw Jane in every woman's face he put his eyes on and felt the accusing gaze. Surely he still had a chance but what idiot leaves a naked woman in his bed. A debate raged in his mind of what was worse of the two evils; to betray his girlfriend shattering his principles in the process or failing a generation-old duty and the unstated male law: thou shalt not walk out on a naked woman in your bed when she needs your attention.

When he got to the small bar downstairs he posed briefly and stared at the shelves behind the bartender. Next to the cigarettes were loads of condoms of all shapes, sizes and brands. There were even the spiky ones that promised a rough ride for those who preferred their intimate moments the scratchy way. He could buy a pack just now, go upstairs and make the men folk, both living and the ancestors, proud or he could walk away not only keeping his principles intact but also holding on to the trust he shared with his girlfriend.

People were still dancing to music from the live band. A stuffy air hung in the room like a morning fog, a thing that didn't seem to bother the revellers, who mostly were in an advanced stage of drunkenness. The place didn't have air conditioning; it wasn't the Sun Hotel. A walk outside would be refreshing; he needed lots of fresh air to clear his mind and think.

He went out and turned west which was better lit. He was in a new place and didn't know just how safe it was to walk around at such an odd hour. Just then an idea hit his tired mind. He walked back to Kgosi where he had left a taxi. He would go back to the Sun Hotel and get his head soaked with as much Martini as he could tuck in. Pumla could wait forever for all he cared. Nothing scared him as much as the pictures of emaciated AIDS victims. He would hate to expire that way.

A cab dropped him back at Kgosi at 6.30 am, so drunk the cabbie had to steady him to get out. The staff at the guesthouse were not least surprised, as this was common in their world. Guests always made themselves a mess, perhaps taking advantage of the unlikeliness of their being recognised. One of the waiters helped him get into his room and onto his well-kempt bed where he immediately collapsed into a deep slumber rumbling with snore.

In his sleep he dreamt. He was in a miry alley, trapped on both sides by heaps of murky rubbish. Faggots, vermin and creeping things were crawling slowly towards him, getting bigger and bigger. Life-size, grotesque viruses were purposely stomping their way after him, stretching their hairy greasy tentacles to grab him. He was running fast, slipping and falling on slippery rotten stuff on the ground. He knew the alley had an exit somewhere but he could not find it fast enough. He had to dig through the rot with his bare hands where he thought the exit was. Quickly he sifted through the rubbish and found it but when he got in he realised it had a dead end. He had blocked the entrance with a huge bin box that the viruses were now forcing open. They banged harder and harder until he could not bear it anymore. He was a trapped man and the creepies would get to him anytime now. *Bang! Bang! Bang!* they went, getting closer and closer into tipping over the box and gaining access. He was absolutely terrified and rounded his mouth for a scream, letting out a horrific shriek that woke him.

He was sweating and hot. Those creepies better not be in his bed. Quickly, he threw the duvet off and looked suspiciously at everything, trying to make sense of where he was. Someone was banging the door and calling his name. Who could that be? A clock on the wall read 11 am, maybe it was the cleaner – but they always waited until the guests were out of their rooms. He dragged himself staggering to the door, careful not to shake his head. It felt like someone had hit him with a torque wrench. Every step he took sent jabbing pains all over his head. It was when he opened the door that he fully comprehended his surroundings and the events of the previous night. Pumla was there complete with two problems. The diamond-ear-stud-wearing dandy by the name Frank represented one and the other was in the form of a seven-feet-tall goon that, thankfully for Kamau, chose to stay outside in the corridor. Pumla threw Kamau a look that said she was going to kill him for real while Frank looked at him like an uncle would at a wayward nephew. Kamau felt awful. He wobbled back to bed, taking a bottle of water from the bedside table, which he emptied with relish, belching after it was empty to the disgust of Pumla. He gestured to them with his free hand to sit down, wherever. Pumla sat at the bottom of the bed whereas dandyboy took the only chair available.

"You look a mess, man." It was a statement from Frank. Kamau nodded, finding words too much of a task but then nodding the head caused a stabbing pain up his throbbing left temple. He grimaced.

"Pumla tells me you're here on big purpose, there're things you need."

"Things I what?" Kamau asked, bewildered. "What things?"

"The papers, Kamau," Pumla put in, feeling awkward. It was important to her that Frank didn't think she brought him out here for nothing.

"Papers?" asked Kamau. Then he remembered 'Operation Destiny' but couldn't remember telling Pumla about it. "Oh yeah, papers."

"Frank here can fix them for you," Pumla said.

"Yeah?" Kamau was now alert though feeling like a boiled

potato in an acidic stomach. He hadn't trusted Frank when he met him at the Sun Hotel and he didn't think he had changed his position.

"I can fix you a passport today but the others probably tomorrow."

"Which others?"

"You want to travel to Europe, right?"

"Right."

"If you want to stay there you'll need more than a passport."

"What I need now is just the passport to get me there. All the others can be fixed there."

"Listen to me, man, I've been there, I know these things. You'll need a job to sustain yourself. They'll ask for certificates, references, police checks, driving licences – the works."

"Why don't you let me worry about those when I land there?"

"If you insist, but trust me I can help you because you're… erm, my friend's friend." This he said throwing a fond look at Pumla that made Kamau shudder. The connection between Pumla and Frank sent jitters into his nerves but he dared not ask. "You're an educated person," Frank continued. "You don't want to regret that you went to school. If you hold a Botswanan passport you'll need all helpful Botswanan papers including a degree certificate from a local university that you can use to look for a job. In fact, we'll put the same qualifications as your Kenyan qualification unless you would like to change it to something that sounds more sophisticated like, say, spacecraft avionics or something like that."

Frank was making sense, a lot of sense, but Kamau had problems trusting him. Guys who sat for several hours to have their hair styled like Frank worried him, yet what choices did he have?

"What's the charge for the whole package?"

"20,000 pula and that's only because of Pumla."

"Twenty thousand?" Kamau exclaimed in disbelief. He made a mental calculation; that came to more than Ksh 200,000. "I can't afford that."

"Eighteen's my final price," Frank said, after a long, hard stare at Kamau. A serious businesslike face had replaced the soft dandy look.

"I can't afford that either!" Kamau cried, and tried to tell Frank he just finished college and was just beginning to build himself. Frank was bored and probably still in the room because of this special mate Pumla, whatever that *mateship* was about. He got up and made for the door.

"Sorry, man, business is business. I put my final price. If you don't want to take the offer, look for help elsewhere. Remember you could buy cheap but end up with obvious fakes that can't even be accepted at a local club membership. Mine are genuine. I can do a passport for you for four thousand for a genuine and three for a fake but like I said it can only take you so far." Kamau wanted to scream but then he let out a scornful laugh.

"What's the difference?" he said. "If you get me a Botswanan passport it will obviously not be genuine and then you talk about another type that you call fake. Both are fakes, man."

"You should know better than that. My genuine type will be a real Botswanan passport from immigration. The paper, signature, serial number, they'll all be from the immigration office. We can even backdate it to whichever date you would like. Furthermore, it will even appear in the official records and in their systems. The fake one will only resemble a genuine Botswanan passport in paper quality but everything else will be fake."

"Hang on a minute, I'm confused now, so you're trying to say that there's a *genuine* fake and a *fake* fake?" Kamau's hangover-soaked brain could not process that information fast enough. Frank shook his head, exasperated, and made to leave. It was a waste of time. In fact if it wasn't for Pumla he could not bother with Kamau. It was obvious Kamau had enough miles to clock on his way out of the woods of naivety.

"Let Pumla know when you make up your mind."

Frank was about to slip out the door when Kamau asked him not to. He really wanted to get over with this thing as soon as possible and travel to Europe. He could now tell Frank was a serious guy when it came to talking business. Kamau had really scrutinised his eyes for signs of deceit but had found none. Either he was genuine or a damn good actor or liar or both.

"When do I get the papers?"

"Like I said, passport tonight, the others tomorrow night."

"That's kinda fast."

"That's kinda my way of doing things."

"Deposit?"

"Normally half then balance on delivery. I know you think I'm a con so I'll not ask for a deposit, and that's only coz of Pumla, better have the whole amount when I deliver though."

"Deal."

"Deal," dandyboy said, and shook Kamau's hand before making it to the door where he paused briefly and seemed to remember something.

"Got a passport photo with you?" Frank asked. Kamau shook his head. Frank asked his goon out in the corridor to hand him a digital, state-of-the-art Canon camera he had brought with him. He knew his trade well, ever armed. Pumla was already busy combing Kamau's hair and before he could protest about being still in his crumpled T-shirt, Frank gently pushed him against the wall and took several shots, looked at the screen and nodded with satisfaction. When he showed the shots to Kamau to choose which one he would prefer to appear on his passport, Kamau nearly swore that it wasn't him. No amount of protestation bothered Frank, making Kamau feel small and overwhelmed. He wasn't in charge of his life anymore.

"Don't worry; they won't give much attention to your picture in the passport. Besides, many still can't tell one black from another," said Frank on his way out. Before he exited he paused again and turned to Kamau. "Oh, before I forget… women have needs," he quipped.

"Yes?" Kamau was lost.

"And if I were you, I wouldn't walk out on a naked, gorgeous girl in my bed at her hour of need, think *sexibly*," Frank added and slipped out into the corridor locking the door after him.

Kamau made a funny face while Pumla smiled mischievously.

She glided sexily to the door and turned the key and the latch to secure it. She then ebbed her way back to the bed oozing naughtiness as her clothes, briefs and strings found their way to the floor.

When Kamau woke up he felt like a buffalo had mauled him. His left leg and arm were numb. He couldn't feel or lift them but then he understood why. Pumla was lying on them clinging to him tightly like a baby, her soft arms and legs twisted around him as much as it was humanly possible. He had to admit she was beautiful, more beautiful than Jane. Her elegant body was exposed, the covers having slipped somewhere to the floor. It was the kind of body you would want to wake up and see in your bed every time. However, relationships were not just about beauty, and thinking of Jane he knew he had a serious problem. What had he done now! Carefully, he attempted to release himself from her entanglement but there was no way that was going to be possible without waking her up. She coughed and moved slightly, slowly opening her eyes, innocently, then closed them again and yawned. She nudged closer for a moment then opened her eyes again and smiled at Kamau sweetly.

"What's the time?" she mumbled. Kamau looked at the wall clock and whistled in surprise.

"Nearly four."

"Nearly… oh, my God," she exclaimed.

"What?"

"Nothing, I'm hungry."

"So am I, could you please ease your weight off me, I'm numb."

"You can handle it," she said. "You're a strong man."

"I don't have to get paralysed to prove it."

"You've already proven it. That was wonderful," she giggled, and nudged closer in childlike delight. She had a lovable innocence at times as well as wild abandon at other times.

Kamau didn't know how to react. He had done what he had sworn to himself never to do. He couldn't even remember using any protection. Regaining the use of his limbs, he trotted to the toilet feeling sick. He was almost surprised to find his willy still intact. He expected it to be halfway through rot. It shocked him how easily he had lost his moral standing. As far as his imagination could go, in a single act of unguarded recklessness he might have brought his life to a nasty deceleration and to a premature expiry. All those hopes of living his dreams might come to nothing. He had to calm himself not to throw up when he looked in the mirror. What he saw didn't impress him. His haggard face read defeat and for what? Instinctively, he looked down at his willy again and cursed the thing: you little doodah, can't you read danger signs? But then the little doodah took instructions from upstairs, aaaaargh! Cars don't read 'no entry' signs, drivers do. A man of principle was supposed to take control of any situation but then wasn't he just human?

The cold water coming from the silver tap felt good on his sweaty skin. The afternoon heat, probably coupled with the events of the previous several hours, made him so hot. He sure needed a coolant and more than a coolant. He wanted to wash away his sins and the guilt of his actions in lots of soap and lots of water. He wished and hoped that perhaps he could also wash off any viruses that probably still hang on him. It took him almost an hour in the bath, lazing in the bathtub and enjoying the cold showers coming from an overhead tap. This helped him sort his mind about his circumstances. When he came out of the bathroom, he watched Pumla turn and wriggle in bed, a satiated woman. He didn't hate her, she was so sweet; probably he was overreacting and needed to calm down. But what was she after? He wondered.

"You smell nice," she said, when Kamau entered the room.

"Well, thanks. You do too."

"You've got a great body, you know," she said, admiring his physique. "It actually looks better when you're standing. I just hadn't noticed how much."

"You haven't seen me standing?"

"Not naked, stupid."

"You're crazy. Get into that bathroom and get ready. I'm famished."

"Me too, I shouldn't be long. What took you so long, scared I was going to eat you?"

"That you've done already."

"Ain't finished with you."

"Get ready!"

She got out of bed, wrapping her naked body with the bed sheet, and glided gracefully towards the bathroom, tailing the long sheet like a bridal gown. She could feel Kamau's eyes admiring her. Without turning, she asked him what he was staring at, before she disappeared into the bathroom. Virus or no virus, Kamau was beginning to think he wasn't exactly unlucky. This freaked out his moral side to bits. *What was happening?*

She came out of the bathroom still wrapped in the bed sheet and full of angelic sparkle. She collected her jeans, top and strings from the various places she had dispersed them on the floor many hours earlier and disappeared again into the bathroom. That was Pumla for you, one moment stripping with ease before his very eyes, the next she couldn't dress in his presence.

"You sounded shocked that it was nearly 4 pm when you woke up. Had other plans?" Kamau asked, once they had ordered their meal. They were at Nando's on Bharathi Road, Pumla's choice. Apparently she couldn't stand the food at Kgosi Guesthouse. The only good thing she could talk about Kgosi was one of its guests who now sat across the table at Nando's with her.

"Had plans? That's an understatement. I was supposed to hand in my assignment today."

"Assignment? You mean you actually are in uni?"

"You didn't believe me when I told you." It was a statement. "You don't have to. Whether I'm in uni or not isn't your business, really."

"I'm sorry, I wanted so much to believe it but you can't always tell when you meet people the first time."

"I see, is that why you walked out on me last night?"

Kamau looked away, embarrassed. It was the issue he had hoped would not come up. She hadn't mentioned it till now.

"Oh no… I… I mean…" Kamau stuttered desperately, searching for words that strangely formed at the back of his mind but for some reason misread the map to his mouth.

"Thought I was a hooker who would give you disease?"

"Don't say that, makes me look... feel awful."

"Never mind, you're a sceptic. Yes, I'm a student if you care to believe me. I'm no hooker if you're already doing your mental sums about how much you think you should pay me. I understand the bit about going to look for a sock, it's the wise thing to do in the world we're living in but running away was, if you allow me, crass. You should have explained that you were not ready for it. Yes, disappointed I would have been but bearable. Walking out on me and leaving me naked in your bed is a different matter. I felt so humiliated, unworthy and cheap. Never do that to a woman. Just explain yourself and she'll respect you for it."

"Then I'm so sorry, Pumla. I..."

"The food is here," she said, cutting him short when she saw the waiter with their order. "Sorry will do, don't have to explain anything." Kamau felt so foolish it almost took his appetite away.

"Which year are you in at uni?" he asked, in an attempt to steer things from his discomfort.

"Second."

"Future plans?"

"I'm not decided yet. Might tour the world when I finish uni for about a year then I'll return and settle down."

"Don't you want to start a new life abroad, America or Europe?"

"Never."

That surprised Kamau who thought every person who could travel abroad should jump at the opportunity. It was unfair that he had travelled all the way to Botswana to get a fake passport to enable him travel yet Pumla, a Botswanan, had little ambition to travel anywhere.

"Don't tell me you don't dream of a better life abroad?"

"What better life? I have the best life I could ever dream of. I've an education, I'm in my country surrounded by friends and family and nobody treats me with prejudice. What more do I need?"

"You probably could earn more abroad," said Kamau, knowing his line of argument was weak. Educated Botswanans earned enough money for their comfort. Pumla laughed at him.

"I've shares in my dad's diamond business which earn me all the money I need."

"Oh, you're full of surprises."

"You have no idea how much more you don't know about me that would shock your naïve mind to the skies," she said, with a smile that suggested that there was much more to Pumla than Kamau would ever know. He felt stupid. It was as if she could read his mind yet he knew he would not get to know the real Pumla and all that went round her mind and heart. She was an enigma.

"Tell me, why then did you decide to make friends with me?" he asked. "I'm curious."

"Don't know. You're yummy and I wanted to eat you so much, I suppose."

"I'm flattered but may I ask do you do lots of this *eating* of strangers?"

"So that you can make up your mind whether you need an HIV test? My advice, do it if it'll make you feel better. No, it does not always happen this *eating of strangers* business but as you probably found out, if you were keen, I wasn't a virgin either."

"And if I may ask, when did you exactly stop being one?"

"Pass."

"I insist."

"Silly boy! I'm sure you don't want to know that."

Kamau shook his head amused. Pumla was something, so frank and easy-going. He liked her and felt embarrassed about all the things he had thought of her.

"Another question whose answer will, to use your words, make me feel better," he said. Pumla nodded her head for him to go on. "What relationship do you have with Frank?"

"I knew you'd bring that up, why?"

"Just want to know."

"Jealous?"

"Who, me? Never!"

"You're so naively transparent. I can tell from your eyes that you're not comfortable with it," she responded. Kamau became all the more uncomfortable, he fidgeted.

"If you really must know then let me just say he does some marketing for me."

"What sort?"

"Precious stones. Thought I told you that Dad deals in diamonds. Frank handles my *special* transactions."

"So you're like his boss or something?"

"Sort of, call it a partnership if you like. That's more like it. I do stuff for him as well."

"What stuff?"

"Pass," she said. Kamau let that off with a thousand question marks dangling in his eyes.

"Do you eat him too?" She shook her head. "Ever ate him?"

"Pass."

"I want to know."

"Knock it off! It's none of your business; your food is getting cold."

# 14

All caution thrown out of the high window, Kamau was under Pumla's spell. She showed him the gist of Gaborone in a way he could never have discovered. Together they travelled places for both fantasy and physical pleasure. Kamau had to try hard to stop thinking about home and his girlfriend. They belonged to another part of him but for now he was better off where he was – under Pumla's spell.

Just before midnight their journey to pleasure adventure was interrupted by a screaming ring of the phone. They were in Pumla's elegant second-floor single-bedroom pad close to Gaborone city centre. This wasn't an ordinary twenty-year-old's pad. The top-of-the-range electronic gadgets adorned the place like Frank's jewels. The rugs were exquisite, handmade cashmere and the leather sofa seats the type you always find in magazines but never actually get to see in anybody's living room. Kamau had trusted her enough to agree to put up with her for the time he would be in Botswana. Not even an inscribed wooden plaque at her door that read 'trespassers will be eaten' deterred him. In fact, he thought the sign was quite funny though a voice in his head questioned his wisdom. Such voices in life tend to get ignored until it is too late.

The call was from Frank's goon, Sam, who was at the main door downstairs and wanted Pumla to collect a parcel. The parcel came in the form of Kamau's Botswanan passport. He was now a Botswanan citizen. It sounded strange but then so much for patriotism if it can only take your dream so far. At least he was still officially an African if that was a consolation. The picture looked strange though and anyone keen enough could tell that he must have been nursing a terrible hangover when the photograph was taken. However, he was exhilarated. He had already overcome the first and most crucial step of his 'Operation Destiny' – the Botswanan chapter. If Frank didn't fix the other papers he would still travel and that's what was most important. Nobody talked about payment. When Pumla brought the passport she didn't ask for the money so he assumed Sam didn't ask for any either. That surprised him but then these people were strange and he had gotten accustomed to it.

Sure enough, there were lots of books in Pumla's pad and loads of photographs taken with her mates at the University of Botswana. Kamau had taken in those facts with delight. How Pumla found the energy to sneak and do her assignments in between marathon lovemaking sessions was a wonder. At last Kamau could relax in the knowledge that the girl was honest, at least on one issue, but crazy to the bone on others. He would bring the issue of paying for the passport later, at an appropriate moment, but now there were more important flesh matters to deal with.

"See, told you Frank could fix it," said Pumla. "It's a genuine one."

"And I'm grateful to the most insatiable tigress I've ever met."

"If that's a compliment I say thanks but I'm also grateful to the hulk who knows how to please a tigress," she said. "Like the photo?"

"Stop being cheeky."

"Looks as wild as you actually are," Pumla said with a chuckle.

"Why did you say it was all right when it was taken?"

"Kamau in any image is still Kamau."

"Very funny."

"Small details like that bother you?"

"You think I'm fussy, huh? How would you like your ID photo to look like a toad with flu?"

"Probably I wouldn't like that, but I'm a woman!"

"Oh, I see, too much for gender whatever."

"Oh, shut up. C'mon love me, the night is still young," Pumla cried, grabbing him and pulling him back to bed while at the same time chucking his passport somewhere across the room. Kamau had been stroking it for a while, glad that things were going so well so far. "Hope you don't mind me throwing the passport to the floor," she said, "but I hate competition, especially from little books. I get jealous."

The following day, Kamau was alone after Pumla went for her lectures. He lazed in her flat, watching videos and listening to music until he had had enough. A stroll into the city sounded a brilliant idea but he could do only so much of that in the blazing July heat. He regretted having turned down Pumla's offer to accompany her to her lectures. She wanted him to meet her friends but he wasn't keen. One thing he hated was to be the centre of attention and struggling to make small talk to a group of excited girls. He could have felt like he was on display, something like 'look what exotic fish me managed to net meself'. Not even Pumla's persuasions to at least accompany her to uni and wait for her in the university library or restaurant made him change his mind. Lying in bed had sounded so cool, especially after the exhausting moments of the night with Pumla.

When he got back from the city, he decided to get snoopy to unravel the mystery that was Pumla but he found nothing much telling or suspicious in the house. He even found a photograph taken with her dad inside their diamond shop with the stones glittering in the background like floating shiny wedding confetti. Maybe he was just lucky or unlucky, unlucky especially when he thought about Jane and his all-important principles. He began to question himself whether he had held himself up like a Waiyaki, his great chief grandfather, but then even Waiyaki was polygamous.

It was already late that day and they had not heard from Frank. Not even a visit to the Sun Hotel produced him. None of his goons had seen him either. Kamau went to bed that night, disappointed that his plans had been slowed. He had to convince himself to relax. After all, he had a passport, which proved that Frank was for real. In any case he could still travel. It was with renewed optimism that he found the energy and will to please Pumla and sleep deeply afterwards.

It was now Friday; four days after Kamau had received his passport. Frank had not been seen and even Pumla was beginning to sound confused when she couldn't get through to his phone. The only reason Kamau wasn't frantic was that he had not paid any money yet. He felt like a sprinter, ready to start an important race yet delayed because of irritating small organisational hitches. Pumla was doing her best to reassure him. He just had to make himself relax or he was going to be a very unhappy person. What Frank had told him about him needing all papers was very sensible. Although the desire to travel and accomplish his mission as soon as possible was compelling, he had to let logic reign.

By Saturday evening things were now critical. Kamau was as agitated as a bull elephant that had been cast out of the herd. He had refused to go out with Pumla who was in the house brooding about staying indoors on a Saturday evening. She was an outdoor person and could live outside with only cloth-change sneaks back into the house. This was a disaster to her. She just couldn't remember one weekend evening she had spent indoors and, to make it worse, with an agitated man who was not in the mood to cuddle her.

As mysteriously as Frank had disappeared, he materialised very early the following day. Pumla was cursing him for incessantly ringing the doorbell before they were out of bed.

"Where have you been, you git?"

"Some breakfast please, I'm starving."

"Go to hell, stupid! You wake me up at 6 am, no explanation where you've been all these days and the first thing you do is ask me to make breakfast."

"Make enough sausages please."

"I'm not your wife."

"No, you're not."

"Seriously, Frank, where have you been? Your phone was off too."

"C'mon, Pumla, is this an interrogation? Can't you heed the cry of a starving man?"

"You're impossible."

"That's why we're friends. If I'm impossible then what do you consider yourself to be? I respect Kamau for putting up with you even for a day. How's he?"

"Magical."

"Silly girl, I wasn't asking about *that*. What makes you think I would particularly want too much information about your bedroom matters? Is he all right?'

"Never better, he's been well looked after, in all ways," she said, full of mischief.

"Your walls are thin!" shouted Kamau from the bedroom. The door was slightly ajar, he could hear everything. They all laughed.

"How're you, my friend?" Frank shouted to him.

"Mine, not yours," Pumla interrupted.

"Okay, my friend's friend."

"That's better," said Pumla.

"All right, now that you're here," responded Kamau.

"See, I knew you're worrying," said Frank. "He's glad I'm here to rescue him from you."

"Oh, shut up!" screamed Pumla.

Kamau had to restrain himself not to demand his papers. If Frank was as hungry as he claimed he was then, it was only wise to wait until he was fed. It was over breakfast that Frank pulled an envelope from his travelling bag and handed it to Kamau. With shaking hands he reached for the envelope and tore it open. Inside were all the papers he needed. There was a birth certificate stating that he was born at the Princess Marina Referral Hospital, Gaborone. There were his academic certificates with a Bachelor of Commerce degree, just like his Kenyan qualification, but this time from the University of Botswana. He found a police check and a bank statement to take with him to the embassy. Kamau was now a happy man.

Whatever misgivings he had about Frank were all gone. Frank could curl his hair and manicure his nails and wear diamonds in his eyes for all Kamau cared. Kamau's money was in cash just as Frank preferred it for whatever reasons. Initially he was so afraid that probably Pumla was some kind of a con. He tried so hard to hide his money but there was no way he could hide that much money when staying with her. The other shocker was the fact that Pumla had lots of money from her diamond business. She wasn't interested in his money. She didn't even want him to take bills when they went out insisting that she was the host.

Frank picked him up very early Monday morning and dropped him at the British High Commission in the Main Hall, off Queens Road. Pumla had left earlier for her lectures, cursing the idiot who thought a 7 am lecture was a good way to start a day. When his turn came, Kamau proceeded to the interview counter, praying that it wasn't going to be like his Kenyan experience. He was very optimistic. There were only a few interviewees and all of them came from their interviews smiling. *Smile and the world will smile with you.* Botswana was doing all right and the world was being kind to her. Never mind that the good economic listings did not necessarily reflect on peoples' lives. It was the way of Africa and in fact other places around the world. The government tried hard to keep appearances in the eyes of the outside world yet did little for its people despite having huge financial reserves. The world embraced it, especially the West, knowing much of the wealth will end up in their banks. They were the big dealers and consumers of the diamonds anyway.

"Hello, Samuel." A smiling lady greeted him when he reached the counter. He almost looked behind him, thinking she was talking to someone else. Few people called him Samuel. He never really connected with the name; it didn't quite register as part of his identity.

"Hello," he said, after a brief hesitation.

"What documents do you have there?" she asked, pointing at the envelope that he was clutching possessively. Nervously, he handed it all to her. She smiled.

"What are all these for, Samuel?" she asked, referring to the load of papers and looking at his passport, which fell off last of the pile from the envelope. "Kamau…" She said the name several times her eyes up on the ceiling, trying to recall something. "Sounds Kenyan. Are you originally from Kenya? I worked there a couple of years."

Kamau's heart somersaulted, flip-flopped, teetered, sank, seized inside his chest a moment then erupted violently sending gushes of blood, mostly to his head. He felt dizzy instantly.

"Yes, I mean sort of, I mean no. It's the name," stammered Kamau, trying hard not to panic. "Dad was a great fan of the country's founding father so he named me after him," he went on, surprising himself. Wherever he pulled that one from!

"Kenyatta he was if my history isn't all gone," she said. Kamau almost screamed to her: *you know too much!*

"Kenyatta was an assumed name, initially a nickname his friends gave him apparently from a beaded belt he always wore that is known as kenyatta, his real name was Kamau wa Ngengi," he said confidently, once again surprising himself. He was doing all right so far.

"Oh really, I see," the lady said pleasantly, obviously glad for the new information. She loved history and she was in fact a member of a historical club that produced a monthly journal. She could write a whole article on the origin of Kenyatta's name.

"How long do you intend to be in the UK?"

"One and a half years."

"And that's for study, right?" she asked, with a flimsy look through his documents which included a letter of acceptance to Middlesex University that Frank had concocted for him.

"Right."

"I'll make that two years just in case the course extends. They always do, don't they? Especially postgraduate courses, had to do mine in three years." That was music to Kamau. She could give him a ten-year visa while she was at it for all he cared. "Enjoy your stay in the UK," she told him, handing back his passport complete with a two-year visa. With shaking hands, Kamau took the passport and nearly forgot to take his other documents. Clumsily he collected them and profusely thanked the lady to her embarrassment. *What's wrong with him?* she wondered.

When he went through the exit gate and on to Queens Road, he rounded his mouth to crow but then thought against it. People waiting to go in turned away in disgust, thinking he wanted to release a jet of spit. Waiting across the road was Frank. He smiled when he saw a happy Kamau approach. Like a good service provider, Frank always felt pleasure when his clients succeeded. He shared in their joy knowing his profile was strengthened. When word travelled around, lots of new clients kept coming and that meant more money and street credibility – especially the latter which was crucial in his exclusively special dealings.

"You'll crease your face permanently if you keep grinning like that," said Frank opening the passenger door of his metallic gold BMW 320 for him.

"Who cares about creases when happy with life?" he responded, beaming with excitement. "Europe here I come!"

"You must be very happy. It must mean a lot to you that you get to travel."

"It means everything," Kamau said. "I've always set my future and my plans abroad. It's as if my life was on hold waiting for this. Everything I ever did revolved around this."

Frank nodded, wondering what the compelling urge to live abroad was all for. He had travelled widely on 'special' business trips around the world but always returned. The network he had set earned him more money than he could earn living abroad; besides, governments abroad were too strict on taxes and businesses of the questionable kind.

"If it means that much to you then it calls for a celebration," said Frank.

"You can say that again."

They went to the University of Botswana to pick up Pumla for the celebration after booking a night flight with British Airways, scheduled the following day. Kamau also called his friend Ben in the UK to inform him about his travel plans. They started with the wines in Pumla's flat, went to the Sun Hotel then to the Cresta President Hotel on Botswana Road. Next they went to the Grand Palm Hotel Casino Resort on Molepolole Road and back to their favourite, the Sun Hotel. In his drunken wisdom, Kamau gave them a lecture about why he thought it was pretty stupid to have a long name like 'Grand Palm Hotel Casino Resort' for a business. Intoxicated to high clouds, he had remembered a few things he learnt in his business commerce class. They had been drinking all day and night, moving from one hotel to the next. It was dawn the following morning when they staggered back home.

When he woke up it was nearly 2 pm Tuesday. He felt like an engine running on several blown spark plugs. Pumla was not in the bedroom but he could hear her humming in the kitchen. Where she always got the strength to arise fresh for the day so early was a puzzle to Kamau. Surely all that partying was enough to drain an elephant. He roused himself with a cold bath and several cups of coffee that Pumla served him with a full meal that combined both breakfast and lunch. He was being well looked after. Surprises were never-ending, he realised that his luggage had been packed nicely in a brand-new suitcase. She must have gone out to buy that or maybe Frank's goons brought it. This was too good to be true. He hadn't noticed just how beaten his old bag looked but now that he had a new suitcase he could see that his bag really did need replacing. *Why is she doing all these things for me?* he wondered. Now all he had to do was relax and wait for his flight. In fact, Frank was coming to drive him to Sir Seretse Khama International Airport. If the world was smiling on Botswana, the gods were certainly smiling on him.

The trip to the airport was full of emotions. Pumla was sulking because he was leaving. She had not even tried to persuade him. There was no point. Kamau was so obsessed with travelling abroad, nobody could talk him out of it. All she had asked was that if it were ever possible he should go back to see her someday. Kamau made no promises but said he would try. He had enjoyed Botswana thoroughly, especially the final week that he had spent with Pumla. There were no regrets, even about morals and principles. He was a man at peace with himself. The puzzle of his life was falling into place.

At the British Airways counter he checked in his luggage then went back to the hall where Pumla sat looking miserable. He hugged her tightly, feeling sorry that things had to be this way.

"Will I ever see you again?" she asked, staring straight into his eyes through her misty ones.

"I think you will."

"Promise?"

"Like I said, I'll make an effort."

"In other words, you might never come back to see me?"

"Please don't make this difficult, Pumla," he said, full of emotion. "You've given me one of the best moments of my life. Don't think it's easy for me going away but then I have to."

"Come with me," she said, pulling his hand.

"Please don't do this," he protested.

"It won't be long." Kamau understood. She was pulling him towards the toilets. Frank, who was several metres away to give them space, shrugged and winked at Kamau then walked outside to his BMW. Being the crazy lass she was, Kamau wasn't surprised. A last kiss or whatever else was possible but then he only had a few minutes before his flight.

When they got outside the ladies, she looked both ways. Seeing no one, she dragged Kamau into one of the toilets. He was horrified and was about to protest strongly and loudly when she put a finger across his mouth to silence him. She gave him a generous kiss, touching him all over while she panted with emotions.

"I'll miss you." She breathed in his left ear and bit it lovingly.

"I'll miss you too," he whispered back, careful not to be heard from outside.

Suddenly she pulled herself away and opened a bag she had brought along. Out came lots of sparkling diamonds. First it was a set of diamond-rimmed sunglasses that she methodically put on his face; then out came diamond ear studs of the clip variety that found their way onto his ears, he cringed. Next came a glittering diamond chain, a diamond-studded watch, and a bracelet then materialised.

"Remember, they are safer worn. If you put them in the bag they might get stolen, wear them until you arrive in your friend's house where you could keep them safe," she said. "Now please remove your shoes."

"Shoes?" Kamau whispered loudly, in bewilderment.

"Sssshhh, quickly, or you'll miss your flight." That was enough to make him remove the shoes in one second flat. She gave him brand-new trainers that somehow had fitted in her handbag.

"Why all these? These things are worth millions, what does this mean?" he enquired.

"Means I value you that much."

"Oh, Pumla, *nooo!* I shouldn't..."

"Shh, you'll miss your flight." She pulled him to her bosom, squeezing her body against him. "Now go on, get out of here, but come back to me some day." She had a quick peek outside then pushed him out of the door and followed a few paces behind, craftily walking round an elderly lady they bumped into at the door. The lady stood erect in shock wondering what the world was coming to. Kamau didn't look behind. The elderly lady's horrified eyes could have haunted him. *Oh Pumla, the things you've made me do,* he thought.

Stepping out into the reception hall he looked like a walking jewellery shop. He was not unlike those rappers he had always watched on music channels who loved wearing jewels, especially heavy, golden chains. Now he wore more stones than they did. Furthermore he had the genuine stuff. He was sure even Frank would be jealous if he saw him.

To his horror, when he got into the hall his name was all over the public address speakers and the digital information display. He was required to board for his flight immediately. He raced to the entrance feeling conspicuous. The jewels glittered and dazzled like disco lights. He looked back one last time and saw Pumla wave, he waved back and disappeared into the inner foyer and into the air bridge that led to the door of the mammoth Boeing 747. The BA pilot wasn't amused to be delayed by a self-loving wannabe whatever, even if his stones looked impressive. What was the use of adorning a five-thousand-pound watch if you can't make good use of it. He had schedules to keep and a long flight to do while the wannabe would be resting his diamond bottom.

As Kamau walked down to his seat in the packed plane, faces

turned eyes caught by the glitter of the precious stones. The ladies were scandalised. It wasn't fair for one man to wear so much stone when they had little or none and certainly not that quality. Why was he wearing so many anyway? Was he a rich gay man or some sort of an African prince?

He was now getting embarrassed. Too much attention always bothered him. He wanted to find his seat as soon as possible. When he did, it was a middle seat with two lovely brunettes on each side. They quickly got into introductions and conversation.

"Wow, that's some precious hardware you got there," said Lyn, who was on his left.

"Oh yeah, may I touch them please?" went Charlene, all excited with sincere admiration.

"Of course you may." Kamau didn't mind now that the jewels made good conversation fillers. He wasn't good at talking to strangers and especially those with accents he comprehended with a time delay, a few seconds after the words had been said. His brains were not used to the true English accent; it took him some time to process words and make out meaning, sometimes only through association.

"Excuse me for asking but are you some celebrity, or what?" asked Lyn, the bolder of the two.

"Oh no, I'm nobody famous."

"Are you a chief, sorry, chief's son, coz obviously you're too young to be chief or are you a prince of an African tribal something… you know what I mean." It was Lyn again.

Kamau considered the question for a few seconds then answered. "Something like that." He felt he wasn't far from the truth. His great-granddad Waiyaki was a great chief. If the traditional chiefdoms still existed in Kenya he would have been royalty, probably even be an heir to the stool after his dad. He was the firstborn son.

"You're a prince then!" cried Lyn. "Oh my God, Charlene, we're seated next to African royalty."

The people in the surrounding seats turned to have a glimpse of the African royalty, terribly embarrassing Kamau. He felt so self-conscious with all those eyes on him; he sunk lower into his seat, hoping no one would get too ambitious and ask questions or, worse, an autograph. Obviously, there were many Botswanans on the plane, a complication because if it came to being put on the spot about his royalty, he knew he would have to lie.

After their meal, the two girls slowly slipped into sleep, still fiddling with Kamau's diamonds. Later on, they each collapsed on both his shoulders. He embraced them both like a protective father and listened to their soft snores, marvelling at how fortunes turn. Barely two weeks ago he was a dejected man, denied a visa by the British and now here he was being thought of as royalty and with two British girls resting on his bosom. He didn't mind the girls though. In fact, it could have been paradise to him if only his mind was settled. Far from it, he was a confused man. Not that he worried about immigration at Heathrow. He had faith they would not find out that his passport wasn't 'genuine' genuine, but rather he was more worried about the implication of all the stones Pumla had piled on him.

His dream was to become reality whether there was immigration scrutiny or not. Somehow he felt he was safe as far as that was concerned. But the diamonds? Did Pumla love him that much? The jewels were worth millions – at least in Botswana's currency – and that was lots of dough in any currency. Why would she want to be so generous to a stranger? Kamau explored several theories in his mind but none seemed logical. Maybe she wanted to come and join him or find him later. Maybe she had fallen deeply in love with him but had no way of expressing it, nor could she convince him to stay. That sounded flattering but knowing Pumla, Kamau had his reservations. She was surely an enigma.

# 15

He must have slowly drifted into sleep because when he woke up they were several hours into their flight. Lyn and Charlene were still stoned with sleep but recovering and now leaned on each other, on Kamau's lap, yawning and making childlike waking noises. They were so adorable, trusting him with abandon he felt protective like a big brother. If they were a reflection of the British people then he had a lot to look forward to. Once in a while, one of them went to the bathroom and snuggled back to the trio's heap around his bosom. Wasn't he lucky?

Eleven hours later they were approaching Heathrow Airport. Amid the rush for the loo that often comes just before descent, as if all of a sudden everyone discovers the plane had a toilet after all, Kamau readied himself for the triumphant entry.

When he got to the arrivals immigration desk he felt embarrassed, with all the people from other flights staring at his glittering stones. It was bad enough to be in a strange and intimidating place but to be centre of attention as well was a bit too much for him. He did his best to avoid their gaze. He needed all his nerves intact when he faced the immigration official at the desk. It wasn't long after when he was next.

"Hello," a slim stern little blonde woman at the desk said, staring blankly at the diamonds.

"Hello," Kamau mumbled.

"Which flight did you arrive on?"

"BA, Gaborone–Heathrow."

"Have you filled your arrival form?"

"Yes, si… ma'am," he said nervously, handing the little slip and clumsily struggling to keep in balance his hand luggage. In a flash, he realised he could have put it on the floor, which was carpeted and impeccably clean.

"So you're a student?" the lady asked, looking at the slip and at his jewels.

"Yes m…" he was about to say 'ma'am' but thought it sounded naff and checked himself. Besides he wasn't sure what title women wanted anymore; mrs, miss, ms, madam, ma'am. Any one of them caused offence depending on the woman in reference.

"For a moment I thought you were a musician or a celebrity," she said jokingly, smiling and taking away a huge chunk off the age that Kamau had mentally given her. That was a good sign.

"I do sing sometimes…"

"Yeah, what sort?"

"Well, all sorts."

"Have you recorded then?"

"Not yet, mostly it's live performances."

"Yeah, live performances as on stage and an audience?"

"Well, sort of… you know… in my bath, in front of the mirror and the hairdryer in hand as the mic." The lady smiled then released a low hearty laugh. Kamau was thrilled. Surely the gods were smiling on him. He knew he would be allowed in without hassle.

"So how long is your study?" she asked, all businesslike now.

"One year, probably a few months on the outside."

"And that's full time, right?"

"Right," he said.

She stamped his passport and gave it back to him. "Enjoy your stay in the UK."

"Thank you!" Kamau hissed breathless and stomped away victoriously to the promised land.

He had trouble finding his way in the crowded arrivals foyer. He meandered his way, looking for a phone to call Ben and let him know he had arrived. He got some coins from the exchange bureau shop and phoned him on his mobile. Luckily, Ben was just a mile away. He would be with him in a few minutes if Kamau could find a seat near the exit and wait for him. Haggard from the long flight, he slumped onto a seat wishing it were a real bed. Just then he felt silly with all those diamonds on him. He was now past immigration. Surely he could take them off and give his neck and wrists a rest. As he reached out to take off a bracelet from his left hand, Ben entered through the automatic doors looking in all directions for him. Kamau waved his hand to attract his attention and stood up, excited to see his friend. Ben quickened his step, trying not to be enthusiastic. He grabbed Kamau with his left hand and punched him lightly on the chest with his right one. They were such blokey blokes. Hugs were a no-no. Emotional embraces were out of the question apart from when they were in uni and went on drunken escapades at Mwimuto, a village on the opposite ridge of their Kabete campus. Many a time they staggered back to the university, shoulder to shoulder or carrying each other.

"Hi mate, good to see you," said Ben patting his friend's back, an understatement of the year.

"Good to see you too. Hey man, what have you been eating? You're big."

"I told you never to trust women. Blame mine."

"And you're supposed to be an unwilling victim, I presume?"

"You don't know what you're talking about. They'll cook for you thousands of calories but eat two leaves of lettuce and a tomato," they both laughed. "This way mate, welcome to London," said Ben, helping him to carry his luggage while leading him towards the exit. "What's all that precious hardware for? Or what did you become that you haven't told me?"

"Thought Her Majesty would be here to welcome me. What a waste, and all I got was broken ribs from your punches, I'm disappointed," Kamau said. Ben chuckled, still puzzled about the diamonds. Just then, three men hurriedly approached them and stood in their way. Kamau and Ben hesitated and were about to walk round them when Kamau saw one with a small placard with his name written on it.

"Hi, Kamau," said the one holding the placard, the tallest of the three. He wore a diamond ear-stud on his left ear.

"Hello," responded Kamau, freaked out to shreds. This was a nightmare. He was just a few yards from the exit. Surely it was not about immigration or he was going to die. His dream was being threatened a couple of yards to its fulfilment.

"Hello Ben, you all right?" said the second one. He was a stocky bloke, smartly dressed in a grey, pin-striped suit. Ben was puzzled. He didn't know who these people were but he hoped his friend wasn't in trouble. How come they knew his name? This didn't look good.

"Yeah," he responded weakly.

"We have an important message for you from Pumla," the studded one said to Kamau. "I'm Shona, Stocky here and Mbane. Pumla is our friend." Kamau was relieved; it wasn't about immigration after all.

"Oh, how's she, what message?"

"This way, mate," said Shona, leading Kamau to the inside of the foyer. Stocky followed close behind. "It's sort of private so Ben you better wait here with Mbane, won't be a minute." Ben looked at Kamau, worried, his eyes begging for an explanation.

"It's okay Ben," Kamau said and followed Shona. The fact that they were headed to the inside of the terminal and not outside was reassuring in itself. At least inside were lots of police and security officers. Nothing outrageously criminal would happen here. As he caught up with Shona, memories of the last few days with Pumla came to him. He missed her already. Wasn't she something? It was a tragedy that he couldn't have her with him every day of his life. Her body was a charm, so bewitching he felt such a desperate craving for its feel but that wasn't going to happen and probably never would. Life was like that, sometimes you meet people briefly but they have such an effect on you that you spend the rest of your life dreaming about them, like Jack and Rose from the *Titanic* film. *Important message? What could that be? Did she want him to return to her? Did she want to visit him here in the UK? Did anything terrible happen to her? Oh please let her be all right.*

Before he knew, it Shona was leading him to the gents. For a second, he thought something wasn't right but he dismissed the thought. This was Heathrow UK and not the police cells in downtown Nairobi where even the cops could blatantly relieve you of your wallet. He was mistaken. When they got in, Stocky quickly pushed him into one of the toilets and closed it behind him. Shona remained outside.

"Be calm, be very calm. Don't say a thing and you'll be all right." Stocky held his collar with a vice-grip round his neck and wagged a menacing finger in his face. Slowly, Stocky released him and stared at him like a scientist would look at a disgusting but important specimen. "The diamonds, quickly, all of them."

Kamau didn't say a word, he understood perfectly. At least this solved the puzzle somewhat. Few people were as generous as Pumla wanted him to believe and he never was that lucky to meet any one of them. All he needed was a few seconds to recover his breath, his neck hurt from Stocky's grip. A few gasps of air and a sheer desire to live long enough to see his dream mature enabled him remove the diamonds one by one and hand them to Stocky who put them away in his inner coat pockets. *Where was that Shona fellow?* When he was finished, he spread his hands in a gesture that he had no more diamonds left. Stocky pointed at the ear-studs, Kamau nodded.

"Just one, the left one," whispered Stocky.

"Why one? Take them all, take all diamonds yourself. I don't want any of them," Kamau whispered back, upset with the whole thing.

"I said one stud, I meant one and that's how it'll be. It's her instructions, I obey and you have no choice either." Stocky levelled his shoulders just to remind Kamau who was in charge here. Kamau knew this could turn ugly if it came to that. People who had the cheek to hold people up in the heart of Heathrow must be ready for any extreme eventuality. He didn't want to find out; he removed the left ear-stud and gave it to Stocky, relieved that this was over.

"Your shoes," Stocky whispered, pointing at them.

"What about them?" asked Kamau.

"Quickly remove them," commanded Stocky. Kamau was

about to protest when he checked himself. It was of no use; they weren't his shoes in the first place. It was the pair of trainers Pumla gave him at Gaborone Airport. People like Pumla and Stocky were not the people who dealt petty with things like shoes. They must have stuff in them; probably the heel was full of more diamonds or drugs. Whatever it was, he didn't want to know. If he was to walk barefoot at Heathrow Airport, the centre of European air travel, on his first day in Europe so be it. Probably people would think he was an African Bushman who was yet to learn the use of shoes or a cultic prophet who was reliving the Moses-and-the-burning-bush experience. Obediently, he reached for the laces. To his relief a pair of new identical trainers materialised from Stocky's coat where the ones he had removed had disappeared. For a fleeting second Kamau was amazed at just the number of crazy skills folks had in this world. How a pair of trainers could disappear so fast into an inside of a coat and not bulge was amazing.

He was still marvelling at Stocky's expertise when he realised Stocky was already outside at the sinks on his way out. Kamau took two seconds to collect his nerves but those were enough to lose Stocky. By the time he got back to the foyer, Stocky was nowhere to be seen and neither was Shona. Kamau could see Ben sitting close to the exit near where he had left him with Mbane. Quietly he approached him, unsure how to break the news to him.

"Let's go," said Kamau, taking some of his luggage from the seat next to Ben.

"Oh, where are the two guys?"

"Probably you should tell me where the third one is."

"He's buying us coffee over there," responded Ben, pointing at the restaurant's coffee bar. "Well, I don't see him now but he was there. I saw him order coffee."

"Let's go, or you'll be thirsty for a very long time."

"Where're the diamonds, what was that all about?" Ben asked, suspecting something was wrong.

"Long story, let's go home."

"Who's Pumla?"

"Part of the story, well, the gist of the story," Kamau answered, fiddling with the remaining ear-stud.

"I'm curious."

"Patience is a virtue pal, later, what I need now is a shower and some sleep."

"Patience is a virtue… shit, you sound like my dad."

"I feel his age right now, take me home."

Ben led the way to the car park where he had left his all-beloved Celica. With exaggerated manoeuvres he steered the sporty car out of the airport and on towards Hatton Cross and the A30. He was disappointed that his friend was not puzzled by all the modernity around him; if he was, he didn't show it. Kamau was in a pensive mood. Whatever had happened in that toilet must be heavy.

The quarter-hour journey home to Hayes was enough for Kamau to drift into lapses of sleep, occasionally peeping through lazy eyes to the modernity around him. All he noticed was the cleaner, quieter environment. As for whatever else, he knew he had all the time in the world to appreciate but for now the quiet would do. It was as if the diamonds had been weighing him down. Now that they were gone he felt lighter, felt peace and just wanted to lose himself to the seduction of sleep. The last few days had been dramatic for him. Pumla had introduced him to a whole new world. It's amazing how people live on the same earth yet such different worlds, that when they have glimpses of how other people live it feels like they have been to another planet. And the climax of it all was in an airport toilet. What an exciting way to end a dramatic experience.

At the Múhíríga's Nestles residence, he was welcomed by Abdi, the only one at home. Abdi was doing an evening dustman job and didn't see the need for another job despite all the free hours. Why die young? There was only one life and if you had food to eat, in good health, paid your basic bills and had a roof over your head that was all you needed. At least that's how Abdi saw it and didn't always agree with the last bit about the roof. He had lived rough at some point and never regretted it. Abdi helped carry Kamau's luggage upstairs while Ben fixed him coffee to take after he took a bath. Kamau got into the sparkling bathroom – well, that's how he saw it then. A carpet adorned the floor, a fact he observed as stupid. Obviously it got wet and mouldy underneath and would stink or get damp destroying the floor but it looked squeaky clean for now.

It was seven hours later when he woke up. Disorientated, he searched around for a familiar thing and then he remembered he had arrived at the land of his dreams. He got out of the unfamiliar bed and strode to the window. The houses and cars parked outside were just as he had always seen them in the movies. He wasn't dreaming after all. It surely felt strange but wonderful. Feeling the lone ear-stud on his right ear, he remembered Pumla. For some reason he didn't hate her. He just thought she was an odd one and wondered who she was to those goons at the airport. Did she control them or were they using her and she in turn used other people? It was hard to imagine a beautiful young university student could also be a baron for some illicit international cartel. Curious about the whole thing, he took the phone from the bedside table but before he called her he decided to call his girlfriend, Jane.

"Hi, love," he said.

"Oh hi, sweetie," she cried. "Where have you been? Everybody's worried."

"Why should they? I said I'd be away for some time."

"It's been weeks, sweetie, and you're supposed to travel to the UK remember."

"I'm in the UK."

"What do you mean, you're in the UK?"

"Exactly that, as in; *I'm in the United Kingdom.*"

"Stop kidding, I know you're a little odd but this isn't funny," she said, with a serious voice. "Why do you disappear like that? You never take me with you and don't say much about where you zoom off to. Are you hiding something, love? Sometimes I feel I don't know you at all."

"Oh really, you don't know me now, huh?"

"Please understand, didn't mean negatively, but this waiting, not knowing whether you're in Congo or Siberia or Botswana kills me."

"Was in Botswana."

"What?"

"Never mind, I'm in the UK now, London to be exact. It's true and it had to happen this way, a long story."

"Why, darling, why?" She wailed with the pain of rejection. Kamau had to explain in so many words why he had to leave without saying a proper goodbye and convince her that he still cared. Finally calm or resigned in the knowledge that there was nothing she could do, she wished him the best and half unconvinced, she promised not to tell the full story and also accepted his vow of commitment to their relationship.

The next person he called was his dad. "Hi Dad," he said when his dad responded exuberantly on his mobile.

"Oh, hi, Waiyaki boy. What're you up to, you porridge head? Why do you have to keep your mama worried like that?"

"I just called her," he lied, intending to call her immediately after.

"Where're you now, when do you travel?"

"I've travelled already, Dad."

"What do you mean, you've travelled already? I don't mean those monkey hide and seek games you play behind thickets, wherever. I mean when do you travel to Great Britain? The minister for transport wants to come to your farewell party."

"What farewell party?"

"I organised one for you."

"Without asking me?"

"I couldn't find you in the Congo rainforest, could I? I'm not as brave as you are to play hide and seek with monkeys."

"Yeah? Tell him it's cancelled."

"Easy boy surely didn't know where to contact you. Even your Jane didn't know so I took the initiative, you don't really mind, do you?"

"Very much father, I do mind. It's cancelled."

"C'mon boy, you know very well we don't disappoint men like the minister for transport. It's a liability."

"Well then, we… I mean you've lost big time."

"Are you drunk? Why d'you talk to me like that? The party is on. Now you listen to me. Get your silly rucksacks on your back and get back here soonest. We need to organise this."

"Sorry Dad, I'm already in the UK."

"What?"

"Yeah Dad, if you looked at the number before you picked my call you must have seen it started with plus-four-four." There was a prolonged silence on the other end. "Are you still there?"

"*Jinga!*"

"Did you just call me jinga, called me a fool, Dad?"

"That's not a Waiyaki way of doing things," Hinga said angrily. "Anyhow, I know a friend to the Kenyan ambassador over there. You may need..."

"Dad, I don't need anybody. I'm a big boy now. If you didn't try to run everything I might have said goodbye the proper way but you just don't stop meddling."

"So I'm now a meddler, huh?"

"Man to man, yap."

"Right then, if you're man enough then work for your own cash. I'm not sending the rest of your fund money."

"Suit yourself Dad. If you're man enough to keep it with a clear conscience then have it." Again there was a long silence on the other end of a man losing grips with a son he always thought weak and ever needing his help.

"Sorry son, I should let you have your life now that you speak like a Waiyaki. I'll send the money."

"Now you speak like Waiyaki," said Kamau, full of mirth.

"You're a Waiyaki remember, son. Live like one."

"Yes Dad, Waiyaki for life."

"Waiyaki for life," Kamau's dad said.

Happy that the call to his dad ended well, he remembered that it was Pumla he wanted to call before he called Jane and his dad. He dialled her number, eager to hear her voice again. Despite the airport incident he missed her very much. She had taken him to fantastic places, to islands of pleasure where he had never been before.

"Hello Pumla," he said, when she picked up the phone. "Thanks for your welcome party."

"Hi love, how're you?" She was very excited like nothing had happened.

"Why, Pumla?" asked Kamau.

"Why what, weren't they good to you?"

"Why Pumla?" he asked again, calmly.

"Because you're naïve and needed some jostling to the real world."

"What if they hurt me?"

"They didn't, they can't."

"What do you mean, they can't? They looked like murderers."

"I can assure you that they are not, my word. In any case, they take instructions seriously."

"From whom?"

"Pass."

"You, Pumla? One of them said something to that effect."

"I said pass, welcome to the real world, my love."

"Don't love-talk me, what do I do with the ear-stud, will they come back for it?" There was a hesitation on the other side. Pumla sighed loudly.

"I'll let you know this, Kamau; whether you believe it or not you're the best thing I've had in ages. What happened at Heathrow was just business, you know, as they say, nothing personal."

"Oh yeah, having me choked and bundled into toilets? Is that what you do to those you care about?"

"The ear-stud," she said, ignoring him and changing subject, "is a souvenir. I would like you to come back to me some day and I mean it. The diamond is worth a lot of money and if I was as mean as you think, I could have taken everything and probably more."

"You used me, Pumla," protested Kamau.

"Okay then, come back to me some day and use me, an offer, I can't be fairer than that now, can I? When you stop being a dreamer you'll realise that being a realist like me is the best approach to life. I value the things that give me an edge in this world. What freedom is there like the freedom of not having to count coins at the end of the day, unsure whether you can afford the next day's bread?"

"Do I need the lecture? You're very strange," he said, impressed at the conviction twenty-year-old Pumla attached to her cause. He liked her and didn't feel she was horrible. All he wished was that he could understand her, you know, get into her psyche. Yes, probably he would visit her some day and take her offer.

"Strange, yes I am. I still got a few more tricks for us, of the intimate kind," she chuckled. "If the English girls are no good just hop onto a plane and come to Pumla."

"Forget it girl," he responded unconvincingly. "I'm not sure I would get out of Gaborone alive."

"I'm not forgetting anything; I know you'll come back."

"And how's that?"

"I'm a woman Kamau. I just know."

# 16

Jane alighted from the creaky, ramshackle of a bus at the Kencom bus stop, frustrated and angry at the same time. She was a very beautiful young woman of medium build. Her chocolate-brown skin agreed often with her favourite semi-bright flowing outfits that she carefully selected to match, making her look so ladylike. Well, most of her outfits were a little tight below the waist, exaggerating the rich curve of her backside. "If you've got it, flaunt it, it can make up for whatever else you lack," is what she used to humorously say, and rightly so because she hated her legs. An adolescence craze for stilettos, thinking they made her look more mature, had left her with hard prominent muscles on the calves of her legs that she thought looked so unsexy. Her hair was, so she thought, also a let-down. It never grew all the way to her back like she would have loved it to. She therefore normally wore a bob that accentuated her long face.

She had just come from Jomo Kenyatta Airport to meet her contact who had the cheek to call off the meeting at the last hour – the second time he had done so. She was beginning to hate him, her nerves all frayed out to limits. Struggling with her bag and the shoving of commuters rushing to pick a bus home in the usual Nairobi manner, she felt lost as she crossed Moi Avenue to the bus stop outside the Ambassadeur Hotel. This was where she was to pick a route 44 matatu to her bedsitter in Zimmerman which she shared with her best friend Maria, a home she had kissed goodbye a second time and wished never to return to.

For all the three years she had lived there it was all right for her, a haven even. It was where she had the first taste of being in charge, responsible for her life without having to explain to anyone why she was late. She was so proud of it she invited her friends for a wild party when she first moved in. Well, the neighbours complained a little about the noise. That was the only thing that reminded her it was not exactly a hideaway mansion on a private island. The noise was never repeated and when the drunk girls woke up in the morning after the 'heng' and collected themselves off each other on the bed and the couch and the carpet and went home, Maria her best mate remained and somehow stayed on, initially on an on-and-off basis. It was hard then to say when exactly she permanently moved in.

That morning, Jane had hugged Maria goodbye and cried so much that she was not going to see her for so long. She had also hugged the walls of her bedsitter that she felt so intimate with. They had watched her, sheltered her too and knew both her happy and sad moments. Now she was unwillingly going back there instead of being in the skies somewhere over the Mediterranean where she had thought she would be by now.

"Don't you dare touch me," she screamed at a tout who attempted to push her into a matatu in their usual rudeness.

"*Iko nini? Ingia ndani ama…*" the arrogant tout shouted back.

"*Ama ufanyeje?*" she screamed back.

"*Wacha kisirani wewe.*"

"You don't have to push me in; I know where I'm going."

"*Wacha maringo, ama uambie chali yako akubaie gari.*"

This was more than she could take. In a rage, she slapped the boyish tout so hard the unexpected strike made him lose balance. He reeled backwards and fell flat on his back. Quickly he picked himself up, seething for a fight to appease his wounded ego but the men who were present stood between him and Jane. They were not going to let a lady be assaulted by one of the uncouth matatu touts that had become a law unto themselves. This created a little commotion, with the mortified tout screaming in agitation and spoiling for a fight while several men roughly restrained him. In the ensuing melee, another crew of a matatu Jane accustomed to work almost every morning sensed trouble. They grabbed her, put her in their microbus and sped off. In the confusion, few people noticed this happen but the crowd kept growing. Soon the brawl degenerated to a skirmish of commuters and touts who appeared from everywhere to rescue one of their own.

When Maria opened the door for her, she suppressed her surprise and let her in without any questions. She knew her friend well and knew she liked to be left alone when she was feeling low. Maria simply nodded that she understood and Jane nodded back and fell on the bed, covering her face with a pillow. The least Maria could do for her was to pull off her friend's shoes and let her deal with her frustrations until she was calm enough to talk about it. Maria switched off the loud and noisy action movie she was watching and put on a slow Michael W. Smith's worship CD that Jane loved to listen to when she needed divine intervention in trying situations. She then took a Ruth Karanja's novel, *A Second Chance,* and spread her petite frame on the couch, contemplating the tribulations her friend had gone through in the past few weeks.

Jane's boyfriend, Kamau, had called three weeks earlier from London to break the good news: he had established a linkman who was to help her join him. Kamau had already paid him £1,500 for the whole 'operation' trusting him on word from many others who reliably had used him. Evidently he had pride in his, ahem, business. His record was so good that he promised a total refund if he was unable to deliver. He hadn't been known to fail. However, due to the clandestine nature of the operation and the man's sensitive position, she was not to let a soul in on this. Of course, Maria knew. She was Jane's trusted confidant. In any case, Maria was the sweetest quietest person on earth. She didn't have enough words to say what was necessary let alone the unnecessary. They talked this over and over again, excited that Jane's dream was becoming true but also sad that they would part. When the contact man finally called late one night they hugged and cried some. It was happening, finally.

"Hello," a baritone growled.

"Hello," Jane said in excitement. She didn't have such a number in her phonebook. It must be the contact. *Please God let it be him.*

"Is that Jane?"

"Yes, yes sir," she responded eagerly. *Sir?* She imagined he must be a big, important man.

"Do you know somebody by the name Kamau?"

"Yes, I do, that's my boyfriend," she said, and felt stupid. Nobody asked her who he was.

"Can I speak to him? Is he with you?"

Jane was alarmed, what was happening? She wondered who it was and feared the deal had gone bust. Oh my God, it's the police! They must be looking for him… no, he was far away; they must be looking for her!

"Who're you?" she asked, defensively.

"I'm his friend, don't worry." Her fear said it all. He just wanted to know he was speaking to the right person. "We should meet as soon as possible. Has he called you?"

"Yes he did, two days ago."

"When are you free?"

"Anytime sir."

"How about tomorrow?"

"It's open, I'm free," she lied. To hell with that stupid secretarial job she did at Fixit Insurance Brokers. Her arrogant boss could type his own letters for all she cared. Hey, she was on the way to the great *UKay!*

"Perfect, meet you at Burger Place, Kimathi Avenue, ten o'clock sharp in the morning, all right?"

"All right."

"One other thing, bring your birth certificate and four passport-size photos with you."

When Jane put the phone down she did a peculiar jig and declared, "And she lived happily ever after" to the amusement of her friend who was watching from her favourite place on the couch.

Early the following morning, Jane called the office and said she was unwell. Her boss was not much older than her, a young man running one of his dad's branches of the big insurance brokerage firm. He ranted and screamed and swore, with Jane holding the phone away from her ear every time he exploded into a fresh foray of expletives. She was used to him by now. She spoke, grabbing the chance when he paused briefly to catch breath before more swearing. She finished the conversation with, "Bye George, see you the day after tomorrow, will miss you."

"I won't, you fu…" he exploded, but Jane hung up on him before he started swearing all over again.

Five minutes before 10 am she was seated in the small but neat restaurant, waiting for her contact man, when she remembered in horror that she hadn't asked him how she would recognise him and neither had he asked. She fished her mobile phone from her handbag and frantically started going through her call register, fearing that she might have deleted the number. Just then, her phone rang.

"Hello," she said, glad that at least he had called first.

"Hello," the baritone growled from the other side, but then the line disconnected. Anxiously she surveyed the restaurant. Maybe he had arrived and wanted to identify her. Devoid of any sign, she looked confused and turned to her table.

"You should have looked here first," the middle-aged, smartly dressed man opposite her table said, and stretched a long, very dark hand.

"Oh my God, sorry," she said, surprised and pleased. She extended her hand and shook his, observing his slim face adorned with a gap between the front lower teeth.

"The good book says you should start in Judea, go to Samaria, then the ends of the earth."

"Actually it's Jerusalem then Judea… my name's Jane."

"Oh, Jerusalem is it? Well, Jane I thought you must be. Mine's Cherono. You're a beautiful young lady, no wonder Kamau is paying the moon to get you there."

"Thank you, sir." she said, nervously caught a little off guard by his easy manner. She could tell he was a very tall man, characteristic of the athletic Kalenjins from the Rift Valley region. His torso towered over her above the table. "May I ask how much it cost?" she asked, and regretted it.

"It's a gift, like a ring, flowers, stuff… shouldn't ask. Just be glad he's doing it for you."

"Point taken."

He nodded his head and cleared his throat, all business now. "I'm an official of the Kenya Amateur Athletics Association. We have a marathon coming, Berlin Marathon, and I'm taking a troop of young people that the Deutscher Leichtathletik-Verband has been sponsoring.

"The what?" Jane quizzed.

"German Athletics Association," said Cherono quickly when he saw Jane's puzzlement. "They'll appear as a guest team and I'm the one drawing the list so that's where you come in."

"Excuse me..."

"Please let me finish, questions later. Most people that I help already have passports but your case is different. Ordinarily I charge more to get a passport for clients but Kamau is a fine young man and I can see his girlfriend is even finer."

Jane looked down, flustered a bit, fidgeting this way and that way. She didn't know how to respond to that. Older men this part of the world rarely complimented women, especially much younger women – unless of course they had bed thoughts. This one, however, sounded sincere, a refined man.

"The passport will take a day or two; the Immigration Department have orders from the Sports and Culture Ministry to do passports for me immediately. We leave in two weeks' time. I'll let you know when we fix the date. I'm sure he told you he paid for everything, including your ticket. When I fix the date I'll want you to travel light to avoid complications with luggage. That means you carry only what is necessary. I'd wish that you kept this deal to yourself because I have enemies. Many of my colleagues would like to fix their people in the list but I can't let them and they don't know of any extras that I take along with me. Please note I may cancel the trip at the last minute depending on the shift my contact at Heathrow is working. Sometimes the shifts are juggled unexpectedly for security reasons. In other words, he may give me notice of only a few hours and if he does I will want you at the airport immediately, the more the reason why you should keep it to yourself. There is no point saying goodbye to people then they see you on the streets the following day. You may ask your question now."

"Did you say the group is going to Berlin?"

"That's right."

"And I'm going to London?"

"Yap, connect flights at Heathrow so between the connection you disappear."

"How will that be?"

"That's my bit, don't you worry none, I'll get you there in the hands of your man. Anything else you want to know?"

"When you cancel our flight that means the whole group stays until the appropriate time?"

"No, one of our officials is already in Berlin. If I cancel, the group travels and the other official receives them on the other side. I then follow, just the two of us, I leave you in London and proceed to Germany."

That's how Jane found herself in a Kenya Airways Airbus A310 flight 46 to London with a connecting flight to Frankfurt Germany at Heathrow Airport. That meant Kamau had paid for a section of a flight she was never going to take but that was a small price to pay for a reunion in the land of the great. Jane was yet to absorb the fact that she was so high up in the skies headed to where her dreams and her man were.

Twice Cherono had postponed the travel until Jane began to wonder whether it was ever going to happen. Maybe he was a con and just wanted to take her on a wild goose chase before disappearing. He looked so honest in a peculiar sort of way though he was doing dodgy business – but don't them hustlers all look convincing?

This was an experience to relish. She was flying for the first time and the trappings of air travel were magic to her. If only her mum knew – she would be horrified then, after the initial shock, she would pray for her safety and finally try to be happy for her. In subtle ways, she had hinted to her family that she might travel out of the country soon but that sounded like all her other big dreams.

They had dismissed her with mock blessings and a laugh. Now it was happening. She imagined the shock on their faces when she would call from London. What more could anyone ask? Scenes from hundreds of movies she had watched replayed in her weary mind. She remembered the exquisite elegance and sophistication she had only fantasised about, considering them way beyond her reach. Now she felt it would soon be reality.

When her boyfriend Kamau travelled out of the country she was happy that he had realised his dream. As days turned into months, then a year, she got depressed as the communication between them reduced to a trickle. No amount of reassurance from Kamau's family convinced her, especially not from Hinga his politician dad. Most times she kept away from him. It wasn't beyond him, she thought, to broker her to one of his politician friends for favours. Jane had adamantly turned down his invitations to parties full of dubious politicians where Hinga always introduced her as part of his family. All she wanted from the Hinga family was her man and she thought she had lost him until he started talking of making plans for her to join him. Beautiful as it sounded, she convinced herself to go it slow lest she got her hopes rocket high only for them to blow up mid-sky and fall sinking to the depth of the sea. It had happened to others whose boyfriends married foreigners to acquire citizenship and others who simply became lost souls sinking into a life of constant revelry and drugs.

After embarking from the plane at Heathrow Airport, she followed Cherono who was so relaxed as if he was taking a stroll in downtown Nairobi. A well-travelled man; he was not overwhelmed by the elegance around him. He had been an athlete of repute himself before he became an official after a knee injury cut short his promising career. Through the air bridge and into the hallway, they turned this way and that way to the waiting lounge for those connecting flights. Her next supposed flight was in two hour's time and she wondered whether the 'operation' would be immediate or whether it would take time. She hoped it was swift, like a visit to the dentist; the sooner you got it over with the better. She wondered how long the anxiety in her would last before it overwhelmed her or, worse, she fainted. Her fears were not outrageous. She had fainted a few times after standing too long in never-ending high school assemblies.

The anxiety now nearly sent her to fits. Beyond those walls was her boyfriend waiting. She was dying to see him, to hug and kiss him. It had been a long excruciating wait, now she felt like the next brief moment before she saw him again would kill her. What if the 'deal' didn't work and she was deported to Kenya? What if she was arrested and imprisoned here? Would Cherono take her with him to Germany if the contact man didn't appear? These thoughts gripped her like a knot, a deep restlessness in her stomach. Cherono was doing a poor job trying to make her relax.

"At least only my best friend knows about this in case I'm deported," she mourned, toying with the coffee Cherono had bought her at the waiting lounge café.

"Relax, nobody is deporting you. I've done this with many people without failure."

"What about the CCTVs?"

"They are machines, no?" Jane nodded.

"They do what you want them to do, shoot what you want them to see like blank walls and stuff, or not shoot at all."

"Who's your contact?"

"A man."

"What sort of a man?" She was panicking. She had heard of girls who were smuggled abroad with promises of better lives only to be sold to pimps and brothels as sex slaves. A wave of hot terror swept through her. "What coins do they use here?" she asked Cherono earnestly. She wanted to call Kamau and tell him where she was in case anything happened. She wanted to hear his voice. It was reassuring just knowing he was there waiting.

"You're very anxious." It was a statement. "It shows all over your face. That's no good; my contact will want you to be sober." He took out his mobile phone and called Kamau.

"Hello, Kamau boy."

"Hello there, mate." He was full of excitement. "You're my

man, Cherono."

"Tell that to your girlfriend, she doesn't trust me," he said, and handed the phone to Jane.

"Hi darling," said Kamau.

"Oh my God, sweetie, it's you! I'm here!"

"Will be seeing you in a little while, feeling great?"

"Now I do. Gosh, darling, I can't believe it."

"You better," Cherono said and took the phone away disconnecting the call when he saw a tall white security officer, about fifty-something, approaching.

Cherono nodded at him and he nodded back. Jane was unsettled when he saw all the security paraphernalia hanging over his uniform. He also wasn't exactly what she expected. She had imagined the contact was going to be one of the immigrant communities, possibly black or Asian and probably a conniving young man. This one was a dignified-looking, middle-aged Caucasian man. Well, an extra penny in any language.

"Will see you someday I hope, take care," Cherono told Jane, shaking her hand, leaving for another section of the lounge without saying a word to the security officer, and taking her luggage with him. "Don't worry, I'm sending this to you by courier. It will be with you before you need the toothbrush tomorrow morning," he said, when he saw bewilderment written all over her face.

"Call me Jack if you've to, follow me immediately," said the officer, walking past the table. Jane was shocked and hesitated a second, then remembered Cherono had told her to do whatever she was told and do it quickly. She hurriedly took her handbag and followed him. After a dizzying maze of corridors and connecting doors she found herself in a closet marked 'Security'. The officer thrust a uniform at her and told her she had a second to put it on. Once again she hesitated a bit, wondering how she was going to change with the man standing there. Then she understood. She was to put it over her clothes.

"You've got half a second now," he whispered, full of tension. That prompted her into action. In a minute and a half she was in an oversize security officer's uniform. The man urgently stuck a security badge on the uniform around her bust and thrust her handbag inside the uniform, scaring her a little. By now her heart was throbbing so hard she was running out of breath.

"When we get out of here, I'll walk very fast. I expect you to keep pace and I'll be shouting at you. Don't say anything, *just follow me*." He emphasised the last bit. It was a command. Jane nodded vigorously with the urgency of the moment.

The tense man was doing long strides down the corridor, swearing and cursing, with Jane following closely, half running to keep pace.

"Who said I'm the one to do all the effing training around here? I got lots of stuff on my hands to do and now what? He brings me a… You got your CRB with you? Morrison's an effing bastard; he should do this himself or pay me more if he thinks I'm that good. Why doesn't he bring in MI5 if it's that critical? What did you say your fu… your name is? Omugwefu… what's the bloody-effing rest of it? Why do you make your names so long, anyway? Haven't your people heard that shit about 'a rose by any other name would smell just as sweet?' better simple. This place is crap. This place stinks… and you want to join. Hell, if you're so hot for it so be it but when you've been here long enough you'll curse your guts wishing you'd become an effing doorman. Your people are good at sports, maybe you'd do fabulous on a track more than this effing stinking hole."

Quickly, unexpectedly, he made an abrupt stop and Jane bumped into him then pulled off, surprised and embarrassed. She felt clumsy. He looked both ways up and down the corridor and shoved Jane through a door marked 'Private'. It led to more doors and corridors and offices. They moved on very fast in what to Jane felt like a dizzying whirl. The boiling adrenaline in her body had risen to a high that made her head feel light but she had to remain strong, hoping this would end in a little while. Jack opened one of the offices and pushed her in, afraid to lose even a second.

"Quickly, take off the uniform," he commanded. This time she was half done before he finished his command. It was like a military drill, orders given and quickly implemented. This was a good one for Jack; she learnt quickly where speed was of profound importance. He quickly shoved the uniform into a locker on the wall and marched out again, Jane close at his heels. She understood now why her luggage could have been a drag.

Fate was watching with a sympathetic eye. Just as fast as this drama had run, so it seemed to end when she found herself in a huge crowded and busy lounge. Jack was still moving fast and she found it hard manoeuvring through the masses of travellers and keeping pace with him. She bumped into many people without pausing to apologise. There was no time for that or she could have lost Jack. One person she bumped into, however, wasn't going to let her off so lightly. He grabbed her terrifying her and turned her round to face him.

"I'm so sorry," she said urgently. "Oh my God, oh Jehovah, Lord God almighty!" She was face to face with her boyfriend Kamau.

"Welcome to London," he whispered to her ear, hugging and kissing her with the indifferent travellers and their loved ones milling past and round them.

"Oh my God, sweetie, it's you!" she cried. "I'm here, sweetie, with you. I've missed you like mad and now you're here."

"Me too, darling, missed you, *sana*," he said. "Come this way." He held her hand, leading her through the crowded lounge.

"Where's Jack?" she asked, tears still flowing down her cheeks. She looked all around but didn't see him.

"Never mind about him, he's gone… quickly, this way. He led her out of the automatic doors of Terminal 4 into a Toyota Celica he had borrowed from Ben, now parked in the car park just outside across the road from main lounge exit. A special girl needed a special welcome. He didn't consider his rickety Rover Metro fit enough to pick a special somebody though he could never say that to anyone; especially not to Ben who always had a dig at him about his wobbly runabout. Kamau gunned the powerful engine and sped off in the fast car. She was in the *UKay* now and she wasn't going to wake up and find Maria on the couch in their little bedsitter in Zimmerman reading her endless novels. She actually pinched her thigh just to make sure she wasn't dreaming and wiped the tears on her face. The last three weeks had been a time of enormous emotional pressure and she found herself crying more often. The tears she was shedding now however, were tears of joy, no, more than joy. It was ecstasy. She was with the man she loved, the only man she ever loved and she was in the UK, a place she only dreamt of. Reclining on the comfortable seat, she extended a hand and touched Kamau's left hand.

"I love you and I'm happy."

"Love you too, I will be happy with you here," he responded, and straightened himself clearing his throat with an air of mock importance. "On behalf of her Majesty the Queen of England and Blair's government, I officially welcome you to Great Britain."

They both laughed.

# 17

Múgo Kíama signed the last file, closed it and grimaced in disgust. The inscription on the pen, 'GK – Government of Kenya' gave him nausea. It was a mark of his ten years of misery in the civil service. He broke the pen in half and threw the pieces out the open window then sat upright listening to the clatter of plastic on the wall and glass as the pen made its way down. Just then, his moment of outrage was replaced by a bout of conscience. What if the pieces hit someone on the ground, two floors below? Quickly he went to the window and peered down to see one piece stuck on a car windscreen wiper. Luckily there was nobody in the car. Guilty, he sighed with relief and looked up the sky. There was a very dark cloud that hung precariously over Nairobi like a collapsing ceiling in an abandoned cottage. A chilly wind blew the curtain into his face, sending specks of dust into his eyes. There was going to be a heavy downpour. He wondered why it mostly rained when you forgot your umbrella at home. He'd better leave now or he wasn't going to make it to the bus stop before the rain started.

He opened the top drawer of the ancient wobbly cabinet his seniors had refused to replace. It probably needed ten signatures and a report by the supplies officer to get it done. Such was the way of civil service. Staff were so indifferent and out of touch with their responsibilities they would do anything to justify their relevance, making the long journey through red tape even longer. Carefully he took a finished file from the desk, afraid that the tattered covers would go into pieces and scatter the contents that he had taken hours to sort. Fortunately the cover was in a behaving mood. But the spring wasn't; just when he was about to stick the file into the cabinet the spring broke, sending papers all over the floor. A tear welled in his eye. A full-grown circumcised African male felt like crying, and for what, a file? No it wasn't the file. He had personally taken it upon himself to help a widow get her dead husband's pension. She had been pushed from one office to another and from one pension officer to another for the last five years. Such was the way of civil service here. Bribery was rife and if she had greased someone's hand her pension woes could have been sorted out in a day. That's how insensitive his colleagues were. They sickened him.

She had come to his office accidentally – instead of the one upstairs with a similar door number – and when he told her it was the wrong office she just collapsed to her knees and wept. Later, when she had calmed down, Múgo had the unfortunate position of listening to her horrific treatment at the hands of his colleagues, and how her children had been suspended from school for lack of fees. Her brother-in-law had robbed her of some of the property her late husband left behind and she couldn't do anything about it because she couldn't afford a lawyer. Múgo had traced every little paper relating to her case and she was to come in the following morning for her pay to be approved, but now every one of the papers in her file was sprawled on the floor.

Like a man in a trance, he knelt down and picked each one of them, muttering incomprehensibly. He was going to sort the file no matter how long it took. He didn't care if they paid him over time or not. There had to be a line between duty and being humane. Where was compassion for other humans? If it was the last thing he did in civil service, so be it, but he was going to see the end of it if only to wipe those tears away from that lady's eyes.

It was close to 7 pm when he finished sorting out the documents and arranging them in the order the senior pensions officer liked to see it if he was to approve immediate payment. The building was very quiet now with everybody having gone home by 5 pm, most of them long before then. Here staff left at will with their jackets hanging on the backrest of their seats to give the impression that they were around somewhere. Thank God it was close to month end when most people worked full days. Not that they didn't wish to do their own errands but they were broke and couldn't afford even a snack outdoors. But today the weather wasn't good and so almost everybody was eager to get home before the downpour. If there was anybody in the building probably it was a crooked pension officer doctoring files or working on one that he had been bribed to do. When he eventually was ready to leave, at the reception, he found the bored guard lazily sprawled on the couch listening to a tiny radio tuned into a station that transmitted poorly organised noise over the crackle of static.

"*Oh, jambo bwana*," the guard said, startled. He didn't expect anybody was still in the building. "Thought with this weather everybody was gone."

"Well, am here," responded Múgo, wondering if the guard would even know if thieves walked right into the building. He was too old to be a night guard and dozed most times.

"Had checked, trust me," said the guard defensively. "We always miss something, don't we?"

"Really?" Múgo was bored. The last thing he wanted to listen to was lies. What concerned him was how to get to the bus stop three streets away without getting drenched. He could call for a taxi but that was Ksh 300, money he couldn't afford. His budget was very tight; so tight that getting wet was the only viable option. After all, he would change into dry clothes when he got home. He reached for the main door and pulled it open. A gush of cold wet draught hit him so hard he gasped and instinctively stepped back, closing the door shut.

"I could lend you my umbrella since I'll be here all night," offered the guard.

"What if it rains in the morning, you normally leave before I come in?"

"I'll sort myself out."

"Yeah?"

"C'mon, take it, I'll be all right. You're a reasonable man without the pride the others have, treat us like dirt." Múgo didn't want to get into workplace politics though the guard's tone was an invitation into a conversation. If the geezer thought he was that good then hey, there was no reason for him to get wet. He took the offered umbrella and dashed out defiantly, his nerves taut with the expectation similar to jumping into a cold bath. He knew the umbrella wasn't exactly an offer. The old geezer always had *harambee* cards for one fundraiser or other. Sometimes it was about an education fund for an orphan somewhere, other times a hospital bill but mostly it was to do with funeral expenses. Múgo never understood western Kenya tribes. Why make such a fuss about dead people? If nobody bought them a suit in life it was no use buying them one in death. However, that was a culture issue and no man had a right to criticise another man's culture – especially about stuff he didn't quite understand. What bothered him though was whether the guard actually surrendered all his collection. Múgo doubted it.

It was quiet outside the treasury building. This was an all business area and remained inactive at night except for some street kids, who lived in the car park opposite the treasury next to the huge skip. Múgo wasn't afraid of them. They all knew him because they had lived there for years and always saw him go to work. However, it wasn't advisable for strangers, especially ladies, to walk that way at odd hours. These kids grew up surrounded by and involved in crime and could do anything when high on adhesive glue and other drugs. Múgo crossed the car park and joined Harambee Avenue towards Moi Avenue.

When he got to Kenya Cinema he crossed Tom Mboya Street, past the Diamond Trust building, towards the Central Bus Station from where he was to pick a matatu to Umoja Estate where he lived. There were lots of people all over, scurrying frantically. Nairobi was always like that when it rained. In a rush to get to the comfort of their homes, everyone, motorists and pedestrians alike, spilled onto the roads clogging traffic in endless jams. The matatu operators then got cheeky and delayed services so they could hike the fares. Wet, cold and late to get home, frustrated Nairobians paid the inflated fares meekly. The matatu crew loved it when it rained. Most of the extra profit was theirs to keep after all. Little of it went to the minibus owners because most of them didn't know or didn't want to know what went on so long as the crew earned their set targets.

Múgo joined the snaking queue at the bus station and bit his teeth in frustration. From the position he joined the queue he figured that he was going to wait for a long time and the guard's umbrella was doing a very poor job of keeping him dry. As he had expected, the matatus were charging double the normal fare. Why were Kenyans so timid? Why did a bunch of thuggish school dropouts push them to the wall without their fighting back? What if everybody refused to pay? But human beings always needed a leader and to be a leader you need to be made of steel because it wasn't guaranteed that people backed you up and you could end up walking home in the rain. He didn't feel particularly heroic today. Besides, like most other commuters, he was concerned about his children and just wanted to go home and be with them. He didn't trust his much younger sister anymore.

She had finally come of age and discovered Jemoo – the name was supposed to be the cool version of James – a dreadlocked freaky matatu tout, apparently the best thing to happen to her. There was nothing he could do about it, at least not now. She was the only one he could have in the house to look after the children without raising suspicion. Any attempt to steer her away from Jemoo had turned into disrespectful outbursts and what he was going through at the moment didn't allow him to have a battle of wills with her. He really missed Wanjikú, his wife. He wondered whether he was insane to let her travel to the UK in search of better prospects. It had been two long years and all attempts of him getting a visa had failed. He had to make one more attempt and if he failed to join her he didn't know what he would do. Probably force her to return which she was so reluctant to do. Didn't she sympathise with the children?

"*Wee kaa square*," barked the scruffy tout when Múgo entered the minibus and sat comfortably, happy to be away from the rain. The minibus sat four people a row but the tout wanted to bring a fifth person to maximise profits. Múgo opened his mouth to protest but realised it was useless. The other passengers had already squeezed themselves obediently to make room. He was going to be a lone protester. A hefty woman was shoved into the limited space with the tout pushing her backside in a rush. This was madness. There was no way the woman was going to fit. When she sat it was simply a battle of might. Múgo, who was next to the window, was squashed breathless against the side.

"Can't travel like this." Múgo finally found a voice after several gasps. "Let me off."

"*Nani huyo mdomo mingi, ukishuka unalipa*. Nobody gets out," shouted the tout, "if you do you pay the full fare."

"You can't treat people like luggage," said Múgo.

"*Kama wewe ni VIP ununue gari yako*, posh people buy their own cars," responded the tout, arrogantly. It was so hard to defeat them alone. By now several of them, mean-looking monsters, some with scary scars all over their faces, were already hovering around in case there was trouble so that they could join in the fight. They hurled abuse saying, "*ati kwa sababu kana tie ya mitumba.*" His wife had sent him the tie and it sure looked foreign but most people bought foreignwear in the second-hand market so whatever looked foreign was considered second hand. He needn't tell them it wasn't *mitumba*, this didn't bother him the least. Frustrated and disgusted with the stench inside, Múgo shut his mouth as more people eager to go home and in disregard of safety were shoved into the already crowded matatu. The windows were misting with a miry concoction of perspiration and humidity. Múgo's stomach churned. Several passengers were hanging on the sliding door, a suicidal venture. They were more bothered about getting home than getting wet. Never mind which home for sometimes accidents happened and some went to terrestrial homes, permanently.

It was an hour and a half later that he alighted from the hell's matatu gasping for fresh air. Thank God for small mercies that Múgo so often took for granted. A journey that normally took twenty minutes had taken forever in a collection of bodies whose owners thought hygiene was an alien hobby. Why did some people smell so rotten? Múgo crossed the road towards Jam City pub that was a block away from his flat. People were revelling inside, gyrating to some fast Congolese tunes played by a live band. He couldn't afford it and not just in finances but also time. The children were priority.

By now, Umoja, which often flooded, was full of lake-like puddles. He meandered his way round where he could and waded through wherever else. His fears were confirmed when he arrived home. Njeri and Kíama his children were alone again. Njeri, the six-year-old firstborn was at the table doing her homework, surrounded by a colourful mess of crayons pencils, and books; close by her side, Kíama flicked through TV channels nursing a cup of milk and a sandwich, no doubt made for him by his caring elder sister. She was a beauty, just like her mother. The round face with big round eyes in it and long curly hair always reminded him of his wife. She was an angel, the girl was. Why would any mother want to stay away from children like these? The children rushed to him and hugged him, clinging to him desperately as if they were afraid he would leave them too.

"You're watery," said Kíama, making a face.

"You're *unwatery*," said Múgo, snuggling his wet face on the boy's dry one.

They were lonely and afraid, left on their own on a rainy evening. Múgo cuddled them reassuringly delighted with the relief on their faces.

"Oh, Daddy," said Kíama, four, a budding little rascal, "Auntie left us alone."

"Don't you worry now, Daddy is home. When did she go?" He said 'when', not 'where'; he had the answer to the latter.

"Soon after I came from school," answered Njeri.

"I see," said Múgo reflectively. "Now you go keep yourselves busy. Njeri, finish your homework, Kíama, choose a channel, I suggest Cartoon Network and stay with it. Papa will fix you proper food."

"I can help you cook," offered Njeri.

"No way, Daddy will be all right."

Múgo entered into the bedroom to change into dry comfortable indoor wear. He stopped a minute to regard his image in the wardrobe mirror, feeling miserable. So much anger welled in him for his sister Dama, short for Damaris. Why did she leave the children alone on an evening like this? It was 9 pm now, a time he preferred the children to be in bed. Njeri woke up early at six to get ready for school and Kíama was too young to be up that late. Whatever demon was controlling Dama was affecting his life too and what was important to him – his children. He had struggled to see Dama through school, afraid she could end up like her village peers – dropping out of school and marrying young. After she did her O levels he took her in, happy that she would help him look after the children when his wife went abroad. An arrangement was made with a neighbour to look after Kíama when Dama attended afternoon classes in ICT. Njeri was already in school so she didn't need much looking after.

Múgo didn't want people to have the impression that he was slaving Dama. Besides, she was better with some qualification if she was ever to be independent. On top of paying for her course, he also covered her expenses and pocket money. She was high maintenance but he didn't mind. She was his kid sister, very beautiful and he wished her well. He had snatched her from the misery of the village and brought her to Nairobi. The transformation was incredible. Already a naturally beautiful girl, she became a stunning city lassie, the talk of the Estate.

This was all well until a local thug loaded with stolen matatu money appeared on the scene. Most touts lived for the day. Their dream went as far as which pub they would 'rave' at and with which girl. The most ambitious strived to become the driver of the newest, most flashy *manyanga* matatu with the heaviest music. Whatever they earned in a day was spent before 3 am the following morning. They earned their money fast and spent it similarly. Women loved them for it. Call it the love for the unpredictable. Probably they craved the crazy adventure, or wanted to milk the money while it lasted or the next girl took over, or their nurturing instincts tragically led them into believing that they could tame these vicious wolves. Unfortunately this bug hit Dama too and

Múgo wasn't sure she attended lectures anymore. He had raised the matter the previous night but it turned out to be like a 'dipping a hand into a hornet's nest' experience.

"So, how's college going?" he had asked, after she had come in at 9 pm smelling of alcohol and sprawled on the sofa, expecting to be scolded. Múgo didn't give her any lashing; he wasn't in the mood. Just two more days and he would know his fate; whether he was going to join his wife or not. Dama would be in Jemoo's safe and caring hands, of course.

"Why don't you first ask me where I was?" she responded defiantly. Múgo suspected she might have been introduced to drugs.

"That I know already, with sweet Jemoo of course, he of the coolest hairdo fame. It's about college that I'm not sure of."

"It's my life, to make or break, besides, not all successful people have college qualifications."

"Like Jemoo I suppose. Hey, it's my life too, I pay for it."

"Want a refund?"

That last statement jabbed at his heart like a thousand screwdrivers. He had squeezed himself, dressing in shabby suits to pay for her course, and what did he get for it? It was thrown right into his face. A cloud passed through his face sending involuntary twitches all over. His eyes narrowed in angst, remembering the things he had denied his children, toys and stuff, just to see Dama through school. He passed a hand through his hair and sighed in exasperation. Even Dama knew she shouldn't have said that but it was too late. She quickly got up and hurried defiantly to her room, banging doors rudely. Múgo sat there for a long time feeling old and used.

Earlier attempts at making Dama see sense had been met with the 'I'm an adult now, it's my life' response. Múgo had even attempted to make his elderly mother intervene but she was no match for the new, city-wise Dama. The only reason he still had her in the house was because he couldn't bring another woman in the house without being suspected of sleeping with her. Employing a houseboy didn't sound very helpful either. It was uncommon here and the few he knew were good at house chores but no good with children. The only options he had were to take the children to his mother, upcountry, or with Mercy, his married sister, and that was a no-no.

Such a longing for his wife clinched him. He missed her so much, her feel, her talk, her laughter, the way she organised the house. She was a true homemaker. He had enjoyed every moment with her, but now he was stuck with a disrespectful sister who thought he was old and senile, missing out on all the fun the world had to offer. In anger, tears welled up in his eyes, remembering the loneliness he found the children in. He opened the wardrobe and stared at his wife's clothes, remembering with nostalgia how she looked in them. Picking one, he sniffed at it lovingly, enjoying her smell that still lingered after all this time. It wasn't going to be much longer before he had her in his arms again. He changed and went to cook for the children.

At 11 pm there was a screech of wheels and an earth-shaking boom of music that lasted for a while outside the gate, no doubt the lovebirds exchanging goodbye kisses. The boom then faded away as the matatu left. That had become the signature announcing Dama's arrival. Múgo had cooked, fed the children and taken them to bed, before sitting to watch English football. Dama fumbled unsteadily with the door lock and came in trying to look as sober as she could. Without saying a word, she slumped into the sofa, staring at Múgo and bracing for a fight. Múgo struggled to remain calm and said nothing. He considered the fact that if he had not come home early, the children could have been alone till 11 pm. What if they had tried to cook for themselves and got burnt or set the house on fire? Why, oh why? What had come over Dama, his sweet younger sister, who could previously have never hurt a fly?

"I'm late." It was a statement, not an expression of remorse.

"I noticed."

"And?"

"And what? I noticed that's all."

Dama snarled and left for her bedroom, leaving her bag on the sofa. A minute later she came rushing and grabbed it possessively. Múgo wondered what it contained. Maybe drugs, maybe beer cans, maybe contraceptives – enough to stock a chemist store – maybe condoms of the spiky variety. She needn't have worried about leaving the bag behind. Múgo didn't want to know its contents. He figured the shock wasn't worth it. One more day and he would know his fate then Dama would have to move in with Jemoo; if he had a home that is or there wasn't some other girl living with him already.

The following day at 2 pm he received the call he was waiting for, the call that was to change the course of his life. Rono, his friend, working at the Haile Selassie Avenue Extelecom – the branch of Kenya Posts and Telecommunication dealing with the country's external telecommunications – wanted to see him urgently. Extelecom was a walking distance from Múgo's office two streets away. Half walking, half running, he arrived there fifteen minutes later, perspiring in the afternoon heat. Rono had been his contact with Chelimo, the Extel personnel boss who was organising a visa for him.

There was a group of Extel employees who had been invited to Malta for a three-month course on telecommunications. Múgo's name had been included in the list – at a fee of course – and yes, he now had a six-month visa to Malta. Rono, the master planner, had introduced him to a cartel of international traffickers who had assured him that they would get him to Britain at Ksh 300,000, inclusive of travel expenses. Trusting his friend Rono, he had taken a loan using his land's title deed as collateral, a thing that could have earned him a curse from his ageing father if he got wind of it. It was a cultural thing with the Kikuyu. The attachment they had with land was incredible; it acquired a sacred dimension, especially among the older generation. That was the major reason they bravely took on the might of the British colonial forces. As for Múgo, precious it was, but it wasn't going to come between him and his dreams. Besides, if he went abroad and struck big he could always buy more land. He was tired of hearing land matters. He never did any farming and images of himself in welly boots pushing wheelbarrows like his old dad gave him nightmares.

The first step in a long, winding climb had been taken and accomplished. He was going to Britain to join his wife, finally. However there was the small matter of his children. Taking them to his mother was the only option now. At least he was sure she would love them and care for them but probably spoil them. She adored her grandchildren. It was going to be very difficult to adjust into the rural countryside lifestyle and worse without him. They had lived two years without their mother and now he was going to leave them for some time. It wasn't easy but it had to be done.

Quickly he left the Extelecom offices in a mad rush back to his office. The Malta group was to leave in the evening the following day and it was only wise that they left together or he was going to answer very hard questions. In his office he picked the few things he valued most, his family's photographs and his documents, and left without telling anybody where he was going. He didn't even leave his jacket on the seat to give the impression that he was still around. It wasn't necessary. Out into the street he looked back at the unimpressive building that had sucked happiness out of him. The only thing that kept coming to his mind were tears of joy the widowed lady had shed earlier that morning when Múgo personally worked her file and saw to it that payment was approved. When the widow finally received the cheque, she came rushing into his office hugging him and crying. She insisted that she would be back with gifts for him, which he didn't doubt; he failed to convince her that gifts wouldn't be necessary. She couldn't believe that he had gone through all that trouble expecting nothing in return. Not after the harrowing experience she had gone through in the last five years. Glad that he had restored faith in humanity into someone's heart, he walked away from the pensions building feeling like one would feel walking away from prison.

# 18

Later in the evening after confirming he was in the Malta trip, Múgo had the uncomfortable moment of explaining to the children that they would have to live with their grandma for some time.

"You'll like it, trust me, lots of playing fields and animals, some you haven't seen before," he went on unconvincingly. Njeri was listening patiently with a 'tell that to the birds' expression. She had heard similar words when her mama left.

"Why are you leaving us?" she asked pleadingly.

"I want to go and get Mama back so we can be family again," he answered, looking at Kíama and knowing Njeri was staring accusingly at him.

"How long will you be away?" she said.

"A month," he lied, "probably a few." The last bit was said with a faltering voice, realising he didn't know either.

"But we don't have to live with Grandma if it's a few months. What about school? We could live with Aunt Dama until you come back," said Njeri pleadingly.

"Aunt Dama will leave you lonely, but Grandma would never do that."

"Oh, Daddy, please stay with us. Write Mummy a letter and tell her to come home. Doesn't she want to visit us?" said Njeri, clinging to him.

"She does want to see you, of course. It's only that it's not very easy because it's a long, long way from here."

Long after winding explanations Njeri resigned herself to her fate and Kíama relaxed in the fantasy of riding on goats' backs. The kids dozed off in his arms for the last time in a long time. He regretted having to leave them and wondered if he would ever have an experience like that again. When he returned they would be a little older and probably they would have grown a little distant emotionally. *A man gotta do what a man gotta do.* Right now he risked losing a wife he loved so much. It was important that he joined her and probably convinced her to come home. He took the kids to bed, tucked them in, and then stood watching their adorable innocent faces before going to bed himself. He had a long day tomorrow so he decided to sleep early. On his way to the bedroom, he instinctively tried Dama's door and was surprised that it wasn't locked. It was usually locked shut to safeguard whatever secrets were inside. She had not come back from wherever but Múgo didn't care anymore. Her time of reckoning was near. She could have all the freedom she wanted now that he was going to be out of her way. On top of the chest of drawers was a picture of Jemoo in all his horrendousness; dreadlocks, unshaven beard, bloodshot eyes, stained teeth and a 'smokable' whatever-it-was in his hand. Fearing a nightmare, Múgo closed the door and went to bed.

Early the following morning he started packing. Soon the lorry he had hired would arrive to take his stuff and furniture to his rural home upcountry. By the time Dama woke up, almost everything had gone into the lorry save for whatever was in her room. Múgo wasn't mean. He thought she might need the bed and the wardrobe to get started with life without him. Those he could gladly give her, and of course the dressing cabinet with its huge mirror for make-up and stuff. She was such a naturally beautiful woman but she hardly left the house without make-up anymore.

Dama staggered into the nearly empty living room battered with a hangover, having been woken by the commotion in the house. She had come in at two in the morning, high as a kite. Múgo was still awake, contemplating the crazy plan his traffickers had of getting him to Britain. He felt sorry for her that she had to learn what life was all about the very hard and horrible way. He also felt sorry for her that she had lost her innocence to Jemoo and wished it were a more decent guy. She surely deserved better.

Dazed, confused and afraid, she dared not ask any questions.

She knew she had been nasty lately but she didn't think her brother would move out without her knowledge. She wished he had tried to kick her out, at least that way she could have pleaded and begged to be allowed to stay but now he was moving out on her. How could she convince him to stay?

All items loaded into the truck, Múgo phoned the landlord and informed him that he had moved out and no longer needed the house. He got the kids into the spacious driver's cabin and left for his upcountry home in Múrang'a, a two-hour journey. Dama sat on the doorstep, lost for words and belief. Nobody told her what the move was all about and nobody said a word. The lorry crew thought she was Múgo's girlfriend and didn't want to interfere in what seemed like a very bad case of domestic fall out. She felt abandoned and unwanted. In a flash it occurred to her just how stupid she had been. Her shame and guilt broke out in floods of tears. It was too late to say sorry.

His aged parents, Kíama senior and Waithera, were shocked to see them arrive unannounced with all their belongings. These new developments were a real surprise. Of course, they were happy to look after the children but hoped it wasn't going to be long. What was this obsession with foreign countries? Their daughter-in-law had better return and look after her family. The old couple didn't care if their children were rich or not. The Múgos had jobs that earned them enough to live on, why the fixation with chasing after shadows?

Múgo had a plane to catch later in the day. Hurriedly he said passionate goodbyes to his children, tactfully avoiding questions about Dama from his mother. Kíama had unhelpful answers though.

"Auntie was crying, didn't want to come with us."

"Crying? Why? Why didn't you come with her?" asked Kíama's grandma.

"She didn't wake up early enough," answered the little boy. "She leaves us alone at night and comes when we sleep and don't wake up early." Waithera looked at Múgo questioningly but Múgo wasn't forthcoming with any answers. The removals crew were waiting for him at the gate. He didn't want them to leave him behind because public transport took longer with all the stops dropping off and picking up passengers. It was 2 pm when they had finished putting everything into his country house next to his parents'. It wasn't necessary to unpack as no one was going to use the house for the next… whatever time span.

It was going to be past 4 pm when he got back to Nairobi and he had a flight to catch at 5.30 pm. Once he arrived in Nairobi he went into Rema Boarding and Lodging on Luthuli Avenue and freshened up in ten minutes flat. He changed into new clothes and left the old ones on the bed. The cleaners could have them. Hurriedly he sprinted to the Ambassedeur bus stop but then realised just how rare the route 34 buses to the airport were. It was 4.30 pm, only an hour before his departure. He took a taxi and told the driver to race to the airport, a thing the cabbie was eager to do. Most customers, worried about the many accidents on Kenyan roads, asked to be driven slowly, what a refreshing difference.

At 4.50 he arrived at the Egypt Air desk to find a furious Rono who had delayed his check-in, to the chagrin of his superiors.

"Jinga Kikuyu, where have you been you fool?" he hissed. "Robbing a bank?" Múgo's Kikuyu tribe was infamous for robberies and alleged love of money. A joke went round that the best way to confirm if a Kikuyu was dead was to drop some coins.

"Jinga Kalenjin, I was running around to see if I could beat your marathon runners." Rono's Kalenjin tribe produced most of Kenya's athletics world record holders.

"Seriously, we nearly left without you. My boss is mad about it."

"Sorry pal, had to take the kids to the countryside."

"Couldn't you let your sister do that?"

"No, she was… never mind. Let's check in then."

Twenty minutes later Múgo shifted this way and that way, looking for the best position on the comfortable seat aboard an Egypt Air Boeing 747 flight A74 to Malta's Valletta Malta International Airport via Cairo. The next major step in the long winding journey had been accomplished.

Eight hours later the huge aircraft landed at Malta International Airport after almost an hour's stopover in Cairo. From Rono, who was widely travelled, he learnt that Malta International Airport was run by Malta International plc, which was a registered company since January 1992. Initially, MIA managed and operated the air terminal but was later responsible for the entire airport. Before 1992, the government's Air Terminal Department was in charge since 1st January 1989 and, before that, by the government's Department of Civil Aviation. The change was definitely for the better with improved services devoid of the incompetence of civil service.

All these details were not of much interest to him. He was in a strange place at night without a clue as to what he was to do next. He hated it when other people took charge of his life. There was nothing he could do about it but wait impatiently for Rono's instructions. Rono led him to the Runway Bistro Restaurant on level 3 and waited for their contact while the rest of the Extelecom staff were picked by their hosts to their hotel. Rono was to join them later. He was a veteran and nobody bothered about him. His boss threw him a suspicious look, wondering if Rono didn't cheat him out of his cut. Probably the rascal charged more than the Ksh 25,000 he claimed Múgo paid him to get a visa. He wasn't wrong but there was no way of finding out. Múgo had paid Rono Ksh 40,000; fifteen thousand was Rono's cut for the Maltese contact. A friend he was but when it came to his trafficking business Rono was a smart operator. He had told Múgo everything, knowing Múgo could not let out the secret to his boss.

A tall and balding man, all muscles and stone, approached their table breaking into a smile. Rono turned and smiled back when he saw him.

"Ello, mon ami," the man said in a heavy French accent.

"Bonjour, Pierre," responded Rono in a heavy Kalenjin accent. "Meet my friend Múgo here."

"Ello, Meukho," said Pierre, regarding Múgo and enthusiastically shaking his hand.

"How're plans?" asked Rono, without wasting time. He believed in business first and whatever else later.

"Fantastique," said Pierre, with a flying kiss for emphasis.

"Very well then, I better leave," Rono said, already standing up. "You'll be in Pierre's good hands," he added when he saw the suspicion in Múgo's eyes.

"Tell 'im, mon ami; Pierre do what he say," said Pierre, patting Rono's back. Rono pulled him aside behind a pillar for a moment of serious hushed exchange – probably about the next 'delivery' job. Múgo didn't see any money change hands whatsoever but these were professionals. They knew their trade well and only they knew how they made payments to each other.

To Múgo's amazement, Rono didn't even come back to say goodbye. He just waved him and left. Múgo couldn't help feeling abandoned. He was now in the hands of a complete stranger. The yearning for a reunion with his wife was all he had at the moment. Pierre came to the table and gestured him to follow. Múgo hoped he would get into some bed soon to rest from the hassles of the previous day and the jet lag.

Out into the car park, the Frenchman led him to a battered old Renault Clio. Trust Frenchmen to be loyal to their own. Through a skill born of experience, tall Pierre fitted in the small cabin though his legs stuck sideways and up towards the dashboard. Múgo thought other drivers could see his knees through the windscreen. Pierre steered the car out of the airport and onto the streets outside, sticking his head out the window slightly above the roof before he somehow squeezed it back into the cabin albeit with a little stoop. By now Múgo felt like he was in vertigo. Jet-lagged and in a strange place at night with a strange fellow, he felt totally disorientated.

"Had good flight, friend?" Pierre asked to break the silence.

"It was all right but I could do with a real bed now." He hadn't slept in the plane, gripped by the uncertainties of the journey ahead. What if the contacts didn't get him through to Britain? He would lose lots of money – a second time. The first time he was to be smuggled through Dubai only to realise he had been conned when he entered the Emirates. Discouraged, he had returned home frustrated and much poorer. His wife had financed his first attempt so when he lost it she was mad with him. Definitely he knew she would go ballistic if she knew how much he had paid for the second attempt. He had told her that a friend was helping him and he was only to pay for the flight. He would reveal everything to her of course when he got to Britain, well, if he got there.

"Bed?" exclaimed Pierre, surprised. "No bed, friend. We leave immediately."

"Where to? But surely… I need some rest."

"Marseille, *mon ami*, we go to France."

"France?"

"*Oui*, my friend, ze best contrie."

"But…" Múgo began to protest then shut up. It was futile.

After what seemed like a run through a maze, they arrived at their destination: the Port of Valletta – Pinto Wharves.

"Zis way," the Frenchman directed, leading the way. "Be'ave *normale*."

Múgo followed without a word to what he now understood was a dockyard. It was 3 am in the morning and freezing. At a distance, he could see rows of boats and ferries floating, some with their lights on, their rays reflecting on the sea like twisted luminous cables. They walked on close to the seaside and entered into an open warehouse near some junked boats that stunk of oil. Somewhere in a hidden corner, Pierre retrieved a box full of smelly fish and told Múgo to put in his light luggage. He had travelled light on Rono's advice. Traffickers hated baggage, apparently. It complicated delicate manoeuvres.

"Why?" asked Múgo, disgusted at the idea of putting his bag into the stinking box.

"Because Pierre said," answered the Frenchman, already on his way out. Through a dark side lane, they criss-crossed a battery of alleys that led them towards some fence next to the shore. Pierre climbed over and had a look, then gestured at Múgo to follow. Clumsily he climbed over, at the same time trying to balance the box with one hand. He fell on the other side with a thud, the box hitting a hard object loudly and spilled part of its contents. Pierre crouched and listened, angry that Múgo had made a noise. Múgo groped for the box and drew it closer to him. He put it back in his luggage and the smelly fish. Up on the ramp, a few men walked in and out of a ferry. One seemed to have heard the box falling and looked their way but then turned away after a few seconds, disinterested. The bright light on the ramp was an advantage. They could see the ramp clearly but those on the ramp couldn't see them. Múgo picked the name *Chevalier de Meditarrenee* written on the side of the ferry.

"When we get up zere you don't say nozing and don't stop even if you're told to," whispered Pierre. "Walk right into ze ferri and go down to ze 'ull. If anybody insists just say Pierre and talk your language, you shouldn't understand much English or French, be stupid." Múgo nodded.

They both went up a flight of stairs onto a pavement that led to the ramp, with Pierre majestically walking ahead.

"Hey, Pierre, where have you been?" the men on the ramp exclaimed almost in unison.

"Malta has delicacies, you know," he winked, and swung his waist suggestively, "and I bring some wiz me, my weakness."

"And who is this?" Múgo's heart jumped a beat but he walked on as if he heard nothing.

"*Mon cherie*, wiz dorado fish, my ozer weakness."

"Hey, you!" the one who seemed in charge shouted at Múgo. Múgo walked on as instructed.

"Shut up, Francois, can't a man be allowed a little pleasure?"

"Both stink," stated Francois.

"Only ze fish and when uncooked, ze guy's fantas…" whispered Pierre, pulling Francois aside.

"Aarg, shut up, Pierre," protested Francois, disgusted. "Get your hands off me, I'm not him."

Múgo walked on to the lower car deck and followed arrow directions indicating 'store' at the end of the deck. This was a very low season or the ferry was in a hurry to go back to France judging by the lack of activity on it. On reaching the entrance, he found an open store full of boxes of Italian wines. He was so tired he just sat down on the floor and leaned on the wall, wishing he could just fall asleep. Pierre joined him moments later, followed by a dozen or so men.

"This place stinks," one of them shouted.

"Yeah, it does," echoed the rest.

"Pierre, can't you have them fresh?"

"Zey're fresh."

"What's your stomach made of? Even your Cherie honey here is sickened, he sits on the floor, and he won't be much fun to you, see," another one said, referring to Múgo. Múgo fidgeted with revulsion that they thought he was gay and wanted to protest but then remembered he wasn't supposed to understand much. The less he talked, the less they asked questions. Later they tried to pull him into conversation but he responded in Swahili. They gave up and disappeared to different sections of the ferry knowing Pierre wanted to have time alone with his catch. Pierre took him to a small room at the end of the store where there was a tiny bunk bed hung up to the ceiling with chains.

"I lie," Pierre said, "you can have bed. Rest, *mon ami,* I know you're tired. Don't worry, me no gei."

"You not what?"

"Gei, you know," said Pierre, pointing to his bum with his forefinger. "Gay, me no gay but zem don't know. It works good for what I do for people like you."

"Thanks, Pierre," said Múgo, thoroughly grateful.

He jumped onto the precarious bed wondering if it could hold as the chains creaked with the strain of his weight. As he stretched himself, he felt the thin but firm mattress take his weight gently. His body felt relief almost immediately as he closed his eyes. But then he remembered his hand luggage in the fish box. If he left it in there any longer it could stink forever. He had to get it but there was a small problem. It had never felt so difficult getting out of bed. His body was just not up to it. Reluctantly, he dragged himself off the bed and walked back to the store. The bag stunk like rotten fish. Now he had another problem: where to keep the bag. If he took it with him, he wasn't going to be able to sleep and if he left it somewhere else, he wasn't sure of security. He decided to take it with him and try to persuade his nose to retire for a few hours. Tired and helped by the soft rocking of the moving ferry, Múgo fell asleep as suddenly as an African sunset, though he spared a second or two to think about his children, haunted by their miserable tearful faces as he left them. If this worked he hoped to make enough money quickly or alternatively convince his wife that they should go back home. To be a family again with wife and kids together would make him a very happy man.

It was early morning four hours later that the Chevalier ferry docked at Port Autonome Marseille. Pierre's strong hands shaking his shoulder woke Múgo up. He opened his eyes and tried to make sense of his whereabouts. The smell of fish on his bag was overwhelming, the last thing he wanted to experience first thing in the morning.

"Ello, 'ad good sleep my friend?" saluted Pierre exuberantly. Múgo nodded, stretching himself and yawning like a hippo.

"We're in Marseille, my friend."

"Oh, what's the time?"

"6 am local time, we've gained some time."

"I see."

"See what? You're still dreaming? Up, up we go."

Múgo jumped from the high bunk and fetched his bag. He could not change into clean clothes because they stunk like a skunk. He retrieved the ones he wore the previous day from under the mattress, where he had spread them to straighten them, a clever move indeed learnt in boarding high school where they had no iron. He wondered what he would do with his bag now that he couldn't use it anymore without making other people's stomachs run. As soon as he got to town he would buy a new bag and new clothes. He was disappointed that he would have to throw away a few African dresses he had bought his wife. But then he had an idea; he could wrap them tightly in several plastic bags and get rid of his bag.

At the Port of Marseille Immigration, Pierre and Múgo waited in the fast-moving queue. Pierre had produced a passport with a picture of a black guy who looked nothing like Múgo but for colour.

"But anyone can tell this isn't me," Múgo protested.

"Do what Pierre say. Zese guys can't tell you apart even if you had no nose."

Whatever that meant Múgo went with it, scared to bits that someone would find out. The passport belonged to a black French guy, complete with all the stampings of previous travel. When they got to the desk, Pierre engaged Múgo in a passionate talk in Arabic; clearly, he spoke a little of the language. Never mind that Múgo didn't understand a word of it, all he was supposed to do was smile and nod and throw in an interjection here and there. Still talking, disregarding the immigration official's greetings, Pierre handed his passport and asked Múgo for the fake one and gave it to the official, then carried on talking like nothing was going on. The official knew Pierre as the passionate Arabic-speaking Frenchman who worked for the SNMC ferries, ever engrossed in fiery discussions. Mechanically he stamped the passports and handed them back, not wishing to interrupt the serious discussion going on with the other man who obviously, he thought, was Pierre's colleague.

"*Merci*," said Pierre, in between a volley of Arabic. Múgo gestured his '*merci*' by nodding to the official and, following Pierre, muttering what he hoped sounded like Arabic words. They joined the throng of human traffic in the morning rush to and from ferries and cruises and walked out into the glory of Marseille in the morning. It was amazing that just the previous day, these were exotic places he only imagined of in his fantasies. Now he was here and in the thick of action, an illegal in the hands of strangers. If only circumstances were different, he wished he had an opportunity of touring these places, relaxed and not looking behind his back. This part of the old Marseille, or 'Panier' as Pierre had told him, had magic of its own if you lived here long enough to appreciate it. The port, the cliff road high above the sea, the wild inlets plunging into the deep blue water for twenty kilometres to Cassis, this was the Marseilles of the tourist guide. But there was the other bit, the commercial port, the airport, which added colour to the mosaic of a city rich in culture and life – the French way. Múgo would have wished to have a taste of all these, maybe he would return some day when the cloud over his life lifted.

Pierre waved a Citroen taxi outside the port after they bought a new bag and chucked the smelly one. He told the cabbie to drive to Marseille Airport. There was no rest for Múgo, though he didn't particularly mind. The sleep in the ferry had been relaxing enough, well, just. The third big step towards his dream had been accomplished. Courage, faith, trust, confidence… the positives began to take root in his psyche. So far things had worked well. There was one more, probably two bridges to cross and he would hold his wife in his hands. Will she be pleased, no excited, to see him? What if she had changed, met someone else or… nooooo! He wasn't even going there. Some thoughts were better buried, no, cremated and the ashes thrown down the Niagara Falls.

At the airport, Pierre took Múgo to a pay bathroom where he freshened up and wrapped his stinking new clothes with plastic bags after spraying deodorant on them. He changed into brand-new trousers and a shirt that Pierre had helped him purchase at a stall outside the port. Pierre was guilty that he had involved him in his dorado obsession. Oh, the power of water! Múgo felt so refreshed, as if he had just had a massage session. He came out to find Pierre absorbed in a football match that was playing on the screen high above the huge hall that was thronging with travellers. Marseille Airport is the third French airport out, excluding Paris, for passenger traffic and second for cargo traffic. It also boasts a worldwide network for passenger traffic with North Africa and Corsica.

"*Appy* now friend?" asked Pierre, regarding Múgo's new outfit.

"Never happier, *merci*."

"Never? No."

"I mean I'm very happy, fresh and all."

"Okay friend, it's been good doing business wiz you," said

Pierre. "Use zat passport, ze one you used at ze ferry port, to fly to London. Here's your ticket." He fished a crumpled air ticket from his jacket pocket and gave it to Múgo. It was a two-way Marseille-Heathrow-Marseille ticket. Keep it safe, someone will use it to travel back here."

"And who'll that be?"

"Don't worry; someone will get it from you."

"How will I recognise him?"

"You don't have to, friend; he will recognise you, now I have to go. Take care, friend, and be'ave *normale*. You'll be all right; your flight departs in twenty minutes."

Múgo was alone now. He was in charge of himself again but it freaked him out. He wasn't a criminal and the thought of doing illegal stuff made him break into a sweat. He had never thought it necessary to go illegal but when the wife you really love goes abroad and can't just return and when Europeans get stingy with visas then that was a different matter. His wife didn't think it was the wisest thing to visit Kenya and use all her savings. It was better to work for some time, save as much as she could, then return for good, probably to open a business. It had been two years now and that was a long time to have your wife away. She could have returned earlier or visited if Múgo had not lost lots of money, her money, to conmen in his first illegal attempt to travel to Britain. He was to blame. Wanjikú felt there wasn't much to return to. She couldn't get her job back and Múgo's salary wasn't enough to provide for the family.

Múgo examined the passport that Pierre had given him. It belonged to a Didier Pemba, definitely someone with African roots, well, if he was real. It could have been a wild name matched with a random photograph or a genuine identity with a random photo to match or actually genuine and belonging to someone who got a cut in the deal. As far as he was concerned, it looked as genuine as they come. Anything else was just detail. He didn't want to know, so long as it got him to Britain, to his wife. Now thinking of her he strode to a payphone and dialled her number.

"Hi, love."

"Oh, hi, honey."

"Been wondering, what's that dish you always promised to make me but never got round to it?"

"What's this dish nonsense, have missed you like crazy and all you go on about is dishes! Can't even tell me you've missed me?"

"Of course, you know I miss you like mad and I've literally been trying to swim the seas to get to you."

"How're the kids?"

"All right."

"You don't sound confident about that. Please tell me my babies are fine."

"Yours?"

"Oh, shut up."

"I was serious about the dish though, could you fix it tonight?"

"What're you rumbling on about?"

"I'm in France…" Múgo paused to let Wanjikú finish screaming on the other end, "arriving at Heathrow on the 14.25 BA flight from Marseille."

"Oh my God, finally!" She screamed again. "France? What the hell are you doing there?"

"Long story but yes, hun, finally."

"The dish," she said cheekily, "will be on the menu. You won't be disappointed."

He went to the BA check-in desk and joined the queue. He couldn't help recounting how incredible his travel so far had been. It occurred to him that many other people in the same queue might have enough of their strange stories to tell; some serious criminals, others probably couldn't remember their original identity. Some were perhaps running from their wives while others were returning to them, bruised and impoverished by the mistress. Whatever stories each had, it expressed what a fake world we lived in. Looks were truly deceptive.

He gave his passport at the desk. It was checked with a mere glance at the previous stamp that had been done at the port. Thanks to those who couldn't tell one black person from another, there wasn't even a hint of suspicion. He walked on majestically with wishes of 'bon voyage' from the BA girl at the desk ringing in his ears. It was better than the Commodore's music, his favourite. He confidently entered the boarding lounge and onto the BA Airbus A340 for his flight to London, finally.

The reunion with his wife at Heathrow Airport was, in a word, dramatic. The hugging, the kissing, the tears and the unmistakable joy left all those around impressed that love still blossoms in a world of hurt and mistrust. The passionate moment was, however, interrupted by a tap on Múgo's shoulder. He spun round, more astonished that anyone was so callous as to interrupt a moment like that rather than being afraid that it was an immigration matter. It was a total stranger, a black guy, so dark, just about the darkest Múgo had ever seen.

"A moment, sir," said a stranger, stretching his hand for a handshake. He then pulled Múgo aside without letting go of his hand. "Won't be a second ma'am," the stranger added politely when he saw the shock on Wanjikú's face.

"What do you…?" Múgo began, but he was cut short.

"The papers, sir." It was a booming voice, commanding but hidden with a tinge of polite language. Múgo understood and smiled.

"Oh that, a minute s…" he said, but choked on the 'sir' bit. He wasn't used to calling just anyone sir. He dug into his bag and retrieved the passport and the ticket that was now a little more straightened out. He had put it inside a *Highlife* magazine.

"Here you go." He handed the stranger the passport and ticket. "Pierre sends his love." The bloke didn't respond to that. He wore a blank face that said nothing. It was as if he didn't know who Pierre was or that probably he didn't. You never know with dodgy cartels. The system was so complicated and obscure it was possible not to know who was who in the business.

"Thanks, sir, *au revoir*," he said and left, nodding briefly at Wanjikú who stood a distance away, confused. Múgo waved him goodbye and quickly returned to his wife.

"What was that all about?" she inquired.

"Let's go."

"Shouldn't a woman know?"

"Business, just business."

"Yeah, one minute in Britain and you're already in business?" she said sarcastically.

"Oh, honey, stop that. You'll know of course, later, the dish now."

Outside the terminal exit they walked and turned left towards the bus stop where they took a H32 free bus to Hatton Cross and from there a 90 bus to Nestles Avenue, Hayes. Múgo was the latest addition to the Múhíríga.

# 19

When Fuso walked into the Múhíríga's Nestles Avenue house that night he was surprised to find everybody in. The mood was pensive with Ben, who had returned from Belgium a few hours earlier, seated at the dining table, high above everybody like a conceited don chairing a meeting with his subjects. Grace was next to him on a lower chair, with an air of an assistant don. Abdi sat on the floor, leaning on the TV cabinet, his long legs stretching under the table. Across the room were the Kamaus, cuddled together on a sofa, trying not to look bored; the Múgos stood close to the door, hating the telling off by Ben. Being the oldest, they felt they should have more say than Ben allowed them.

Immediately, Fuso knew he had chosen the wrong time to visit. It was difficult to find everybody in the house at the same time because they all worked different places and shifts. If it were not for Ben's insistence that Fuso stay, he wanted to excuse himself and leave immediately but Ben said there was nothing to hide. Ben was his friend of many years and for some reason Ben always pretended there were no secrets between them, though Fuso knew so little of Ben's other side. Fuso had met Kamau and Njambi in Kenya and he coped well with the rest of the Múhíríga, especially Abdi who was so welcoming. It was as if Fuso was an external member of the Múhíríga and they trusted him not telling on their status though they envied him for being in uni and having his immigration papers in order.

Fuso's friendship with Ben stretched way back, a long time ago, when they were teenagers and found themselves in the unfortunate position of being interested in the same girl-angel, Múmbi.

She was born Rose Múmbi, an angel, the last born of Mr Bethuel and Siphirah Gicheru. She was a gorgeous being, a gentle, comely beauty that made folks rush to the verdict that some real angels lived among mortals. One had no choice but to love her. Her skin was ripe *kambara* banana skin, like she was mixed race, her eyes a luminescent African sunset, between brown and a glowing flame. She had these long dark eyelashes that contrasted well with her skin and which coiled upwards and downwards like a doll's. When she blinked, it was a slow, lazy, gracious converging of the eyelids, which then consulted a while before agreeing to let the eye see again. People held her, neighbours cuddled her and women in public places reached for her cheeks and tickled her to endless smiles. She always smiled back, happy and radiant.

Gíturú village fussed over her and even Kangarí, the nearest big market, heard about her. The friendly June weather consented. The casual farm workers who picked her father's tea wanted to have a glance of her before they went down to the sprawling green carpet of tea bushes. Gícherú's homestead was on top of a hill from where there was breathtakingly beautiful scenery. Across to the north was Ngúrweiní ridge, to the south was Ndakainí, where a coiling deep valley immediately after the huge dam formed a spiralling fog in the morning, giving it a sacred tinge. To the west, not too far away, was the Aberdare Mountain Range that overlooked the Great Rift Valley. Nothing was like watching the evergreen tea estates on a clear morning with the mountain, grey and towering in the background. Next to Gícherú's farm ran the main road to Gatanga and Thika towns. People admired his estate. It was well tended, the tea bushes so well trimmed. From a distance, the tea bushes gave the illusion of a well-mowed golf course. This is where Múmbi grew up.

To her parent's relief, she grew up well. Little of the much fussy adoration she received got into her head. She was obedient, minded her own little affairs like an adult and was always ready to help in whatever was required of her. Her three sisters and one brother had left home and started their own families; save for one, her immediate elder sister who was in a boarding teachers' college. There was such a big age difference between her and her bigger sister. Múmbi had been born almost as an afterthought or an accident if not an incident of her parents' rejuvenated spark in old age. The end-of-year rates for tea bonus payment had been high when she was conceived. Gícherú had pocketed close to a million of the crispiest notes. You can't rule out well-fed wallets boosting amorous instincts. The product of this re-found vitality readily did much of the housekeeping when she got a little bigger and did a marvellous job of it. She couldn't let her now ageing mum break her back cleaning after her. She kept everything tidy, the house well organised, her clothes always well pressed. Her home's neatness was the talk of Gíturú village, a place relatively tolerant of grime, and her fame extended beyond to Ndakainí, Gíthumu and Gatiainí.

She went through her elementary education at the local village school, Gíturú Primary School. Her sisters tried hard to take her to an elite private boarding school but she refused. She didn't want to leave her parents behind. In her adult-like reasoning, she felt they needed her, arguing that she was born late to keep them company and look after them; this wasn't entirely untrue. Her sisters were not impressed. The village was not the best place for their angel sister to grow up. In their eyes it was so remote, primitive even. They feared she might pick the villagers' dreamless, stoic and tragic approach to life. True, they too grew up here but now all well-educated and successful, they had realised what a handicap such a background could be. Unfortunately their little angel had a mind of her own. Perfect and gentle as she was, there was no way of making her do something her mind was set against. She put her foot down. It was the village for her till she went to secondary school.

Like all the other children, she stuck the place out. Well, at least she had shoes and nice leather bags and designer school uniform but lived the dull life like everyone else. The better wear didn't make her look down upon other kids. She wasn't that kind of person. Everyone seemed to accept that she was special. She was made a prefect from day one of her school life, an automatic leader of whichever group she joined – from discussions to play to Sunday school groups saying choral verses. She was very active in church. Every Sunday she arrived early to help clean the pews at the African Christian Church Gíturú where she worshipped. Service was her second nature. She had a strong faith in God.

To her the church wasn't just a social gathering; it wasn't just something of a culture, like most people took it. It was here that she felt most peaceful. Her spirit quietened, she could whisper exultations to God. She felt Him all around her and in her heart too. She was a passionate and intense *Jesusite.* Flowing in the spirit she could sense people who were hurting. She could walk up to them and give them a word of encouragement. For that reason therefore, folk also feared her. When she looked unblinkingly at them with those blazing, innocent eyes they felt naked before her. It was as if she saw right through them. It was hilarious how folks who indulged in sin the previous night, frantically devised ways of keeping out of her way as much as they could. *God bless you sister* they shouted, rushing out to never-appointments that were suddenly remembered.

The rains came and the dry spell followed, reducing the loose tea-zone ericaceous soil to fine powder. Tea was picked and the bushes pruned to ugly dark stumps that, behold, sprouted all over again with re-awakened vigour and green freshness. The seasons rolled with a conveyer belt sequence, complete with some unusual breaks of unexpected showers and dry spells as if the conveyer got stuck somewhere. Múmbi swam in and out of each of these seasons, totally immersed in the activities of the village, a country girl, if only a little exposed, courtesy of holiday visits she made to her siblings in Nairobi.

She was soon to sit her Kenya Certificate of Primary Education examinations that were to determine which secondary school she would join. In her childlike innocence she wrote a letter to Jesus. She felt Him that close, like a friend she always had a chat with. She kept the letter under her pillow from where it was retrieved at bedtime for a re-read and reference. She imagined Jesus was reading it too, over her shoulder, like those Western dads she had seen in movies, when she visited her sisters. She liked the way they read bedtime stories to their children.

*Dear Jesus,*

*Thank you Lord for creating me and loving me. Thank you also because you've always been gracious to me and answered my prayers. You have taught me how to trust in you, I've seen your faithfulness. Now please, Jesus, I've a request to make. I'm about to sit for my exams. Lord I need your help. I really need you now more than ever. Please give me a good memory when I'll be writing the exam. I know the little things I've done for you haven't been in vain and you will remember me like your promises say. Help me pass my exams and I'll always love and obey you.*

*Your loving daughter,*
*Múmbi*

Like the good Lord He is, Jesus didn't disappoint her. When the results were out, she led her class. She had 68 points out of 72, a remarkable achievement that had not been attained in the school for many years, less so by a girl. Mr Múthengi, the headteacher, was exhilarated. He basked in her glory, insisting his sound leadership produced winners. Never mind she was the only one who joined a National school that year. She was admitted at Loreto Convent Girls' High School in Limuru for her secondary education.

Within two terms in secondary school, adolescence hormones ambushed, colonised and raged wild within her. When she returned for August holidays she caused an emotional uproar. Men were scandalously tantalised. She had grown tall, become elegant, a rose in full bloom. The clothes she used to wear now felt uncomfortable. The curves of her body threatened to burst them. Her waist had narrowed; her bum bulged generously in that full, peculiar African curve. She felt strange when she walked. Her now unfamiliar hips swung this way and that way, not unlike those of a healthy deer. Her bust felt big and sensitive when clothes rubbed on her and the cleavage formed a cascading 'V' as if giving the impression of an arrow pointing to a sign reading 'touch here'. Most discomforting was the drooling, shameless stares she was receiving from men, including much older ones, like whimpering, hungry puppies watching their master eat meat. *Oh God, what's happened to me!* She resolved to stay at home as much as she could.

Word moves fast. The talk of this extremely gorgeous young lady reached the ears of the entire hormone-charged troops of teenage boys with their amateur tactics of wooing girls. The dirty old men too heard about her. Specifically so Bwana Dawa, a wealthy pharmaceutical tycoon from Mairí who was known all over for his deflowering of young girls, some underage, but nobody had the stomach to complain. Such men were the law here. The authorities were aware but all were at his beck and call. 'There was need for the 'real men' to make way for the weak boys,' Dawa revoltingly unashamed would say.

It was not surprising then when his gleaming maroon Mercedes Benz 500 SEL was seen making rounds in Gíturú. His scouts had certainly told him about Múmbi. Strategic plotting thus made it possible that he appeared as the beautiful young lady was on her way home from church one Sunday during an August holiday. The sparkling huge car rolled lazily and stopped beside her.

"Hello, young lady," Dawa saluted, grinning lustfully. Múmbi wanted to faint. She knew this was going to happen when she saw the famous car approach but now she didn't know how to react. She felt vulnerable when her friend Múrugi jumped over the fence and ran down the nearest footpath, *so much for friends in need.* It was a scandal even to be seen near the contaminating man.

"Hello," she responded smugly, trying to catch her breath.

"You want a lift?" Dawa asked. He didn't wait for an answer. "Beautiful young ladies like you need a treat. C'mon, will drive you home."

"Got strong legs, I'm okay walking," she said, biting her lower lip, afraid and angry. She couldn't quite tell what the monster could do.

"Yeah, can see them. Oh c'mon, can I take you to some fun place, huh? Somewhere you could show me all the leg you got…

you know… can buy you what you want. You know who I am… money isn't a problem. C'mon, show me what you've got for Uncle Dawa."

Múmbi got mad. The old fool disgusted her. She wanted to scream or throw something at him. "I have got nothing for an old fool like you," she screamed at him. "Oh, and about a lift, please take that ramshackle to a scrapyard, the one I love has so much he wouldn't ride anything as lowly as that."

"And who might that be?" Dawa asked sarcastically. They always played hard to get initially but he always got his way finally.

"You really wanna know him?" growled Múmbi in righteous anger. Dawa was thrilled. She was a bomb. He imagined that sweet growl in private with him and felt hot blood rush all over him. Her pretty face stern in naïve indignation excited him. He now felt he needed her. Oh, she was something all right – the real thing.

"Yea, I wanna know the lucky guy. I'm sure he can't take care of a beauty like you better than I," he said earnestly, drunk with the urgency of his lust.

"His name is Jesus," said Múmbi with a seriousness that startled Dawa.

"Who?" he wasn't sure he got that one right.

"Jesus," she said with finality and walked on home. Bwana Dawa was stupefied for a moment, looking for something to counter her reply. Formerly a religious person, he partly recognised the existence of supernatural beings. His policy was that he didn't bother them and they didn't bother him. From the look of things, the girl was downright emphatic and she had invoked the name of Christ. He didn't want Jesus to bother him so he was not going to provoke him. He maddeningly did a three-point turn and sped off in the opposite direction, his big car blasting and scattering gravel in all directions. He was honourably embarrassed, scandalously furious. 'At least I lost to Jesus,' he consoled himself, and bit his teeth so hard he thought he heard something crack.

Next in line from Mr Dawa came the love-struck boys. There was a collective crisis that needed a collective solution.

Consultations were made on how to handle the challenge at hand. Múmbi had become a phenomenon that needed a pooled approach, something to do with that 'united we stand, divided we fall' adage. A consensus was reached; it was better to let the most prospective of the local boys have the chance than all lose out to brats from Kangarí who always snatched the best girls from them, luring them with rides in cars 'borrowed' from their parents. The lucky appointee was Stevoo, the name supposedly a sexier version of Stephen, a bright enough lad if at times guilty of obnoxiously overestimating himself. The lot fell on him because he was the only one within Gíturú who was at Njiiri's, a school just a few ridges away and which was close to Loreto's level. At least his English was a trifle more refined, his tongue past confusing 'R' and 'L', a common difficulty among the Kikuyu – something they called 'shrubbing'. The less mother-tongue influence you had, the trendier you were considered; an asset in the teenage dating scene.

Unfortunately, Stevoo had strong competition. Fuso had met Múmbi when he got in favour with a school prefect who slotted in his name to visit her school for a debating contest. He was in his first year of secondary education, a 'mono' as the first formers were spitefully called. *Monos* were equated with lowlife, vermin and the like. If possible, they were not to be seen and absolutely not to be heard. Like most boys-only or girls-only high schools have 'their' girls or 'their' boys, Mang'u High School had Loreto Convent or 'Reds' as they fondly called them. They were their girls for first loves, to kiss and to hold. They used to do lots of joint stuff including cheering each other's sports teams when they played in interschool leagues. Loreto's red uniforms were a little too bright but there's something about women in red that men find fascinating.

Being the only *mono* on the bus trip to Loreto was a nightmare for Fuso. Seeing so many angelically glowing girls gave him jitters; he was used to the geeky, shabbily dressed village wenches. When he saw Múmbi he wanted to cry out of emotional overload. She was so beautiful, way out of his league, and he knew there was no way he could get to talk to her. The star boys among them got to first pickings and the rest of the lesser lads scrambled for whatever else was left. The only *mono* in the lot was to go last if he was at all lucky. Fuso's chances of talking to a girl therefore, let alone one like Múmbi, were as many as his mum had trying to make him take a daily bath when he was in primary school.

Whoever disputes miracles do happen needs a little faith. Múmbi flatly refused to talk to Jizzy, whatever his name meant, the trendiest most hip Mang'u boy, a son of a cabinet minister. To the disbelief of all the other boys she walked straight to where Fuso was, coiled, miserable and afraid, and asked him for a dance. The boys were scandalised and the girls wanted to know who that cool lad was who caused the popular Jizzy embarrassment. Fuso danced with Múmbi very afraid that he might crush her toes, freaked out by all those eyes on him, petrified of the trip back. It was obvious he was in more trouble than he wanted to think about. The unstated law was clear. A *mono* wasn't supposed to shine and taking the girl the likes of Jizzy were interested in was simply poking fingers into the eyes of the gods of fury.

To his amazement, he learnt that Múmbi was also in form one but somehow she had turned into something of a Miss Loreto within the two terms she had been there. Luckily he also learnt that she was from Gíturú, about twenty miles from his home. He had to see her again during the holidays.

By the time Fuso appeared on the scene, Stevoo, the brainiest lad in the village, had failed to convince Múmbi that he was the thing she had been missing all her life. From then on, Stevoo grudgingly settled for 'good friends'. At least he could visit her at home and once in a while join her for a walk or send a seasonal greeting card. His status had changed immediately to a privileged position, unlike the lowly fellow villagers that were still at the peering level.

With blessings from Stevoo and the envious Gíturú boys – who also helped him conjure a poem in exultation of the object of their feelings – Fuso promised not to let them down. They were comfortable with him, a stranger who was from a different location, making a move on her rather than their sworn neighbouring Kangarí rivals.

The almighty moment came after a day of stalking Múmbi, almost developing cold feet at the last minute when he needed all the courage. Fuso had travelled to Gíturú early that morning, determined to declare his love by whatever means. If he had to kneel or lie prostrate doing it, fair enough, but he had to do it. After much trouble, he tracked her down to Kírúga tea buying centre where she had gone to help her father's workers. When their eyes met, she acknowledged his presence with a nod. Fuso considered that a good start. The girl remembered him all right. How could she forget? That clumsy dance at Loreto and the sweet talk they had afterwards excited both of them so much, especially him who was out of breath most of the time. Never underestimate the power of instant love.

What followed was an endurance test. Fuso couldn't move. He didn't know what he would say if he went to where she was. Besides, she was in a group of adults; older men and women with whom she was deeply in mature conversation. Oh hell! How was he going to tear her away from them? She sure was a mystery; adults treated her like a peer, respected her. While he was still agonising on the best way to approach her, she suddenly cropped up by his side without his notice.

"Hi Fuso."

Startled, he furiously fumbled with the best response to give.

"Sawa, okay… cool, okay, fine. You?" he somehow finally got to say something after a near choking sensation. He extended his hand for a handshake.

"I'm well," she said, still shaking his hand which she held while she studied his face with her blazing stare. "How's Mang'u?"

"Oh, school… fine," he answered, nodding his head vigorously, his mind frantically searching for what to say next. He desperately wanted to take control of the situation, "and Loreto?"

"Mind walking with me home as I tell you all about Loreto?" she asked. With that, she led the way out of the Centre.

"Oh no, not at all, don't mind," Fuso answered, angry with himself for sounding too eager. He followed her out quickly, only turning his head slightly to acknowledge the thumbs-up sign from his support crew, so far so good.

They talked much, mostly about their schools. Fuso didn't have a clue how to steer the talk to the mission at hand. They shared their early days' hilarious experiences of first-form naivety, about their language problems and ridicule for 'shrubbing', having come from rural primary schools like theirs, about the horrible food and new friends. Soon, maybe too soon for him, they found themselves at her gate.

"Am, aah… can't visit today," he stuttered, after she opened the gate. Fuso wasn't sure his mannerisms wouldn't let him down. He feared he might spill tea on the sparkling tablecloths he had been informed about by his spying support crew, or blow off involuntarily. Besides, he felt he might sweat more in a confined place. Fuso was already doing too much of that and his handkerchief was nowhere to be found, though he was certain he had one in his pockets somewhere.

"You must come and have a cup of tea please," she said, "it's your first visit, you know."

"Oh, sorry, I can't. We've formed a discussion group… with… aah, Joe and Maish my pals to handle the tough topics in physics. Had agreed we meet today… so… have to travel back as soon as possible." He was lost for words. His hands motioned this way and that way in meaningless gestures. Regretting what he had just said, a lie, he was sure Múmbi could see right through it.

"Oh, great scientists in the making, huh?" she said, tongue in cheek. "Some other day then, perhaps? Will see you around then, huh? Thanks for visiting and for the company, bye." This she said inside the gate and was about to close it when Fuso made to say something, stopped then stood there confused. He didn't want to leave.

"Yes? Changed your mind about coming in?" she inquired.

"Actually, no, I wanted to tell you something." Fuso's heart pumped hard, the pressure increasing in his head so much the veins showed on his face. One thick one run in the middle of his forehead and a few smaller ones criss-crossed and cascaded to join the ones around his temples.

"What about?" asked Múmbi, trying to put him at ease. He shifted his weight from one foot to the other in general unease. *A man gotta do what a man gotta do.* Now that he had started it there was no retreat without losing face.

"I want us to be friends." He blurted it out and felt relieved immediately.

"But we are friends, Fuso. We've been since the dance."

"Not just friends, special friends."

"We are special friends, Fuso. Why do you think I welcomed you? I didn't ask any of those other guys to escort me?"

"You don't understand. Special as in *special.*" Fuso touched his chest where he thought his fluttering heart largely dwelt. "My sweetheart, my girlfriend, special…"

Múmbi stared at him for a full minute. To him it felt like an uncomfortable eternity. Fuso read pity in her eyes.

"Oh, Fuso, I feel flattered. Let's just try what we have now – good friendship. Trust me; you're not ready for anything else yet."

He felt small. He felt stupid. He actually felt unprepared for a relationship; saw the folly of imagining he could start a relationship in his first form complete with kisses and all with this beauty. How could he handle it? Now it felt inappropriate, foolish even. Fuso wondered if he should give her the poem written in the combined creativity of his local support crew but decided against it. It would look silly now. Feeling it in his trouser pocket, he resolved to destroy it immediately afterwards but unfortunately his uneasy hands accidentally removed the envelope. In his haste to get it back it fell at Múmbi's feet. She picked it up for him only to see her name on it.

"This is for me?" she asked.

"Oh yeah… almost forgot."

"Who from?"

"You'll know when you open," said Fuso, now resigned to fate. When she started to open it he wanted to run. "Please, later," he managed to gasp, and begged to leave but she was already too engrossed reading it she didn't hear him excuse himself.

"What're you reading?" asked a tall guy who materialised from nowhere. He was much taller and slightly older than Fuso. His designerwears instantly made Fuso's neatly washed and pressed clothes look like old haggard sisal bags.

"Oh, some poem my friend here wrote," she said. "This is Fuso, the Mang'u guy I told you about. Fuso, this is Ben my boyfriend, he is in form three at Thika High," she added, and hugged Ben tightly. Fuso wanted to die as Ben stretched his right hand over Múmbi's shoulder to shake his while the other stroked her back. Thika High and Mang'u High were bitter rivals. Now the rivalry was about to turn personal.

"Oh yeah, hi, Fuso," he said. "Múmbi told me about you." Fuso felt like a small boy whose teacher knew he admired the teacher's girlfriend. "You must have come a long way."

"Yeah… I mean not really," he stammered, "had visited relatives of mine at Makomboki and thought of seeing Múmbi just to say hi," he lied.

"I see, so you write poems?"

"No, I mean… well, I try."

"May I see that one?" Ben asked Múmbi.

"Never," she said, and put it away. Fuso honoured her for that, a wise girl indeed. Fuso made a desperate plea to be excused to leave. He walked away sick with embarrassment and defeat, wondering why he had come all that way to bruise his ego. That was his first real heartache. It hurt so badly.

Much later after that heartbreaking experience Fuso visited Robin, one of his friends at Kabete campus of the University of Nairobi, only to realise Ben was Robin's roommate. Now both adults, Ben and Fuso were pursuing undergraduate studies with dreams of making it in life. Fuso, having gotten over his first heartache experience, struck a rapport with Ben that matured to true friendship. He had gotten over Múmbi, though she was still the most gorgeous woman he knew and she got better as she developed into a young, mature woman. Múmbi and Ben were still together, even toying with the idea of marriage and suggesting names they would want for their children. If they had survived this long then this relationship was for real. Grudgingly, Fuso admitted Ben was probably the man for her if only he could slow a little on the bottle. Admittedly he was smart too, smarter than Fuso by far and he was about to graduate whereas Fuso still had two more years to try and keep his eyes open in lecture theatres.

# 20

There was no bad blood between Fuso and Ben over Múmbi, although Fuso hated what Ben had done to her when she arrived in the UK. It was such a waste; spoiled Fuso's chances and he couldn't take her now. It didn't feel right for him although when he thought of her his principles wobbled precariously; she was so beautiful. However, there was too much baggage in the way, furthermore – bastard or not – Fuso had much respect for Ben. He liked Ben's determination and the way he was fearless in chasing his dreams though he had changed so much after graduating. Ben's methods were questionable. Ben respected Fuso's stand to run his life in the light. The Múhíríga, too, respected Fuso's stand to stay legal and wished they were in his position. He had emphatically turned down a request to let Dan and Kamau use his papers and also categorically refused to allow Ben use his bank account for his deals. Ben respected Fuso for that. He knew he could never get him into his dubious business.

"I go away for a few days and you won't give my *wife* a moment's peace," Ben said, putting emphasis on the wife bit. All in the room rolled their eyes and even Grace herself adjusted her position on the chair to cover her fidgeting. She didn't know they were married.

"What have we done now?" It was Múgo. Ben looked at him then at Múgo's wife Wanjikú and told the latter just how much trouble her getting into the bathroom before Grace had caused that morning. Grace had picked a speeding ticket, scraped somebody's car in her rush to get to work, arrived late and received a telling off from her superior and, because of that encounter, she was now listed for a transfer to a hospital outside London.

"This has to stop," said Ben, "it's the only civilised way. You eat what you've bought from the fridge, stick to your bathroom time and you..." He pointed at the Kamaus.

"What?" said Jane on the defensive.

"You keep that rusty contraption out of the driveway."

"Yeah? Contraption?" Kamau loved his rickety Rover Metro and hated anyone who spoke ill of it. "Well, your *Ferrari* is supposed to be parked in the garage, at least that's what your insurance thinks."

"I mean it, Kamau. This isn't about what you drive, it's about where you park. I don't care if you park in the driveway yourself but just don't block anyone in. I never do when I find you in the driveway."

"Okay, point taken but still my car is a sensible stable runabout."

"Without the gusto of a Celica, of course," Ben stated.

"Oh shut up, it's only an old Japanese motor," retorted Kamau.

"Will you two go argue about cars outside, I always say walking is healthier," said Abdi, who could traverse London and back on foot any day. "Fuso is here and he shouldn't be drawn into our domestic squabbles. Let's give our guest some attention, pizza anyone?"

That was Abdi, ever generous, ever an angel. He was such a contradiction coming from a warlike lot that were his people. He was born in Garissa, a town close to the Kenya–Somalia border. The Somali people were separated when the colonial powers drew borders. The dry semi-arid region drew little attention from the Kenyan government and crossing the border was no big deal, you just walked right through it. Besides, it was better to let the people who had everything in common with their cross-border neighbours interact. Many had relatives across the border. Most times they didn't really feel they belonged to separate countries. This helped when war broke out in Somalia; many Somalis simply escaped to live with their Kenyan relatives. The Somali warlords fought for control of whichever region or parts of town they thought lucrative. They offered security for hire and controlled trade in their region, the most profitable ones being the Port at Kismayu and the airports. To move from one part of the city to the other you had to pay a fee to the militia group controlling that area. It was crazy but that is the way of Somalia, a nation of almost entirely one tribe.

Other African nations have tribal tensions but, lacking the tribal excuse, the Somalis took it a notch lower to clans and allegiance to war lords, tearing at each other with fatal outcomes. One could buy almost any type of gun in Somalia. You could buy an Uzi or a bazooka in the open-air markets. Guns sometimes were more available than a good hotel where you could buy a decent meal.

The Americans had tried to sort them out but to them America and Satan were bedfellows. It appears that they are hopelessly allergic to the stars and stripes. That probably explains why America underwent a gnawing humiliation with their botched intervention 'Black Hawk Down'. Of course, Americans were embarrassed. Many American soldiers were massacred here in a fire fight and their bodies dragged around the streets. The inhuman act prompted the US congress to lose its stomach for humanitarian intervention. What they didn't know was that many here hold crazy principles about honour and stuff. To settle scores, vendettas go on and on in a cycle of revenge and violence. Isn't it senseless? Not in their perspective. To them that is how you hold on to your honour. The Somali therefore didn't need Americans to settle their scores for them.

Abdi grew up in both Kenya and Somalia. He tasted the conflicts when he frequently sneaked to Somalia to visit his cousins, war or no war, despite the beatings he received from his fiery dad. He walked right past the militia unbothered. An unusual creature Abdi was. He had no fear, had no care in the world. Saying he lived by the day was too ambitious, the guy lived by the hour. All that bothered him when he walked through the war-torn country was why man was so senseless he couldn't live peacefully with his fellow human beings.

On his twentieth birthday, he hopped onto a lorry that was

transporting cattle to Nairobi. He wanted to see the big city that he always heard about but never got to see. His father would kill him if he returned but that was another day, he would worry when it came. It was important that he stayed around and helped his dad with the camels and goats but then the old man would never let him travel anywhere now that his older brother had travelled to Europe. The old man could not stand not having a son around to fight family and clan battles if need arose. At Nairobi he was employed by a fellow Somali at Eastleigh Estate to sell *miraa,* which he quickly became an addict of, though he hated the green murk it left around his mouth. Unable to cope with the fast life in Nairobi, he travelled to the border town of Namanga where there were many Somali refugees living in the Kenya–Tanzania border town. This is where he got the desire to travel abroad like his elder brother Hassan.

Most refugees were easily allowed to travel to Europe now that the world knew Somalia was up in smoke. Many Kenyan Somalis took the advantage. There was no knowing who was Kenyan Somali and who wasn't, they were one people and helped each other acquire papers from each of the two countries as need be. Abdi wrote a letter to Hassan his older brother in Denmark and let him know that he wanted to join him. Hassan sent him money to buy a Somalia passport from sleuth fixers and brokers that he used to travel to Dubai. He couldn't get a Danish visa so, like many other Somalis, his journey to glory land had to be taken in phases, sometimes taking years. His brother's wife was still held up in Sweden, after two years trying to get refugee status, and their two children were in Holland with an uncle who had succeeded in getting his status approved. When his brother's family was ever to live together remained an illusion; a very sad situation indeed. Hassan's children lived desperately longing to have their daddy with them.

In Dubai, Abdi got a job as a spanner boy, so to say, in a business that dealt in stolen second-hand Japanese cars. Most of the work was to change the right-hand drive cars to left-hand drive for the Central and West African market. The change was shoddily done, overlooking all safety and technical considerations. Abdi hoped the cars didn't kill anyone but he couldn't guarantee that. He prayed to Allah every day asking him to forgive him and forgive the secretive powerful Chekov, the Russian owner of the business. The business' name was El-Majid Autos to give it an Arabic front, complete with Arab managers who operated like the owners. Abdi humorously called the business El-Majidsky.

After Abdi had been one year in Dubai, the Danish authorities approved his brother's refugee status. This was music to Abdi. Hassan sent him his passport, which he used to travel to Copenhagen. His music soon turned to noise when he became stressed with the unbearable language barrier. He had just never appreciated how sweet understanding what people said and being understood was. There was no way he could live like that. With his brother's papers he travelled to London and posted the passport back to him without explaining why he had to leave.

In London he took buses at random, finally ending up in Northolt. He didn't know anyone here but that was no problem. Little matters like worrying where to sleep didn't bother him. He had survived in the jungle and war-torn Somalia sleeping rough, lulled to sleep by the whine of passing bullets and gunfire; he could just as well survive in modern and peaceful London. There were people around all the time, the town was well lit and it never really went to sleep; besides, no one was trying to shoot anybody else.

When his money ran out he could no longer afford those ten-pounds bed and breakfasts that were only slightly more than rat holes and took to sleeping in Rectory Park on Ruislip Road. It was so quiet and peaceful there and so long as he had collected enough reject *miraa* from the vending kiosks in Southall to chew all night, sleeping in the cold at night couldn't kill him; it wasn't winter yet. Soon he realised he could sleep inside Northolt train station which was warmer. This became his home.

During the day he visited Southall, which was like Mogadishu or Nairobi's Eastleigh Estate to him, there were so many Somalis. The shop owners gave him chores and errands for pay, Abdi having refused their offers for donations. He cleaned and mopped and did lots of lifting loads and running about, then retired to the train station for the night. Few people knew where he lived, having refused to divulge that information. It bothered him when people felt sorry for him and loved it when he lived his life his way.

It was in the course of his shop-to-shop errands that he bumped into Ben in a barber's shop. Ben had gone to Southall for a haircut. One of the things that Afro people find difficult to locate when they travel to Europe is a good hairdresser who knows how to do their curly hair. After Abdi had cleaned the salon and left, the barber told him about Abdi's life. Ben got interested. He liked a man who stood on his own feet despite what everybody else thought. He liked the fact that Abdi never took donations or wanted anyone to feel sorry for him. He was his own man, the captain of his life, regardless of sleeping rough. A few days later, Ben strolled into the barber's shop again and met Abdi. He skilfully engaged him in conversation and slowly won his confidence after many days.

Abdi was free to join him at Nestles Avenue house if he wanted. He could pay whatever he could afford for rent but he didn't have to until he found a proper job. Ben had guaranteed him a job and refugee papers. The only condition Ben put on him was to quit chewing those disgusting *miraa* leaves Somalis seemed to consider sacred. The greenish murk they left at the edge of the mouth was revolting; Ben couldn't stand it. Abdi liked the idea, sort of. Giving up the disgusting twigs wasn't going to be easy but he had been trying to give it up for a long time. Maybe this was the time, it had messed his teeth so badly and he had begun to believe what people said about the weed messing the libido too. He had little sexual drive, only had a passing interest in having a woman though he found almost all of them gorgeous and delicate and needing his help. Abdi was also persuaded by the fact that Ben wasn't a Somali. He so much disliked the squabbles, fights and unnecessary arguments over small issues among his people, finding living with them stressful.

There was no way Abdi could escape Ben's smooth talk though actually Ben wasn't up to any tricks. He just liked the live-by-the-minute attitude and a man who kept his pride, even when he lived in a tube station. Abdi offered to do all house cleaning to make up for whatever balance he couldn't afford on rent but Ben would have none of it. Abdi joined Ben and the Múhíríga in Nestles Avenue but still cleaned after them to Ben's despair until Ben got him papers and he got a job that could afford him rent.

# 21

In the course of Fuso's visit when he bumped into the Múhíríga's meeting, long after Abdi's pizza had been delivered, and quickly devoured by the Múhíríga who were eager to put the tensions of the day behind them, Fuso learnt what had transpired that morning to warrant convening an emergency Múhíríga meeting.

Grace had woken up with a terrible nightmare, sweating and panting. Disorientated, she looked around the room, scared and expecting to find flames and billowing smoke. With relief, she realised it was the alarm on her mobile phone that had gone off and not the fire engine she had dreamt about. She reached for the phone, switched off the alarm and threw the phone to the floor. Slumping back to bed she wondered why they made the damn thing so loud. The clock on the wall read 5 am. She had an early shift today at the hospital.

Reluctantly she dragged herself out of bed, glad that she had no one to compete for the bathroom with at this hour. She was wrong. Just when she was about to leave the bedroom she heard the bathroom door close shut. But that's wrong. Everybody knew how crucial it was for her to get to work on time. Her superior was a hefty, no-nonsense Zimbabwean nurse who took nursing to a different level. She even believed starching your uniform wasn't an option, it was a must. It was Wanjikú, a nurse too, who had beaten her to the bathroom. Apparently she thought she should go to work earlier to sort some paperwork she had left unfinished the previous day.

"Get out of there!" shouted Grace, not caring she could wake the rest of the Múhíríga.

"Won't be a minute," said Wanjikú, knowing she should have let Grace take a shower first but then Grace always took too long tending her coveted long hair.

"Yeah, fifty-nine seconds now!" snarled Grace. She went back to her bedroom to iron her uniform.

Ironing done, she ran downstairs to make herself breakfast. As she went past the sitting room to the kitchen she noticed how much it stunk of stale perspiration. Three souls slept here in a complicated arrangement. In her wild thoughts she suspected Njambi, who slept on the top bunk, joined Dan in the lower one in the cover of darkness but there was no way of finding out. Abdi, the all-time best person and the one who slept on the sofa, would never tell on other people unless what he had to say was positive. Grace stopped briefly, listening to Abdi sprawled on the sofa and snoring softly like a baby. He was so good, an uncomplicated soul and they all loved him.

When she opened the fridge door she was horrified. Her milk, eggs and stuff were gone. Anger welled up in her so much she nearly broke the whole fridge to pieces when she slammed the door with fury.

"Damn!" she screamed. "When'll people get civilised? Whoever used my stuff I want it back immediately."

Initially they used to do combined shopping and cooking. Dan cooked on Monday. He was horrible at it, prompting everybody to find an excuse to give his culinary disasters a miss. Some 'worked late' while others supposedly met friends who invited them to dinner. Grace cooked Tuesdays and Wednesdays, Wednesday being Ben's day, but he was either too busy or away somewhere. Nobody was brave enough to trust him with their stomachs anyway. Njambi's duty was on Thursdays, while the Múgos fed the Múhíríga on Friday and the Kamaus on Saturday. Abdi's day was Sunday when everybody was guaranteed a pizza. But then some people got dodgy with the arrangements. Some failed to cook on their days while others obviously took advantage, always hanging around the fridge to have a bite of this and a sip of that. Food and drinks ran out quickly, overshooting reasonable budgets. The split was inevitable. Now everybody did their own shopping but nicking other peoples' foodstuffs was rampant; some even thought it was funny, something of a practical joke. It wasn't to Grace. Not in a morning like this when she was at risk of running late and getting a telling off by an unsmiling big Zimbabwean nurse.

Seething with rage, she went back upstairs and knocked on the bathroom door. "Get out!" she shouted.

"A minute," responded Wanjikú.

"A minute," she sneered back quietly, hating the woman on the inside. *A minute.* That annoyed Grace so much she rudely kicked the door with her foot, so hard her foot hurt. Just how long was a minute? Her leg hurting, she limped back into her bedroom wishing Ben was there with her. She felt like crying and could have done with a cuddle but Ben was away on another make-it-big trip. He had called from Belgium. *Belgium! What the hell was he doing there?* He hadn't even told her he was to go to Belgium. All Grace knew was that he had gone to the Orkney Islands, off the north-eastern coast of Scotland. *Whatever he went to do in places like that!* She even wondered if there were other black people in Orkney.

How he ended in Belgium was anybody's guess. As much as she loved him, she had begun to worry about him. Maybe she should have let that Múmbi girl have him, but hell, she didn't have lovely tresses like hers, why have him. Ben was hers for life. She was getting jealous and knew it. Oh, how she had loathed the month Múmbi stayed in the house. The newcomer was so gorgeous; she always reminded women of what they wished their bodies were. If Ben had not wisely disappeared, Grace was sure she would have gone mad watching him eye her up and probably regretting that he had to dump such a beauty. She admitted grudgingly that the girl was beautiful – both in body and personality. For the one month she stayed in the house, though, Grace mostly ignored her; but Múmbi surprisingly still managed to carry herself with dignity. Grace could sense, in a way that only a woman can, how deeply betrayed Múmbi felt but the girl showed little of it and bonded so well with everybody else. Grace could almost read what was on the Múhíríga members' mind: *Múmbi was the better option!*

When she heard the bathroom door click open, she took her towel and dashed out. At the door was Dan with a towel wrapped around his waist, his hairs sticking out of the shapeless legs below and the bare chest above. He was waiting to get in after Wanjikú.

"Won't be long, a minute," he said to Grace. One look at him said it all; jog off mongrel.

By the time she came running downstairs she was met by a waffling smell of cooking sausages, eggs and coffee.

"Have made you breakfast," said Abdi.

"Really?" She couldn't believe it. "Aaww you're an angel," she said, meaning it. He knew how important breakfast was to her. Normally she ate nothing in the day, finding the smell of hospital too much. It took her appetite away.

"Why Abdi?"

"Why what?"

"Why can't everybody be like you?"

"You mean squeezing a seven-foot body in a five-foot sofa?"

Grace shook her head and took her breakfast standing in the kitchen. She didn't have time to sit down. Abdi was the most selfless person she had known. She was sure he heard her complain and had run to the 24-hour service BP petrol station past the Hayes and Harlington train station and bought breakfast. It was obvious he had not used her stuff – he could never do that, but he hated conflicts and seeing people unhappy. He didn't expect anything in return though the Múhíríga always rewarded him individually. They bought him presents like clothes and pizzas, first having to find ways to convince him to accept them. When the Múhíríga stopped shopping together, each called Abdi to show him which stuff was theirs in case he needed anything. Rarely did he take the offer though – a curious character indeed. It bothered him that people living in the same house could hoard stuff. Life to him was about loving other people and sharing. He was so different from his volatile Somali roots where folk had been attacking each other in a state with no government for many years.

Grace thanked Abdi profusely and ran out into the thinning

darkness to find Kamau had parked in the driveway, again. He was so annoying! She had always told him not to park in the driveway if there was another car already there but he was such a habitual animal it never got into his allegedly 'royal' head. Mad with rage, she ran back into the house, taking three stairs at a time, her impeccably white uniform creaking at the seams with the strain. She banged at Kamau's door so hard her fist hurt. It was Jane who opened the door, a bed sheet wrapped around her like a sculptured Madonna. One look at Grace and she knew it was about the car.

"A minute and I'll move it out of your way," she said. *A minute!* That's what all those who messed her day that morning said. Losing it, she stormed into their bedroom to Jane's shock, without caring if Kamau was naked, and grabbed his car keys on the table. She ran out of the house, reversed Kamau's car and then threw the keys at Abdi to drive it back into the driveway once she got her car out.

Jane watched from her bedroom window wondering what had gotten into Grace lately. But then there was that Múmbi girl who had made her so insecure for a whole month and now Ben was off again to wherever. It was difficult when your hubby was not there when you needed him. Thinking of hubbies, she glanced at hers sprawled on the bed, so handsome, and smiled. She let the sheet wrapped around her cascade to the floor. Gracefully and seductively she slithered back to bed, enjoying the desire in Kamau's eyes as he watched her through sleepy eyes. 'To hell with irate Grace,' she thought.

But Grace was important to her. As an illegal immigrant, there was no way Jane could use her passport. For some reason, Kamau didn't particularly fancy getting one fixed by Ben. In the meantime, Jane had to work. Like what Njambi, Ben's sister, and several other friends who were all illegal did, she used Grace's passport and National Insurance number to register with employment agencies. Thus one of the worst mistakes you could ever make was to call them by their real names at their workplace. No one noticed that the photo in the passport was different, even though Jane had a much lighter complexion than Grace. They all wondered how nobody from Inland Revenue noticed the huge amount of hours Grace supposedly clocked in a week. But then several of the agencies they registered with paid in cash, dodgy about their own tax issues. If Inland Revenue were to notice, and the worst came to the worst, she would claim identity theft. Jane and Grace would then have to move house in case someone came snooping but so far everything was all right.

# 22

Múgo opened the massive seething dishwasher and stepped back from the steam billowing aggressively from the hot machine. He wiped his sweaty brow and felt streams of sweat cascade down his back and armpits. There was nothing he could do about the armpits unless he took off his sweaty T-shirt, which stuck uncomfortably to his body. That wasn't an option in a restaurant kitchen. This was his second day at an on-site canteen at Dale Electricals, a big firm that dealt with electric and digital advertising at Brooklands Industrial Park, Sunbury-on-Thames. The sink was full of dirty pots and dishes that still needed his attention. Apparently he wasn't as fast as he should be. He took too much attention to the dishes, the chefs said. A meticulous perfectionist, he couldn't help feeling disgusted to see the blackened stainless steel pots and tried to scrub them shiny clean.

"You all right darling?" Jenny the lady restaurant manager asked him. Múgo's bowed head made nodding movements, though inside he felt like rubbish. *Don't darling me, cow!* It was hot this summer and doing dishes in a hot water sink and a steamy dishwasher wasn't helping the situation at all. His hand was dipped inside the sink trying to unblock and drain the miry water while trying to figure out how he would clear the pile of pots that accumulated by the minute. The sink was nearly full, a mistake because hot water sipped into the rubber gloves making his hand soggy and uncomfortable. He dipped the hand deeper to reach the plug, scooping more water into his glove. It wasn't coming off easily because of the pressure. He applied some force, twisting it a little, which worked but then splattered his face with murk from underneath. Trying not to cry with disgust, he reached for a tissue and wiped off the murk and a few drops of tears from his face. Some things unexpectedly break a man's confidence.

Being lunchtime, lots of mostly young staff queued for their meal. When he went to pick the never-ending flow of used plates and cutlery from the restaurant, he could tell they pitied him, wondering how on earth a man could do dishes all his life. Someone said life wasn't a straight line, a fact Múgo now believed should form a basis for a religion; it was an absolute truth. For goodness sake, he had an education, formerly a respected pension officer, but that was now only in his fading memories. Here he was doing dishes and everybody thinking he was an uneducated asylum seeker. In fact, most people didn't understand when he spoke to them for the first time. Not expecting him to speak English, they had to ask him to repeat what he said to confirm they heard him right the first time.

"Oh, you speak good English," some exclaimed to his chagrin. And how was he supposed to respond to that? 'Thank you' or 'Hell, I was taught in English since I was five, you moron'? Nobody seemed to think his qualifications and experience as a pension officer were of much importance.

Tired of waiting for a good job when he settled in London, he had given up and registered with an employment agency which had kept him busy for the last year in all sorts of warehouse jobs, from mail sorting to security and cleaning. His lack of a visa wasn't much of a problem. Ben had seen to it that he got a Ugandan passport, complete with a visa and a new name. When he complained about the new name, all Ben said was, "It will save you, some day" – whatever he meant by that. Of course it cost him – or to be exact, his wife – lots of money. Múgo didn't have any money left on him.

Wanjikú, his wife, had gotten disillusioned with the lives they were leading and to Kamau's joy returned to Kenya to look after their children, Njeri and Kíama. She had some six thousand pounds she had saved to start a business but that was never to be. The cost of living in London was too high and Múgo never got to save any money. He had therefore defaulted on payments to service the loan he had taken to cover his travel to London. Their small farm in Kenya was at stake, the bank threatened to repossess it. Múgo's elderly father was so incensed, he had threatened that if the land was repossessed he, Múgo, might as well never return. So in his wisdom Múgo remained behind when his wife, who was mad with him too, returned home and used almost all her savings to clear the loan plus interest and defaulting charges. With whatever remained of her savings, she opened a small shop that all it afforded the family was a basic livelihood.

Múgo was a caged man. He couldn't return worse off than when he left. Everybody expected people who went abroad to become successful and if they didn't then they were horrible losers. His wife, though, had swallowed her pride and returned for the sake of the children. If it wasn't for the loan, the six thousand pounds she had saved; it was a lot of money in Kenya, enough to open a business. For the last year, all Múgo had was a meagre eight hundred pounds to his name, whatever else he saved he sent back home to his wife to boost the stock in the little shop. At that rate he was to stay in the UK for a very long time if he was ever to make any substantial savings and that didn't look likely. No way, this wasn't a way to live. He didn't even have a moment's rest because there were just too many bills to pay. In fact, he couldn't have taken the washing-up job against his resolve never to do it again were it not that he had not found work for the first two weeks of that month. That way, he figured he couldn't afford rent come month end, a situation the no-nonsense Normandy landings veteran landlord wouldn't consider exactly funny.

By 3.30 pm he had miraculously finished washing the dishes and mopping a kitchen floor the size of a football pitch. Most of the kitchen staff had left except Jenny and the head chef, a huge Scandinavian ogre more suited to be a rugby star than dribbling meatballs on pans. He was making orders for the following day, consulting with the lady manager who kept peering to see whether Múgo was doing the floor properly. This made Múgo's blood race with rage. Earlier in the day she had taken Múgo through a thorough lesson of the wonders and function of a vacuum cleaner. He had listened attentively, acting amazed with this new and marvellous technology. When she wanted him to try it he pretended he was unable to control it. He pushed it dangerously towards her sending her hopping scared out of his way. Shocked, she couldn't trust him with such a sophisticated gadget, she hoovered the office herself.

"Say," Jenny had said at tea break, "hope you don't mind darling but d'you wear clothes where you come from, you know, like these?" Jenny pointed at her dress. "Or is it skins or leaves?" Múgo looked at the shabby clothes from a budget high street store and felt sorry for her. His wife Wanjikú would never be seen dead in such tasteless, cheap apparel. For a moment he was tempted to say: *no ma'am we use banana leaves around the waist and a few more around the bust for women.* He didn't.

"Clothes, ma'am, we wear real clothes."

"Oh, really?" she said, surprised. Múgo nodded and felt pity for her rather than anger. She was so pathetically dim. "What about the Mesei, those ones do as well?"

"The Maasai."

"Whatever," she said with a dismissive brush of hand.

"They live in Kenya and Tanzania," said Múgo, remembering the stories he made up about the Maasai to the exhilaration of his colleagues in the various places he had worked in London. Most believed all East Africans were Maasai and revered him in the belief he had killed a lion to become a *moran* initiate. What most excited his listeners was the Maasai tradition that members of a clan-set could share wives. All you had to do was stick a spear outside the door or in the compound to announce your presence inside and all other men, the man of the house included, kept off. That was like paradise to his male listeners and a few women as well. Some suggested that they would always stick a spear outside their doors then go out on a spear-sticking spree outside other men's *manyattas.* The idea fascinated staff in one of the places Múgo worked so much they booked holidays to Kenya en masse. Múgo had smiled knowingly, unsure any would have an opportunity to stick a spear outside anyone's *manyatta*. He was sure they managed to stick spears of a different kind elsewhere though, but then you could stick those anywhere and don't need to travel thousands of miles to a *manyatta* to do that.

"No, not all do, some wear cloaks instead."

"Fabric?"

"Fabric."

"Oh," she said, unconvinced.

"Been to Africa?" Múgo asked.

"No, never. There's lots of trouble down there, inn't? I would love to see the animals though."

"I see," said Múgo.

"Too much disease, too many hungry children. Why do you African men give your women all those children that you can't provide for? Don't you have pills there or is it the heat?"

"Probably," Múgo said, keen to let the discussion die.

"Oooh must be the heat. You African men are hot, you don't give your women a moment's rest, even a minute to take the pill, your men should do the vasectomy thing," Jenny said and broke into a cheeky guffaw. Múgo left the table with Jenny's laughter ringing in his ears.

Now done with the mop and bucket, he put them back into the store and walked to the changing room feeling a total failure. The safety kitchen boots he had been given felt heavy and coarse inside. He stood in front of the mirror above the sink, regarding his image with disgust. What he saw was a reflection of someone who looked knackered, beaten and silly in a dark green apron. The shabby suits he used to wear working in civil service could have looked like designer wear in comparison. What he couldn't tell anyone back home was that the drudgery of his civil service office back in Kenya was paradise compared to how he lived now.

"Thanks for your help, darling," said Jenny, signing his timesheet. "Will call the agency if we need you again. Did you enjoy it here?" Múgo's Adam's apple did a jig and his throat went dry. He couldn't answer that; words escaped him. "Well, it isn't bad really, there are worse days, believe me," Jenny went on, thinking probably he didn't understand the first question. Many who were sent from the agency didn't understand much English. It wasn't unusual. Múgo just nodded, thinking he wouldn't want to experience the bad ones if today was good. "Oh, one other thing, please don't give up your day job yet," advised Jenny as Múgo turned to leave.

"What's that about?" asked Múgo, head bowed without turning.

"The singing, you've been humming and occasionally singing all day."

*Stupid!* Múgo thought. The African sing not to perform but to lift their spirits, fill their troubled souls with inner peace. They will sing at work, they will sing in the streets and they will sing anytime. The really good ones perform and that's good, everybody else sings, right notes or not. Who cares about right keys or notes? Let the soothing rhythm feed the soul. Ask the slaves in America what kept them going. They sung.

"It's the food for the soul," said Múgo to Jenny and walked laboriously away singing 'Swing low sweet chariot'. Jenny watched him leave and shook her head. *Strange creatures these.*

Out in the summer sunshine he walked on, a dejected man, through the Tesco Sunbury parking yard, past Sunbury Cross shopping centre, across the Staines Road, and found his way to the route 235 bus stop. He had junked his car when it failed MOT inspection, needing a lot of money to fix and the insurance became too high for him. It was impossible to afford another car just yet. *Oh the freedoms of owning transport.* If he still had transport he could have been home in Feltham, where the remaining Múhíriga members now lived, within minutes. This would have taken ten minutes by car but now he had to wait for the bus for twenty minutes or more and take another twenty to reach home. He needed to get home as soon as possible to catch some sleep before going to Weybridge for a second job, another all-night dishwashing job. A man can only take so much trouble. Múgo feared he would snap soon.

The journey to Weybridge was one ordered from Sheol, the devil's stronghold. He had to take the train to Weybridge Station then change onto the Guildford, one alighting at the Byfleet-New Haw Station. A fifteen-minute walk through unkempt yards completed his journey at the mammoth Tesco distribution warehouse. That wasn't even the worst bit: the journey took an hour and a half due to the connecting train's timetable difference. It wasn't even the nightlong dishwashing. What was a real spirit breaker was going home in the morning. The first train to Weybridge Station arrived at 6.25 am, a whole hour after he had finished work, and the next one to Feltham at 6.50 am. Nothing killed him like the wait in the freezing weather, especially in winter, all alone in the train station. He couldn't wait at Tesco until train time. He feared he could fall asleep and miss the train, which would have meant being late for his day job that started at 9 am.

Alighting at the Feltham High Street bus stop, he crossed the road to the opposite side where what remained of the Múhíríga lived. He picked up mail from the letterbox, putting the ones belonging to the others on the lounge table. He now shared the house with Abdi, Ben and a bloke called Kariúki who had joined them. When Grace left, the place wasn't the same anymore. A month later, Kamau and Jane decided to find a place of their own. Njambi could not stand living with four blokes after Wanjikú went back to Kenya. Grace's suspicions of her sneaking into Dan's lower bunk bed were not outrageous after all. Njambi moved in with Dan somewhere in Teddington where they were spotted so often trying to sneak behind benches and trees in Bushy Park on Sandy Lane to canoodle – old habits die hard.

The blokes did little in the house, expecting Njambi to sort their mess after them. They still had traces of the African traditional male mentality you see, ever kings to be served by their subjects – women. Now that Grace had left, Njambi had been doing both Dan's and her brother Ben's stuff: washing and cleaning after them. Ben always joked mischievously that the greatest wonder of this century was a washing machine. He said that he never understood how he could dump dirty clothes into the laundry basket and get them clean and pressed out of the wardrobe! Between the two, she figured she would rather wash for her man Dan, though she owed her brother so much. She knew Ben would flip his lid when he returned from wherever he was and have to contend with the fact that she had moved in with Dan. Ben tolerated Dan only just, but she didn't care anymore. She was a big girl now. Since Ben broke up with Grace he got stranger. No one exactly knew where he was most times. He slipped in and out of the house at such unpredictable schedules there was no point in asking him where he had been. Not that he wouldn't answer but because it wouldn't be true. The good thing was that he paid all his bills and even stocked the fridge, though he rarely used the stuff he bought.

Múgo went upstairs to his room. The bed was invitingly well spread. He took off his clothes and sprawled across it, feeling its softness sooth his weary body. How he survived with only a few hours' sleep a day was amazing. Mostly he finished catering jobs at half three in the afternoon and warehouse jobs at five o'clock. It then took him an hour or more to get home, depending on where he was working. His wake-up time was 7.45 pm so he could get ready for the 8.10 pm train to Weybridge. This was like riding a whirlwind. Why couldn't life be simpler?

Before he knew it he was snoring like an ancient diesel pump. In his routine way of falling asleep, his mind always replayed bits of the day's activities. He must have thought last of the letters he picked from the letterbox because he dreamt of hands, just hands, giving him a letter offering him a job at the Home Office. Gladly he accepted the offer though it bothered him that he was going back to civil service – words that almost induced trauma in him. But hey, it was better than dishwashing. Suddenly a heavy weight lifted off his shoulders. He didn't have to mop anybody's floor or wash anybody's dishes or wear stinging warehouse boots that hurt his toes so much. When he woke up it was with optimism, a renewed hope for a better day only to realise he had been dreaming. Disappointed, he slumped back on the bed and stared at the ceiling. Just then the alarm on his mobile went off. It was 7.45 pm, time to get ready to go to Weybridge. Damn! How he hated the sound of that alarm! It traumatised him, made his body cringe. He reached for the phone and turned off the alarm then tossed the phone to the floor in annoyance. If it were not for the carpet the phone would have broken into pieces.

Múgo stretched his hand to the bedside table reaching for the letters. He hadn't read them. One was a BT phone bill, one from Hounslow parking 'terrorists' for a parking ticket he had acquired several months ago when he still had a car. A parking warden had told him it was okay to park there only to find a ticket on the screen when he returned. He had refused to pay and now they were sending bailiffs to him. There were five other junk mails, promotional stuff ranging from insurance on anything including, hilariously, his anatomy to getting partners. The last letter was from Barclays Bank. Its contents weren't new. This was the third time they were sending him a promotional letter on the joys and peace of taking a Barclayloan. Why let financial needs bother you when they were there to help you? *Oh, how kind!* Probably he should take their word for it, and why not? He remembered a joke he had read in the Reader's Digest; *a bank is a place that lends you money if you can prove you don't need it.* He smiled, how true!

Múgo sat bolt upright and listened to voices in his mind. A bright flash of insight engulfed him like the ancient sages in the line of Confucius, that Eureka guy, and Newton. If this is how they felt the first time it hit them then it was wonderful. It was peace, nirvana. Who was that nirvana fellow? Buddha, that's him. This must have been what he talked about. A flow of insight so deep and so high it set you above everybody else. The good thing about it is that other folks didn't know you were operating on another level. You could sit back and watch them, knowing that you knew more than they did and that they didn't have the foggiest clue that you did.

He jumped out of bed and went to his computer at the right-hand corner of the room. Weybridge could wait, perhaps forever. Let the chefs wash the plates themselves if they had to. Right now he had a higher calling, one that would redeem the Kíama family. He opened his Barclays online account and he was greeted by that all so welcoming invitation that he had a pre-approved offer and that he was eligible for a loan of up to fifteen thousand pounds. The offer had been there for the last two months but he had not thought a thing about it. In fact, the only thing that came to his mind the first time he saw it was how callous the bank was, dangling carrots he could not reach. Like a man under strong inspiration he clicked on it and applied for the loan, which was approved immediately. He printed off the agreement form so excited beyond belief. Unable to wait until the following day lest the inspiration wear off, he signed it and ran out towards Feltham High Street to buy a stamp and to post the form.

A happy man, Múgo strolled back into the house in a state of euphoria, amused about the way of the world. The bank had an option of taking a loan protection with them. In other words, they were giving an insurance cover supposedly to protect customers in case they had trouble, say, an accident, while in actual fact they were covering themselves in case one defaulted. They never lost, and woe unto anyone who had a claim. Compensation was never as automatic as made to be at application. They rode on the backs of emaciated customers in the guise of a caring service. Talking of a caring service, he remembered a hospital insurance cover the bank made him take when he applied for an account. It was supposed to cover him in case he was hospitalised. What was a bank doing in hospital insurance? Múgo had taken the cover anyway, afraid that they might take too much time trying to persuade him about the wisdom in it and notice something unusual with his Ugandan passport. In all ways the passport looked genuine but Múgo always feared it probably had something that could betray him. Besides, knowing Ben, he couldn't rule out someone else having an identical copy. But he was grateful to Ben for the passport. It enabled him to work and even open a bank account. In fact, the mystery of the fifteen thousand pounds loan limit was all to do with Ben. For the last six months, lots of Ben's money was coming through his account from strange places. He was afraid that it would explode into trouble but he couldn't do much about it. If he told the police, his identity could have been discovered. The traffic in his account looking busy and healthy, the caring bank could not help but offer to supposedly support him to absolute financial health with a loan, its interest so high even its managers were reluctant to take it.

That night he made himself his favourite meal – chapati and Thai chicken curry then sat to watch football, all cares about night dishwashing jobs in crazy places like Byfleet Industrial Place gone like a fart. He loved Ben, he was a pain and attracted trouble but a life coach, this world did not belong to the afraid. Conquer fear and you could conquer anything. Ben could go anywhere and do anything. He didn't even need to have money. How he got it was something else but he got it anyway. The sneaky fella could sell you his dirty socks if he had to. Múgo remembered the words he told him about the passport. *It will save you someday.* How true, brilliant, the guy was a genius – in the order of Confucius.

Three days later he called the bank to hear the news he had been waiting for; he was required to go down to his branch to sign some forms. He had not gone to work for three days and had switched off his mobile phone like one on a hermitic retreat. Concentration was paramount or so he convinced himself. The reality was that he was too tense to work. For the first two days, he spent most of the time pacing up and down the house. When he sat down, all he did was rock back and forth in spasms of anxiety or stare blankly at the TV screen, legs shaking. To calm himself down, he got himself to adopting Sting's *Englishman in New York* to *African in London*, his version that depicted his own life and his predicament in a foreign land.

When he walked into the bank he felt like fainting. What if his identity was queried? He remembered the thousand voices that always told him 'they can't tell one black person from another'. But that wasn't true of course. Just as many as couldn't, lots of Britons could and you shouldn't put your hopes on that alone. *A man gotta do what a man gotta do.* He walked purposefully to the vacant personal banker's desk where a business-faced young lady welcomed him.

"Morning, sir," she said, "please take a seat. What can I do for you?" Múgo loved the 'sir' bit. Soon he would be one, hopefully. Fifteen thousand pounds in Kenya was over two million – a lot of dough.

"I applied for a loan which was approved and was asked to come in this morning to sign some forms."

"Right, do you have your account card with you?" she asked. Múgo fished for his debit card from his wallet and handed it to her. Immediately she opened his account and went through his security details with him, confirming or changing whatever needed to be changed. Everything done, the lady printed the forms and gave them to him to sign.

"I see you've taken a loan with protection. Do you understand the benefits of taking the cover?"

"Perfectly," answered Múgo with a grin. *So that you can cover your backsides,* he thought.

"Any questions regarding your Barclayloan?"

"How soon can I access the money?"

"As soon as you walk out of that door."

"Perfect, thank you…" he said, and paused to read the name on her badge, "thank you Danielle, I won't forget you." Danielle squinted quizzically, won't forget me? *What the hell is that supposed to mean?*

"All right sir, have a good day."

"And you too, have you been to Kenya, Danielle?" She was surprised with this twist of conversation; she thought she had dismissed him.

"No, why?"

"Lovely country."

"I'm sure it is. Next please!" There were too many people to serve to dwell on one happy customer.

When he walked out of the door into the bright sunny day he felt reborn. Music came live in his mind, translating into whistling and humming tunes like Louis Armstrong's 'What a beautiful world'. *And I say to myself… what a wonderful world… terereere.*

The following day, he went to the bank and wrote a fourteen thousand pounds cheque to Uchumi Motors, a car dealership that was a front for a money transfer and exchange bureau owned by an Asian family of East African origin. The remaining one thousand pounds was for his flight ticket and a little shopping. He then went to the Uchumi office in South Harrow to take the payment slip. These were professionals, or veterans, or whatever you would call them. There were many people who used the bureau to send money back to Africa because they charged much less than the established businesses like Western Union or the banks themselves. The amount didn't matter – a factor most customers appreciated. They could send as little as twenty pounds or even ten pounds, ridiculous amounts to send through banks, which would charge several times over for the service alone. They didn't charge much for services and they had a branch in Nairobi and Kampala. All they did was inform the Nairobi or Kampala offices who to pay how much. No real transfer was necessary.

Few questions were asked and when huge amounts of cash were transferred through their business they just didn't want to know the details. The sooner they were done with it and made their profit the better. They understood that times were hard and if one of their fellow Africans broke through the ice, who were they to frown? Back in Africa there was a huge divide between the black and the Asian people of African origin but here in the UK nobody wanted to know. They were one and the same. All felt they didn't belong and forged a fragile unity based on a common identity of origin.

The papers were done and all Kamau had to do was wait. How they were able to transfer huge amounts of money without a trace was a mystery.

"You understand we've to wait four days for the money to be credited to our account," said Patel, the sleuth, pot-bellied proprietor.

"Yes, of course, I understand."

"This is a lot of money so what's the name of the account you want us to deposit the money in?"

"Cash, I will collect it in cash."

"Cash?" He looked up at him. "You're travelling to Africa

then?"

"That's right."

"Right, your passport," he said after hesitating a moment with a look of a smooth operator who has been there, seen it all and done it. "Choose your password then, the money will be in Kampala in three days," he added, studying the passport briefly and handing it back. No copies made, they were not necessary.

"Kenya, I prefer Kenya." Patel looked at him a moment then nodded.

"Kenya it'll be, password?"

"Dreamsooth."

"Dream*what*?"

"Dreamsooth," repeated Múgo spelling it out slowly. That was from William Butler Yeat's poem 'The Song of the Happy Shepherd'. He loved the poem so much he always recited it in his mind, especially the bits about singing and seeking and dreaming for this is also sooth. On his way back from Uchumi Motors he mumbled the words in the bus to the amusement of other passengers. He was a happy man and being thought mad was the least of his worries: *Dream, dream, for this is also sooth.*

Five days later, Uchumi Motors confirmed that they had received his money. It was a relief, not that he was much worried about raising suspicion. He was somewhat confident that this would go according to plan. There was a peace hanging over him since the insight had hit him like it did the old sages. He didn't have to run around the cage looking for an exit whereas all he needed to do was to look up, see the open roof and fly free. A trip to Staines High Street, his favourite, was in order. Some shopping wouldn't do him any harm. He scouted through Maplin, Marks and Spencer and Woolworths buying a few items like clothes, shoes, jewels and little fancy electrical gadgets that he thought his family would appreciate. He also bought a top-of-the-range digital camcorder he always fancied that cost almost five hundred pounds.

That evening he checked for a flight ticket and was horrified by the prices. It was in the high summer season when everybody was travelling. The cheapest ticket to Nairobi was six hundred and eighty pounds excluding taxes. That was about Ksh 70,000, enough to buy a plot of land. He wasn't going to spend that kind of money on a plane ticket. Wisdom was reigning in him like torrents of a heavy downpour. It was now evident that his moment of make or break had come. Like his people said in Kenya, everybody had one major opportunity to cross the poverty valley to the other side where riches smiled at you. If you missed it, well, too bad. Most people never got it again. He wasn't going to waste his. No way, he was too clever for that.

Early the following morning he packed the few things he considered valuable to him including the few gifts he had bought for his family. He had bought some expensive jewels for his wife, which he figured not only would look good on her but also were a valuable asset. All along he had not told his housemates that he was returning to Kenya. It was better that way because he didn't want to draw any attention to himself. When asked about the several days he had not worked, he claimed the employment agency had not found him any work. Abdi had even offered to talk to his boss at Thorpe Park where he now worked, and who he was on good terms with, but Múgo insisted that it wasn't necessary. His catering agency had promised to fix him a deli bar job, which was clean and all right. The housemates were afraid that come the end of the month he wouldn't be able to afford the rent and they would have to bail him out.

All packed and ready, Múgo went to a telephone booth several blocks away and dialled 999.

"Hello, thanks for calling Feltham Police Station, how can I help?" a male police officer answered.

"I would like to give some information that I think could be helpful," Múgo said with a screechy fake voice.

"Yes sir, what about?"

"Some illegal immigrant."

"Yeah? That would be helpful, sir. Can you identify him...her, male or female?"

"Male."

"Name?"

"Múgo, Múgo Kíama."

"Do you know his address?"

"902A Hounslow Road."

"And what's your name, sir?"

"I can't identify myself. It's risky."

"But sir…"

"He's home at the moment, he may be dangerous," Múgo said, and hung up. Sprinting, he ran back into 902A Hounslow Road, an uninhabited building a few blocks away from the Múhíríga house. Whatever had happened to its owners he didn't know but what he knew was that it was popular with squatters who came and left. At the moment it was unoccupied, the gods were smiling at him. He ran upstairs to one of the bedrooms he had spent hours cleaning. He had done his best scrubbing and getting rid of tonnes of rubbish previous squatters had left behind. In a similar room a few blocks away in the Múhíríga's house, he had nursed his sorrows and loneliness for the last year since his wife went back to Kenya. He walked to the window and pulled the blind a little. The clock on the wall read 11 am, funny that the squatters had not nicked it. He waited, surprised at just how much he had changed in the last few days. His audacity surprised him. Obviously, he wasn't an adrenaline junkie like Ben and his cohorts but he was eager to see how this would go.

At 11.10 am he heard the sound of a siren from a distance coming from the direction of Feltham train station. *That might be it,* he thought and waited. The police siren grew louder and louder, too loud perhaps, but then he realised why. There were three police cars racing down Hounslow Road and that wasn't all. Not too high up in the sky emerged a Eurocopter twin squirrel helicopter, the tat-tat sound of its rotor setting the beat to complement the sirens in a crazy song.

Outside the house, the cars screeched to an abrupt halt, sending the other traffic into confusion. Stern looking policemen jumped out and ran to the front door while others ran to the back surrounding the house in case somebody escaped through the backyard. The chopper hung precariously above the house, swaying this way and that way in a hop dance movement. Múgo watched the drama through the slightly drawn blind and smiled. *They're so wasteful*, he thought, *but then such things helped when the Police Department presented budgets*. He stretched himself on the bed, going through the pages of a magazine waiting for the bang. It came with so much force the door lock snapped like a biscuit. Heavy boots ran everywhere, some thundering their way up the stairs. Three policemen in their protective gear burst into his room, the first one with a gun at the ready.

"Don't move!" he shouted, pointing the pistol at him. Múgo raised his hands, letting the sports magazine he was holding fall on his belly. The policeman noticed there was no need for the gun and put it back into the hip holster. "Are you Meu-go?" he enquired, giving the nod for his two colleagues to begin the search.

"Múgo," he pronounced it the original Kikuyu way, "that's me."

"Any identification please?"

"I… I'm… erm, yes." Múgo fetched his Kenyan passport from the pile of papers on the bedside table and handed it to him. The fake Ugandan one was in a thousand shreds somewhere in the sewage system.

"Hhhmmm, Kenyan," he stated. "I don't see any UK visa here, how do you explain that?" Múgo stared at him blankly and said nothing.

"Mr Meugo, how do you explain that?"

"Because there's none, sir."

"And how did you enter Britain?" The policeman studied the passport again, tilting it at an angle, the way ageing folk who are losing eyesight do. "…from Malta? Two years ago?" Múgo looked away and shook his head. "What have you been doing with yourself for two years?" Múgo shook his head again.

By now, the commotion in the other rooms had quietened somewhat. Bored by finding the rooms with nothing suspicious, the other half a dozen cops joined their colleagues milling about and watching Múgo like a suspicious poisonous specimen. The other two cops who searched his room collected the few papers that were around, mostly lottery tickets and junk of no importance. If they asked what he did for a living he would simply say he never got employed and used to hawk pirated DVDs on the high streets, an explanation he hoped they would swallow albeit with a choke. He was so sure they would be more interested in deporting him than finding out how he had been earning his living.

"I think you'll have to come with us to the station to write a statement. We are arresting you on the charge of violating immigration rules. Anything you say..." He went on reading Múgo his rights, as Múgo stood up. He turned around ready for the handcuffs, hoping this was going to work out his way. It was an outrageous thing to do but then if it worked he would have the final laugh. If they didn't want him around then it was going to be at their cost.

He was led downstairs and outside of the front door to meet a crowd of people who milled outside to watch the drama. Enough of them lived in the neighbourhood and knew him. Even if they didn't know him personally, they had seen him around. They wondered just what he had done to justify a raid by loads of policemen and a helicopter back-up. He seemed such a decent bloke who bothered no one. The policemen cleared the way and let him into the back seat of the middle car sandwiched by two policemen. They left in a huff, sirens blaring and the chopper hovering above them – a thing Múgo thought was unnecessary but then the drama had to be right.

At Feltham Police Station he wrote a statement. There wasn't much to say really, *keep the lie simple, you won't have trouble retelling it.* He had flown to Malta from Kenya from where he was smuggled by a boat and dropped at the shores of Bournemouth. He couldn't recall the name of the boat, nor did he know the men who smuggled him. He simply paid money to be taken to Britain and at the coast he was picked by men he didn't know who showed him the best route to avoid authorities.

Later in the afternoon, at around 4 pm, Múgo was led to a van that had just arrived at the station. Inside, he found seven other blokes in various stages of misery. There were two Pakistanis, a Ukrainian, one Turk, two Nigerians and a Congolese. They were illegals like him. Their faces said it all; it was the end of the world, it was almost the end of their lives, like one who was being led to the gallows. Some pondered on what was the worse punishment: facing jail or the thoroughly disappointed faces of their families. Many preferred the former if only to buy time and seek to appeal for their asylum applications to be reconsidered. If they were deported, some were never to pick the pieces again. The cloud of doom and gloom hung on them like a galey winter storm.

They travelled to Cambridge in silence, each man deep in his own thoughts. Nothing bothers a man more than the possibility of a bleak future. Being a natural provider and expected to stand on his feet, the thought of ever being under a boot or permanently labelled 'loser' is the worst feeling – worse than any physical pain. Their destination was Oakington Asylum Centre in Cambridgeshire which catered for people claiming asylum on a 'fast-track' processing, a period of seven to ten days during which time their initial petition for asylum is assessed. The place contained several hundred immigration detainees and was run by both a private custodial service company and by the prison service.

The first night and most of the following day they were each locked in their own room with only some magazines to read. Múgo was bored to high skies but compared to the condition the others were in, he must have been the happiest. On the second day, a legal adviser with an offer of free legal representation visited him if he wanted to contest his deportation. *How nice? You arrest people you would like to tip down abandoned mines but also give them legal representation.*

"And how long do you reckon that'll take?" Múgo asked, out of curiosity.

"There is a huge backlog of cases right now. All I can say is that the shortest it can take is six months and not in this centre."

"Wow," exclaimed Múgo.

"However, even then the outcome depends on the

circumstances. It can even take years but then you'll have to be taken to a centre like Kidlington in Oxfordshire."

"That'll not be necessary."

"Are you sure?"

"I would rather go home than spend years cooling my feet in Kidlington."

"Kenya isn't bad mate, I've been there. Why would anyone want to run away from all that warmth to this mother's chiller?"

"You need to be warm elsewhere to enjoy Kenya's warmth."

"What d'you mean?"

"The wallet, sir, the wallet."

"The wallet, of course," the legal officer stated and instinctively reached inside his coat pocket. He noticed the deviation from the purpose of his visit and became all business again.

"I'll be here tomorrow if you change your mind. However, if your decision remains, fair enough, then you'll be out of here in less than ten days."

Four days into his detention, Múgo's decision not to contest his deportation became official. He was allowed to make a call to his housemates who brought him his packed bag, feeling sorry for him. They had no clue he had planned all this and they were already speculating on a few people who might have betrayed him. The extreme way of settling scores when illegals fell out was to tell on each other to the police. Unfortunately, sometimes that was done out of jealousy. If one was doing very well, someone could tip the police about their status and have them deported. Múgo was a nice man and was never in conflict with anyone. Wondering who could have a grudge with a bloke like him, the Múhíríga and his friends wished him well, consoled by the realisation that at least he was going back to his family and he didn't look particularly distressed. They were going to hold a fundraiser for him on top of paying him his dues from their welfare's risk fund. They had a society of immigrants contributing ten pounds a month to cover each other's big issues, say, a wedding, a birth of a child, or a misfortune such as deportation or the death of a loved one. Múgo was in luck; if all went well and considering his popularity in his welfare association, he estimated he might get more than three thousand pounds.

# 23

Múgo walked down the row of seats inside the Kenya Airways Boeing 767 following Inspector Alistair Brooks and closely followed by Derek Banks, both officers of the asylum removal of the Prisons Department. At the door, the young and beautiful ebony member of the Kenya Airways cabin crew bade them a good stay in Nairobi as they took the stairs down onto Jomo Kenyatta International Airport. It was 6.30 in the morning – a bit chilly but not freezing. To the east of the airport the rising sun peered behind the Ukambani hills in a beautiful golden glow, silhouetting the acacia trees on top of the hills like in a landscape painting. Múgo was excited. This was home, as he knew it. It had been two long, trying years but finally he was home. Far off at a distance he could see Embakasi village and the aircraft hangar close to the Embakasi barracks. Farther up, next to Mombasa highway, he could see cars and buses and matatus slide past the mammoth Kenya Pipeline Company petroleum tanks. He was home and it felt good.

When they entered the arrivals lounge, three Kenyan immigration officials met them. It was apparent they had been informed of an arriving illegal. A Mr Ogwok led them to an office past the lounge opposite the arrivals desks and offered them seats while he went to look for Inspector Kimathi, his senior. The other two, Corporal Kirui and a Mr Karim, engaged the two British officials in useless talk about the weather. When Kimathi came into the room, the mood immediately changed. He was a massive seven footer with a face that commanded respect and a charisma to match. After introductions, he directed his attention on Múgo.

"So you're the people giving this country a bad name, eh?"

Múgo shifted nervously and said nothing, all eyes on him. The rest of the men in the room were surprised at the anger in Kimathi's voice but did not show it. None wanted to look at his face.

"You won't talk, eh, *Unanyeta?*" growled Kimathi. In one swift but brutal move he rose from his chair, smacking Múgo across the face, sending him sprawling on the floor. Mr Brooks went pink while Banks entertained a glee in his eyes.

"Sir, that won't be necessary, he's been very cooperative and..." said Brooks, shocked with this turn of events, fearing it might boomerang on him. The last thing he wanted to be accused of was inhuman treatment of detainees.

"*Eh, jinga wewe*, stand up!" barked Kimathi, ignoring Brooks. Before Múgo could even collect himself from the dishevelled position on the floor, Kimathi reached for his collars and lifted him so high up his feet were suspended above the floor. Múgo wiped off a drop of blood at the corner of his mouth, sending shivers down Brooks' spine. When Kimathi let go, Múgo dropped back onto his chair with a thud, hurting his back a little. Inspector Kimathi ordered Corporal Kirui to handcuff Múgo and take him to the car outside as he turned to Brooks and Banks. "We're all going to Nyayo House," he told them, all business again as he straightened his uniform, "the immigration headquarters, to verify whether that scum belongs here." The 'scum' bit was said in everybody's hearing. Brooks didn't know what to say.

In the Nyayo House immigration office, Múgo was made to sit on the floor by a more ruthless officer than Kimathi, a Mr Tanui, to Brook's dismay. Mr Tanui roughly took Múgo's fingerprints, badly staining his shirt cuffs, before leading him through signing reams of forms after his passport was verified as genuine and his identity ascertained. All done, Tanui shoved him back to the floor seething like a caged bull.

"I think we'll leave the matter in your hands now," said Brooks, eager to get out of the room. He couldn't stand watching anybody tortured. "It's up to your authorities to decide if you would like to prosecute him," he added.

"Thank you very much, gentlemen. You've been very helpful.

I'm sure the world would be a better place without criminals like him." He pointed menacingly at Múgo, with his right foot ready to drop on his face but checked himself when he saw the horror written on Brooks' face. "They give our lovely country a bad name," he added. *And you give your country even a worse one*, Brooks thought.

"We're glad that we've been helpful. We shall leave now, gentlemen, if you'd excuse us," Brooks said, pulling Banks away. Banks lingered to watch another slap find its way onto Múgo's face.

"I hope you'll enjoy it here for a few days before you travel back," said Tanui as he bade them goodbye and locked the door behind him. Everybody stared at his smiling face and smiled back.

"Get up, *rafiki*," he told Múgo, lending him a hand. Múgo hesitated, unsure of this sudden friendliness. "*Jinga wazungu*, who gave them a visa when they colonised us?" All the others except Múgo laughed. "'It's up to you to decide if you want to prosecute him'," Tanui said, mimicking Brooks. "*Jinga yeye*, you're free *rafiki*, sorry for the slaps. We've to make them happy, you know. Show them we don't encourage our nationals to migrate illegally. You're going home to your woman's bosom and your children."

"What do you mean?" Múgo stuttered.

"I mean what I've said. You're free, you were never here this morning and you were never in the UK, that's what I mean."

"Really?" he said excitedly, like a child who's been offered a full box of candy.

"Really," said Inspector Kimathi, who had been unusually quiet since they arrived at Nyayo House. "They get their visas at the airport, just filling some forms, guaranteed, yet they won't let us travel to their country and then what do they do? They deport you back, guarded by two or three at a time as if you're Bin Laden then go on a safari and enjoy themselves over here and they expect us to prosecute you. They should get Osama first if they're so hot about safeguarding their cosy castles. You were simply trying to better your life. These are hard times *bwana* and we understand a man's gotta sneak up an aircraft's undercarriage, if it comes to that, to seek a better life for his family. Get the point?"

"Kind of, but what about those forms I signed?"

"Ever heard of a shredding machine?" asked Tanui. Múgo nodded his head in perfect understanding. "A perfect invention if you ask me."

"All too well, gentlemen, all too well, but may I ask, what's the catch?" Múgo was very suspicious.

"No catch, friend, but now that you mention it, don't you think this requires serious celebration?"

"It surely does, what's the tab on the party?"

"Aah, sensible man," said Kimathi. "I'd say twenty-five thousand but that's just an estimate. I don't know what the others say."

"Sounds reasonable to me," Tanui said.

"Twenty-five thousand it shall be," Múgo said, excited at how easy this was. That was only about two hundred pounds.

"Good man," said Tanui. "I'll leave you now in the able hands of Corporal Kirui who'll drive you home and let you know where the party will be. You'll have an official escort all the way from London to your doorstep, how do you like that?"

"I'm honoured," said Múgo, sincerely glad that it was all over.

"Before you go, I would like to show you something." Tanui walked to the corner of the office and put the forms Múgo had signed into the shredder and switched it on. "No comebacks, *rafiki*."

Corporal Kirui expertly steered the police Hyundai Sonata through the morning traffic towards Buruburu where Múgo's family lived now. All along, he engaged Múgo with talk about the imbalances in the world and what drove citizens from Third World countries to do anything to enter Western countries. He was full of stories about lots of deportees they received almost every day from all over the world.

After about forty minutes, Múgo knocked at his family's door. Being too close to the door, Wanjikú couldn't see who it was clearly from upstairs but she could see a police car at the gate. Her heart assumed a turbo mode instantly. In a second, all possibilities why the police would come for her flashed through her mind. Surely the few times she broke the law, like getting off a bus without paying the fare, didn't warrant an arrest. She walked downstairs, worrying that probably her shop at Umoja market had been broken into or probably a relative was in trouble or been in an accident, *dead?*

Before she opened the door, she herded the children, who were ready to go to school, into their bedroom then walked to the window and peered through the curtain.

"Oh my goodness!" she screamed as she struggled with the lock that all of a sudden wouldn't open. When it finally did, she literally flew into Múgo, almost knocking him down. She hugged and kissed him and said unintelligible things and cried all at the same time. Kirui, who stood leaning on the police car, watched the drama and so did scores of neighbours and the children Kíama and Njeri. Curious and attracted by their mum's scream, they came out only to see their daddy and they too jumped on him sending them all to the ground into one passionate happy pile.

When they began to recover, Múgo looked at Kirui and waved at him. Kirui waved back, got into the Hyundai and backed out of the driveway. "Super Mambo pub, Friday!" he shouted before he drove off. Múgo put his thumb up to him, too emotional to say anything. This was all he lived for, his lovely family.

Early morning of the second day since his return, Múgo walked into the offices of Uchumi Motors on River Road. He went to the counter and asked for the Indian manager Mr Rajat to whom he gave the password 'dreamsooth'. Rajat led him into an inner office and asked him to wait for a couple of minutes. When he came back after fifteen minutes, he brought a laptop with him, which he logged on to a webcam. Rajat told Múgo to face the tiny camera above the desk then say a few words on the mic. Patel's face appeared on the screen from London and waved at Múgo.

"*Jambo, rafiki,*" said Patel.

"*Jambo,* Patel," Múgo responded, waving back at the manager of the Uchumi Motors, UK branch.

"*Endelea Rajat, iko sawa,*" said Patel.

"The boss is satisfied so you'll have your money in a minute. I hope you have security," Rajat said, closing his laptop.

"Yes, I do have security. How'd you know if I wore a mask?" asked Múgo.

"It's not the face; it's the voice that's more important."

"Oh really, I don't remember Patel asking to record mine."

"Well, he didn't ask, you want to sue? You've been away too long. Trust me; this is for everybody's benefit. Do you have security?"

"Waiting outside."

"As you might know, these operations are purely on trust. The money is correct. Fourteen thousand pounds came to Ksh 1,820,000. It's all in the briefcase. If you'd like to count it, it's up to you but I can assure you that will not be necessary. The cost of the briefcase is on the house."

Múgo picked the briefcase and walked outside where his old police friends, former high school classmates Thúita and Mbete, waited. They were off duty but for reasons Múgo didn't want to know, they still had their official pistols with them. Quickly they got into a car Múgo had borrowed from his uncle Seth and drove the few streets to the Queensway branch of Barclays Bank. Múgo's conscience was clean-ish. The money was from one Barclays bank branch to another, well just several thousand miles apart. If he had changed banks that might have been *kinda 'dishonest'* but he now felt BB wasn't losing everything, ironical as that might be. *Ona núgú ígítunywo mwana nííkagirio múngú* – roughly translated that even when snatching a baby from a monkey's hands, you first throw it a banana. Huge deposits were sometimes scrutinised but Múgo had arranged with a cousin who worked in the bank to handle the deposit. In case anybody asked, everybody expected people to come back from abroad with lots of cash. Probably the mode of delivery was a little unorthodox but who cared?

# 24

"To deported friends," said Inspector Kimathi in a slurred voice, raising his glass drunkenly for a toast.

"To illegals that are legalised again," added Tanui, stifling a chuckle as he raised his glass too. Corporal Kirui and Mr Ogwok joined in the laughter and raised their glasses as well.

"To those who swim across oceans, fight the ogres and bring back magic portions to their people." It was Thúita this time, normally a quiet fellow but loosened up by a bottle too many. Everybody crackled delightedly; more amused by the fact that quiet Thúita had come up with a catchy line than what he actually said.

"To those who appease the blood of our fallen Mau Mau heroes who died fighting for our land that was so ashamedly taken by slave driving Johnnies," Mbete said pensively, in mock sorrow for the departed ancestors. Then he burst out laughing, joined by the others.

"To Múgo, my good kinsman, for making my boss smile at me for bringing such a 'bankable' customer, cheers mate," said Joshua, Múgo's banker cousin.

"*It's up to your authorities to decide if you'd like to prosecute him,*" said Tanui, mimicking Brooks. "Oh yeah, prosecuted, found guilty of having a go at colonisers and sentenced to a night's endless flow of beer, at his cost." Everybody at the table broke out into prolonged laughter.

"C'mon, Rhoda," Múgo shouted at the big-bottomed waiter who served their table. Tanui's joke was like an inspiration. "Let the river flow." He pointed at the empty bottles of beer on the table. 'Rhoda' was what people called all female pub waiters, a tag borrowed from a common character in Wahome Mútahi's humour column in the *Nation* newspaper. Their Rhoda dashed off, exaggeratedly swinging her huge, rounded African bum seductively. She knew the men were drooling lustfully, imagining the possibilities, and she too imagined how it would be if she could afford rent which was due the following day.

When she returned she had loads of beers, enough to keep the already drunk revellers wet all night. Purposefully, she swung her generously endowed behind towards Thúita whose jaw was somewhere close to the table, agape with desire; but that's all he ever did. He could never muster the courage to talk to women. To rescue the situation, Mbete stretched his hand and fondled Rhoda's bottom to the delight of the drunken men. "Censored," he exclaimed and rolled with laughter. Rhoda let out a seductive chuckle and walked away knowing whom to target next.

The mood in Super Mambo tonight was party. Though it was normally a crowded but chaotically fun place to be, especially on a Friday evening, the patrons could tell that the bunch of boys at the extreme right rear corner were unusually happy. Many knew Tanui and also knew he was from the Immigration Department, just the person to see if you had an immigration issue. Passports were still a hassle to acquire – a fact that Tanui had personally dedicated to correct, especially if you saw to it that he neither got thirsty nor his wallet complained of malnourishment. This corner table was almost always reserved for him, his unofficial office.

Múgo had kept his word to meet him here as directed by Corporal Kirui. Not that he had a choice. Even though his deportation papers had been shredded, these were not the people one short-changed if one cared about living without accidents. Besides, this whole thing needed a celebration and what better way than with a bunch of boys full of mischief. Alcohol kept flowing to the wee hours of the morning. In the course of their drinking, Múgo had followed Tanui to the gents and handed him an envelope containing Ksh 25,000, the booze and meals tonight were on him, a bonus. He was now a free man in a free country, more or less.

It was around 4 am when they staggered to their cars, all except Mbete who had disappeared mysteriously, no medals for guessing where. Rhoda had given special attention to him all night. The drunken men leaned on each other for support and sang traditional circumcision songs, each in their tribal language. Kenyan drunkards believed all they needed was help to get in their cars but once they got behind the wheel they would find their way home. Some even joked that they had driven the car home so many times that surely the car must know the way home. Reckless as it might be, it was considered almost heroic managing to get home with only a few scrapes after downing a crateful of alcohol.

Of course, many never got to tell their story but were honoured all the same by their fellow drunkards, like fallen soldiers. They turned up for funerals of their fallen comrades impatiently going through the rituals of funerals. As soon as the earth covered the coffin, they quickly sneaked off to pubs, the only way they knew how to deal with grief, and the cycle went on and on. The police didn't have enough breathalysers, the resources or the willingness to get the drunks off the roads. Few people stopped to wonder why there was so much broken glass on the roads, mostly on Saturday and Sunday mornings, but many women painfully knew. Not keen on binge drinking, they let their husbands and boyfriends join the boys to get 'smashed'. Many ended up in hospital or in the morgue. The boys' nights out were a constant source of trauma to their women. It was impossible to relax, knowing they could receive that dreaded call. In fact, many quietly rejoiced when their men sold their cars or the car broke down. Some even prayed for circumstances that would make their men not afford to drive. They preferred walking or using public transport than being driven around by a drunkard – when he was around, that is – and spending nights lonely or worse. They could soon end up widows or caring for a paralysed man the rest of their lives.

When Múgo arrived home that morning, he fiddled with the lock at the gate to no avail. His unsteady, drunken hands could not find the keyhole. *Why do they make them so tiny?* he wondered as he squinted with one eye to get focused. Frustrated, he looked up and saw the bedroom light was still on. *What is that woman doing up there? Watching silly soaps at dawn? She should come and open for me.* He went back to the car – the one his Uncle Seth never let anyone drive but had lent Múgo hoping for a delicious gift from the UK – and honked twice. When the security light came on, he heard the front door click. Soft steps came to the gate and undid the lock then the gates swung open. There stood Wanjikú in all her night splendour. Her laced nightdress was wrapped in a gown to keep her warm but Múgo could see those seductive laces at the hem sticking below the gown. She was beautiful. Without saying anything, he got into the car and shot it right past her, overshooting the driveway and rammed into a laundry-line post smashing the right-side headlamp.

"See what you made me do?" he shouted at her. She locked the gate and said nothing. "Should open the gate immediately," he rumbled on. Wanjikú looked him in the eye and said nothing. She went to the door and waited for him to lock the car; he didn't. He just staggered out and went past her into the house. She went to the car, switched off the lights and locked it. By the time she got into the bedroom, Múgo was sprawled on the bed like an ogre in his shoes and clothes, snoring like a badly tuned engine. Standing there for some time, she watched him and shook her head, wondering when men will ever learn. She then went to a settee she kept in the bedroom where she lay awake for a long time.

Woken up by the smell of food, Múgo stumbled downstairs, leaning heavily on the banisters and struggling to carry his head, attracted by the smell of eggs and bacon. His head hurt badly from the previous night's drink. He hadn't eaten much the previous day.

"The English did you good," he stated, referring to the breakfast on the table. His wife barely responded with a mumble. "I didn't hear you get out of bed," he added, feeling guilty. When he woke up and found his shoes and clothes still on, he knew he was in trouble. The fact that a blanket was on the settee was no consolation either. Wanjikú stared at him for a long time and shook her head.

"That's because I wasn't there."

"Why?"

"Why, Múgo?" She spoke slowly, putting emphasis on each syllable. "You want to know why?"

"To make me an English breakfast of course."

"If that's an attempt to be funny, cut."

"Hey, what have I done now?"

"Go to the window and have a look at your uncle's car."

Múgo went to the window and looked outside. He turned to her, confused.

"What happened? Don't tell me that rascal son of yours hasn't learnt to shoot a ball straight. I always said Beckham wasn't a good role model."

"Stop it Múgo. You're not funny and you know it. Thanks for that, now I know Kíama is my son and not yours. When did you arrive from the UK, Múgo?"

"Hey, am I on trial or what?"

"Wednesday, I'll remind you. We spent a good time together. What did you do on Thursday?"

"I went upcountry to see my parents."

"And returned yesterday, Friday. What did you do last night?"

"Can't a man catch up on friends?"

"Of course a man can catch up on friends – but all night at the expense of his family?"

"I protest. That's not fair. I told you I had to see someone from the immigration."

"And I suppose he didn't turn up until 4 am in the morning?"

"Okay, so I didn't come home early enough. That was bad, I should be forgiven because it's just that once."

"We've spent little time together, Múgo. For a whole year we've been apart and for two years our children missed their father."

"Don't you forget you had left them with me for two years."

"This is not a forum to trade accusations, love."

"Okay, it happened once, it won't happen again, the bacon is getting cold."

"Yes it was this once but it could turn to many more times. This family needs you here. I need you to be with me and your children need you. Surely you need to catch up with all of us. See how Kíama has grown? He needs a male figure in his life, a model, and you're a perfect man, Múgo; that's why you're my husband."

"That's the statement you should've started with."

"I mean it, honey. I need this family to be on track again. Out there are sharks waiting to cannibalise you. Everybody knows you just returned from abroad. They'll want to dip their fingers into the honey jar as well. I say this because I love you, I need you, and the kids need you, pleeease."

Múgo stroked a hand that was now on his shoulder. 'Never underestimate the power of a woman' his granddad always said but all she said made sense.

"Okay, love, point taken," he said. "Can I have my breakfast now?"

"Of course, love, oh, the headlamp costs Ksh 3,500, you don't want your uncle to find his car like that. He comes for it at noon today, that's only two hours away."

"Aaaargh!" he snarled and resolved to be a very good boy in future. "Should have told me that after breakfast."

"And that might be just an hour to noon."

He bit his lip and looked across the room at the toy Mini Cooper with the Union Jack painted on its roof. He had bought it for Kíama, imagining how excited the little boy would be, playing the remote-controlled imported thing. To his disappointment, the boy had given it as much attention as you would an undersized inner garment. The boy had grown so much he was more interested in bikes and stunts and hanging around when Daddy watched *Top Gear*. Múgo had expected to find him more or less the way he had left him. Three years can't be that long. But he was surprised to find the noisy, chubby-cheeked little one transformed into a quieter, lean and tall lad. Oh, what a difference time could make.

Múgo stared at the British flag on the toy Cooper again and

smiled. He had been doing lots of that lately. There was no need to hang like a wet discarded coat anymore. The world had been kind to him; a wife that he couldn't change for any bulimic model and now this recent British 'generosity'. The only thing that checked him from soaring was his younger sister Dama.

When Múgo visited his parents, Dama was dying in shame and guilt. He found her in a state, a shell of the former beauty and no qualifications – she had dropped out of college. What Múgo saw was a young woman who had conceded to a beaten life and stopped caring how she looked. She didn't lack food for there was plenty in the highlands, but she had no money. She therefore couldn't afford to buy all the beauty stuff Múgo used to provide. The hair was roughly plaited to tame it, her skin looked dry and tired, and her eyes had become distant and acquired a slight squint, probably to see less of her troubles. Obviously it didn't work out with Jemoo – he of the coolest hairdo. And now there was another problem. He found little Meja, a nephew that he had never met. The name was the Swahili derivation of Major, a popular tag with the 'toughies'. Múgo had shaken his head, sad that Jemoo had left a lasting legacy in his family. He gritted his teeth and wished he could persuade Dama to change the poor boy's name.

His parents were ageing and with Dama and her son about, Múgo knew they worried constantly. Being the last-born, Dama always only had a slap on the wrist for her sins. She grew up pushing boundaries far beyond what her siblings were allowed even to imagine when they were growing up. To Múgo's annoyance, his parents blamed him for not sorting her out. Mercy, his married sister, was in the clear because she lived far and *belonged* to another family. Thinking about it now, he thought he might as well sort her out else he would have to look after the little boy and educate him. Besides, he loved his younger sister. Despite her foolishness she deserved another chance. He hoped her misery had instilled some sense in her and that she was not too depressed to stand on her feet again. Why do some people seem only to learn the hard way?

The deportation had saved him a cool Ksh 70,000 on a ticket home. He could extend this British generosity to Dama for starters. Seventy thousand was enough to open a small business, say, open a general retail shop. If Dama succeeded without another Jemoo to distract her, or the old one returning, God forbid, then Múgo could help her expand with the money he was expecting from the diaspora welfare contributions. If he did return, Múgo entertained the idea that he might consult Inspector Kimathi to fix the vermin Jemoo in a cellar somewhere. For a minute, he wished he was the kind that arranges accidents but he reasoned against it. Wisdom calls that interfering with matters of the heart, between two people who have shared intimacy, have a way of blowing in the interferer's face. All Múgo wanted was Dama to be sensible so she would look after her boy and stop giving his parents high blood pressure. This was his new dream. If it worked out, his joy would be complete.

He had hoped that all would be well. What more would a man want? He stuck some grated cheese on a wedgy toast, threw in a slice of bacon and sliced sausage then raised the sandwich. "To the British," he said to the amusement and bewilderment of his wife.

# 25

High up, somewhere over the Sudan, the huge British Airways Boeing 747 tore through the clouds. It was on its night flight to London from Jo'burg via Nairobi. Mr Brooks sat next to the window reading the *Highlife* in-flight magazine. In the next seat sat Banks, absorbed in some rock music on the in-flight entertainment. Brooks leaned forward and tapped his colleague's shoulder. Banks took off the headphones and looked at his boss quizzically; that look in his eyes always worried Brooks.

"How did you like that Carnivore Restaurant place?"

"Brilliant, had some real fun with a tight ars… enjoyed myself."

"If I had time I would have gone on safari."

"Not for me, don't care about animals. People are lots more interesting. I liked the place though, efficient handling of criminals."

"Don't you think they were a bit rough on that Mewgho fellow?"

"Hardly."

"What about human rights? That's what modern society and civilisation is all about. Human beings should be treated with dignity no matter what they've done."

"A criminal is a *criminal* if you ask me. No one thinks about the rights of others when they commit a crime. Why do they expect to be treated different?"

"But there has to be distinction between the way we treat offenders from the way criminals treat their victims. Two wrongs don't make a right."

"Tell that to a woman who's been raped or to those whose

loved ones are senselessly murdered in cold blood."

"But still..."

"Brooks, I liked the way that bloke smacked our geezer," said Banks, cutting his boss short. "Whack!" he added, swinging a clenched fist, glee pasted on his face and a sparkle in his eyes. Brooks recoiled. "That's what those vermin we deal with and those bastards in north and east London need."

"Seriously, d'you think it'd solve crime?"

"Off record?"

"Off record."

"Brilliantly," he said excitedly, his fist clenched so tight it went pink. "Smack them, shove them to the floor, put a heavy boot on their necks, and crush their balls so they don't reproduce little vermin like them. Give them real heart attacks."

"As in silencing them permanently?"

"Why not? Means less nigg...I mean bastards on the street." Brooks leaned back on the backrest, sinking into his seat horrified. He knew just who to watch in his department. It was crucial that he retired in honour. May there never be even a hint of racism or human rights violations in his department.

# 26

"You're a debtor," exploded the big-eyed lady behind the desk, pointing a wagging finger at him the way Fuso's mum taught him never to. He was taken aback; a few seconds earlier she had just smiled at him and called him 'darling'. "If we can't allow local students to pay in instalments, I believe you shouldn't either," she added menacingly her lips quivering.

"But I've been paying in instalments." Fuso tried to put a defence. "The international office allowed me to."

"Who in particular?" she lashed at him. "It doesn't happen and shouldn't."

"I spoke to a Ms Hossling and Mr Osman, they said it was okay at the Penrhyn Road main campus."

"First of all, we don't have anyone by those names at Penrhyn Road International Office. Second, I need a letter of proof authorising you to pay in instalments."

"I've a cheque to clear the balance and pay this term's..."

"We don't take cheques here. See, they take more than nine days to clear. If you have that money in your account you've to go withdraw it and pay in cash."

"But..."

"No buts, bring the cash and a letter authorising you to pay in instalments."

Dejected, Fuso went back to his car feeling like he had just had a glass of acid laced with salt, vinegar, bleach and an assortment of bitter herbal concoctions. She had no reason to shove him like that, he thought, even if she was having a really bad day. Now she had messed up his as well. None of the campus's hillside attractions or the leafy grounds blending beautifully with Kingston town centre a few miles away could cheer him up. The modern buildings of glass, aluminium and steel standing on beautiful, landscaped gardens and the large Victorian house that once gave the country estate based here pride, were usually a source of fascination to him but not today. There were more serious matters at stake.

It was Monday and the first lecture of the second term was starting later that evening. It was crucial that Fuso registered and got done with it. There was little time to spare and he wasn't sure he would get a free day any time soon. His employment agency would be cross with him although he had done lots of work for them in the last few months. He had been working like crazy, kindly assisted by *Nyagúthií,* his sweet fifteen-year-old little three-door metallic-grey Ford Fiesta. Nyagúthií, is a Kikuyu girl's name meaning one who loved to travel.

Aggressively, he reversed out of the car park and out of Kingston Hill campus of Kingston University, venting all his frustrations into a single manoeuvre. He had to be in Penrhyn Road campus as soon as possible before they took lunch break. Waiting an hour for the offices to open after lunch would kill him.

At the Penrhyn Road campus he spent twenty minutes looking for parking. Being the main campus on an opening day, it was bustling like an African open-air market. The campus is the hub of student activity in Kingston. It's fantastic cosmopolitan atmosphere, Students' Union headquarters and central facilities such as the gym, health centre and the main library attracts students from all other campuses.

When he finally found a place to park he raced to the sports centre, where registration was taking place. To his dismay, queues appeared to snake all the way to Lokichogio. This was Fuso's interpretation, Lokichogio being a town in the remote northwest region of Kenya, which was far removed from the rest of the country. He tried hard to be calm and enjoy the wait – a thing he thought nobody ever taught him properly. Queues always did his head in. It is the one single thing that most raised his stress levels so high he couldn't sit through it without devising a hundred ways to beat it. But this was Britain where, like someone said, 'Show the British a queue and they'll politely ask for directions to the back of it.' If it was Kenya, he could have somehow found a way to the front. When he finally reached the front of the international students' registration desk he came face to face with Mr Osman. For good reasons, Fuso didn't mention the Kingston Hill incident but reminded Osman that he had previously allowed him to pay in instalments.

An understanding man indeed Osman was. Somehow Fuso had managed to convince him to pay in instalments when he first enrolled for his Masters in Environmental and Earth Resources Management course. Fuso didn't even have the minimum amount Osman wanted him to pay for his initial admission. In fact, all the money Fuso had was a credit facility of eight hundred pounds and some three hundred pounds he had saved from his odd jobs. Fuso had to borrow another eight hundred pounds to raise the amount Osman needed if he was to enrol. Luckily, nobody bothered him about fees payment until the semester was over. A letter only arrived from finance office in summer to remind him to clear the previous term's balance ASAP. Being a holiday, nobody was going to kick him out of the university or deny him access to facilities and services – he didn't need them. The finance office had to wait till the opening of the autumn term while he figured how he would pull through.

The only problem Osman had was that Fuso's cheque crossed two academic years. His suggestion was that he should clear the balance in cash then pay the new term's fees by whichever method he chose. Before he enrolled him, he sent him to River House to see the International Students coordinator Ms Hossling for advice about his payment. Luckily, she had no problem with Osman's suggestion. Fuso was free to register any way Osman deemed right.

Racing from the International Office, he quickly found his way back to the sports centre. A crowd was milling outside with stern security guys standing at the door. The fire alarm had gone off and they were not letting anyone in. Trust things to go wrong just when you can least afford it. Fuso had been on his feet so long that day his whole body ached. All he needed was to get done with registration, and now this. If it was a drill, then whoever thought of it wasn't funny. There was no fire anywhere but nobody was let in until the frantic security and fire marshals approved. Fuso wanted to cry. What if Osman changed his mind? What if that abrasive Kingston Hill woman called Penrhyn Road?

An hour later he was done with enrolment, complete with a new student ID and a Student Union card. Osman had no reason why Fuso shouldn't enrol. In any case, he had already paid five thousand pounds, almost double what EU students paid for the whole course. With exhilaration, he found his way out of the maddening queues. *Down with abrasive women!* he almost screamed, remembering the dismissive treatment he had received at Kingston Hill. He fantasised going down there and shaking his new ID at her face, a scornful laugh spicing the gesture – *heheheeee.* You never know what bothered some people. They might be in horrible domestic chaos that they project to the public to ease their inner hurt. Majestically, he walked back to his rickety Fiesta that had given him so much freedom. The car helped him roam all over at odd hours doing odd jobs in odd places. If one owned transport, the employment agency sent you to places that were inaccessible by bus. Fuso didn't mind that at all, it meant getting lots of work if sometimes going till late in the night. He desperately needed the money. Sadly, he hadn't reciprocated Nyagúthií's kindness. She badly needed a wash but five pounds for a car wash wasn't always affordable. And then there was that noise that had a nasty habit of squeaking loudly, mainly when Fuso's girlfriend, Louise, was around. It always made her turn crimson. That could wait until whatever it was fell off or Louise refused to ride in the car anymore. He feared that would happen soon.

From a distance, he could see a notice on his car window. Getting closer he realised that his car had a warning notice on the driver's window. Apparently he had parked in contravention of Kingston University's traffic and parking regulations. It said that he shouldn't attempt to drive the car before contacting security as if driving it was possible with the clamp on the front right wheel. Determined not to let anyone mess his day, Fuso stifled lots of unchristian words already forming in his mind. He nearly succeeded but one managed to come out of his mouth. "Terrorists," he muttered. Why should a university behave like street parking wardens? He had to walk back down past the sports centre and the computer centre to the security office next to the main reception.

"My car's been clamped," he said to the tall black security officer standing next to the desk talking to someone on radio. It helped if you were black to get a security job this side of the world. The dark skin was supposed to look mean and scare any lawbreakers. Its opaque nature hid mysteries within and people always fear what they don't understand.

"Yeah?" he said, as if that was a riddle. "Hhhmm, I wonder why."

"Says I don't have a parking permit."

"Oh I see, you student?"

"Yeah."

"You pay the fine then apply for a long-term permit or you'll be paying for daily permits."

"Look man, I'm from Kingston Hill Campus and only came here to register. I'm a student of Kingston and won't be coming back here soon. Why should they charge me? The place is so crowded because it's opening day. Surely they should consider."

"Regulations, you're clamped, you're fined."

"Then I didn't know, it's my first day and I get clamped? What a welcome."

"This is your first day, new student?"

"Yeah mate," Fuso lied, and felt horrible about it. If it turned out bad, he would have to lie again.

"Can I see your ID?" He gave it to him knowing it was new and postgraduate students' IDs didn't indicate which semester or year one was.

"You look young for a master's student," the security guy stated, examining him with curiosity. "Environmental and

Earth Resources Management… saving the planet huh?" Fuso shrugged. "Take me to your car." Fuso led him round the several blocks to where he had parked.

"Get a permit mate or you'll be in lots of trouble, okay?" the security man said as he unclamped the car and let Fuso go without a fine. Today he was in luck, despite that Kingston Hill virago trying to spoil his day; the luckiest bit was that his loan money had been credited to his account only that morning. Who doubts miracles happen?

His luck had started a week earlier when his bank thought he was good enough to do serious business with and offered him a loan. This was after several months of body breaking, life-shortening work. Summer had passed Fuso almost unnoticed. He worked day and night in several places all over Surrey and Middlesex, like one possessed. A week was like a day and quite frankly sometimes he didn't know which day of the week it was, the days just flew like feathers in a storm. Several months earlier he had asked the bank for an overdraft which they refused, then he asked them to raise his credit limit which they too refused. Frustrated, Fuso immersed himself into work, clocking upwards of seventy hours a week. Top of his anxieties was how he ever was going to pay his fees when uni opened. He already had a balance and they wouldn't let him register when the new term began. Enrolling was crucial because he was to renew his visa in October. He had to have enrolled to show why he needed to extend his visa.

When he saw that all-important message in his online account it was heaven for him. Apparently, someone had noticed his sudden increase in income. Trust banks on that one; *they are places that lend you money if you can prove you don't need it*, someone said. There was a pre-approved offer for a six thousand pounds loan, which he applied for immediately and luckily got approved. But the transactions dragged on till the morning of the enrolment day. Whoever doesn't believe in miracles! And talking of miracles, how he was going to service the loan on warehouse jobs was a matter best left to their performers.

That evening he was glad to meet his classmates in the first lecture of the new term. The module had a wide international representation from Brunei to Nigeria to the Caribbean to Greece. Greece had the majority of students for reasons perhaps only Aristotle and Plato could explain. In his class, Fuso was an intellectual colleague, a shining African brain ready to take his exotic knowledge back home to change the course of miserable Mother Africa. Nobody needed to know what he did in the day. As far as they were concerned, he was a full-time student spending most of the time buried in huge books and drinking more of the waters from the well of knowledge. And who could doubt it? Fuso was as articulate as everybody else, if not more, and discussed issues with the competence of a master.

What they didn't know was that he swam in sinks in the day, giving swabs to murky dishes. They didn't know that he understood the psychology of a dishwasher so well he could tell when it was deliberately getting temperamental or when it genuinely needed medication. What they also didn't know was that he owned a battered, toe-stinging pair of boots that sat at a funny angle because of the awkward trips, twists and turns it did in warehouses all over Greater London. Fuso could spend a day doing dishes and mopping floors, rush home to freshen up, dash for an evening lecture and leave immediately after for a half or an all-night job. All they ever saw was the trendy Fuso who came to class in hip attire, confident and fluent in good, though accented, English.

# 27

Njambi entered the squalid bathroom and shuddered. She lifted her eyes to the mirror above the sink and squirmed at the image staring back at her. Her face had lost all radiance in the six months since she returned to join Dan, her boyfriend who was deported from the UK a year before. She loved him to bits though sometimes she wondered why. Dan too loved her in a way she knew only he could.

Dan was a loser, a fact that didn't escape Njambi. The reason why he was deported was evidence enough. He had picked too many parking and speeding tickets, which he couldn't bother to pay. Even when he was summoned to court, he didn't appear, despite having received three reminders. When he was finally arrested after a string of warning letters, he couldn't produce a valid visa. The visa had expired a couple of years previously to his arrest, but he didn't apply for an extension with the Home Office. It was too much of a hassle for him. It didn't matter that, unlike most of his friends, Dan had nothing to be afraid of. He was in Britain legally, although he had dropped out of uni. He just didn't have the willpower to take responsibility for anything including his own life.

Having no savings, Dan was all right only for a while with the little the immigrants' welfare group, which he was a member of, managed to raise for him after he was deported. He was now broke and jobless and too lazy to look for a job. All he did was dress, talk and behave as if he was still in London. To fill his time, he surrounded himself with loafers who were keen to hear about his exploits in the UK. His pet subject was his alleged escapades with white girls. Most of his tales were lies but if it tickled their fantasies it tickled his too. This was his way of avoiding confronting his shame. Unfortunately, quite a few people knew he had been deported penniless. It wasn't going to be long before everyone in Kayole Estate, where he and Njambi lived, knew.

Njambi had a quick shower and fled from the dingy bathroom, afraid that she might pick up an infection. Back in the bedroom, she paused briefly at the door staring at Dan who was in bed fast asleep, a man at peace without a single care in the world. Her eyes strayed to the open bedside drawer where her passport was partly visible. She still had a valid UK visa, an indefinite leave to remain status. How Ben, her mysterious brother, managed to get it was his secret that she didn't particularly want to know. At the moment, she had a more urgent problem at hand. She had to do something about her life and Dan's. They had lived together long enough for Njambi to know that he was the man for her despite his flaws. She was therefore determined to do something about their circumstances. They couldn't live like this for the rest of their lives.

When she was all dressed up and had breakfast, she rushed out to catch a bus to work at Uchumi Supermarket on Agha Khan Walk. On the bus ride to the Nairobi city centre that day, Njambi was full of thoughts. Sitting at the till all day was not her idea of a fun job. It didn't even pay enough for one person to live on, let alone two. And with Dan lazing about, whatever savings she had brought from the UK were dwindling fast. She could just about afford a cheap air ticket. She knew if she delayed any longer the money would soon be gone and she would be stuck. It therefore broke her heart what she had resolved to do.

A couple of weeks later, Njambi explained to Dan that she had to return to the UK for the sake of their future. Who knows, she might even arrange for him to join her. Dan didn't even try to dissuade her. He was a man resigned to whatever came his way. This frustrated Njambi so much at times it felt like looking after a four-year-old child. She promised that she would send him money to pay rent but he had to do something for his upkeep. She also explained that she was not leaving him and promised to return to him as soon as she made enough money to start a small business.

Dan just shrugged and switched on the TV.

Once in London, Njambi re-registered with a care employment agency she had worked with before in Islington. The manager, Mrs Knight, was glad that she was back because a Mr Higgins, a sickly and senile old man Njambi used to take care of, was constantly asking for her. He always tried to chat her up saying how much he liked Jamaican women. At some point, he had proposed promising Njambi a substantial inheritance. Njambi had scoffed at the idea and didn't bother to explain to the dirty old geezer that she wasn't Jamaican. The thought of his shrivelled body on her made her sick but now she wondered whether this was her ticket out of poverty.

When the old man finally fully died, his brain and heart having long been working part time, Njambi realised that she would have to be deployed elsewhere. Mr Higgins used to shower her with money thinking that it would soften her heart. She took the money without remorse and hardened her heart all the more. *Let the pervert pay penance for his sins*, she reasoned. The money kept coming, enabling her to save quite a tidy amount. Njambi wondered what he was like in his youth if all he thought at his deathbed was a lay.

Frustrated by having to wipe frail old people's bottoms day in day out, one late spring evening Njambi went drinking. In a booze-triggered recklessness she intentionally provoked Gaetano, a fiery local Italian tycoon who had interests in Islington's local government politics. She said something to the effect that she had no respect for a fake don whose willy's health didn't match that of his bank account. The outcome, though unplanned, worked like clockwork. The volatile Italian knocked out several teeth from her drunken loud mouth and consequently received a letter from her lawyers the following morning. In it was a choice: what line did he wish the lawyers didn't pursue, the assault or the racial?

When Lewis Jnr, her lawyer from Lewis and Sons Advocates on Camden Park Road, received the letter back from Gaetano it had a clenched hand drawn on it with the middle finger sticking out. Lewis Jnr decided to visit Gaetano Foods headquarters on

Torriano Avenue for a chat with its CEO.

"Well, sir, in the light of your political ambitions I think sending the letter back with your artistic impression on it proves you're a brave man, fit to be mayor," Lewis Jnr said, adjusting his geeky round-rimmed glasses. Mr Gaetano looked at the thin shabbily dressed black or mixed-race fella sitting across him with disdain and made a mental note to fire his secretary if she could allow vermin like the one before him time to see him.

"I'm glad you're impressed. Now Lewis – I believe you said that's your name – I'm a busy man and if you think I'm paying a penny to that slutty *la scimmia* nigger then think again."

"Excuse me sir, did you just say 'nigger' or am I losing my hearing?" said Lewis Jnr, adjusting his small frame to look taller and running a nervous hand over his bald shaven head.

"You heard me. You and your lot, all you niggers think you can get away with anything coz all you do is cry racism and you become untouchable."

"Well, I wanted to ask for a fifty thousand pounds settlement now that I suspect '*la scimmia*' has something to do with the zoo I've doubled it." This he said softly, ever the humble gentleman.

"What? Up yours, scum nigger. Not a penny, do you get that into your round-barrelled nose?" bellowed Mr Gaetano.

"That makes it two hundred thousand pounds."

"Are you kidding me little imp?"

"Now two hundred and fifty."

"Get out of my office now or I throw you out," he growled menacingly as he stood up, ready to carry out his threat.

"Hey, not so fast," said Lewis Jnr as he retrieved papers from his briefcase and handed them quickly to Mr Gaetano. The recipient gave them a glance and froze mid-step. They contained all his tax-evading deals that he had done importing food from Italy and the Mediterranean. With a cold stare at Lewis Jnr, he backstepped to his desk and pulled out a drawer. When his hand reappeared, Lewis Jnr was staring at a .45 automatic complete with a silencer.

"Bad idea," said Lewis Jnr, shaking his head like a clever child who catches an adult doing something naughty. "Lewis and Sons and other *special* people have copies."

Mr Gaetano looked at him long and hard and thought of the mayorship he so much needed. He lowered his gun. Unblinkingly, still staring at Lewis, he produced a chequebook. He was about to sign when Lewis Jnr spoke.

"Make it two hundred and seventy thousand pounds sir. The gun scared me a bit."

"Don't flipping mess with me man," shouted Gaetano and threw his Parker pen at Lewis, narrowly missing him. Lewis ducked in time. "I'm calling your boss and you and all that shit Lewis firm will know what it means to mess around with me."

"Be my guest, call him but most likely they'll say he left to see one Mr Gaetano."

"You!" screamed Gaetano when it dawned on him. "*Mama mia* a git like you is the senior? They do come a dozen a penny these days."

"Lewis Senior died a couple years back, I'm his son." Lewis Jnr said meekly.

"Wait a minute, my secretary said someone wanted to see me, a bigger lawyer than you, git. This is blackmail and you've just been struck off the bar register." Gaetano said as he picked up the phone and called his secretary. "Hi Sharon, who did you say was the big lawyer guy coming to see me?"

"He's the chairman of the Islington branch of the Law Society," Sharon's voice came from the reception.

"Chairman of the Law Society? Send him in... you'll never practice again." The last bit was said to Lewis Jnr.

"We'll see," muttered Lewis Jnr.

"I sent him in sir. Mr Thompson, Lewis Thompson Jnr," came Sharon's reply.

"What... you?" Gaetano said in disbelief then defeat. He produced the chequebook and another Parker pen. "Can I negotiate? She surely provoked me. Is she worth that much?"

"Every bit and more. Count it as gain, I'll tell the Law Society members you're cooperative."

Gaetano signed the cheque and felt sick. At least his political ambition or rather his life was safeguarded. His Sicilian friends crawling among the huge Italian community in Islington were not supporting his campaign to fail. He had guaranteed them serious connection and heavy business on his victory. They didn't like failures very much, especially not where their money and 'that thing of ours' were involved. Being steamed in tar was one of the possibilities to whoever failed them.

"The copies," said Gaetano after he handed the cheque to Lewis Jnr, his face contorted with nausea.

"What copies?"

"Don't mess me up, Lewis."

"There were no copies, Gaetano, just a messenger I sent to your Sicilian friends to let them know you've been profiting in ways they don't know."

"*Mama mia*, you didn't!" exclaimed Gaetano, worry written all over his face. The taxman he could face, his Sicilian pals he had no courage to confront.

"I could stop him before he delivers the message."

"Please do, please Lewis. Lives are in danger here."

"Will try."

"Don't just try, do it Lewis. And this is between us Lewis. I'm dangerous."

"Ha, you don't look it right now. Anyhow, who do you think I am, a kiss and tell hooker? Besides, this is not about my woman client or about those papers. The papers alone are worth millions. If I were interested in money I would have asked for millions. I have more money than I need. All I would like you to know is that, for reasons I can't discuss now, the Islington branch of the Law Society would like to work with you."

"That's good, very good."

Thereafter, Njambi received her compensation, some two hundred thousand pounds, the rest of the money was termed as legal fees. She visited her disillusioned man in Kenya with assorted goodies, a set of gold teeth in her mouth included, to put a smile back on his face. He didn't care if his woman was sleeping around when she had bought him a block of property and given him enough dough to spend as he wished. He didn't care how she had acquired the money. In any case, he figured there wasn't a way of finding out exactly. Let her lovers knock out all her teeth for all he cared and pay for gold replacements every time. He figured he might knock out the gold ones himself some day and sell them for a fortune. What he didn't know was that Njambi was absolutely faithful to him.

With over Ksh 25,000,000 in her purse, Njambi's return to good old motherland was victorious. She had a miniature Kenyan flag in her hand, and songs like 'Home sweet home' came easy to her lips. Villagers at Karia-iní where she grew up were blown with a generous flow of free booze as she traversed the dusty roads in a neat second-hand Mitsubishi Pajero packed with her cousins and their girlfriends. Dan watched all this from the comfort of the Pajero's front passenger seat, powerless to do anything about it. Now if there was anything the villagers frowned at, it was that. This was the hottest gossip of the moment. In such a patriarchal community, no woman should reduce her man to an impotent zombie and no sensible woman would go out binge drinking and 'raving' in the company of teenage cousins and their girlfriends. The last bit was a matter beyond taboo. That Europe place must be dodgy; the things it turned people into were strange indeed.

# 28

Fuso turned right off Wellesley Road into Bedford Park next to the imposing Lunar House, his destination. Happy to find an empty parking space, he reversed the car into it and killed the engine. He was glad that his map reading skills did not desert him at his hour of need like they so often do. Looking around, he took in the surroundings to familiarise himself; it was still dark. There were movements and the glow of lighted dials in the other cars parked close by, some with engines running. Fuso realised why. It was very cold that early morning and the folks inside needed to keep warm. *Oh no, please don't tell me it's Upper Hill, Nairobi all over again. Please tell me Croydon Home Office won't be like that traumatising British High Commission in Nairobi.* It was 5.30 am and the folks all around seemed like they had been there for ages.

After locking the car, he checked the parking charges. At least charges start at 7 am and that was a whole one and a half hours away. He would have thought of something before the car-clamping terrorists descended. Meanwhile, he strolled to the reception, glad that it was only a few people who had arrived. *It shouldn't take long to extend my visa*, he thought. At the Lunar House main reception, a black security officer directed him to a waiting area to the right of the building. Fuso asked him about parking; he advised that Fuso should move the car to a private parking opposite the building because he won't have time to go feed the parking metre with coins once he was inside the immigration office.

"Will it be long, I mean extending the visa?" he asked.

"Oh yes, might take several hours."

"But there're only a few of us here."

"Oh no, mate, better go and grab a position in the queue now or it'll take you longer," the security officer said. "Sort the car first though, they're strict, they tow them away."

"Terrorists." Fuso muttered his favourite adjective for parking attendants and walked out after thanking him.

*It was Nairobi all over again*, Fuso began to suspect. He decided to have a quick look before he moved the car. Entering the waiting bay, he found about five-hundred people in the queue already. They looked like a one world UN party. Almost every colour, every shade of it, every nationality was represented here from Fiji to Antarctica and all the specks between. This was madness, when did they get here? But then he saw heavy shawls and coffee flasks. Fuso understood. Some had arrived the previous night to take positions in the queue. Now so worn out, some sat on the dirty floor, more concerned with resting their weary bodies than dirtying their clothes. Fuso looked at this mass of humanity and felt sorry that they have to go through this, him included. It was a chase after a dream, a chase after happiness, and a chase after a better life. Was it a chase after waterfalls then? Was the dream realised or deferred like in Langston Hughes 'A Dream Deferred' poem?

It can't be described simply as chasing after wealth alone, for many came from wealthy backgrounds but their ambition for what they thought would best offer a better tomorrow. That wasn't necessarily all about money. Was it hunger for deferred dreams?

Two blokes were arguing that one had sneaked in a girl in the queue. The accused fellow tried to explain that the girl in question was actually his wife and that she had just gone to grab something from the car. The other guy was having none of it, rambling on menacingly; he was spoiling for a confrontation. A giant security officer came in time before fists were traded and quelled the tense moment. Folks watching turned away, disappointed that someone would want to stop the only thing that would entertain their gloomy morning. Fuso was amazed that anyone would find the energy to argue and fight at 5.30 in the morning. He liked approaching the day quietly, gradually warming up to it like a charcoal stove.

Nothing bothered Fuso like standing in a queue with nothing to do. The book he brought along couldn't be read in the poor lighting. He was so bored and restless and from what he heard from those in the know, the offices were not to open till 8 am. Well, 'patience is a virtue' someone said but he always struggled with that. He shifted this way and that way like one with biting ants inside his trousers until finally he decided to do something about it. Facing the Indian guy behind him, he let him know that he was going to move his car to a private parking. One had to make their neighbours in the queue register their face when taking a break or one might end up with a very black puffy eye and a bleeding nose when they returned to take their position in the queue. Endless standing in queues had a way of shortening tempers and raising tension.

Back in the queue, the guy ahead of him engaged him in a conversation. Fuso was glad the stranger was Kenyan. Talking about home came naturally and they shared the tribulations of foreigners. He lived somewhere in Bristol and had to take several trains and buses to be in Croydon early in the morning. Unfortunately, in a hurry to get to Croydon, he must have forgotten to clean his teeth, his bad breath was nauseating. Fuso offered him a mint chewing gum but to his disappointment, Smelly declined the offer. The guy said he would have one after he ate his breakfast sandwich later. Fuso's prayer was that he would have been out of the queue then. Luckily, a cousin called all the way from America with all the latest gossip from home. Her mother had visited her a month earlier and generously updated her with the current village talk, including Njambi's escapades.

At last Fuso was in the front of the queue. His cousin's hour-long gossipy call certainly had made his queuing less stressful. A huge security guy ushered a bunch of people to the reception and through the metal detectors, his hands bulging sideways off the thousand paraphernalia and gear he had on him. Fuso wondered if it was necessary to dress like Rambo in a civil office that only dealt with visas but then what did he know? These were troubled times indeed.

It was now 9 am and Fuso had been standing in the queue for almost four hours. With only three guys ahead of him to the payment desk, the security guy guided ten people ahead of him. This was outrageous. He wanted to scream but then he remembered they were on appointments. That's what he should have done but being a procrastinator par excellence he had delayed calling the Home Office until the previous week when it was too late. The only available booking was three weeks away and by then his visa would have expired. The only way to do it now was by traditional means: stand in the maddening queue and gnash his teeth, careful not to dislocate the jaw. Maybe it was worth it to spend the time he stood in the queue thinking of the meaning of words like 'patience' and 'initiative'.

Done with payment, Fuso took a seat as advised. How much was it again? Two hundred and fifty pounds! Multiplying by the thousand plus souls present that morning, that was more than two hundred and fifty thousand pounds, a lot of dough. Multiplying that by the week was mind-boggling but then the charges were justified, perhaps. If folks wanted to overstay their visit, charge them the moon for the privilege!

It was another tedious wait. Luckily, there were seats inside and the hall was well lit. He could do his reading. Before he took out his book, he quickly studied the people around him. A few rows in front of him a woman was furiously sending text messages from her mobile phone. A security officer approached and pointed out that it was clearly prohibited. For goodness sake, there were a thousand notices to that effect all over the place.

"Nice phone you've there ma'am," the security guy said.

"Aye?" the woman muttered, raising her bowed head and shaking off her long hair from her face.

"You shouldn't use that here, should be switched off."

"I'm only sending a text," she responded defiantly. She didn't seem to think that warranted prohibition, it was not making a call after all. The security guy's mixed-race complexion did little to hide his irritation. He turned a shade redder with the look of one about to curse.

"Well, that too. Switch off the… switch it off," he commanded, sheer willpower making him manage not to shout. The unstated words on his lips were obvious: *switch off the flipping phone, idiot*! Next to her, a friend of hers was glad he had not seen her text too. She pulled a magazine higher to hide the phone and continued to text, undeterred, as if the world would stop if she didn't send the messages.

In the middle of the next row of three seats sat a Chinese guy. A couple politely requested him to move to the next seat so that they could sit together. He adamantly refused.

"But I came here first," he said, his small round face burning with aggression.

"They don't follow the queue here. The numbers are called out so it doesn't matter."

"No, I come here first, you come last, go sit back."

"It doesn't matter; they call out numbers when they prepare applications and not in order of sitting." An elderly lady in the row behind tried to intervene. The Chinese guy shook his head, reading conspiracy.

"*Túkumbabu tútú twa Shaina*," the man said to his wife in Kikuyu, loosely translated into 'these little Chinese morons', as they moved away to look for somewhere else to sit.

Fuso was probably the only other person who understood what the man said. He felt embarrassed that such a seemingly dignified man should resort to insult but luckily the Chinese guy didn't understand. The Chinese guy leaned towards a Chinese girl in the immediate row in front of him and whispered something to her. They both smiled and made rude gestures on their faces. Fuso didn't quite understand what they said but he imagined they were equally rude. Well, fair enough.

Further on in the hall, a mother had three babies, one in a pram and two budding rascals wandering about. She had trouble controlling the two boys, especially the younger one who had a moment earlier climbed onto the counter to the annoyance of the officer at the desk. People watched and sympathised with her. No one wanted to help though. This was the UK and not his village in Múrang'a where babies were looked after in communal care. One had to be careful here.

When finally Fuso's reference number appeared on the screen above, he moved to the counter. All his papers in order, it took only a short while to be attended. Having enrolled at the university, had his first semester's transcripts and bank statements that looked impressive, thanks to the loan, there was no reason not to extend his visa. The bank statements looked healthy only because he had been working like crazy last summer.

"I can see you've been working," said the interviewer, a bloke of about thirty-five but balding fast.

"That's right."

"How many hours have you been doing?"

*Upwards of seventy, mate, this is an expensive country!* "Twenty," he said. That's the hours students are authorised to work a week.

"Right then, you've got nine months to finish your course, I'll give you one year's extension. Is that all right?"

*No mate, give me a couple of years mate, got that loan to repay, you know.* "Yeah, that's all right. Thank you."

In the next counter to his right, an Arab-looking guy was having a tough time convincing the interviewer that he had been in the UK for the last year without a bank statement. His explanation, he had been using a relative's bank account. Unconvinced too, Fuso turned to his left where the couple who had a confrontation with the Chinese guy were being attended. As they conversed in Kikuyu, his first language, Fuso was eager to talk to them. However, just before he saluted them and said a thing about Kenya he saw the interviewer hand them their passports – the passports were Zimbabwean. *Zimbabwean Kikuyus?* Fuso smiled knowingly. *An African sometimes gotta do what an African gotta do.* A long way from home this Europe was, he thought, and perhaps it was better if he minded his own business. He sat rocking back and forth like he had sensory modulation difficulties while his interviewer photocopied his papers.

"The visa processing will take three hours so you could either wait here or go out and come later," the interviewer advised.

"Do I have to queue again?" he asked, alarmed. Queues traumatised him.

"No no, just use the side door and tell security you've returned to pick up your passport. Show them your receipt."

On his way out, he struggled to get through a crowd of applicants that were hovering near one of the counters. A black staffer was having a hard time trying to convince them to move to the seats. Everybody would be attended when their numbers showed on the screen. There was no need to crowd at the counters. Some heeded, others didn't. They went on to squat or sit on the floor near the corridor, blocking the exit.

"They are like flipping stupid sheep," the staffer hissed to a colleague; he moved back inside, frustrated.

"Call security," his colleague advised.

When Fuso finally managed to get through the crowd, he passed near a door marked 'prayer room'. Apparently, though unstated, only Muslims were expected to go in there. He entertained the thought of deciding to go in there and say his Christian prayers. It didn't read 'Muslims only' anywhere on the door.

Staying away from controversy, he found his way out and into Croydon High Street where he had lunch in an Italian café. Braving the chilly weather, a stroll after his meal came handy to kill the three hours before his visa was done. He also took a short trip on a tram for the first time. Well, he had seen them in movies and pictures but never travelled on one. Marvelling at modern technology, he felt sorry for Africa. Will she ever achieve all these modern technologies? Kenya still operated ancient diesel locomotives that rivalled steam engines in billowing smoke and froth. Well, Kenyans needed to learn to stick to rules first. They needed to learn that it wasn't bravery to jump the red lights before trams were introduced or they would die trying to beat trams at the traffic lights.

Just after 3 pm, Fuso walked out of Lunar House with another year's permit to live in the land of the Queen. That was a plus but still he had the matter of six thousand pounds plus three thousand pounds interest to pay and hopefully have some serious change by the time he returned home. How he would perform that miracle was a matter for the Almighty but in the meantime he had to live on. When he went to redeem Nyagúthií, his Fiesta, from the private car park, it made him thirteen pounds poorer – a lot of money in his frame of budget. Fuso walked to the attendant's booth to pay after the temperamental pay machine rejected his notes. Expertly, he guided the little old girl out of the winding car park towards the exit. The attendants smiled and waved him goodbye, ever the gentle robbers. Why should parking a car be so expensive?

Within minutes, he was past the A23 Brighton Road and onto the M23 motorway, gunning the little car like crazy. He could afford to push her now that he had the mandate of another year's leave to remain. On his way to Croydon he had been afraid to do more than 50mph on the dial, afraid that the stuttering old Fiesta wouldn't survive the trip but now he didn't care. If the car died, fine. She had served her purpose and for only two hundred and fifty pounds – which was her purchase price, six months earlier – he could afford to dump her somewhere on one of the bushes along the M23 motorway if she became troublesome.

Keen to prove him wrong, Nyagúthií behaved well. Ladies are mostly sensible when it comes to divorce and would do anything to keep the marriage, especially when it's the man who is entertaining straying thoughts. She tore through the M23 with the libido of a Ferrari, unafraid of the monster Range Rovers and the mammoth trucks. Along with Fuso she hummed as he sang: *Oh happy day.*

# 29

That evening he left home a little earlier for a midweek fellowship meeting in his church in Staines. Fuso had enough things to thank God for, the chief of them being that he would be able to continue with his studies and second that he had managed to extend his visa. He wasn't ready for Africa yet. The loan had to be repaid and also he had to get some heavy change on the side. There was no way he was to return to Africa with only his university qualification to show for his stay in Europe. Despite good prospects of getting a good job, he needed some money to get him started in Africa.

The speaker in the fellowship was a South African bishop, a friend of the minister who was a regular visitor on his numerous church businesses in Europe. He spoke about the value of freedom. Coming from South Africa, he had experienced apartheid first hand. He therefore tried to paint a picture of how it felt to come out of a system that legally allowed putting signs like 'Dogs and natives not welcome' and this happened even outside some churchyards. To the discomfort of the congregation, he spoke about how British people – having had centuries of freedom – took freedom for granted and that Britain was bending backwards to please everybody and losing part of its freedom and status to strangers.

At the door stood Angus, the cheerful Scottish church minister, to bid his congregation goodbye. It was a wise public relations move or else he lost members and found himself in the scary position of preaching only to his disinterested wife.

"Good of you to come to fellowship with us tonight," he said to Fuso, shaking his hand vigorously. "We love visitors, please do come again if you can, I don't think I caught your name though."

"No, I don't think we've met, my name's Fuso," he said. "I worship in a church called Shalom, in Staines." Angus's face made a transformation through all the shades pink and red could go, finally settling on raspberry. He always called Fuso all sorts of names and even addressed him by a different name several times the previous Sunday afternoon in his house. He had invited Fuso to his house after the Sunday service to join him and his wife for lunch. Now he didn't even recall Fuso's face! If the minister had invited a group, that would have been understandable. However, Fuso was the only guest that day. Mixing names was all right, Fuso did lots of that himself, but forgetting the face of a person you had personally invited and entertained in your house had to be defined by a new term.

In extreme embarrassment, Angus hugged him and mentioned something about Fuso, looking somewhat different. "Aah, it's because you cut your hair," he exclaimed, avoiding eye contact, "and where are your glasses today?"

"I don't wear any," Fuso whispered in his ear, more amused than offended. He might as well have meant to invite somebody else for the previous Sunday's lunch. *Oh dear,* Fuso thought, *I might have eaten another guest's meal!* Fuso left Angus reeling with embarrassment, his wife standing by with that 'when will you ever learn?' look. He walked off to the car park where his girlfriend waited. *Can't tell one black face from another.* This replayed over and over in Fuso's mind as he reversed out of the car park. Maybe it was true, that some people could not tell black people apart. How come the minister's wife could tell everybody apart but Angus couldn't. Fuso looked at Louise, his girlfriend, in the front passenger's seat and hoped she didn't mistake another bloke for him.

Near Staines High Street, Fuso and Louise got into McDonald's on Mustard Mill Road for a snack before he drove her home in Egham and later picked Abdi from work in Thorpe Park. The restaurant was a little busier than usual with diners who had just streamed out of an early film show at the Vue Cinema. Next to the restaurant, a South West train from Waterloo was picking up speed after pulling out of Staines train station, a few hundred yards away its steel wheels making that annoying screech. He looked hard at Louise sitting opposite him and marvelled at the turns life take. When he left Kenya he had a girlfriend, who was, in all respects, the best thing to happen to him. For a long time he dreamt of a future together with her, convinced that it was best if people married their own kind. Fuso had not appreciated just how different his Kikuyu culture was from the British culture. When he did, he thought it was so difficult to have a relationship with a white English woman in the light of such glaring differences.

When that belief crumbled he couldn't tell, but what he least expected to happen to him was exactly what did happen. Fuso's fears came to haunt him. He simply felt different about Lulu, his Kenyan girlfriend. Slowly an English friend took over his heart and before he knew what hit him, she was all he wanted and bad.

He looked at her now, seated across the table, and smiled. Could she ever understand where he was coming from? Did she know he didn't wear shoes to school for eight years of his primary education? It is not that he didn't have shoes but wearing them to school was frowned at unless your parents were teachers or the village who's who. Many pupils didn't have any at all so if you ever wore shoes to school you were considered a show-off. How could his girlfriend understand that he had to fetch twenty litres of water after school from the river – quite a distance away? And that that was just part of the chores he was expected to do. Fuso milked the cows as well, went to the fields to fetch fodder for the cattle. How could she understand that his childhood involved tilling the land till his palms were rubbery with calluses? That he carried loads of disgusting manure to the farm on his back and from the age of five was not left out when the family picked coffee berries all day in their small farm?

Could she understand that that wasn't child labour or abuse but what he helped Mum do? She had so much on her hands and with Fuso's dad away at work in the city she couldn't handle the seven children in the family without them helping. Could his girlfriend ever understand that they had no electricity and no TV in their house until past their teenage years? Fuso was a country village boy through and through, only modernised by education in good schools. What Louise saw now was not the raw peasant lad but an eligible, refined, prospective spouse. He shook his head, resigned to fate. *Na liwe liwalo* – so be it! If they were meant to be together, so be it. Sometimes it was futile fighting destiny.

"You're staring at me," she said.

"I know."

"Why?"

"Because."

"What?"

"Am I not allowed to appreciate pretty English girls?" She pretended to look behind her.

"Don't see any back there," she said and smiled sweetly, brushing her long blonde hair and giving a shy flutter of her blue eyes. She was going to be a spectacle if she ever visited his village.

Not so high up, almost directly above the McDonald's, an Airbus A320 rumbled from Heathrow Airport, about five miles away, on its take-off climb into the falling darkness. Fuso could clearly see that all too familiar red and white KQ logo on the tail; it was a Kenya Airways plane. A weird feeling gripped him for a moment as he watched the plane bank to port, pick bearing then rise steadily in a southeast direction, most likely headed to Kenya. For an instant he thought about Múgo, and marvelled at his audacity. Although Fuso couldn't do what Múgo did, he wasn't sure who was happier between the two of them. A nudging feeling pointed at him but he dismissed it. The straight and narrow wasn't always the easier one but mostly gave the last laugh.

"Anything the matter?" asked Louise, extending her soft hand to touch his. He looked down at her hand with fascination. The contrast between their skin colours was incredible. "You look worried."

There was cause to be. Ignorant supremacists had thrown a few insults at him when he walked with Louise in the streets. That so agitated Louise but Fuso had learnt to live with it. Most black people had suffered insults for so long they had either built a buffer or resigned themselves to their fate. One needed not to let it sink in or one became depressed. Fuso couldn't be bothered to stop and challenge his detractors. His main concern was safety. If he and Louise were safe, then the racists could scream themselves hoarse for all he cared. Fuso knew people would always question his motive for being with her and especially question his honesty or her sanity.

His people had issues of their own too. Already one of his friends had maliciously congratulated him for hitting a jackpot. If he meant being lucky for getting a good woman that would have been fine but he meant that Fuso had stumbled into riches. There was no way of explaining to this lot that his girlfriend had no money and neither was he interested in changing his citizenship. In his wildest dreams he entertained thoughts of getting into politics or becoming some big fellow in Africa and that wasn't possible on a foreign passport. Like all relationships that defy people's expectation, he knew this was going to be very difficult. What he had gotten himself into scared him. *It was big! Oh you silly heart, won't you ever learn to love appropriately!* The only consolation he had was that his family and kinsmen would treat Louise like a queen because they respected him and so they would his spouse.

"No darling, it's nothing." Even as he said it, a nostalgic feeling, a moment's dream of a soothing return home, overwhelmed him. For an instant he wondered in the light of the new developments if he would ever return back home to Africa.

Joel Mwangi was born in Nairobi Kenya… not too long ago. He graduated with a Bachelor's degree in Education from Kenyatta University in 1997. He taught English and English literature in several secondary schools in the country and later worked for the Kenya Literature Bureau. He then moved to the UK to pursue postgraduate studies, graduating with a Master of Arts degree in Education (Special Educational Needs) from Brunel University London in 2005. He also holds a postgraduate diploma in leadership and management. Joel has worked for several local authorities as a special educational needs officer. He is married and a father of three. He continues to dream in London.

Printed in Great Britain
by Amazon